An Experiment in Time and Memory

Debbie Coll

"Concussion-inducing car chases, coffee addictions, memory loss, and gloriously plot twist-y time travel. If that doesn't make you want to read this book, then I don't know what will. You should probably reconsider your life choices if you don't want to." -- Rebekah O'Donovan, co-host of *Ballads of Beyond*

"Time travel, international organizations, daring escapes, car chases, gun standoffs, amnesia, shady men in black, newspaper clippings, and coffee—yes, coffee—this book has it all. With a blend of humor and action that brings the characters off the page, Debbie Coll manages to bring to life one of the best time travel stories I've ever experienced." -- Bojidar P. Marinov, writer friend

"I feel like it's my...book niece or something. I'm proud of it for being released." - Lauren D Fulter, author of *The Unanswered Questions* series and book aunt to *AEITAM*.

"You should be proud of yourself for writing something when you were nineteen, that still holds up five years later. You peaked." --my sister, of course

"I rooted for Lucky and Amber and was SO happy by the end. Their chemistry was better than I expected." -- Tip, certified time traveller

For the Uncle Tony Band

12:41PM 14 FEBRUARY 1998, JFK INTERNATIONAL AIRPORT

You cannot change history.

I thought it was supposed to be a seven-hour flight.

Stephanie Heile stepped out of the airport, pulling three bags of luggage and wishing it was still February 13th.

So this is New York, she mused, then smiled excitedly to herself. *The taxis really are yellow.*

The small cars streamed past the exit to the airport, steadily picking up their passengers and ferrying them away. Other travellers bumped past her, heedlessly dragging suitcases and children. Some were hugging friends and family in what should have been a heart-warming scene.

But Stephanie's eyes just glanced over them tiredly. Somehow being 'just thankful to be alive' made it hard to be grateful for anything else. It had been a long and stressful journey to her first solo holiday, and now that she was here, she was determined to enjoy it.

After a nap.

Two men came out of the airport's doors, shivering in the brisk cold. They leaned against the wall, watching the people shuffle past. Stephanie recognised one of them: young and fair, with dirty-blonde hair and an Irish lilt to his accent. When the flight had completed its emergency landing in Fiji, he'd been there to make sure they were all fine and ready for their connecting flight to New York. She'd seen the older one, tanned with dark hair and a thick Spanish accent, around the plane, but hadn't taken much notice of him.

'Carl,' the young man said. 'Where's Amber?'

The Spanish man folded his arms. 'I told you before. The records said she never got on the plane. So I'm her replacement.'

'So what happened to her?'

'Ask Neil,' Carl snapped. 'Get him to ask Shinichi what happened. The report just said that when something minor went wrong, she panicked and fell apart. I guess she just couldn't keep calm under pressure, and you know this mission requires a lot of that.'

Stephanie paused. *Mission?* She hadn't meant to eavesdrop, but this seemed almost confidential.

Lucky frowned, but turned his attention straight ahead, his face tense. 'What's she been doing this whole time?'

'She was probably taken back to ARCHIVE as soon as I left.'

Archives? What archives?

'Neil? What have you heard?' the Irish man asked.

Neil? Stephanie glanced around, but no one was looking at him except Carl.

'Ah, hang on,' Lucky said, and Stephanie turned back to see him looking at her. 'Hello. Stephanie, was it? How can we help?'

She froze. *How does he remember my name?* 'Ah, sorry, I wasn't—I mean…' She swallowed and tried to move past the question of whether she'd been listening in. 'Actually, I just wanted to… to thank you for helping us all out today. And… I wondered if…' She latched onto an idea belatedly. 'If I could buy you some dinner? Or—lunch, I suppose.' She choked out a laugh. 'Timezones. Um… to say thanks?'

An awkward silence descended. Lucky glanced at Carl, then forced a tired smile. 'That's very kind,' he said slowly. 'But you don't have to. And… I don't think we'll have time.'

Stephanie nodded, keeping her smile secure. 'Ah that's okay. That's what I wanted to say, anyway.'

'Thank you, though,' Carl said. 'Have a good time in New York.'

'Thanks,' she said, smiling at both in turn. 'You too.'

'Do you have a ride?' Lucky asked, and she noticed Carl shooting him a glance.

'I was just going to hail a taxi,' she said, gesturing to the flow of taxis just across the pavement.

He nodded. 'Good. Take care.'

She shook their hands, then turned back to try to find herself a taxi to take her to her hotel. *I have to call mum when I get to the Cresthaven,* she thought. Her mum would have been following the news of the plane. She was more nervous about this trip than Stephanie was. *I'll tell her that I'm safe, and that I think I met two secret agents on the plane.*

It's like that woman said… it felt like so long ago that she'd met her, at the airport back in London. She'd warned Stephanie not to take it for granted that the plane would reach New York in one piece.

She'd been right.

Stephanie shook her head in bemusement. *It's almost like she's from the future,* she thought, settling into her seat.

PART ONE

- Memory -

*Always arrive at ARCHIVE on time for your
mission briefing.*

A RCHIVE was bustling when Luc walked in.

How can there be so many people here already? he wondered, yawning. He glanced at his watch with a grimace. If Commander Haste was watching, he would have shaken his head and given a lecture on punctuality and how it showed you cared about your work.

Amber must be here, he thought, setting off amidst the bustle. *She cares about her work.*

'Ah, you're here,' said a voice behind him.

'I'm here,' he agreed, turning to his partner, Amber. 'You can relax now. The world is saved.'

She laughed, shaking her head. 'Mr Lucky Holmes, my three-minute-late hero.' Grinning, she added, 'Hey, new development—'

'Ooh, I like new developments.'

'Then you'll like this.' With a little excited bounce, she set off among the ARC-researcher's desks, beckoning for Luc to follow.

Her black ringlets bounced in time with her steps as she wound around people. With her olive skin and pleasant, youthful features, Amber could have been on ARCHIVE posters, advertising office safety with a shining smile. It was almost embarrassing to be her partner; she outshone Luc, whatever she – or he – was wearing. He'd quickly learned to accept that people would be nicer to her than they were to him.

Amber pulled up in front of the mission board, a shiny TV filled with agents names, times and locations. 'Tadaa!' she called, pointing to a row toward the top.

Luc's hopes rose. 'Do we have a new mission?'

'Yep.' She grinned. 'Not a very exciting one, but a mission nonetheless.'

Luc read aloud the description. '*Retrieving Timebox 3.0 from Movarian Laboratories.* Yeah, sounds… thrilling. But why is the ARC-researcher spot blank? Are we not worthy?'

Amber shot him a look. 'I looked it up while I was waiting for you,' she replied. 'Movarian Labs is just across the city. We shouldn't need ARC-researchers.'

Luc pursed his lips, but nodded. 'Haste is probably saving them for other missions,' he replied. 'I suppose since we're not Travelling, it's not really a mission anyway.'

Despite this, the day was filled with preparations. They were briefed on the security questions they might be asked, taken through the paperwork that had to be presented, and finally given directions to Movarian Laboratories. As Amber had said, it would only be an hour's drive each way.

Just after lunch, Luc received a text from Commander Haste, sending him Movarian Lab's location. He replied,

> Sir, we noticed that we won't be given ARC-researchers on this mission.

> Yes, that's correct. I need my ARC-researchers elsewhere, and there's already two of you.
> Haste

Well, that was pretty much the answer I expected, Luc mused, replying with an *ok*. He turned to Amber, the new-mission bubble of excitement building in his chest. *It's not a proper mission,* he told himself, but that didn't stop him from feeling like the *Men in Black,* slipping on his sunglasses as opened the door to the ARCar. 'You ready?' he asked.

She laughed. 'Luc, it's just a new timebox. Don't be so theatrical.'

He slid into his seat with a gallant toss of the head. 'Theatrical's my middle name.'

Movarian Laboratories

'That's… it?' Luc said, instantly regretting the words.

'That's it,' Dr Whitehall replied dryly. 'Two PhD's, forty years of research, billions of taxpayer's pounds, a nuclear reactor dedicated to powering it, three hours-worth of security clearance for anyone who wants to *look* at the thing, and it's transported in a polystyrene-filled cardboard box.'

Amber didn't look too sure about it either. 'It's… it must be small.'

The professor shrugged. 'So is a cell. Both are more complex than you can imagine.'

He looked tired, but to Luc it was like he was always tired; it had wrung out his skin, and no amount of sleep would refresh him anymore. His grey hair was falling out, he had lines on his face and bags under his eyes, and he carried himself dejectedly, as though he felt personally responsible for all the agents who had ever died in the depths of history due to his innovation.

Luc picked up the cardboard box just as the lab's phone rang, hefting it experimentally. It was about as heavy as a small book, and if he had to guess, Luc would have said it contained a small laptop or tablet.

'I thought we'd have a suitcase to chain to a wrist,' Amber whispered to him.

He shrugged, a small mischievous smile forming. 'Do you think we'd be allowed a peek inside?'

She sighed. 'I think the Commander might notice—'

With a snap, the lights went out. Natural afternoon sun streamed in through the windows along one wall, but the dimness was uncomfortable for a moment while Luc's eyes adjusted.

'Is this normal?' Amber asked.

As though in answer, an alarm blared.

The door banged open, and a man strode in. He was of middling-height and weight, with dark hair and a neatly trimmed beard. 'Lucky Holmes.'

Luc's eyebrows rose. 'Yes?'

'That's the timebox you got there.'

Part of Luc, probably the part influenced by Amber and his mother, told him not to reply.

The other part felt that stupid questions deserved sarcastic answers, and he quickly decided to listen to this part. 'Actually,' he said, 'it's a cardboard box.'

'Luc…' Amber groaned.

The man ignored the comment, pulling out a gun and aiming it at the professor. 'Give it to me or—' he swore as the professor ducked behind a lab bench, surprisingly quick. A gunshot rang out, a bullet punching a hole in the wall behind them. Luc followed the professor, pulling Amber down with him.

He pulled out the keys and ripped into the box.

'What are you doing?' Amber whispered, peeking over the desk. 'He's coming.'

'I know,' Luc replied, digging through the polystyrene chips. He finally pulled out what must have been the timebox. 'Seriously, when he said small, he wasn't kidding.'

He put his hand back in, in case there was something else, but Amber rolled her eyes, grabbed the box and upended it. Polystyrene chips scattered everywhere. A book, charger cord and cover clattered to the floor, and Amber snatched them up.

They each pulled their pistols out of their holsters. With timebox in one hand and a pistol in the other, they both began to army crawl around the desks.

I could do with an ARC-researcher right about now, Luc thought, gritting his teeth.

To hear his final words, if nothing else.

'Doctor,' he whispered.

'I'll get out by myself,' Dr Whitehall whispered back. 'Get that timebox out. I don't want anyone but ARCHIVE to have my technology.'

Luc nodded. 'Be careful.'

'You too.'

They crawled to the end of the desk, and Luc tried to judge the distance they would have to run without cover. It was about ten metres to the lab's door, then, if he was quick, he could close it and use it as a shield. He nodded to himself.

'You ready?' Amber asked. It was almost funny; just at the start of their mission, he'd asked her the same question.

Now it had a very different weight.

He nodded, his jaw set and his eyes fixed on the doorway. Ten metres.

'You go first,' she said. 'I'll cover for you. Then Dr Whitehall, and then you cover me when I get out.'

They all nodded, and Luc counted down. 'Three. Two. One.'

Protecting the timebox with his body, he jumped up and sprinted for the door, a bullet-hole appearing in the wall just in front of him. But then more shots were fired – he assumed it was Amber, because suddenly the air around him was clear of flying metal, and he was out the door panting and shaking.

The inventor barrelled into him, and he pushed him aside, aiming his gun on the intruder. He didn't want to hit the man; he just wanted to make him feel threatened enough that he wouldn't be able to take aim. Amber ran into him, and the door slammed shut behind her.

Dr Whitehall whipped out a key, locking the man inside the laboratory.

'Go,' he ordered, and this time, Luc didn't hesitate.

He ran.

★★★

Amber only noticed the raindrops when she reached the Labs' carpark. The sun was on the horizon now, and a light rain had begun to fall, forcing Luc to protect the timebox as best as he could by tucking it under his jacket during the mad sprint to the car.

Gunshots rang out behind them, and the laboratory windows shattered. 'Start the car!' the intruder yelled, and immediately, one of the engines revved to life. Mismatched headlights flicked on, one white and one yellow-tinged.

He has an accomplice.

They reached the car, Luc unlocking the doors as they slid in.

'Here, keys,' Luc said.

Amber groaned. 'Why am *I* driving?'

A bullet hit the window near Luc's head, embedding itself in the bullet-proof glass. 'We can't change now,' Luc said. 'Come on, Amber!'

She tore out of the carpark and down the road, keeping to backroads and sharp corners. When she couldn't see the glow of the headlights anymore, she parked the car, turned off the engine and slid beneath her seat.

Luc slid down his seat, under the window line. Amber tapped the touch screen between them to wake it up, then swiped through the listed features. She'd gone through this list in training, but there were still some surprises. Finally, she found the one she'd had in mind and selected it, then folded herself into the footwell. Outside, tiny tiles that interlocked all over the body of the car separated slightly, flipped over, and settled back together to create a seamless shell identical to the way it had been before. Identical, except for a change in colour.

The sleek black paint had been replaced with a gaudy yellow, and a wide scratch had appeared along the backseat's door.

Amber only hoped that their pursuers wouldn't notice the bullet hole in Luc's side window.

Mismatched headlights streaked around the corner. Inside the car, Amber held her breath. Luc offered a small smile to Amber, which she returned, trying to bolster his spirits. The car raced past them, wound through a roundabout and went on.

Amber released her breath. She pulled herself back up to the seat and twisted the key in the ignition while Luc changed the car's colour back to black. Rain steadily pattered the roof of the car, sloshing away from the wipers as they switched on again.

Luc opened his phone and began directing her back to the highway. In their chase, they had crossed four suburbs and added another hour and a half to their travel time. It was now ten past seven. Commander Haste would still be waiting for them back at ARCHIVE, and he would not be happy. The thought put an uneasy twist in Amber's stomach.

Luc crossed his legs and the timebox nearly fell into the gap between the seat and the centre console. His hand slapped down on top of it to stop its fall.

'Careful!' Amber snapped. She closed her eyes for a moment, tightening her hands around the steering wheel as though that would also tighten her grip on herself. 'I'm sorry,' she said quietly, but couldn't quite keep her misery out of the words.

Luc repositioned it on his knee. 'It's okay. I'm sure they made it strong enough to survive being knocked around.'

'Yes, but it's worth more than we are.'

He laughed. 'It's sad, but true.' He offered her a reassuring smile. 'I know you're worried. Let me concentrate on the box of historical influence, and you can concentrate on driving. Deal?'

Amber nodded reluctantly, focusing on the road ahead for a few seconds.

Finally, she gave up trying to ignore it. 'Really? *Box of historical influence?'*

'I told you before. Theatrical is my middle name.'

Amber smiled, shaking her head. *Just concentrate on driving,* she told herself. *Imagine what Haste will say if you crash.*

'Was that always green?' Luc asked suddenly.

'I don't know,' Amber sighed, turning a corner. 'I thought the *box of historical influence* was *your* responsi—oh no.'

'I'm sure it was orange before. What's wrong?'

Behind them, headlights flickered on and a car pulled away from the side of the road.

The speed limit was forgotten. Amber put her foot down on the accelerator, as far as it would go. The engine roared, and the car felt like it was trying to pull away from under her.

'One yellow, one white,' she breathed, shifting the gears. 'It's them.'

Luc's hands moved to hold onto the timebox a bit more securely. The lights were getting steadily larger. Amber shifted from fourth to fifth gear.

'When do I turn to get back to ARCHIVE?' Amber said, her voice rising in pitch. Luc pulled out his phone and retrieved the maps, quickly turning the brightness down from blinding to too-bright-but-bearable.

'Not for a while. Keep speeding up. When we turn off, we'll be heading towards ARCHIVE anyway,' he said. He was distracted by the light flashing on the travel box. 'The light on this thing's flashing faster.'

The headlights were only fifty metres away, now. Amber was driving at sixty miles an hour in a road marked at twenty-five. Rain spattered the windscreen, obscuring the view of the road ahead, and the car was buffeted by strong winds. Amber had to wrestle with the steering wheel to keep the car on the left side of the slippery road. Somehow, the men behind them were going faster. The speed limit went up to sixty. The speedometer climbed to seventy-five. Amber could feel her heart rate speeding up. 'Luc,' she said.

'Yeah?'

'I don't want to go any faster. We're going to crash.'

'We won't crash,' she hoped he would say. *'I know you're scared, and it's hard to drive when it's dark and raining and windy, but you're a good driver. You can do it.'*

But he didn't say anything.

Eighty miles per hour. The engine roared, the ground slippery and treacherous beneath the tires. The rain had only gotten heavier, and now it spattered thickly against the windscreen, obscuring the road ahead.

The car behind was tailgating now. 'When do I turn?' Amber breathed, fighting rising panic.

'Just keep going along this road,' Luc replied calmly. 'I'll tell you when to turn.' Amber wasn't sure how he was feeling, but he radiated reassured confidence. For once, it helped to calm her down. She took a deep breath and concentrated on the road ahead.

Suddenly Amber was blinded. She squinted through the bright light. 'What happened?'

'They turned their headlights up to high-beam to blind us,' Luc replied grimly. 'Clever, but slippery.' He pulled out his sunglasses and put them on to cut the glare. 'That almost helps. Do you want yours?'

'I can barely see the road in front as it is!' The steering wheel twisted on the side of the road, almost coming free of her grasp. Trees lined the road to the left. *If we crash into them, Luc will die first,* she couldn't help thinking. Her eyes flicked his way. His window was half-open, and his wrist and hand were trying to aim a pistol at their pursuers.

Luc, what are you doing? 'There's no way you'll hit them!' she yelled.

Luc opened his mouth to reply, then nodded and twisted back to face the front.

The acceleration pedal was almost touching the floor, and the car was coasting at eighty-five miles an hour.

Gunshots rang out, echoing off the houses and across the parklands on either side of them. The bullets lodged themselves in the thick rear window.

'Turn right here!' Luc said suddenly.

Amber jumped, then swung the steering wheel hard to the right.

The nose of the car behind hit the corner of their bumper. The ARCar swung out of control, spinning doughnuts into the grass. Amber screamed. Luc grabbed the wheel to help Amber steady themselves, as the car skidded along the wet road. It hit the curb and tipped as its momentum carried it onto the nature strip and into a fence, but Amber felt more than saw their impact. Her vision was temporarily blinded by the timebox as it flew through the air, hit her window and fell into her lap.

Pain lanced up her neck and for a moment she couldn't breathe. An airbag blew up into her face, further smothering her, and as she blindly pushed it down, smeared blood decorated the front. She couldn't have said where it came from. *Maybe it's Luc's.*

Heaving breaths, she gave a groan and rested her head on the windscreen before finally giving into the darkness.

The timebox let out a cheerful beep. Three words appeared on its digital screen:

Ready to Transport.

Outside, two men approached the silent car cautiously, peering in through the windows.

'The woman was driving?' the older one, by Luc's window, asked. He fidgeted like he wished he had a weapon in case the agent woke up. 'Is she there?'

The other man still had his gun from the ambush at the lab. 'Nope. But guess what *is.*'

He held up the timebox, its green light flickering steadily. A countdown flicked by on its screen. *6… 5… 4…*

The older man smiled, then glanced down at Luc's unmoving body. 'I was worried for a moment, but it seems it all turned out better than I expected. The boss will be pleased.'

There was no reply. The man looked up. 'Harry?'

Muttering to himself, he slammed the car door shut and went around the front of the car. 'Harry, you idiot, what are you—'

There was no one there. Harry had disappeared along with the driver.

And, he noticed, the timebox.

8:45PM 12 OCTOBER 1868, WALHALLA, AUSTRALIA

Do not let the locals practice their medicines on you. If you are injured or ill, contact ARCHIVE immediately.

A sticky smell clogged Amber's nose. Her skull ached, inside and out, and as she opened her eyes, light blinded her.

'Ah, she's awake,' a deep voice said beside her.

'Well, her eyes are opening at least,' said another voice, still masculine, but not as deep.

She blinked a few times, chasing away spots that danced in her vision. Strange, whispering voices seemed to whirl around her. 'Where…' she croaked. She was sure her voice wasn't meant to sound like that. She cleared her throat and tried again. 'Where am I?'

A man moved closer to her face, blocking the light from the open window with his body. Although he was slightly silhouetted, Amber could see his dark beard and heavy eyebrows. He wore a snug jacket that came down to his knees, and a tie poked out underneath his collar. 'Good evening,' he said, his voice matching the first one that had spoken. 'My name is Richard Johansson. This is Doctor Somerton. I took the liberty of taking you into my home, as you were in a very poor state when we found you this morning.'

Amber squinted, glancing around her, spreading her hands on the fabric. She was in a bed, she realised. She could feel beams poking through the thin mattress, but the doona was warm and soft, and she sank her sore head back into the pillow with a sigh.

A young woman came into the room, wearing a wide-hipped green dress and apron, her curly brown hair held back by an off-white handkerchief, and followed by a young boy of about six or seven. The woman carried a small bowl full of water, and had a white towel draped over one arm. She sat down next to the bed, dipped the towel into the water, and started cleaning Amber's head. Dark red blood came away on the towel.

Johansson cleared his throat. 'What's your name, miss? Do you have any family we should call?'

Amber opened her eyes. She hadn't realised she'd closed them. She grimaced as the cloth touched an injury near her eyebrow. For a moment, she almost answered.

But the moment passed, and she realised that she had no idea what her answer would have been. She glanced at the doctor. 'It's… it's the strangest thing,' she said. 'I can't remember what my name is.'

Johansson looked at the doctor over the bed, as though hopeful that he could fix her.

'What specifically can't you remember?' the doctor asked.

Amber thought hard. She knew that she was in a bed, so she could remember basic things like that. She also knew that the man's accent sounded Northern, as though she remembered what Northerners sounded like. But she couldn't remember anything about herself; what she looked like, what she liked to do, whether she had any family. Her brain was foggy, like it was a wet, soggy sponge, and each pulse reverberated painfully through her head. She shook her head. 'I don't know if I have any family,' she said. 'Or what my name is. Or who I am.' The woman cleaning her injuries shook her head sympathetically.

'Amnesia,' Doctor Somerton said, rising from his seat.

'What?' Johansson said.

'Amnesia,' the doctor repeated impatiently.

The man frowned at Somerton's tone. 'I heard you the first time,' he muttered. 'I was simply questioning your movement to leave. Aren't you going to medicate?'

Doctor Somerton shut the briefcase and went to the door. 'There's nothing I can do,' he replied simply. 'I'm not a doctor of the mind. I suggest you send a telegraph to Sale and advertise in the paper there to see if her family gets in touch. Sometimes the memory comes back on its own; sometimes nothing helps. Good luck.'

The doctor, unhelpfully, left, with a scowling Johansson in his wake. Amber looked at him tentatively. His dark eyes flicked to her face, and she quickly looked away.

'Well, I suppose you can stay here as long as you need to,' he said finally. 'We've got plenty of space.' The woman choked, then looked down at her hands, her eyes wide with shock. Johansson looked at her with half a smile on his lips. 'Is there a problem, Miss Mollie?'

Miss Mollie shook her head quickly, murmuring approval. Johansson nodded.

'Miss,' he said, turning back to Amber. 'Let me know if you remember anything. I will advertise in the paper, as Somerton suggested, and do what I can to help, but I can't remember for you.'

Amber nodded, surprised by his kindness. 'Thank you, sir,' she said.

Johansson made a grunt deep in his throat. 'I'll talk to the Minister and that botanist fellow too; I hear they have some medical experience and may come up with some good ideas. And my son can make up a name for us to call you by until you remember your own.'

Amber nodded tiredly, settling back into the pillows as the man left. *Should I trust him? I don't remember meeting him before – rather, he doesn't seem to remember me.*

But it wasn't like she could get up and walk out. So, resigned, she closed her eyes and waited for sleep.

Look after your partner before you look after yourself. Look after any civilian before you look after your partner.

L uc stopped in front of Haste's office, steeling himself for the battle ahead.

If Commander Haste were to describe himself, he would probably use words like *kind but fair; level-headed; a team player.* He was about fifty, mentally and physically fit, with a good income and a successful enterprise going on in the desks surrounding his office. He was the sort of boss who, if he read a pamphlet saying that an hour of exercise increases brain activity by 75%, would implement compulsory hour-long exercise sessions for all his workers.

The Commander, as most people called him, was the best boss anyone could hope for.

Luc knew that this was what he was meant to think.

What is this feeling of terror welling up within me? he thought sarcastically as he stepped forward and knocked on the glass wall of the office.

The truth was, Luc didn't particularly like Haste, and the man's opinion of himself was only part of it. Of course, Luc knew that the other part was mainly the exercise that Haste so cheerfully enforced on his field agents. *Why wasn't I hired as an*

ARC-researcher? he sulked inwardly, not for the first time. *They don't have to exercise.*

'*Try it, Lucky,*' Amber had said when the idea had first been introduced. '*Who knows? It might actually do you some good.*'

Laura had laughed at them. '*Lucky's allergic to exercise, Amber,*' she'd replied for him.

Normally, Luc would chuckle at the memory. Now it just brought a painful stab in his gut.

Where are you, Amber?

He knocked on the door, entering at the genial 'Come in!'

Haste was standing at his desk – "*standing desks not only improve work efficiency but also eliminate harmful effects of sitting all day*", as he'd told his employees when they'd been introduced – typing something on his computer. He smiled at Luc, gesturing for him to close the door behind him.

'How was your day off yesterday, Agent Holmes?' Haste asked. Luc shrugged. He didn't remember most of it. He should have taken today off as well, his aching head reminded him, but he ignored the throbbing and forced himself to focus. He had too much to do to take sick leave.

Haste folded his hands in front of him, the smile now gone. His face was mainly clear of wrinkles, but his hair was grey, and there were some small creases around his eyes and mouth. He wore an expensive-looking blue suit with a striped red tie.

'Agent Holmes,' the man sighed. 'I have to admit that I wasn't expecting you and Agent Elkhoury to fail your mission the day before last. I assumed that the mission was quite simple.'

'The thing is –'

'I'm sorry, Agent, but I wasn't finished.'

Luc closed his mouth. *Fine,* he thought irritably. *Finish your point.*

Outwardly, he gestured graciously for the man to continue, trying to curb his normally moderate temper. *What's wrong with me?* he wondered. He wasn't usually snarky. He shook his head, filing the issue away for later while Haste continued.

'I've made my expectations clear. Of course, there were some difficulties, but every mission has unique challenges that ARCHIVE agents must overcome by themselves.' He spread his hands out in front of him. '*Si Periculum.* Do you know what that means, Agent Holmes?'

'*At whatever risk.*'

Haste nodded. 'Now, what were you going to say earlier?'

Luc had been going to point out that they hadn't anticipated being ambushed at the laboratory, nor had they been in control of the car crash. And it wasn't like Amber had kept to the speed limit out of respect for local residents. But Haste had already dealt with that point. *Si Periculum.*

Instead, he opened his palms in a sign of surrender. *I'll talk to him in his own language,* Luc decided. *He'll love this.*

'Sir, as an agent, I won't try to make excuses for why we didn't finish our mission,' he said. 'And I know that if Amber were here,' he stumbled for a moment, then hurried on, 'she would already be thinking about how to get the timebox back to ARCHIVE. I want to learn from my past mistakes, and use them to move forward. All I need is your permission to use ARCHIVE's resources to try to find Amber.'

Haste didn't seem impressed.

'And the timebox, too,' Luc added. *Stupid timebox.* 'Of course.'

The phone on the desk rang, but Haste ignored it. He studied Luc carefully, mulling over what he'd said. 'I did have other missions I wanted you to look at, Agent Holmes,' he said finally, as though disappointed. 'But I value your ethic. Learning from mistakes is impor—'

'I'll do those missions too. I can investigate this in my own time.' Luc shook his head in desperation. 'Amber was unconscious, maybe even dead, when she disappeared. I believe the timebox sent her back into some point in the past. I just have to find her and bring her—'

'Holmes,' Haste stepped around the desk. 'Amber has the timebox. She'll come back when she's ready.'

Luc shook his head, running his hands through his hair. He'd had enough. 'No, Commander,' he snapped. 'Obviously it's been too long since you've been on-field. Amber has the timebox. It's been two days. If she was fine, she would have come back by now. Why would she program the thing to come back *a full week later than she left?*' He was yelling at the Commander. He stepped back, breathing deeply in an effort to steady his nerves.

The Commander didn't seem rattled. He eyed Luc calmly, then shook his head. 'It may have been a long time since I was on field, Agent,' he said quietly. 'But I am your Commander, and you need to speak to respect me.'

As infuriating as it was, Luc knew that the Commander was right. He tried to make himself sound contrite as he mumbled an apology, but he didn't think he succeeded.

'However, I do find your logic sound,' Haste went on.

Luc felt strangely satisfied.

'You must finish this mission, Agent Holmes.' Haste said, his gaze boring into Luc's head. 'Find that timebox, whether it is in the past, or, perhaps more likely, if it's the present with the men who ambushed you at the labs.'

Slowly, Luc raised his gaze to meet the Commanders. A minute ago, he hadn't been sure if he would make it to the carpark. But now that Haste had given him a mission, his head cleared with resolve. 'Yes, Commander,' he said, and it sounded slightly more submissive this time.

'*Si Periculum,*' Haste said.

Luc clenched his fists to stop himself from rolling his eyes. *If ever I have to prove my* si periculum-ness, *it's now,* he thought.

5:00AM 12 OCTOBER 1868, WALHALLA, AUSTRALIA

Communication through time is possible using timeboxes, regardless of make. This is the most efficient way to contact ARCHIVE if communication with your ARC-researcher is disrupted or compromised.

Harry hadn't expected to travel through time. So, when he opened his eyes, still clutching the timebox, he was stunned to see small weatherboard houses, stables and dirt roads, with the sky lightening just over dark, tree-covered mountains.

So this is history, he thought.

History. His eyes flew open. *Where's the timebox?* He patted the fallen leaves and ribbons of bark around him, blinking as his eyes adjusted to the pre-dawn gloom. Finally, his hand patted something hard and metallic, and he pulled it out. An amber light on the sight blinked patiently. He tucked it into his jacket safely, then began to look around.

He was standing beside a well-packed dirt road, wide enough for two cars, but completely devoid of life. White weatherboard houses lined the road ahead, shaded with verandas and on an angle, as though standing aloof. There couldn't have been more than four or five within eyeshot, each one dirty and quaint.

Harry headed for the buildings, keeping an eye out for anyone who could tell him where and when he was.

He wondered how ARCHIVE agents discovered this sort of information. *They probably use newspapers and billboards and those sorts of things,* he concluded, searching for them. Unfortunately, wherever he was seemed like a less dusty Wild West, but there were no billboards or discarded newspapers. It was too remote.

He sat down on a veranda and decided to wait for the sun to come up. *ARCHIVE agents don't need newspapers,* he thought bitterly. *They have the timebox to tell them where and when they are.*

It took him a moment to realise that he'd just had an idea. He pulled out the timebox, scowling at his own stupidity. By the light of the rising sun, he could read a small sentence on the screen.

Walhalla, 0516 12 Oct 1868

He pressed on it experimentally, and it expanded to show a calendar and map. *Fancy.* He zoomed out of the map until he could see a recognisable coastline.

Australia?

According to the map, he was in the south-eastern tip of Australia.

Before this, Harry had never left the United Kingdom, and his geography was sketchy as a result. Australia? That was the other side of the world – he knew that much because he'd always used that fact as an excuse to never learn anything about it.

He zoomed back into the map. Fact boxes sprung up around the screen. Apparently, Melbourne was the capital of Victoria, the colony he was currently in. But, as he zoomed in closer to his location, he realised that he was more than a hundred miles from even the edge of Melbourne.

He was in the middle of nowhere.

Walhalla was nowhere.

His research was interrupted by a flashing notification.

Unread message

He pressed on it, and the box expanded.

Hey Amber it's Luc. I'm still in 2019. Let me know when you are and if you're okay. The timebox must have turned on at some point and sent you somewhere. Reply to this message if you can and we'll see it on the timeboxes here.

Harry read the message a few times. *Amber must have been the missing driver,* he decided. *And Luc is her partner. I wonder if she's here.*

Harry took a photo of the message with his phone, checking the battery life as he did. 68% left. He'd have to be careful; he didn't know when he could get back.

Or how to use the timebox.

'Timebox,' he said, hoping it would blink awake and verbally ask him what he wanted to do.

Nothing happened.

Apparently the scientists spent all their budget on making it a time travel machine, so they had nothing left over to make it actually functional, he thought bitterly.

He found a home icon on the screen and pressed it. The date and time came up once more, as well as a few other options.

Travel | Send a message | Make a note | First Aid | ?

He tried *Travel,* but a message came up, warning that he did not have fingerprint access to initiate Travel.

His knuckles turned white around the box, his teeth grinding. It took all his self-control not to throw the thing in the dust, stomp on it and storm away.

He checked his watch, but he had no idea when he arrived. *Surely it was at least close to an hour ago,* he thought, and decided to wait it out.

Once I get back to 2019, we can move on with the plan, he thought. *I just have to keep this safe until then.*

1:03PM 6 MARCH 2019, ARCHIVE

ARCars are fitted with GPS, dash cam and in-car recordings. No matter what happens to the car, this data is uploaded in the ARChronicles.

'*Why am I driving?*'

Luc pressed the fast forward button on the computer, skipping forward a few minutes. Behind him, the elevator beeped and an agent he didn't recognise left the ARChronicles for a different level.

The ARChronicles, the ARCHIVE records, was home to copies of every document, newspaper, magazine and record ever published. It spanned the entire bottom floor of the ARCHIVE headquarters, a maze of overflowing shelves. No one bothered to use them anymore. Instead, every computer was occupied by field agents using the digitised records and search engine.

Luc sat at the computer farthest from the door, his headphones on as he listened to the black box recording of the night of the crash, saved on a USB that was now plugged into one of the ARCHIVE desktops.

'*What happened?*' he heard Amber ask on the headset and skipped forward a little bit more.

The sound of screeching tires filled the headset, making him flinch. The sound seemed to last an eternity, drilling into Luc's ears and bringing back terrifying memories. He squeezed his eyes shut, forcing himself not to skip any further ahead. Finally, just when he thought he couldn't hold his breath any longer, it stopped. There was a loud crunch, the sound of airbags inflating, then silence.

Luc sucked in a breath. *One, two, three—*

He hadn't gotten in a full five-second breath before more sounds came through.

The voices were badly distorted and crackly, but Luc could just make out the words.

'That's odd.' It sounded like a man. 'Where's the driver?'

Luc's heart dropped in his chest. The men didn't know where Amber was. They weren't keeping her as a hostage.

So where is she?

He kept listening, his pen poised above his pad.

Harry? he wondered. *Who's Harry? And where did he go?*

He strained his ears, but the only sound was the slowly-fading footsteps of the other man. Impossibly, Luc's heart sunk further, feeling like a brick in his stomach.

Did this Harry Travel as well?

'No, no, no, no, no way,' he whispered. If Harry had Travelled too, it would mean that *he* had the timebox. Wherever—whenever—Amber was, she was stranded. If she was still alive, she had no way to get home.

Of course, it was frighteningly possible that Amber was already dead. Agents had to be at peak health and fitness before they Travelled, and she'd been concussed and unconscious. Could that kind of thing kill her?

The recording was playing static, with the occasional car passing by, so Luc stopped it. He went to get up, but paused.

Finally, he sat back down and played the recording from the start.

The car doors slammed, and he heard Amber say, 'Oh, the traffic's eased up. It should only take us an hour now.'

She sounded so naïve in hindsight, and Luc grimaced as he heard his own nonchalant reply. *Little did we know,* he thought.

He closed his eyes. As though tattooed onto the backs of his eyelids, he saw a vision of Amber. Unconscious. Bleeding.

Dead?

He was fairly confident she hadn't Travelled dead. He'd seen dead people as a police officer; they were… different. Unmoving, unbreathing, unsettling. He'd be able to tell if she was dead, right?

In an effort to make himself concentrate, he put his pen on the paper and forced himself to write out his thoughts.

Amber's not a hostage, he told himself.

That means she could be… anywhere. In all of history.

Work backwards, he told himself, still writing.

The timebox must have been tested while it was being developed, so it must have been already calibrated to a time and place. He could ring the labs and ask them where and when it had been calibrated to. Assuming its settings had not been changed since then, it should have sent Amber back to wherever the lab had set it to.

But to do that, he needed the phone number for Movarian Laboratories. *Ah, the timebox manual.* That might hold some clues such as where it was calibrated and how it could have been accidentally activated. He'd heard there was an app that could link to the timebox; maybe it had a tracking function.

So the first step would be to read the timebox manual.

Nodding to himself, he stood to leave, but the room dipped. He had to lean against the desk until it righted itself. As his head cleared, he risked a step forward. *Well, I'm still standing,* he thought. *But I might need something stronger than Aspirin.*

I wonder if I'd be allowed to go home.

He shook his head resolutely, but wavered when he saw the time.

I have to stay here until five? he thought. The mere thought of the next two and a half hours before he went home was exhausting. He wasn't sure he'd make it to the car now, let alone after the afternoon of work.

I suppose I have to keep going, he decided. *Amber's life could be at stake.*

With that thought, he nodded and took the elevator up to the main floor.

Agents muttered into earpieces, bustled around with papers and tablets, creating a busy but not chaotic hum. To Luc's tired mind, it was distracting. It sounded like a drill and felt just as painful.

He didn't know where he was going. He vaguely thought of asking someone where the manual had been put – maybe Haste would have it – but he found himself in a small kitchenette just off the main floor and decided to make himself a coffee instead.

'Oh, Lucky, I've been looking for you,' came a voice behind him.

It took him a moment to realise that he was being addressed. Most people called him Lucky – Amber was the only one who didn't – but the voice had sounded far away, so he had initially ignored it.

'Oh. Laura,' he mumbled when he realised who was talking.

'Don't sound so excited, it's only me,' she replied sarcastically. Her hair was messier than usual, and something about her eyes made her seem older and tireder than she had when he'd last seen her a few days before.

'Sorry,' he said. 'I'm just…' he didn't know how to finish the sentence. *Weary? Achy? Depressed?*

'You look half dead,' she replied bluntly. 'You could go home if you wanted to.'

'I want to,' he replied, closing his eyes and leaning his head back against the wall. He saw Amber in his eyelids again, as a flash. 'But I have work to do here.'

When he opened his eyes, Laura was watching him, her arms folded. 'Right. *"Work."* Go home, Lucky. You were in a car crash not two days ago. I think you can afford some sick leave—'

But Luc shook his head.

She sighed, going up to the sink and starting to fill a drink bottle with water. 'How productive do you think you'll be in your state? Even if you find where Amber is, you won't be allowed to Travel to find her until you've rested.'

She had a point there.

'I just need to find the manual—'

She turned to him, shutting off the tap as she did so. 'You *just need* to go home.'

'But—'

'End of story.'

'Do I look that bad?'

He hadn't meant it as a joke, but she laughed. 'You know that I always wish you were out of sight, but I mean it this time. You're so pale, it's a wonder you're still standing.'

He decided to ignore his spinning head even more than before. He folded his arms, trying not to lean against the wall or massage his aching temples. When he almost thought he looked kind of normal, he asked, 'Why were you looking for me?'

She pursed her lips. 'Don't try to change the subject.'

'Sorry.'

'But since you asked, I was wondering what you were up to with Amber. Finding the manual?'

Luc nodded, relaying his findings to her as briefly as he could.

When he finished, she smiled, and to Luc it was a warming smile. It revived the hope in his heart that Amber could still be alive, and helped him to stand a bit taller.

'You've made good headway,' she said. 'Good work, agent.'

'I just want to find the manual and then I'll go home.'

Her eyes narrowed. 'And read it?'

He almost nodded, but rubbed his face instead. 'Honestly, I'm so tired that I can barely see straight.' She raised an eyebrow, and he knew that he'd proved her point. 'Okay, fine. I'll go home. But after I've had some painkillers, and a good sleep, I'll read it through.'

She nodded slowly. 'Fine. Manual, then home.'

He rolled his eyes. 'Yes, mum.'

It was three days before Amber woke up again, hungry, sore, but less dizzy. She sat up tentatively, then, leaning on a bed post, she attempted to stand.

Her head seemed to float for a moment, then her vision focused and she found herself feeling fine. A bit sore and bruised, but she could take her hand from the bedpost and not fall over, which seemed to be a good sign.

She looked down at herself, puzzled. Sure enough, dark bruises stained her arms and chest, but somewhat stranger was her clothing. It was so different to what she'd seen the doctor, Johansson and Mollie wear. Her pants were tight around her legs and hips, and she wore a black singlet underneath a short, loose shirt.

Her stomach growled, and the spell was broken.

Finding food was not difficult. She asked Miss Mollie and was rewarded with some cold beef and an omnibus of tales about Richard Johansson, Mollie and herself.

'Mr Johansson came out to Australia for work, see,' Mollie said. 'Met Miss Winters on the deck of the ship and was married the day they landed. But she was the type that's permanently sick, if you know what I mean, and recently she was just worse than usual, and then suddenly she died. Personally, I think it was the trip through the mountains. No idea why Mr Johansson thought it a good idea to come out so far with someone so ill.'

Amber didn't know what to say. 'How long ago did she die?' she asked quietly, hoping she wouldn't take offence.

'About a year back,' Miss Mollie replied. 'Left poor Master Richard with poor Master Arthur to look after all on his own. Well, he has me, I suppose. But I'm not the same.'

Amber nodded solemnly, chewing slowly and swallowing. 'I understand,' she said, to fill the silence.

Mollie dipped a cloth in the water and wiped down the table. 'Though I think having you here will do those two a bit of good. It'll give them something else to think about. Master Arthur hasn't been able to stop talking about you since you turned up.' She stopped her wiping to smile at Amber. 'What I wouldn't give just to know who you are, dressed like that, beat up in the middle of the night.' She shook her head, then turned to plop the towel back into the water basin. 'Let me know once you regain your memories.'

Amber frowned. 'Do you think I will?'

Mollie shrugged. 'I'm not a doctor. I just assumed that since the body can heal, the brain can too. It's part of the body, isn't it?'

Amber shrugged.

'Speaking of memories, Master Arthur's already given a name for you.'

Amber's eyebrows rose. 'What is it?'

'Rachel Winters. He wants to name you after his mother. That's sweet, isn't it?'

Amber forced a smile, hiding her choked breath with a nod. 'I suppose.' *Not as good as knowing your real name,* said the rueful part of her. She quickly shut that part of her up. *Sooner or later I'll run into someone I know,* she thought. *They'll recognise me and help me.*

Until then, she was Rachel Winters.

★★★

In return for his care and hospitality, Amber tried to help out as best she could. She often helped Mollie to cook and clean, running errands that she suspected the maid dreaded. Mollie seemed to feel embarrassed asking her to do things, but sitting in the bed all day while everyone else had their jobs to do felt wrong. And since Amber knew nothing about herself, an inkling that she liked to be active was direction enough to get her moving.

She found out that she was in Walhalla, in South-East Australia. There were not many people at all living there, and many were there simply because of the rumours of gold. They gossiped that larger companies were on their way, preparing to lug heavy machinery through the mountains and even build a railway.

She slowly came to know the local shopkeepers and prospecting families. Most of the inhabitants were in good spirits, hopeful of wealth and the better life it would bring. A few were jealous, bitter, or lonely, and everyone was interested in everyone else. There were more than enough rumours about the new Miss Winters Winters, even before she met Christopher Alpine.

She'd been searching for a fruit and vegetable market, but, due to the heat, had been suffering some dizzy spells. In the middle of the road, the world had spun around her, and the next thing she knew she was on the side of the road, a man's arm around her shoulders, hearing him shout as he fanned her face with a small notebook.

He had such kind features – smooth brown hair, a wide, pleasant smile and beautifully kind blue eyes. And he'd seemed somewhat familiar.

'Luc?' she asked dizzily.

The man's smile became a concerned frown. 'No… my name's Christopher Alpine. I don't believe we've met, ma'am.'

No, he can't be… who? What did I say? She felt strangely disappointed, though she couldn't remember why, like the sadness left over from a dream she couldn't remember. She pushed herself up from the dusty ground.

'What happened?' she asked, taking the flask he had offered her.

'It must be the heat,' the man said. 'You were in the middle of the road, you seemed lost and disoriented, and suddenly you fainted. I saw it all from my house, over there.' He pointed up the road to a tiny weatherboard cottage tucked into the trees at the bottom of the mountain. 'I was just going to visit a friend.

Jack and his horse were coming, so I stopped it and carried you here to the shade. I hope I didn't cause offence.'

Amber swallowed her mouthful of water. 'None at all,' she said, smiling at him to add warmth to her words. Her smile prompted another from him.

'I don't believe I've seen you around before,' he said. 'What's your name?'

Her smile faded. She handed the flask back and said, as confidently as she could, 'Rachel Winters. I've been here for a couple of weeks, but I've been… ill.'

The man nodded. His eyes glanced at her hairline for a moment, as though he'd already noticed the scabs on her face.

He clearly doesn't recognise me or know what happened to me, she thought. *That's probably why I felt disappointed.*

'Interesting. My mate Harry came two weeks ago too, though he's over from England.'

'You think I came from outside Walhalla?' Amber asked without thinking. It hadn't occurred to her that she might have come from a different town altogether. Maybe a different country, even… That would explain why no one recognised her.

'I assumed you were from overseas,' he said, helping her to stand. 'From your skin, I'd guess… Arabian? Am I wrong?'

Amber smiled, dusting off her dress. 'I didn't realise it was so obvious,' she replied as casually as she could. 'I tried so hard to fit in as a local.' She picked up her basket and thanked him again for his assistance. 'Would you be able to show me the way to the fruit market?' she added sheepishly.

'It would be my pleasure,' he replied.

Good ARCHIVE partnerships do not come through teamwork, but through understanding. Learn how they think, how they strategise, and become the best team you can be.

Luc wasn't sure if he was dreaming or just remembering, if he was awake or asleep. He knew the memory was real, but he felt strangely immersed in it.

Every year ARCHIVE had its annual Christmas party. Luc had been recruited by ARCHIVE only a few weeks before, and was in training to become a field agent. He'd been standing in the corner of the decorated ARCHIVE HQ, sore and bruised from his training and wishing he was anywhere else. He'd already met about half of the party, but was having trouble remembering who was who. If he could observe them for a time, he might be able to remember names without having to ask for them again.

The ARCHIVE agents congregated in groups according to their jobs, but otherwise, they didn't seem to have much in common. ARCHIVE recruited people from all over the world, with various training and capabilities. Luc himself had been a police officer in Dublin when he'd been referred to ARCHIVE, but he'd heard of detectives and dentists, psychologists and social workers, teachers, firefighters, medics and musicians being recruited for their expertise.

There were a few that he could name easily within the bustle. Over there was Commander Haste. He'd never talked to the man, but he was featured in the ARCHIVE brochures and consequently was well-known from Luc's theory training. There was his trainer, Philip Farmer, talking to another agent.

People were sitting on desks chatting, eating the small sandwiches and drinking soft-drink and beer from large red cups that had been filled and placed on the tables. The lights were on bright, though the sun had gone down, and forgettable music played over some speakers.

'You must be Lucky Holmes,' said a voice next to him.

Luc jumped. 'Commander Haste. Yes, how did you know?' He shook the offered hand as the Commander laughed.

'I know all my agents,' Haste said. 'And I'd like to introduce you to someone.'

Luc had no one better to talk to, so he nodded, following Haste into the middle of the party. A small group of people were talking in hushed, gossipy tones. Three of them seemed around Luc's age: two from east Asia and one seemed Filipino. An older Jamaican woman Luc wasn't sure he recognised was trying to start a side-conversation with a young woman.

Haste elbowed his way into the centre of the group, Luc following close behind. 'Agent Elkhoury,' he said, and the woman looked up. At Haste's beckoning, she excused herself from the group. 'This is Agent Lucky Holmes. You two will be partners when you join ARCHIVE next year.'

Luc stared at the Commander for a moment too long. *My partner? Does that mean I've passed my training?* He'd never done better than scraped through the timed races and obstacle courses, and he'd been hoping that if he failed, he might score a desk job. But if this was his partner, then that meant he would pass.

He was going to travel through time.

'Nice to meet you, Lucky,' Elkhoury said, and he tried to come back to the present, returning a mumbled 'you too'. She was shorter than him, fitter than him, and had a warm smile that he instantly liked. 'Interesting nickname. What makes you lucky?'

'It's just a shortening of my name,' he replied, offering his hand. 'You are?'

'Amber.' She spoke with a soft East-London accent. He led her closer to the wall, where the ambiance was quieter and they could talk in peace. 'I take it you're still in training?' she asked.

Luc nodded. 'Honestly didn't think I'd pass until about ten seconds ago.'

She laughed. 'Congratulations.'

'Have you been working here long?'

Amber seemed startled. 'Me? No, I finished my training about a week ago. I was a psychologist beforehand. I think ARCHIVE took notice of me after a case I testified in.'

Luc raised his eyebrows. 'Impressive. My sergeant referred me. I was a police officer, and he said I was going to move to London. I assumed it was just a change in post, but I'm not complaining. I love history.'

'Maybe that was why he referred you?'

Luc shrugged. There were stories he preferred not to tell.

'I'm glad I got to meet you,' he said instead, and he meant it. He'd been fighting nerves about his first missions all throughout his training. But this woman seemed warm and friendly, and somehow that gave him confidence that it would be okay. He opened his mouth to say this, but it seemed too honest for a first impression. She didn't seem nervous, but maybe if he admitted to it, she would.

It hadn't mattered in the end. By their first mission, they'd both confessed to their nerves and feelings of inadequacy. It was hard to believe you belonged in the "best of the best" when you'd failed your Historical Drivers' License, and couldn't remember where the ARCHIVE toilets were.

They'd told each other that it couldn't go wrong. After all, ARCHIVE worked according to existing records. If they were tasked with saving a malfunctioning plane in the 1990s, then they had to succeed. It was recorded.

Somehow, against all their training, they'd been wrong.

Amber had been sent to London City Airport in the late 1990s, plane ticket in hand. Luc had been sent to Fiji to meet the plane with medical support and directions to their connecting flight. But when the doors to the plane had finally opened, he was met with a sour Carl Mendoza.

He'd found her in the ARCHIVE break room, sipping a cup of tea, her face pale.

'Amber?' he called, sliding into a chair opposite her. 'What happened? Are you okay?'

She looked up, tucking a stray curl behind an ear. 'Hey, Lucky. Did the mission finish well in the end?'

Luc stared at her. *What happened?* he wanted to demand. *Why did no one know where you were?*

He licked his lips. 'It's fine. That's not what I asked.'

Her lips twitched, but she looked down at her hands, cupping her mug. 'I'm fine. I just… I got held up.'

'By Carl?'

She half nodded, half shrugged. 'He said I never got on the plane. He said I couldn't handle the mission, and he needed to do it instead. Or else everyone would die, and it would be my fault.'

'That's not true,' Luc said without thinking. It couldn't be true.

She watched him for a moment, then smiled. 'It's not. I'm okay, Lucky. I just had… something else to do.'

Luc wasn't sure what to say. He'd been rehearsing his condolences, trying to think up things that might help her to feel better. *We're still learning. Carl's just a jerk. You're a fantastic agent, and you have plenty of missions to prove that.*

But she didn't seem upset at all. If Luc didn't know what had just happened, he would have said she was… amused.

Her words finally landed, and he squinted at her. 'What did you have to do?'

She shook her head dismissively. 'I'll have to tell you later.' Her shoulders picked up, and she spoke louder. 'By the way, I thought of a new nickname for you. Can I call you Luc? Not *Luke*, but *Luc*, like the first three letters of Lucky. Get it?'

Luc stared at her, trying to keep up. 'Why?'

'You don't like it?'

'I mean…' he tried it out in his head. 'It's not my name.'

She shrugged. 'That's the point of a nickname.'

He thought it about it. 'I thought you said Lucky was cute.'

She rolled her eyes. 'Sure it is, but this is…' she shrugged, as though she wasn't sure how to describe its appeal. Finally she gave up. 'Can't they both be cute… Luc?'

'Are you *sure* you're okay?'

She grinned. 'I'm sure. But thanks for looking out for me all the same… Luc.'

He rolled his eyes. 'Fine. Somehow, when you say it, I don't mind.'

6:15PM 29 OCTOBER 1868, WALHALLA, AUSTRALIA

ARCHIVE medics recommend that you avoid local food and water, to avoid food poisoning. It's recommended that food is cooked thoroughly and water is boiled before consumption.

'Do you remember anything yet, Miss Winters?' Arthur asked.

Amber put her knife down with a barely-contained sigh. 'Arthur, I *told* you that if and when I do, you'll be the first to know. You don't have to keep asking.'

His smile widened into a grin as he made sure she wasn't mad with him. She didn't mind him checking in, but so far, the answer hadn't changed. And her early concerns were starting to grow into anxiety.

His most burning question answered, Arthur began his detailed recounting of his morning at school and his afternoon with his friends. Mollie said there were nine children at Arthur's school, but each child had a first name, a last name, a nickname, and a description. Amber couldn't tell who was who anymore.

As Arthur recapped his day, Johansson came in from the workroom at the front of the house, wiping sweat off his face with a handkerchief. The windows on the front of the workroom caught the sunlight late in the day, and Amber had quickly learned to stay out at that time if she didn't want to be baked like their roast beef.

Arthur interrupted himself to say good evening to his father, who gave a formal *'good evening'* back.

'Mr Johansson,' Amber said, before Johansson's attention was captured completely by his son. 'I asked at the post office if there was a brain doctor around, and he said there was one who's just landed in Melbourne. I'm thinking of going tomorrow, to ask him to examine me.'

Johansson paused. 'In Melbourne?'

Amber nodded.

'How are you going to get there?'

Amber's confidence shrank a little. 'I could... walk?'

His eyebrow rose a little. 'Will you? It's four days from here. Possibly more, seeing as you're still recovering.'

'Four days?'

'Aye. You could take the post next fortnight. I reckon you'll have more chance of getting there in one piece. You don't want to be going through these mountains on your own, walking or no.'

Two weeks? 'I couldn't trouble you for that long,' she said quietly. 'I didn't realise—I thought Melbourne—'

Johansson looked away. 'No trouble. We'll wait for the post and see if you don't get better before the carriage comes. In the meantime, I've sent an advertisement to the paper in Melbourne, to say we found you.'

'Thank you,' she murmured. A new thought occurred to her. 'How far is Sale?'

'About a day's walk. You want to try there for a doctor?'

The thought didn't appeal to her as much as Melbourne did. Melbourne was a city, with people coming in and out on their way to the goldfields. There might be a doctor in Sale, but she wasn't confident that he would be able to explain what had happened.

She wasn't sure *she* could explain what had happened.

'I'll keep thinking,' she said, gingerly prodding at the gash on her forehead. 'I don't have any money to pay for a doctor, anyway. And even if I did, I don't know he'd say anything I haven't already thought of.'

Johansson's other eyebrow rose to join its mate. 'Heavens, woman, he's a professional. What, have you finally remembered that you're a doctor too?'

Amber tried to ignore the sarcasm, but couldn't stop a frown from forming on her face. 'No, I—don't ask how I know this, but I do. I have amnesia, that's fairly clear, but the question is, how did I get it?'

'I've been wondering that too,' Johansson said, folding his arms.

'Long-term amnesia can come from two things:' She held up a finger. 'A brain tumour'—another finger— 'and severe childhood trauma, like in Dissociative Identity Disorder.'

Johansson looked ready to nudge his son behind him to protect him from whatever spell she was summoning. 'Miss Winters, you were unconscious. You were covered in injuries. You're overthinking this.'

Amber shook her head. 'Bumps on the head can cause *temporary* amnesia, but not long-lasting amnesia. My memories should have been localised to the event, or they should have come back by now. Brain cancer would mean my condition deteriorates. I've been improving, while my memories stay constant, so I'm assuming it's not that. And the childhood trauma doesn't account for me forgetting my *entire identity*. If I went through some severely traumatic event through my childhood, why did I forget people I know as an adult?' She looked down at her hands. 'Maybe I'm just an exception?'

Johansson cleared his throat. 'We'll wait for the opinion of a professional,' he said.

Amber threw up a hand. 'Maybe *I'm* a professional,' she muttered, which made Arthur giggle. Johansson only threw her a glare.

'You're a woman with no memories,' he said, sitting down to eat with them.

She nodded tiredly. *I had a life before this,* she wanted to scream. *Someone somewhere knows my story.* But just as they bowed their heads to give thanks for the meal, she said quietly, 'I could be anyone.'

Johansson didn't bother to reply to that.

Don't underestimate the power of rest and recuperation.

Luc slept for the rest of that afternoon, then called in sick the next day.

Laura called to say that they'd searched the ARChronicles for a mention of Amber's name, and hadn't found anything outside her usual timeline that resembled her.

'What did you do yesterday?' she asked.

'I slept till nine, then did some housework, then watched a historical documentary for the rest of the afternoon.'

He heard Laura laugh on the other end. 'How many *Horrible Histories* episodes did you watch?'

Maybe Laura knew him too well. 'To be honest, I'm not sure,' he laughed. 'I fell asleep again.'

Even though she'd stopped laughing, he could hear her smile through her tone. 'You've had a rough week, Lucky. This will be good for you. Go to the doctors today or tomorrow to see what they say.'

'Will do,' he replied. 'Thanks, Laura. I really appreciate everything you're doing for me.'

'Pleasure.'

They said their goodbyes and hung up. He was left with simultaneous feelings of despair and deep happiness. He knew Laura was putting on a brave face, trying to keep him from giving up hope, and he appreciated the effort.

But mingled with that warmth was crushed hope. *No mention of Amber in the records.* He'd already looked her up quickly and found the same thing, but it was still concerning. *The ARChronicles include the obituaries of every person who has ever had one written about them,* Luc told himself. *That means that Amber hasn't died, or at least that she doesn't have an obituary.*

And, as he kept reminding himself, she may be using a fake name for any number of reasons. If her name wasn't in history, it didn't mean that *she* wasn't.

For now, he picked up the timebox manual and flicked it open.

Bed rest was fine.

Luc liked to read in bed.

★★★

What Luc had thought to be the timebox manual was really a guidebook for ARCHIVE field agents. It was about three-hundred pages long, with four chapters dedicated solely to the new timebox. Luc opened a notebook and prepared to take notes; he didn't want to have to trawl through three-hundred pages of how-to-ARCHIVE twice. Most of the manual was things he already knew from his onboarding training, so he skipped to the timebox chapters.

By the time he'd finished the four timebox chapters, he had some points written down and a good idea of where to go next.

- *Timebox is voice activated, but for more accurate/delicate stuff use the manual controls*

- *The timebox can only transport one person at a time. there is a 1 min gap between ppl. It will transport 1, then countdown 60 secs on its screen. When it reaches 0, it transports the next person if someone is touching it. It repeats this until no one is touching it, then transports itself.*

- *Location of the earth no longer has to be calculated!! The timebox does it for you*

- *Travel history can be accessed on the timebox!! Lab also has access to this!*

- *Timebox screen shows location, time, any extra info.*

- *Is this the only timebox? Are they making others?*

And underneath was the most important point:
- *Lab phone number: +44 20 8463 2691*

Luc pulled out his phone and punched in the phone number. The tone rang a few times, then he heard a click.

'Hi, this is Movarian Laboratories. What can I help you with?'

'Hi, I'd like to talk with Dr Stephen Whitehall, please,' Luc said, remembering the name he'd been sent to on his mission with Amber.

'Your name?'

'Lucky Holmes. I'm an ARCHIVE agent.'

'One moment, please.' The receptionist put him on hold.

Luc reviewed the list he'd made. Most of the information on the timebox had been about how to use it; how to turn it on, calibrate it, put in the desired location, and so on. As Luc didn't have a timebox, this was useless to him.

However, there were some interesting points in his notes. He was impressed that they'd made it easier to use. Before, the agent needed to do some difficult calculations to make sure that the old timebox would land him on the earth, instead of deep in outer space. If they were travelling from midday in summer to late afternoon the previous winter, the position of the earth in its orbit around the sun would have changed, and this change would have to be taken into consideration. It seemed that agents no longer had to worry about these calculations. *What a relief,* Luc thought. Those calculations had been headaches, and they'd been required to triple check them before trying new coordinates.

More importantly, there were clues in how Amber had been accidentally transported. If one of them had accidentally triggered the timebox's transporting mechanism through their conversation, or if one of them had bumped its 'on' button, it would explain how Amber and the timebox had disappeared. *It had been jostled around a lot when the car was spinning,* Luc thought, feeling a pang of guilt as he remembered nearly dropping it even before the crash.

The hold music on his phone abruptly stopped and a man's 'hello?' sounded from the speakers.

'Hi, Doctor Whitehall,' Luc said. 'It's Lucky Holmes.'

'One of the agents who picked up the timebox, aren't you?' the man said.

'Yes, that's me.'

'What can I help you with?'

'Can you access the Travel history of the timebox?'

'Yes…' he said slowly. 'If this is about the other night, I already told Haste that they went to 1868. Didn't he tell you that?'

Luc nearly dropped his phone. *1868!* Before he could forget it, he wrote the number in his notebook, then underlined it twice. 'Uh… he… he didn't mention it. But I'm investigating from home this week.'

'Didn't he?' he said quietly, then muttered something under his breath that, if Lucky had repeated in Haste's hearing, would have had him fired. 'Haste is making you work from home, but he didn't tell you the findings of the timebox?'

Luc frowned. 'No, he… should he have mentioned something?'

There was silence on the other end of the phone for a long time.

Lucky held his breath. 'Where did you say the timebox Travelled to?'

Whitehall paused. 'I didn't.'

Luc picked up his pen, poised above the paper.

'Walhalla.'

Luc wrote the word frantically. *Where on earth is—*

'Walhalla, Australia, 12 November 1868,' Whitehall said shortly. 'Now go and get my timebox back.'

12:15PM 7 November 1868, Walhalla, Australia

Once you know how to use it, the timebox is not difficult to use, but it is important to know it thoroughly. Ask your ARC-researcher if you have any technical troubles, or call our help line.

Despite the past two weeks, Harry still hadn't made any progress with the timebox. Whenever he tried to Travel, it complained that his fingerprints were not registered on the ARCHIVE database. He'd looked up the 'Help' button, but it had simply asked him if he wanted to

> 1. Contact an ARC-researcher
> 2. Submit a question to our online forum
> 3. Find ARCHIVE agents near me
> 4. Read/watch our timebox manual

(which opened a window that unhelpfully told him that there was no internet access and no files were downloaded).

He'd searched through every link, every window, zoomed into every picture and still there was nothing to get him back to the era of concrete pavements and disposable coffee cups. *What's the point of having a timebox and no internet?*

He'd been forced to use a room at the local hotel in exchange for doing odd jobs around the place. It was a terrible room –

no running water, a tiny, rickety bed with a few sheets, and a small window that only showed the dirt and tree trunks on the side of the mountain. He'd scavenged some old clothes from the lost and found at the hotel, and pored over maps to nearby cities, and useless timebox functions.

As he'd researched, he'd tried *Find ARCHIVE agents near me,* expecting no one to show up in the hemisphere. To his surprise, one red dot appeared on the small screen. He tapped it.

Agent Amber Elkhoury is 0.8 miles away.

That was a bit closer than Melbourne, let alone London. He snatched up the timebox, took his hat off the bed and set off down the dirt path of Walhalla.

★★★

Amber threw her chopped carrot into the pot, nodding absently.

'My mum always said she missed the birds in England. She said in the morning, you'd wake up to gentle birdsong in the trees outside, but here, they're loud and squarkish.' Mollie turned over the pot she was scrubbing, pushing stray hairs back with her forearm. 'Thing is, I never thought they sounded like someone laughing. Do *you* think they sound like they're laughing?'

Amber looked up. 'What?' She'd assumed not even Mollie was listening to herself anymore.

She was saved an answer by a sharp knock on the front door. Mollie set the pot into the trough with a sigh. 'I'll get that.'

Amber handed her a towel and picked up a new carrot.

'No, sir,' she heard Mollie say. 'You must have the wrong house. I'm not Amber.'

There was a pause as the man at the door said something.

'The only other woman here is…' there was a shorter pause. 'Maybe…' suddenly the woman shouted. 'Miss Rachel! Come quickly!'

Amber knew what Mollie was thinking. She'd been thinking it herself. *Maybe this man knew me before my accident. Maybe my real name is Amber.*

She dropped her carrot and knife, pulling off her apron as she ran to the front door. *I'll probably know him as soon as I see him,* she reasoned. *And I might get all my memories back too.*

The man came into view, filling the doorway in front of Mollie. She didn't know him. Her memories didn't come flooding back. But something deep inside her started pounding on her, screaming that she should run.

'Is this Amber?' Mollie said.

He looked her up and down with distaste, then glanced at a strange box that he held in his hand. 'I… think so, yes.'

Amber frowned. 'You think so?' she repeated.

'We've never met before,' he said. He had a Northern accent and spoke with the air of someone who thought that he was in charge, an impression that was dampened by his homeless look.

'Then how do you know my name is Amber? Do you know a friend of mine?' *Should I ask him if he's responding to the paper?* she thought, but kept her mouth closed. If he was, he would mention it.

The man shook his head, his mouth hanging open. There was something about him – maybe his scruffy appearance, or his unsure way of handling himself, or just his foreboding face – that made Amber hesitant to trust him. 'Why do you think I'm Amber?' she asked again.

Again, he glanced at his mysterious box. 'It's a long story,' he eventually sighed. 'I'm... Harry. I was looking for...' -- his eyes narrowed – 'for the *archives*, and I was told that someone named Amber Elkhoury might be able to help.'

Amber raised an eyebrow. 'This is a tailor's,' she replied flatly. 'Good luck finding any archives.'

She turned to leave him in the doorway, but he darted past Mollie and grabbed her arm, stopping her. 'Amber, wait!' He took a deep breath. 'I… I'll give you this,' he held up the strange box and looked at her like he hated what he was doing. 'I'll give it to you if… if you can get me back home.' He let go of her arm. There was fear in his eyes, but also an intense desperation.

Amber held out her hand. 'Let me see that.'

He handed her the box hesitantly. His hands were shaking. She turned it over, inspected its buttons and numbers. It was slightly heavy, but its weight and heft was unfamiliar.

'What does it do?' she asked, still inspecting it.

The man's eyes widened. 'What do you mean, *what does it do?*' he yelled. 'You're the ARCHIVE agent – you're meant to know! Now get me back home!'

'I don't know where your home is, or how to get you there,' Amber snapped. 'Please keep your voice down.'

'Maybe you should check the police archives?' Mollie said. 'They might know where your home is if…' Mollie looked at Amber tentatively. 'If you can't remember who you are.'

The man rounded on the poor girl, yelling at her. 'I know where my home is! And if you go to the police, I'll… I'll take that thing back and you'll never see it again!'

Amber looked at the box again. He was ascribing a lot of value to it; apparently it was both a guarantee of his freedom and of his safety on his way back home. *Should I keep it? Or give it to the police?*

But she didn't know what it did. It seemed completely useless.

Harry stepped forward to Mollie, straining himself to appear taller as he tried to intimidate her. A cold indifference settled into Amber's stomach. He couldn't demand she help him, threaten her and try to intimidate them, then expect her to roll over. 'I don't know what this is,' she said, slamming the box into his chest and pushing him away. 'And I have no interest in it, when you're going to be so rude to us about it. I don't know where your home is, or how to get you there, but whoever I am, I'm not Amber Elkhoury. Get out, and if you ever come here again, I'll call the constable.'

She pushed him out the door, slamming the door behind him and firmly locking it. The door shook and rattled, but she pressed her back into it, closing her eyes.

Harry, she thought. *Is this Christopher's friend?*

She opened her eyes to see Mollie hugging herself, her face pale and stiff.

'Are you alright?' Amber asked. Mollie nodded.

'Good. Is it okay if I have a lie down? Just… fifteen minutes.'

Mollie gave her a sympathetic look. 'Of course. You're still recovering, after all.'

Amber's makeshift room was a small converted storeroom behind the shop. It had a small window that was covered by some old cloth, leaving the room cool and comfortably dark. She closed the door and leaned against with a sigh.

Her mysteriously-sourced injuries left her tired most of the time, and the dresses Mr Johansson had given her to wear weren't very helpful, either. They were heavy, hot, and constricting, making her feel dizzy when her head wasn't hurting.

She stopped at the small mirror on the wall, staring at her reflection. Tanned skin, dark curly hair, thick, dark lips… *Who are you?* she thought. Shaking her head, she knelt next to the mattress and let herself fall onto it.

Lying still helped her head to clear. Harry probably had the wrong girl. In the long list of potential people, she could rule out one name. But then, even *he* couldn't say for sure that she wasn't Amber Elkhoury.

She sighed heavily.

Maybe I'll have to resign myself to the name Rachel Winters forever, she thought. She wasn't sure why, but the name didn't feel right, like a mis-fitting shoe. Keeping it until she died made her feel… lost. She tried to imagine marrying someone and becoming Rachel… *Alpine?* she thought with a small chuckle at her childish thoughts. *Just because he was nice to you once, doesn't mean he likes you enough to marry you.*

Strange questions started crowding her mind. *What if I'm already married? Do I have a husband and children looking for me? What about my parents?*

And, the inevitable, *why does no one know who I am?*

It was like she'd dropped out of the sky into the tiny town of Walhalla. *Maybe I'm a goddess, thrown out of the heavens to live among mortals.*

The joke didn't amuse her.

Christopher must be right. She must be from overseas. She'd gotten off the boat, hit her head and forgotten who she was.

That feeling of wearing an ill-fitting shoe came back. She twisted on her bed, trying to feel comfortable in her tight clothes.

Trying to figure out who I am… it's like trying on dresses, but each one is either a size too big, or a size too small—

She sat up abruptly. *A size too big? What does* that *mean?*

She lived with a tailor, and she'd never heard him, or anyone, say 'a size'. As though a size was a measurement, like an inch.

Strange. Her own thoughts didn't seem to fit in here, judging by what the others said. It was like she spoke a different dialect – no, it was more than that. It was a different culture.

The thought sparked a memory, and Christopher's words floated through her mind. '*My mate Harry came two weeks ago too.*'

The same time as me.

She flopped back onto the bed, regretting it as pain lanced through her head and she winced. *I've never seen anything like that box he had, either,* she thought. *It looked like some kind of low-tech iPad.*

She sat up again, more slowly this time, and looked around the room. 'Come to think of it,' she said quietly. 'I haven't seen an iPad here.' She searched through her memory, listing things that she'd missed. *Television, plastic, RnB music…* the more she listed, the more hopeless and out of place she felt. It was longer than she'd thought it would be.

She pushed herself off the bed, a new resolve building inside of her. *I need to talk to Harry and investigate that thing more,* she thought. *It's not an iPad – I don't know what it is; but wherever I'm from, Harry's from there too.*

She passed Mollie and Mr Johansson on the way out, giving them both a nod. 'I'm going out,' she said.

Johansson raised an eyebrow. 'Now?'

She nodded. 'Now.'

As Luc walked through the office doors, he shot a text off to Laura, asking to meet her. Almost immediately, he got a reply.

> I can swing by your house this afternoon after work.

'I'm at work now,' he said, finding her bent over her phone.

She looked up as he approached, disapproval already written clearly on her features. 'You're not well—'

'I know where Amber is,' he interrupted. 'She's near Melbourne, in the 1860s.'

Laura's eyes widened, and all concern about his well-being was forgotten. 'Are you going to Travel to get her?' she asked quickly.

'I didn't think that *not* going would be an option,' he replied slowly. 'But there's something… a bit off about this whole thing.'

'A bit off? What do you mean?'

He shrugged, lowering his voice, even though no one around them seemed interested in their conversation. 'I talked to Dr Whitehall from the lab this morning, and he was suspicious. He said he'd already told Haste where the timebox was.'

Laura's eyes narrowed. 'What are you implying, Lucky?'

He held up his hands in defense. 'I don't—No. I'm not implying anything. I'm just... confused. It's not like Haste *couldn't* contact me to tell me where and when she was. And it doesn't seem like something he would just forget about. So why didn't he tell me?'

Laura folded her arms, an eyebrow rising. 'Maybe he knew that as soon as you knew, you would Travel, and since you were in a car crash the other day, that wouldn't be good for your health.'

Luc hadn't thought of that. His brow furrowed slightly. 'You think the Commander will actually *stop* me from going?'

'I think he should,' Laura replied. 'You have stitches in your *face*, Lucky. And you know it's dangerous to Travel when you're not in peak health. If *he* doesn't stop you from Travelling, one of the medics will.'

Luc nodded thoughtfully. 'That's true. Do you think there's a way to Travel without having to go through the check-up?'

Laura stared at him for a long time, her face blank. Stepping away from him, she shook her head. 'I shouldn't have to answer that.'

Thinking through it, it would be risky for him to Travel after being injured just a few days before. Laura's reasoning kind of made sense.

But the thought of sending another agent in his place, or leaving it until he was better, twisted his heart painfully. He remembered searching for Amber in the masses of people who had disembarked the downed plane, and remembered the panic at not seeing her. And the confusion when he'd recognised Carl.

If Amber was hurt, *he* wanted to be the one to help. He didn't want someone to go in his place.

'Laura,' he said, trying to keep his voice at a normal register. 'I just read the ARCHIVE manual. Well, the bits about Travelling, but that was enough.'

'So?'

'So, it explained why it's unsafe for people to Travel when they're sick or injured.' He thought back, hoping that he could explain it clearly and convincingly. 'The main problem is the risk of infection. When you Travel, you're exposing your body to all the infections and diseases that survive between now and the time you're Travelling to.'

'Is this supposed to convince me?'

'Yes. Hear me out.' Luc took a deep breath. 'Say you Travel to…' he tried to think of an era on the spot. *1868,* his brain said unhelpfully. 'you Travel to 1019, for example,' he said slowly. 'You're exposed to one thousand years-worth of pathogens, but your body is also squeezing one-thousand year's-worth of healing into that moment of Travelling. So, even though I have stitches in my face, it shouldn't be a problem, so long as I take some kind of disinfectant—'

'Lucky, listen to yourself,' Laura said. 'Whatever you say, you don't know better than the medics. Go and get a check-up if you want to be sure, but they won't let you Travel.'

Lucky sighed heavily. 'But if I don't go, then who will?'

She shrugged, laying a sympathetic hand on his elbow. 'Why don't you talk to the Commander about it? Maybe you could listen in as an ARC-researcher or something. I'd be happy to go, if he's looking for volunteers.'

'You're not a field agent.'

She glared at him. 'I'm still more ready to go than you.'

He sighed, but couldn't think of another argument. 'Fine, I'll talk to Haste.'

She nodded, patting his shoulder. 'Lucky, we want Amber back too. We just don't want to risk losing both of you in the process.'

He nodded, taking a deep breath. 'I know, Laura. I know.'

Haste's Office

Any higher-ranking officer is able to withhold information from you at their own discretion. As their subordinate, it is not your place to ask them questions. They will give you what you need. Go and do what they tell you.

Luc took a deep breath, confident that he already knew what the Commander would say.

Haste put down his phone, and gave his attention to him. 'Agent Holmes, I thought I heard you'd called in sick today.'

Luc nodded slowly. 'I know where Amber is.' Haste didn't react to the information, disappointingly. 'I just need permission to get her.'

Haste nodded immediately. 'Yes, I agree,' he said. 'As soon as possible, in fact.'

'What?' the question was out before Luc could stop himself. His hands tightened on the arms of the chair he was sitting in. 'Um… as—as soon as possible?'

The Commander seemed surprised. 'What answer were you expecting?'

Luc didn't want to remind him that he was injured, in case that changed his mind. 'I talked to Laura earlier and she… expressed concern… since I was…'

'Since you're so close to the case?'

Luc gestured something that could have been taken as a nod or a half-cough.

'I think there's no one better to send,' Haste replied. 'You, of all people, know the importance of getting the timebox safely, and I'm sure you won't come back empty-handed again.'

Last time I came back empty-handed, I was also lying on an ambulance stretcher. 'So I can leave… today?'

Haste leant on the desk, his face deadly serious. 'Agent Holmes. The man who held up Movarian Laboratories also Travelled back with Agent Elkhoury. *He* has the Timebox. If you value everything this organisation has protected for more than fifty years, why would you delay?'

So that man did *Travel back with Amber,* Luc thought, his heart starting to beat quicker. 'Of course, Sir,' he said quickly. 'So… who can I have as an ARC-researcher?'

Haste frowned. 'An ARC-researcher? Would you need one of those?'

Luc paused. 'Well, traditionally…'

Haste shook his head thoughtfully. 'From memory, I don't have any spare ARC-researchers. I can double-check, but I don't think you'll need one. It should just be a simple in-and-out.'

No spare ARC-researchers? What were they all doing? There were more ARC-researchers than field agents, so there were always at least a few on leave or stand-by. Even Laura or a spare medic would be better than nothing. Otherwise he'd be Travelling while injured, with a clearly hostile enemy waiting for him on the other end, without any chance of back-up. Even *he* knew that would be stupidity.

'Sir…'

'Agent Holmes,' Haste interrupted. 'I'm sure I don't need to tell you how important this is. I am anxious to get the timebox out of that man's hands as soon as we can.'

Luc nodded briskly. 'Of course, of course. But still—'

'*Si Periculum*, Agent Holmes.' Haste fixed Luc in a hard glare. 'The timebox, and everything it represents, is at stake. You *must* get it back, no matter the risk.'

Stupid si periculum, Luc thought, closing his mouth. *You can't argue with it.* 'Can I at least borrow Amber's file?' he asked.

Haste nodded vaguely. Grabbing a piece of paper, he scribbled on it:

I give specific permission for Agent Holmes to carry out whatever investigations he deems necessary. If you hinder him you will answer directly to me.

Commander Haste

Luc's eyebrows rose even higher up his forehead. 'How can this be specific permission if—'

'Agent Holmes,' Haste said, handing him the piece of paper. 'At the moment, I am not only trusting you with my reputation as Commander, but also with the fate of the world.'

Luc closed his mouth and took the paper silently.

Haste's hands were shaking. 'Do not let me down.'

***

Laura protested for a long time, asking the same questions and throwing the same protests around that Luc had been thinking since his meeting with Haste.

Luc tried to answer, or at least listen, as though she could change his mind. 'Laura,' he said finally. 'I *know*. But this isn't me being stubborn anymore. Haste *ordered* me to go.'

'At least get an ARC-researcher,' she said. 'He can't claim he has none; there are more of them than there are of you. Get one off-the-books; it won't cost him anything.'

Luc nodded, though he wasn't sure how that would work. 'I will, Laura. Can I have some clothes?'

She looked at him for a long moment. 'Fine.'

She put together two outfits: one for his hopefully short stay in Australia, and one for Amber, assuming she only had her clothes from the crash and might like to change when she got back to ARCHIVE.

Laura,' he said while she tutted over sizes. 'You're Australian—are you from near Walhalla?'

She shook her head, choosing a brown suit. 'I'm Kaurna.'

'Is that… close to that?'

'Nope.'

'Oh. Well, either way, you grew up in Australia. Anything I should know before I go?'

Laura had looked at him for a long moment, a small smile threatening to twitch on her lips. 'When are you going to? November?' Luc had nodded. 'Well, that will be late Spring over there, so it'll probably be hot. In hot weather, you have to watch out for snakes in long grass and bushland.'

Luc nodded, filing the information away. 'Anything else?'

She shrugged. 'Most of Australia's reputation for deadly animals is overstated. If you leave the wildlife alone, they will leave you alone. The only exception for where you're going is the magpies.'

Luc paused. 'Birds?'

She nodded. 'They will swoop at you and try to poke your eyes out.'

Luc stared at her for a moment. *She's joking,* he decided, and tried out a laugh.

'I'm serious.'

He swallowed. 'Great. Watch out for the birds.'

Luc's next step was to figure out how to convince an ARC-researcher to work off the books, against Haste's orders. He took the elevator one floor down to the ARChronicles floor. Although the ARChronicles covered the floor, there was a small pocket in the back corner used for general mission supplies and more sensitive files. Luc headed there, and was soon greeted with an empty reception desk. Behind the desk was a wall covered in colour-coded files: yellow for field agents, red for ARC-researchers, green for admin-staff and white for the medics. More of these files were scattered over the desk in a chaotic rainbow.

With a start, Luc read the name on the front of a red file. *Shinichi Samejima.*

Come to think of it, he hadn't seen the Japanese ARC-researcher for a while.

The attendant was nowhere to be seen, so Luc tentatively, slightly guiltily, picked up the file and opened to the first page.

There was a black stamp over the front that read, *Agent resigned,* and the date *19/02/2019* was scrawled on the line beneath it.

Resigned? Luc thought, frowning. *Why? Wasn't he Amber's ARC-researcher at London City Airport?*

Maybe there was a connection.

Either way, it gave him an idea. He pulled out his phone and made a note of Shinichi's address, then carefully put the file back on the desk the exact way he'd found it.

When he was sure it was perfect, he took a deep breath. 'Deng?' he hollered.

There was the sound of something smalling, a curse, and finally Deng strode out from behind the bookshelf, an unimpressed look on his face. 'Can't you read?' he snapped. 'If I'm not here, ring the bell.'

Luc had missed the sign. 'Sorry. I need an earpiece, please.'

'Do you have a mission?'

Luc pulled out the paper from Haste a bit sheepishly.

'That's not specific permission,' Deng said, an eyebrow raised.

Luc shrugged. 'That's what I said too. But I can have it verified that he wrote it.'

Deng waved his hand dismissively. 'Nah, don't worry. It's his handwriting, and if anyone tried to forge it, they at least would have tried to write something vaguely understandable.'

'Yeah, only Haste can make something that would otherwise make sense not make sense but still make sense.'

Deng laughed. 'I reckon you're coming in a close second there,' he replied.

'I do my best. So… the earpiece?'

Deng handed over a small box. 'Anything else?'

Luc opened the box, staring at the small earplug inside. 'Actually, can I get an extra one? For Amber? She's stuck in… somewhere in history, so I'd like to give her one when I find her.'

'Fair enough.' Deng handed over another one. 'Who's your ARC-researcher?'

Luc swallowed. 'It… hasn't been assigned yet. I'll make sure they let you know.'

He half expected Deng to ask for the earpieces back. But Deng only glanced at his computer screen, then handed back Haste's "specific permission" slip. 'Good luck then,' he said. 'Hope you get a good one.'

Luc forced a smile, taking back the slip. 'Yeah, me too.'

Shinichi's Flat

The next point on the to-do list was a name.

Shinichi Samejima.

For such a quiet, reserved man, he was swathed in mystery and rumours at ARCHIVE. He'd worked as an ARC-researcher for over twelve years, and, apparently, he'd never lost an agent.

Luc felt his heart beat a little bit faster as he lifted his hand and rang the doorbell.

He stood on the balcony outside a small block of flats that seemed crowded by the tall buildings on either side. The white walls were clean but faded, and each window along it was small and blocked by curtains. Shinichi lived at number eight, on the far end of the second storey. Faintly, he could hear classical music playing through a tinny speaker inside, and next door someone was vacuuming.

The door clicked, and a second later it opened a crack, revealing the corner of Shinichi's face. The one eye that Luc could see was narrowed to an unimpressed slit, and he stared Luc up and down. 'If you're selling something, I'm broke. Go away.'

The door shut.

Luc sighed, ringing the doorbell again. *I don't have time for this,* he thought, wishing once more that he had Shinichi's number. But he'd tried to call his phone, and it seemed he'd disconnected that phone since he'd left ARCHIVE.

'Shinichi Samejima?' he called.

'What?' Shinichi called back, not bothering to open the door.

'I'm Lucky Holmes, from—'

The door opened, cutting Luc off. Shinichi wore a blue sweater and jeans, slippers on his feet. His black hair was dishevelled, and he was clean-shaven aside from a small goatee that accentuated his angular face. 'You're that ARCHIVE agent, aren't you? Amber's partner,' Shinichi asked. Despite his years living in London, he still carried a heavy Japanese accent.

Wow, he remembers me, Luc thought. 'Yeah, that's me. Look, I have a favour to ask.'

There was a pause. 'Is it for ARCHIVE?' he asked quietly.

'More for Amber,' Luc replied and, quickly as he could, he explained the situation. 'She's missing. I think she's in trouble, and I don't want to go in alone.'

Shinichi stared at him, his eyes hard. 'Why didn't Haste give you an ARC-researcher himself?'

Luc repeated once more what Haste had told him. 'I just don't feel safe going without one,' he finished. 'So if you're not busy…'

'You want me to be an unofficial ARC-researcher for your mission?'

Luc swallowed. 'Yeah.'

There was a pause. 'Does Haste know about this?'

'Well… no.' Luc cringed, hoping that wouldn't put him off.

But Shinichi was nodding thoughtfully. 'He won't take kindly to finding out that I'm involved,' he said quietly. 'I didn't leave on good terms. He can't find out about me. And I'm not going to ARCHIVE, okay?'

'Okay.'

'I can connect everything from here. Does anyone else know?'

'I… haven't told anyone, no.' Luc frowned, Shinichi's words suddenly seeming significant. 'Wait a second… do you mean you'll do it?'

Shinichi sighed heavily. 'I think I have to.'

Finally, someone agrees with me, Luc thought. Haste only cared for the timebox, and Laura valued Luc's health and safety far too much. But Shinichi seemed to get it. 'For Amber?'

Shinichi's eyes caught his, and he almost seemed ready to nod. 'I'll need an earpiece,' he said instead.

'Oh.' Luc dug around in his pocket, then held out the earpiece. 'Here, but I don't have the… code… or whatever it is you need to connect them.'

Shinichi shrugged. 'I'll figure it out. When do you Travel?'

'Probably as soon as I get back to ARCHIVE.'

Shinichi stared at the earpiece. 'Great. Send me the date and time before you go.'

Luc breathed out a sigh of relief. 'I didn't know where I'd go if you said no,' he said, but Shinichi was already closing the door.

'Let's get this over with,' Luc heard, just as the door shut.

1:10PM 11 NOVEMBER 1868, WALHALLA, AUSTRALIA

The timebox has been designed to be unremarkable to those who don't know what it is, but keep it with you at all times.

'Christopher!' Amber called, raising her hand.

The man flashed a smile and crossed the street to meet her. 'Miss Winters! I was just on my way to see you! Are you busy right now?'

Amber nodded. 'But only for a little while. Christopher, you mentioned that you had a friend here named Harry?'

The flash of emotions across Christopher's face only reflected how Amber herself felt about meeting the man again. The surprise, disapproval and disgust were quickly smoothed over, but his voice remained neutral as he said, 'You're going to see him?'

She nodded again. 'He came to meet me, but he was talking nonsense. I just wanted to ask him a few questions.'

Christopher didn't try to remove his frown this time. 'Are you quite sure that's… wise?'

I'm quite sure it's not wise, Amber thought. 'I'll be fine,' she replied, shoving down the discomfort she'd felt. 'I don't think he's dangerous.'

He raised an eyebrow as though he disagreed. 'May I offer to come with you? I'll stay out of his sight, so he won't know that I'm there, but if anything turns untoward, I can step in. I don't want you to be hurt, and he's not a predictable man.'

Amber was about to refuse, but stopped herself. While she was sure that Harry wouldn't be able to hurt her, she would feel better to have someone beside her. *Besides,* she thought. *Christopher knows him. He might be able to make more sense of his ramblings.* 'Sure, you can come,' she replied. 'But I'm warning you, he wasn't making any sense earlier today.'

Christopher smiled a half-smile and offered her his arm. 'That man rarely does, Miss Rachel. Do you know where he lives?'

She shook her head and he laughed, leading her down the street. 'Do you?' she asked.

'Yes, he's staying at the local hotel. We'll have to ask which room; I always forget.' He frowned. 'What was he saying earlier?'

'He had this… box-thing, and he kept offering to give it to me if I would take him "home", but I've never seen the man in my life—at least, not that I can remember…' She was learning that the latter clarifying statement reduced the effect of her statement considerably. 'And he didn't even recognise me.'

Christopher didn't reply for a moment. 'A box-thing that would take him home? That is very strange.'

The hotel was not what Amber had expected, though she wondered if her expectation was another "Rachel-only" expectation, and not one that those around her shared. It was a large house on the north side of town, weatherboard like the other houses, and had charming dark green awnings and balcony railings. The landlord showed Christopher and Amber to Harry's room immediately.

Amber knocked on his door, while Christopher waited just to the left of the door, so that when Harry opened the door, he would be blocked from his view. Amber took a deep breath, hoping against all hope that she was mistaken, and this man was a different Harry.

But the man who opened the door was most definitely the man she'd seen at Johansson's house.

He stank of sweat, and he fidgeted with his fingers and feet constantly, his eyes darting over Amber's shoulders and making her itch to see if there was someone behind her.

'Amber,' he said, sounding surprisingly relieved to see her. 'Amber, I'm sorry about before. I've been so desperate and I forgot that you're in the same position as me – neither of us have any way of getting back on our own. So I was thinking, we should collaborate. Together, we can get back home, and then you never have to see me again. I promise.'

Amber glanced at Christopher, uncertainty creeping over her. He sounded genuinely desperate, but she *couldn't* help him. She wasn't the right person. But she hardened her heart and forced the conversation in her own direction.

'Where did you get that box?' she asked.

Harry's eyes narrowed, but suddenly his face cleared and he shook his head. 'Of course, you were unconscious the whole time. I... took it after the car crash.'

Cars. Another thing that are strangely missing, but that I remember. I must be from the same country as Harry.

She schooled her face to keep herself from giving away her questions. She needed to control the information he gleaned from her.

But then the other thing he'd said sunk in. *I was unconscious?* 'What car crash?' she asked slowly.

Harry laughed, as though she'd told a funny joke. 'Who are you acting for?' he cried, still laughing. 'There's no one around but us. And I've already figured you out, *agent.* You're an ARCHIVE agent, the one from the lab, and from the car we chased. The timebox sent us both here accidentally. It says you're Agent Amber Elkhoury.'

Amber could feel Christopher's eyes watching her, waiting for her to explain this. The trouble was that she couldn't. She had no idea what Harry was talking about. *London? Timebox?* She wanted to scream from frustration.

'I'm surprised you survived that crash,' Harry went on. 'Really. You only got a few cuts and bruises, but that car was spinning doughnuts, if you remember. I wouldn't have been surprised if you both died in there, but obviously you're still alive. Maybe your friend wasn't so *lucky.*' He laughed louder, spitting his foul-smelling breath into Amber's face. 'Get it? Lucky? Like Lucky Holmes?'

Am I meant to know what that is? Amber folded her arms across her chest, finally letting her disapproving scowl through in the hope that it would make the man shut up.

It didn't.

He laughed, oblivious to her stretched patience. 'I bet he hears that joke ten times a day. It just makes it better.'

'Who?' Too late, she realised. *Is Lucky Holmes a person?* She shook her head, banishing her perplexing thoughts. 'I don't know who you are, Harry, or what you're talking about.' At first, she'd hoped that Harry knew who she was. But whatever he was talking about, she wanted no part in it. It couldn't be her. Car crashes? Labs? *Agents?* Agents for what? 'I can't help you. You've got me confused with someone else.'

It was like she'd slapped him. His eyes widened, and his laughter stopped abruptly. He reached out, grabbing her wrist. 'Amber, I'm not a local—'

'Who's Amber?' she yelled, trying to twist away from him. From the corner of her eye, she saw Christopher move, but he didn't come out of hiding to help her. Summoning as much strength as she could, she punched Harry in the stomach, then wrenched her hand away from him while he was doubled over in pain.

'Keep that stupid… thing,' she hissed, then turned and stalked out of the hallway, ignoring his cries for her to come back.

Amber kept going until she came to the stairs, and as soon as she'd twisted out of sight, she tried to calm herself. Her hand ached, and terror thrummed through her. She'd never punched anyone before. *Have I?* Maybe she *was* someone who got into fights, who knew strange madmen and… *was I in a car crash?* Finally, she heard the door click shut behind her and Christopher's footsteps hurrying to catch up.

'Are you alright?' he asked, offering her his handkerchief.

'I'm fine,' she said, taking a deep breath to soften her tone. 'I can't believe I did that,' she whispered. 'Was he okay?'

'He's… okay.' Christopher watched her face carefully. 'But why did he call you Amber? And who was… Holmes? Do you know?'

Amber shook her head, heading down the rest of the stairs. 'He has me confused with someone else.'

At least, I hope he does, she added silently.

11:24 12 November 1868, Just outside Walhalla

There may be occasions where you are separated from your partner, with no way of contacting them. This will present you with a choice. Search for them, or stay where you are and wait for them to find you. If both agents are able to search, the general ARCHIVE advice is that the female partner waits and the male partner searches. You may change this with your partner, but be clear before you Travel.

Perhaps Travelling with a headache was a bad idea. Luc opened his eyes to harsh sunlight, peeking through tall trees, then quickly shut his eyelids again.

Growing up in the UK had taught him that the sun wasn't too bright. It was friendly. It came out some days when it was feeling nice and made the hills a bit greener and the laundry a bit drier.

But this sun was mean.

He could smell composting leaves and mulch, and the air felt moist and stale, even as the sun heated it. Sticks and rocks dug into his back. Nearby, a flock of birds screeched as they flew past.

He peeked an eye open again. It seemed he was lying on a dirt track. Enormous trees towered above him, and grass lined the road to either side. Not far beyond that, the ground just fell away. His gaze went beyond that, and he gasped despite himself.

The side of the mountain was steep and covered in ferns as tall as he was. Trees lining the side of the mountain further down stretched far above his head. He felt like he'd made it to some strange fantasy world.

He looked around him, frowning. *Have I forgotten something?*

Suddenly he jumped up, glancing nervously at the grass and shrubbery around him. The world dipped as the blood rushed from his face and he stumbled a bit. He rubbed at the stitches on his temple. Travelling was difficult enough when in the peak of health, and Luc was frankly surprised he'd passed his medical. 'Uhh… Shinichi?' *Please be there; please be there; please be there…*

'Yes.' There was a beep, then the sound of clicking computer keys came through the earpiece along with Shinichi's voice. Luc let go of the breath he'd been holding.

'I'm here too!' came a distinctly Australian voice.

Luc frowned. *Laura?* 'Aren't you at ARCHIVE?'

'Yeah, I'm on a break. Shinichi told me you'd Travelled, so now I'm joining in through a very complicated phone-ear-piece-set-up thing.' Luc could imagine that the very complicated set up was really just a phone in front of Shinichi's earpiece.

'Anyway, you sound nervous,' Laura went on. 'What's wrong?'

Luc glanced around him again, her warning still fresh in his mind. *Spiders, snakes… what else could be hiding in the under-*

growth? His head whipped up – *ouch, too fast* – and he scanned the treeline. *These stupid trees are too tall,* he thought, squinting against the unreasonably angry sun. *I can't see if there are any magpies around.*

'Lucky?' Laura said. 'You alright?'

He swallowed. 'Yes, yes, I'm fine. Just… in the middle of a forest.'

There was silence from the other end. 'And…?' Shinichi asked.

'In *Australia,'* Luc added.

Laura understood. She clicked her tongue. 'Come on Lucky, you won't get bitten by a snake. Just find the main road where you can at least see them before you step on them.'

He took a deep breath and licked his lips. 'Well, I'm on a track,' he said slowly. 'Which way should I go?'

'Go west,' Shinichi said.

Luc clenched his fists and took another deep breath, wishing his head would stop spinning.

He couldn't be bothered waiting until he was ready. He closed his eyes and took a step forward. 'Well, I didn't faint,' he muttered to himself.

'Wow, you sound as fit as ever,' Laura remarked. 'I still can't believe you passed the med exam.'

'They were probably laughing so much at your permission slip,' Shinichi said, sounding distracted.

Laura laughed. 'Lucky's going on an excursion and needs the Commander's permission.'

'His *specific* permission.'

Luc rounded a bend, and, half sliding, half walking down a steeper section, he came to a sealed road that ran at an angle to his track. It was empty as far as he could see until it twisted around the mountainside and down into a valley. He guessed that would lead to Walhalla, where Amber apparently had Transported to.

Luc took his jacket off and draped it over one arm, noticing that it was covered in grass seeds and dirt. He'd have to brush them off his pants as well before he went into town. 'I covered my stitches with my hair before I went in for the exam,' Luc replied absently.

Laura laughed again, and even Shinichi gave a chuckle. 'Ah, that would help to hide the injury from them,' he replied dryly. 'Anyway, are you at the town yet?'

'Not yet.'

'What's the weather like?' Laura asked.

'It's 11.29am, just outside Walhalla, in 1868,' Shinichi said. Unwittingly, he sounded like a news reporter. 'Currently 38° Celsius, bright and sunny in ways England rarely sees. Weather for the rest of the day…' Shinichi paused. 'At four o'clock it will be… 18°. *With showers?* How is that possible? That's twenty degrees less within two hours.' Luc heard keys ticking as Shinichi double-checked his weather report. *As though he can double check a report that's two-hundred years old,* Luc thought, rolling his eyes.

'It's typical weather for Victoria,' Laura replied. 'Four seasons in a day. Melbourne's famous for it, and the mountains will just make it worse. Sounds like a nice day, but I have to go. I have a call with Ria about a 16th Century pirate disguise.'

'Who's getting the pirate missions?' Luc asked.

'Me,' she said cheekily. 'It's for a costume party, and I have a reputation to uphold. Be careful!'

'I will. Bye, Laura.'

There was silence after she left. Luc could hear clicking as Shinichi typed. Walhalla didn't seem any closer than it had at 11:29. *I should change my watch,* he realised. He didn't stop as he fixed it and his phone's time, tucking the phone into a hidden pocket when he'd finished.

'What's your plan once you get in?' Shinichi asked.

'Ask around for Amber, or someone that looks like her...'

'Yes, I suppose that a look-alike will do just as well as the real thing,' Shinichi said.

Luc rolled his eyes. He didn't explain himself to Shinichi; the man knew what he meant. He moved onto his next step. 'If I don't find her, I'll stay a few nights and explore. Haste said that someone else had Travelled with her too, and I might be able to find him instead. When I do find her, I'll let you know to take us back to the present.'

'I see a few flaws with your plan, but let's find her first,' Shinichi said, frustratingly matter-of-fact. Luc didn't ask what the flaws were. He knew them.

'Will you check the cemetery too?' Shinichi asked.

'Yes.' *If just to get rid of the suspense of not knowing whether she's alive or dead.* 'I'll ask the minister if they found a corpse, too. If she *is* dead, it's most likely she's in an unmarked grave.' Luc was surprised that he had said that sentence without hesitating. But then, the possibility that she wouldn't be there hadn't really sunk in. *She may be dead,* he told himself firmly. He still didn't quite believe it.

'You're approaching Walhalla now,' Shinichi said. 'We won't be able to talk for a bit, so I'm going to get a coffee. Don't get kidnapped.'

Luc rolled his eyes. 'I won't. But you'll stay on the line?'

'Of course.'

The road was hugged by two mountains on either side, but there was still evidence of a town nearby. To his right, a few tombstones clung to the mountain side halfway up. To his left, the mountain was barren, a few small saplings evidence of the forest that had once stood there.

As he went, the road showed more and more evidence of use. A small creek ran parallel to it as far as he could see, and more horse dung and chickens started to populate the road. A few small weatherboard houses climbed up the mountainside, with paths snaking down to the main road like ancient rivers. Lining the main road were the commercial buildings: a general store, a few churches, a tailor's, and a school house. Townspeople wound through on their daily business, surrounded by dogs, chickens, horses and darting children.

He stepped onto the main road of Walhalla, heading toward the church. The search for Amber had finally begun.

11:31AM 12 November 1868

One of the most important lessons you will need to learn as an agent at ARCHIVE is how to learn and move on from mistakes. If things don't go to plan, reassess and see what you can do. Don't dwell on failures except as an avenue to help you learn.

'Mollie,' Johansson said, coming into the kitchen with a few coins in his hand. 'The allowance for the groceries.'

Mollie nodded at Amber. 'Give that to her. That's her job today.'

Johansson turned to Amber, raising an eyebrow. 'And why's that?'

'It's laundry day!' Mollie grinned. 'And Miss Winters doesn't know how. So I figured she can do the shopping, and I'll do the clothes with Winnie and Philippa.'

Johansson shrugged, and went to Amber. 'Well, Miss Winters, you know what to do?'

Amber nodded, taking them and putting it in her basket. It had been more than five weeks now, and they hadn't had a single response to their advertisement. As little as she wanted to admit it, she was stuck. She couldn't move and risk missing an inquirer to their advertisement, but she was beginning to lose hope they'd ever come.

Harry was the only one who'd offered a name, but she hadn't seen him since she'd gone to his hotel room with Christopher. She'd asked Christopher if he'd seen him, and he'd shaken his head, hypothesising that maybe he'd gone to the city, or perhaps back to England. She was glad to accept that if it meant she would never see him again.

But a small part of her almost wanted to go with him, to see if England was her home.

After all, she knew so many things that were foreign to those around her, and the list only grew every day.

Arthur had hit his head falling out of a tree, and she'd checked him for concussion before declaring that he would be fine with a bit of rest. Mollie had looked at her strangely, and asked where she'd learnt medicine. Of course, Amber didn't remember.

She didn't understand the local currency; she knew what pounds and shillings were, but everything seemed so cheap here. Why? Were things more expensive wherever she was from? And why had she been expecting dollars and cents?

Why did she know and use words that no one else knew? Simple words like 'okay' or 'k', 'like' in place of 'um', 'hey' instead of 'good morning' brought strange looks from everyone around her.

Everyone, that is, except Harry.

Sighing, Amber picked up her basket and went to start on the groceries. She had a list with her of what she needed to get.

Farmer Eugene had his market stall out that morning, tables covered in colourful seasonal fruits to entice customers further into the shop. 'Morning, Mr Eugene,' she called.

He smiled at her and waved. 'Morning, Miss Rachel. How are you today?'

'Fine,' she replied. 'It's a beautiful morning, isn't it?'

'That it is. What can I get for you today?'

Amber surveyed the crates of fruit. Stone fruit, tomatoes, lettuces, all fresh produce. She picked out some vegetables she needed for a stew, then decided to treat Arthur to some fruit. 'How much are the peaches?' she asked.

She didn't hear his reply.

A young man came up to the stall. He had dirty blonde hair, an excited smile that made up for his otherwise plain features, and wore a crumpled, dirty brown suit. 'Hey,' he said quietly, ignoring the farmer.

Amber smiled back at him, returning the greeting before calmly speaking to Eugene. 'I'll take four peaches, please,' she said to Eugene. 'And three nectarines.' Christopher had said that he liked nectarines; she could take them to him as thanks for his help.

The farmer told her the price, then turned to the young man. 'I haven't seen you around here, I don't think, sir. Fresh off the boat?' he asked.

'Um, yes, something like that,' he replied. Amber lingered at the stall, wanting to find out more about this man, though she couldn't have explained why she thought he was important. With a start, she realised what it was.

He said hey.

No one else here says hey like that.

'What's your name, then?' Eugene asked.

'People call me Lucky,' he replied. 'Lucky Holmes.'

Amber's eyebrows rose, and she risked another look at him. *Lucky Holmes. That was the man…* Amber thought back to what Harry had said. *That was the man Harry had thought had died in a car crash.*

So *this* was Lucky Holmes.

Amber smiled at him, trying to decide if he was a disappointment compared to what she'd expected. *He's definitely alive,* she thought, wishing she could rub it in Harry's face. He was younger than she'd thought; he couldn't be much older than her. But she had also expected someone scruffy, which he certainly was. Though his face was clean, his tousled hair, on closer inspection, was full of twigs and leaves. *Not scruffy,* she mentally revised. *Dirty.*

'What makes you lucky?' she asked, unimpressed.

He laughed. 'You know, I get that question a lot,' he grinned. 'Some say it's my great personality that is good fortune in and of itself. Others say my abnormally good looks make me lucky in love.' He shrugged, as though he thought himself modest.

Amber couldn't help it. She laughed at him. It was all a well-rehearsed act; a modest presentation of his exaggerated virtues, when it was clear he didn't think himself as possessing a great personality or abnormally good looks. If someone else had said the same things, it would have been annoying. But somehow, when *he* said it, it was funny.

He grinned back, happy to have made her laugh. 'May I buy an apple?' he asked.

Eugene rolled his eyes, though he seemed amused too. 'Anyone else, I would say yes, but you?' he said sarcastically. 'What do you think they're here for? Display?'

'Point taken,' Lucky replied, picking out an apple. 'How much?'

***

'Have you found her?' came Shinichi's voice in Luc's ear, apparently back with a coffee. 'Where are you?'

'Not now,' Luc murmured, glancing at Eugene as he carefully counted out his change and handed it back to him.

Luc thanked him, but his excitement was making it hard to think. *That was Amber! Right there! Alive!*

But before he could say anything more to her, he realised that he was opening his mouth to empty air.

He swallowed, going back to the farmer. 'Mr Eugene, that woman that was there, where did she go?'

The man shrugged. 'I didn't see; I was counting your change. She probably had errands to run. That family always does.'

'Family? What family? Does she have a family?'

'The Johansson family. The tailor?' He laughed at Luc's face. 'Don't look so shocked, lad.'

Luc closed his mouth, then glanced back where he'd thought Amber had gone. *Amber has a family here? Did she get married?* He shook his head. *Wait, how long has she been here? Whitehall said this was the day she'd come, according to the timebox.*

'Lucky,' Shinichi said in his ear. 'Come back, Lucky. Focus.'

He took a deep breath and tried desperately to think objectively. *According to Dr Whitehall, she's only been here for a day,* he told himself. *She can't be married.*

'I just… I didn't see a ring on her hand,' he said. It wasn't exactly a lie; he hadn't seen a ring, but he hadn't thought to look either.

That only made Eugene laugh harder. 'She's not married.' Luc forced himself not to sigh in relief. 'Blimey, if you saw her and the tailor together, you'd know that if they married, we'd be in for a right show.' He shook his head, still chuckling. 'No, I don't know what relation they are, but there's no romance between them.' He laughed loudly. 'If you want to try your famous luck on her, you'd probably have Johansson's blessing to take her away, Mr Lucky.'

Luc forced a laugh. *Wow, what a hilariously original joke on my name.* 'Thanks very much, Mr Eugene.'

Luc turned back to the road, peeking between houses and into shop windows to see if she'd come this way.

I need to fill in Shinichi, he remembered. He continued down the path, munching on the apple and still looking, unsuccessfully, for Amber.

A small gravel track veered off to the side, and, curious, he followed it up the mountain. This track was surrounded by trees, and, shielded as he was from the main road, he decided he could easily talk to Shinichi without fear of being overheard. He trudged up the steep hill, wondering where the track led to.

'I was talking to a farmer at a market stall,' Luc said quietly, glancing around just in case. 'Amber was there. Speaking with—'

'I'm sorry, are you talking to me now?' Shinichi asked.

Luc sighed. 'Yes.'

'Okay, I'll pay more attention,' he said. 'Don't sigh; it's always hard for us to know who you're speaking to when we can't see where you are.'

'Do I need to start again?' Luc asked. He could hear Shinichi typing.

'No. You were talking to a farmer. Amber was there. Lucky, I can hear your conversation through your earpiece; you don't have to repeat it to me. The important question is: where did Amber go?'

'I don't know. She was right next to me, but it was like…'

Like what? Like she didn't recognise him? But it was more than that. It wasn't like she hadn't expected to see him there, so hadn't recognised him, it was like… He stopped walking.

Like she'd never met me before.

He couldn't say it.

'Like what?'

Luc shook his head. 'I don't know,' he whispered.

Shinichi was silent for a moment. 'Did she say anything?' he asked eventually.

'She… I said my name was Lucky Holmes, and she asked what made me Lucky.' Suddenly, the fresh memory was replaced by another, older one. *ARCHIVE Christmas party. When I first met her and she asked me the same question.*

'That's weird.'

Yes, thank you for summing that up, Shinichi.

It felt more than weird. It felt… wrong. Unsettling.

'Could she be trying to tell you something? Maybe it could have two meanings,' Shinichi suggested.

Luc thought about it, finally taking another laboured step. The exertion was making his head spin, and he felt a bit sick. *What makes you lucky?* Maybe she was asking why he was looking for her, but that seemed like too much of a stretch. 'I don't know, Shinichi,' he said, then forced himself to elaborate. 'She looked at me, smiled at me, like I was… like she'd never met me before.'

There was another silence as Shinichi digested this. Luc heard him type again. What, was he writing a novel, with all that typing? 'It's strange,' Shinichi said quietly. 'That you saw her at all. You were bedridden for a day after the crash, yet she's walking around doing errands the day after.'

Luc nodded slowly. 'Yeah, I could tell as soon as I'd seen her that she didn't arrive here this morning. The timebox must have glitched or something.'

'Glitched? Is that a word?'

'It means it… it's broken.'

'Hmm. "Glitched."' There was a short pause, then he said, 'How old did she look?'

'The same age. But she didn't have any cuts or bruises on her face.'

'Aha,' he sounded triumphant. 'So we can assume that it's been between a month and… a year? How much do you think the timebox… gri… gli…'

'Glitched?'

'Yes, glitched? Sorry, it's a hard word for me to say. Glitched.'

Luc shrugged. 'I don't know. Look, no matter how long she's been there, I need to find her again and bring her back for a medical check-up.' He couldn't shake the feeling he'd felt when he'd first seen her. *Like she'd never met me before.* He shivered.

The track ended, and he looked up, startled.

He found himself in a garden of tombstones.

He shivered again.

'Yes. And the timebox.'

Ah yes, the accursed timebox.

A branch snapped behind him, and Luc turned, surprised. A man he didn't recognise stood behind him, arms raised above his head and brandishing a thick, solid, eucalyptus branch. Raising his arms to protect his head, Luc gave a yell and dove to the side, narrowly missing the man's swing. He tripped and rolled down the mountain, his fall only stopped by a tombstone slamming into his back, winding him.

'Lucky? Lucky? What's going on?' Shinichi asked urgently.

He scrambled to his feet, heaving for breath. 'I'm being attacked by a man with a—'

The stick found its mark, and Luc found himself on the ground, the world out of focus and sounds distant.

Luc could do nothing. Dimly, he heard Shinichi's voice in his ear, but he couldn't figure out what the man was saying. He moaned.

He vaguely made out the stick above his head and, with an enormous effort, raised his hands above his face as though they would help to protect his poor head.

It didn't help. The stick came down. Everything went black.

11:35AM 12 November 1868, Walhalla, Australia

Outside of your mission, do not attempt to help the locals, even those in poverty or hardship. You cannot afford to be distracted from your mission. Keep a professional distance between yourself and all locals.

Amber decided to take the nectarines to Christopher immediately. She had no other reason than that she would feel embarrassed to take them home, then tell Arthur that they were reserved for someone else.

She went down to the church at a leisurely pace, enjoying the fine morning. The day was sunny, promising heat in the mid-afternoon, but pleasant in the meantime. And the lack of wind meant there was no dust in her face as she walked.

She came to the track up to the cemetery and veered up it. As she climbed, she was surprised to see Lucky Holmes – in the flesh – walking further up the track, muttering to himself. The track wound to the right and he continued up, disappearing from her view.

The man presented many questions. Honestly, Amber had assumed that he was a figment of Harry's imagination, created to somehow back his claims and help him to convince her that she really was Amber Elkhoury. But now he was here, in Walhalla – newly arrived, he'd said – and, if anything, it only disproved Harry all the more. Lucky Holmes hadn't recognised her. She couldn't be Amber Elkhoury.

She stepped up to the front door and knocked. In her four weeks here, Christopher had been the only one who had accepted her without demanding answers. She felt calm around him, released from the pressures of trying to fit in. He was patient, asked thoughtful questions, and always seemed to know how to make her feel better.

That was the *only* reason she'd bought nectarines for him. He was a good man, and that was *all*.

He answered her knock, smiling warmly when he saw her. 'Miss Rachel! How are you?'

'I'm well. I hope I'm not disturbing you,' she said.

'No, I was just drawing a new weed I found nearby. What can I do for you today?'

Amber smiled and held out the basket for him to take. 'I brought you a token of appreciation. To say thank you for helping me these past few weeks, I bought you a few nectarines.'

Christopher's eyebrows rose. 'Well, I—' he took the nectarines with a grin. 'You remembered! Thank you, Miss Rachel. Please, think nothing of it. I can't resist a mystery, and you uncovered a great one in Harry. I'm intrigued. Did you ever find out who that Miss Amber was?'

Amber shook her head with a small smile, though her chest tightened. 'No, thank goodness. I haven't seen Harry since I went to his apartment with you.'

Christopher's face cleared. 'Good. I don't trust him.'

'He's an odd one,' she agreed. 'Enjoy the nectarines. I have a few other things to do before lunch.'

'Of course,' Christopher smiled.

His face lit up with an idea. 'Just wait here one more moment,' he said, then hurried back into the house.

Amber waited curiously. A few moments later, he returned without the basket and presented her with a long, narrow leafy sprig with a beautiful little red flower on the end. 'I just finished drawing this,' he said, holding it out for her. 'Thank you,' he said.

She laughed nervously. 'I don't think you understand how thanking people works,' she said. 'The nectarines were—'

'I want you to have it,' he said quietly, pressing it into her hand with both of his.

She didn't know what to say. 'You… you don't need it?'

He smiled. 'There are plenty more out there, Miss Rachel,' he replied quietly.

'Then thank you,' she said, admiring it. 'It's really beautiful.'

He nodded. 'Almost as beautiful as you,' he smiled. 'Have a good day, Miss Rachel.'

Amber's mind froze, and her cheeks went red as he closed the door. *How can he say that so casually?* she thought, numbly turning to go back home.

A small bubble of warmth rose in her chest, and she couldn't stop a smile from forming. It was such a cheesy line, but for some reason it didn't make her laugh. It made her feel special.

She glanced up at the graveyard as she walked past it, expecting to see Lucky.

He wasn't there.

Another man was standing there, panting and holding a bloodied branch.

She narrowed her eyes. *What…?* All thoughts of Christopher vanished from her mind. *What's he hitting? A rat?* she wondered, moving slightly until she could see in between the tombstones.

She gasped. Lucky Holmes was lying on the ground, with his face covered in fresh blood. He raised shaking hands above his head, just as the man brought the stick down with a sickening crack. The man raised his head and dropped the stick, and finally, her scream dying in her throat, she recognised the attacker.

Harry.

Amber's heart thudded in her chest. She wanted to call out, to scream, or to at least check that the man was alive. But she couldn't move. Shock coursed through her body, blinding her mind and keeping her feet cemented in the path.

What has he done? She wanted to believe that Harry must have his reasons, but Harry wasn't like that. He was the kind of man who might attack another man and steal his wallet while he was visiting a friend's or relative's grave.

Harry straightened, throwing the stick to the side without another thought. He glanced around, and Amber ducked behind a tree, peeking around so that she could watch without being seen.

Holmes wasn't moving. He seemed completely unconscious, which wasn't surprising, considering the open wounds on his head. He would need medical attention quickly if he didn't want terrible brain damage.

Harry carried the strange box with him, the one he'd shown her in an attempt to get them home. He tinkered with it, watching the screen intently. He pulled out a phone and typed something, then turned back to his box.

Amber glanced back at Holmes. He still hadn't woken up, and blood was soaking into the grass. He'd need a doctor.

Harry knelt next to Holmes, and Amber watched for him to start searching his pockets. Harry said something to Holmes, laughed, then picked up his limp hand and pressed the box into it.

Amber frowned. *What is—*

Harry stood, and, without warning, he disappeared.

Harry wanted to go home, she thought. *That box must be their mode of transport to go home. But he couldn't go by himself; it must only work for certain people.*

Lucky had been one of them, but Harry hadn't, so he'd stolen his fingerprints. *He wasn't meant to go home.*

She shook the thoughts out of her head, picked up her skirts, and ran up the path.

3:04PM 10 March 2019, London

*ARCHIVE has five core values that must
be upheld at all times. They are: Intelligence,
Commitment, Bravery, Compassion, and, above
all, Integrity.*

Laura ran the length of the toilet cubicles before picking one close to the door, locking herself in and sitting on the floor.

She pulled out her phone and messaged Shinichi.

> What's going ooooooonnnnnn?????????

Please reply please reply please reply…

It was better than that. Her phone vibrated, the screen taken over with Shinichi's name and the quacking ringtone echoing off the bathroom walls.

'Hello? What's going on?' she asked. The toilet block was empty but she lowered her voice instinctively.

'He's found Amber,' Shinichi said immediately. Tears of relief rushed to Laura's eyes.

'Thank goodness.'

'Yes, that's the good news,' he went on. 'Apparently she doesn't know who he is.'

Laura frowned. 'What? Why?'

'We're… not sure yet. Apparently one of the men who ambushed her Travelled with her on the night of the crash. Maybe he's been following her around…'

She fiddled with her lanyard thoughtfully. 'So she pretended not to recognise Lucky in case he found out that he's an ARCHIVE agent?'

Shinichi grunted. 'But that man was at the lab and the crash. He'd recognise Lucky.' He sighed. 'I think Lucky will need to get her alone somewhere quiet and ask her what's going on. I wonder if she's been there longer than we thought, but I'm not sure how long. I think something has been going on to make her keep her distance from him.'

Laura nodded. 'And the timebox?'

Shinichi snorted. 'Who knows? It's not Lucky's priority at the moment,' Shinichi said, and Laura rolled her eyes.

'You might have to remind him that it's his mission,' she replied.

Shinichi chuckled. 'I do, frequently, and it's like talking into a voice recorder. "*Get the timebox, Lucky.*" "*Ah, yes, must get the timebox.*" Then he forgets.'

Laura laughed. 'Sounds like Lucky. So what *is* the other news?'

'Lucky's not responding.'

'Is he okay?'

'I think he's unconscious.'

Laura tried to be surprised, but gave up immediately. 'Is he?'

Shinichi chuckled dryly. 'If you're struggling to pretend to be sympathetic, this may help: I think he's been knocked out by someone.'

She grimaced. *I hope it doesn't involve that other guy…* 'Should we be worried?'

Shinichi shrugged. 'Probably, but there's nothing we can do from here. Normally I would contact Amber, but obviously that's not an option this time. The only thing we can do is monitor his heart rate and vitals, and try send in back-up if anything goes bad. At the moment, he's quite stable. The rest might actually do him some good.'

Laura snorted. 'Yeah, and the bump on the head might knock some sense into him.'

'We can only hope,' Shinichi replied dryly.

'Is there anything else? I need to go soon.'

There was a small pause. 'Well, there's a lot, and I'd rather talk about this in person. Can we meet up somewhere?'

Laura flicked through her mental to-do list. It was too long. 'After work, maybe. Where?'

'Do you know Leon's cafe? They have good coffee.'

Laura groaned. 'That's half an hour out of my way!'

'Good, it's settled then. I'll meet you there when you finish work.'

She sighed. Of course Shinichi would pick his meeting rooms based on coffee quality. 'I'll see you there,' she said.

★★★

Laura's stomach wasn't feeling less queasy by the time she climbed the step to Leon's Coffee. It was a small corner coffee store with a hipster feel, nestled between a grocer and a camera shop. Light streamed through large windows onto reading seats and coffee tables. A small bookshelf labelled 'Little Library' squatted in the corner, filled with second-hand, second-rate books. Laura's eyes flicked around the small café.

There were about four customers. One was Asian.

She would have recognised Shinichi immediately anyway. Theirs had been a curious friendship while he'd been at ARCHIVE. She'd first met him when his agent had spilled wine on her Tudor ruff, and though they hadn't talked often after that, she enjoyed it when they did. If she was honest, it had taken her a few days to notice when he'd stopped coming.

But she'd been shattered when she'd found out why.

She went over and announced herself by putting her laptop bag next to the chair. Pulling it out with a teeth-grinding screech, she plopped herself down unceremoniously and waited for him to acknowledge her presence.

Unwillingly, her eyes flicked around his elbows.

No coffee.

It's still being made, she told herself. *He'll get it soon. In fact, I doubt he'll start this without one.*

It didn't make her feel better. Neither did telling herself that the ARCHIVE superstition that it was bad luck to see Shinichi without a coffee before a mission was just that: a superstition.

'Do you have the ARChronicles on your computer?' he asked.

Laura jumped. 'Uh… no. Just a few documents that help my designs, but otherwise I just go downstairs if I need something. Only the ARC-researchers get the privilege of constant access.'

Shinichi's eyes flicked from one side of his screen to the other. 'Oh. How sad for you. But that shouldn't be too much of a problem. You're not going to order?'

Her stomach flipped at the thought of coffee, and she shook her head. 'I don't feel like drinking coffee right now,' she said quietly.

Shinichi nodded. 'Good. It will strengthen my own break from coffee.'

Laura's heart dropped through the floor. 'Your *what?*'

'I don't drink coffee anymore.'

She closed her mouth and turned her head as though squinting at him would help her see through him. 'You're lying.'

Shinichi's eyes flicked up and held hers for just long enough that she knew.

She knew, but she couldn't believe it. Shinichi… without coffee? It was like tasting a saltless sea, or walking through a peopleless city. Coffee… *defined* Shinichi. It was the root of his rumours, his one and only love, his—

'Here's your macchiato,' the barista said, setting it down next to his computer.

'Perfect,' Shinichi said, a hint of a smile twitching at the corner of his mouth. 'Thank you, Carrie.' He sipped the coffee, unsuccessfully hiding his smirk.

Laura waited for the young woman to leave before she sent across her most withering glare. 'Nice to see you again, too, Shinichi.'

He smiled. 'Always. But yes, we have more important things to talk about. I always knew that Haste would have fun covering this up. I didn't know he'd have *this* much fun.'

Laura frowned. 'Fun? Covering what up?' She leaned in and dropped her voice. 'Lucky said Haste was acting strangely.'

Shinichi nodded. 'We all know he was. If you need an example, he didn't assign Lucky an ARC-researcher and sent him back in time even though he wasn't in good health.'

'He wants his timebox back. It was Lucky's mission.'

Shinichi shrugged, clicking something on his computer. 'I have some leads. I'll take you through them.'

He turned his computer around until she could see the screen. It looked like a pdf of a report, the page filled with a large table populated by 12-point Times New Roman scientific words and tiny but elaborate footnotes. In the footer was a copyright symbol and the name 'Movarian Laboratories.'

'This is a report of the testing the timebox underwent before it was given to Lucky and Amber,' Shinichi said. 'The scientists at Movarian Laboratories Travelled to various locations under various conditions, but look at this. This is the final "test", and it took place after the results were finalised and the timebox was deemed safe.' He used his cursor to highlight the final row in the table, and Laura read it aloud.

14/02/2019 ML | 12/10/1868 Walhalla, VIC Australia

Timebox ran smoothly with no problems. A THD was left in Walhalla for research purposes.

'I assume ML is Movarian Labs,' Laura commented.

Shinichi frowned. She tried again.

'What's a THD?'

A nod. She was getting closer. 'A Traveller's Homing Device,' Shinichi replied. 'It's like a bookmark in history. With the new timebox, you can leave a THD in a particular moment and place in time, then when you Travel, you'll automatically go back to wherever and whenever the THD is, no matter where the timebox is scheduled to go.'

So that's *why that was significant,* Laura realised. 'Wait, so they were testing this THD, to make sure it was connected to the timebox and everything, but after placing it, they never Travelled again to make sure it would take them to 1868?'

Shinichi shook his head. 'No one Travelled, until Amber did.' He scrolled through the file until he found a special report and handed it to Laura. She read out the section he'd highlighted with his cursor.

'One trip,' Laura whispered. She felt sick to her stomach. 'This wasn't an accident.'

Shinichi shook his head. 'Add to the story the little-known fact that the timebox can be turned on remotely, so long as the remote and the timebox are both at the same time.'

Laura's head felt light. She rested it in her hands as Shinichi's theory crashed in. 'You think the lab Transported Amber there on purpose?'

Shinichi shook his head, pulling the computer back around to face him. He clicked around on it, and finally turned it back to him, this time with an email that was signed with Dr Whitehall's name. 'Read this.'

Laura reluctantly read the paragraph he pointed to.

I tried, on multiple occasions, to convince Haste that this was not just a bad idea, but unethical, illegal and unsafe. He kept calling it an "experiment", but I'm sure there was something deeper than curiosity motivating him.

'I don't understand,' Laura said in a small voice.
'Keep reading,' Shinichi said, sipping his coffee.

It is illegal to take someone to a place against their will. How much more to send them back in time?

Laura choked on the words, tears filling her eyes unbidden. She tried to keep going, but the words were blurring and as she blinked the tears away, she realised that she could only see the back of the laptop now. Shinichi calmly kept reading for her.

Finally we compromised, when he said that he would warn the agents that they will Travel, to test the timebox and the THD. While I am by no means satisfied, it is the best I can do. So now, we plan to give them the timebox and have them Travel the night they take it.

Shinichi put the paper down, and Laura fought to compose herself.

'I'm sorry,' he said quietly. 'I should not have shown you this. I should have known that you would be affected by it.'

She shook her head. 'No, it's fine I…' Taking a deep breath, she forced her voice to steady and was almost successful. 'Did Haste tell Luc and Amber that they were going to Travel?'

He watched her face for a moment, then seemed to decide that he would continue the conversation despite the difficult topic. 'We must assume the best of him,' he said eventually. 'Maybe he meant to tell them to Travel when they got back to ARCHIVE.' He shrugged. 'But then Dr Whitehall says, *"I gave Haste permission and access to activate the timebox remotely. Despite our eventual agreement, I still felt there was something wrong with the idea. But eventually I had to trust Haste, as the rest of ARCHIVE trusts him."* '

'It…' Laura couldn't say it. 'It was deliberate?' she whispered. 'But why?'

Shinichi shrugged. 'I don't know for sure. That's as far as I could get without the ARChronicles.' He picked up his mug again, staring into it. 'Although I have a good—' he stopped abruptly, looking alarmed. He touched his right ear. 'I'm here,' he said randomly.

Laura frowned. 'What—' Then she remembered. He had his portable earpiece that he'd taken from the office.

Lucky's awake, she thought.

2:24PM 25 November 1868, Walhalla, Australia

Luc awoke – once more – to a blinding headache. He opened his eyes, but his left eye wouldn't respond. Something soft was pressing against his face, blocking out light and almost smothering him. While he could *just* breathe, the feeling of being suffocated wasn't helping his state of mind. *Where am I? What on earth happened?*

'Shinichi?' he croaked, trying to muster strength to push away whatever was blinding and smothering him.

'I'm here,' Shinichi said immediately.

'Oh, you're awake,' came a familiar voice. The cloth was lifted and bright light shone down on him.

Amber? he moved his head toward her voice. *Am I dead?*

Something brushed his eye, and suddenly he could open it, and he could breathe freely. He blinked a few times, his eyelashes slowly unsticking. It *was* Amber sitting over him, smiling encouragingly. Her shawl and hands were smudged with blood. His blood.

'Take it easy,' said Amber. 'You had a massive hit on the head, so don't rush yourself.'

Luc smiled and closed his eyes tiredly. 'It's so good to hear your voice again,' he mumbled, waking up just enough to glance at her face.

Amber's smile faltered slightly. She pressed the shawl up to his face once more.

'Lucky, can you talk to me?' Shinichi asked.

'Shinichi, Amber's here,' he mumbled. 'She's here. I can't believe she's here, right next to me.'

'Well, I was going to ask where she was, but now I don't have to,' he said sarcastically. 'Do you remember what happened?'

'Uh…' He forced himself to concentrate on the memory as he thought back. 'I was at the cemetery, talking to you…' When he swallowed, his throat scratched against itself, and he wished he had some water. *Maybe Amber has some,* he thought.

'Anything after that?' Shinichi asked.

Luc blanked. 'After what?'

'Mr Holmes,' Amber said, only adding to his confusion. 'Can you hear me?' she held up her index finger. 'Follow my finger.'

Shinichi sighed. 'Lucky, can you give the earpiece to Amber?'

'What did you call me?' he mumbled.

'Lucky!' Shinichi snapped. 'Pull yourself together, agent. Give the earpiece to Amber.'

'She just—'

'Do it!'

His head spinning, Lucky reached up and, with fumbling fingers, pulled the earpiece out of his ear and held it out to Amber.

She stared at it in confusion, then shook her head and took it from him. 'I assume whoever you were talking to is in this,' she said, putting it in her ear.

Luc closed his eyes, thankful that his eyelids blocked out the sun.

'There was a man here, his name's Harry,' Amber said. Luc opened his eyes, wondering if she was talking to him. 'I don't know his last name. I saw him knock out Mr Holmes. Then while he was still unconscious, he… he gave him that box-thing, picked it up again and….' her forehead creased.

'And?' Luc asked.

'He just… disappeared. I think the… the timebox… must have sent him back to… wherever he came from…?' She listened for a moment to Shinichi, but her gaze stayed on Luc. Tentatively, she reached into his pocket and pulled out his phone, but didn't seem to know what to do with it beyond that.

What's happened to her? Luc wondered. *And why is she calling me Mr Holmes? It sounds so weird. No one calls me Mr Holmes.*

He took the phone from her and opened it. Now that he could remember how to think, he knew what Shinichi had told her to do. He opened an app on his phone and turned up the volume until Shinichi's voice clearly came through. '…both be able to hear me.'

'Yep,' Luc said. He tried to sit up, but his head spun as soon as he did. Amber gently pushed him back down, bundling up her shawl and placing it under his head as a pillow.

'Can you breathe okay?' she asked him.

'Yeah.'

'How's your vision?'

'A bit misty.' He held out his hand, and Amber took it in both her own, but didn't pull him up. She just held his hand in her own warm ones, as though offering mental support through the contact. Somehow, it helped Luc's head stop spinning a little; gave him something to ground him.

It was a bit distracting, though.

'So this Harry has the timebox now,' Shinichi said quietly. 'We can assume he came back to the present.'

Amber frowned. 'What do you mean?'

There was a pause from Shinichi's end, and Luc glanced at her. *Her hands are really soft,* his mind said, and he shook his head.

There's something wrong, he thought. He pulled his hand away, forcing himself to sit up even as the world dipped and spun around him. 'Is...' his voice sounded too breathy, but he continued anyway. 'What's going on?'

He saw her look away, and his stomach turned to ice. 'Why are you calling me Mr Holmes?'

Shinichi spoke up. 'Amber, is there someone tailing you?'

'Am I meant to call you something else?' she asked Luc.

He frowned, trying to analyse the question for a hidden meaning, but couldn't see anything.

'Do you want me to call you Lucky?'

Unconsciously, he moved away from her, confused. He'd been so sure that his mission was over. Okay, so Harry had the timebox, but he had Amber! Right next to him, alive and frankly in better condition than he was and… and… suddenly the feeling he'd had earlier crashed back down onto him.

She looked like she didn't know who I was.

Hot, angry tears came to Luc's eyes. *I came all this way. I went through all of this.* 'Amber, what's wrong?'

Amber looked uncomfortable under his gaze. 'You were knocked out and—'

'We know that much,' Shinichi said impatiently. 'Laura's joining the conversation.'

'Amber, we're all ears,' Laura said. 'You can tell us in a code if you need to.'

Luc also turned to Amber expectantly. She was staring at the phone, silently, shaking her head. Her mouth was compressed into a tight frown, and her hands were clasped rigidly in her lap. She kept shaking her head. 'I…' she started. 'I don't…'

Luc pushed himself up a bit higher so that his whole back was leaning against something hard. *A tombstone,* he realised, feeling slightly sick. He felt so thirsty. Later. He could find water later. 'Amber, what's—'

'I'm not Amber!' she exploded. 'I don't know who I am, but please, I don't want to be Amber! So stop calling me that!' She stood, and took a few paces back. Luc's heart sank further in his chest.

He didn't know what to say; his mind was drawing a complete blank. He stared at her, trying to find what part of her wasn't her. *Her eyes, her mouth, her whole face is exactly as I remember,* he thought. *Did I get the wrong person?* 'If you're not Amber,' he said tentatively, 'Then who are you?'

'I don't know,' she snapped. 'I woke up one day and I couldn't remember who I was, and no one recognised me. For five weeks I've had no idea who I am or how I got here.'

'Maybe you found your look-alike,' Shinichi suggested, unhelpfully. 'I mean, she doesn't sound like her.'

'Yes, she does!' Laura cried indignantly. 'You know nothing—'

'I was her ARC-researcher on her mission to 1998, and she didn't sound like that,' Shinichi protested.

'Then I don't know who you were talking to, Shinichi,' Luc replied. 'I'm sorry, but you look like her, and you sound like her, to me at least. And your story fits with Amber's—'

'I'm not Amber!' Amber protested, 'I can't be!'

Luc watched her wordlessly. Confusion didn't begin to explain what he was feeling. 'Why not?' he asked softly.

'We weren't sure that she was still alive, because it's so dangerous to Travel when you're not at peak health,' Shinichi said calmly. 'There was an immense chance that she'd died, or been severely concussed because of the mixture of the crash and the Travelling. It's not impossible that it would cause her to lose her memory.'

He'd summed up what Luc had been thinking. If Amber had forgotten her whole life in the present, it meant that she'd forgotten him too. *But why is she so adamant that she's not herself if she doesn't remember who she is?*

He looked at Amber, about to ask her his question, but stopped himself. Her shoulders were hunched, her mouth drawn in a straight line. He softened, beckoning her back over. *The confusion I'm feeling now must be tiny compared to how she feels,* he thought suddenly.

'Harry said that I'd been in a car crash,' she said quietly, 'And that I could work that… that box. But I… I don't think…'

Luc wanted to sit next to her, hold her and tell her it was all okay. He wanted to desperately. But he knew it wouldn't help. Not only was he too weak to sit without support; from her point of view, he was a complete stranger. She wouldn't find any comfort in him. no matter how much it hurt him to watch her as she was so lonely and helpless, he couldn't do anything about it.

'Why don't you tell us exactly what happened?' he suggested. 'We might be able to help if we know all the facts.'

She nodded, taking a deep breath. 'I was found lying just outside Richard Johansson's home about a month ago. Apparently I looked like I'd been beaten; I had cuts and bruises all over my face. They asked me who I was and I… I couldn't remember.'

Luc nodded silently.

'Mr Johansson kindly offered to allow me to stay at his house. His son, Arthur, chose the name Rachel Winters for me, after his dead mother.'

That's right, the fruit seller called her Miss Rachel.

Amber described her meeting with Harry, then her second meeting with him, in the hotel with Christopher, going to confront him about the note. 'That's when he mentioned you,' she said to Luc. 'He said that he was surprised that I – or Amber – had survived the car crash, and he said that maybe you weren't so lucky.'

Laura snorted. 'I bet he thought that was funny.'

Luc didn't even have the energy to roll his eyes.

Amber then related the events of that day leading up to helping Luc in the churchyard. When she finished, she looked at Luc, as though expecting him to give her answers.

There was silence on the phone. Luc half-expected, and half-hoped, that Shinichi or Laura would say something. But he knew they were waiting for him.

He looked up at Amber's face, judging her emotions as best as he could. He could see the confusion, the hurt, the tiredness on her face. Then, more than ever, he wanted to wrap her in a hug and Travel back to ARCHIVE, where they could go to the medics and make everything better. He didn't trust himself to say what she needed to hear.

'Do you… do you want to hear my side of the story?' he asked quietly. Amber gave a small nod.

So he told her. Starting back at the car accident, he told her how he'd found the manual, how Laura had searched through history, and when he'd found her, how Haste had sent him to retrieve her and bring her back. But when he'd come, she hadn't recognised him.

She was quiet for a long time. 'I just… I don't want to be Amber Elkhoury,' she whispered eventually.

Luc couldn't help himself. He shuffled closer to her and reached out an arm, but to his discouragement, she pulled away from him. He nodded once and went back to the tombstone. 'Why not?' he asked quietly.

She shook her head. 'Well, she's a bad driver, for one thing,' she said.

Luc laughed. 'I can't deny that,' he replied. 'Is that all?'

She shook her head, but stared at the ground like her gaze was too heavy to lift. 'It's… Harry,' she went on softly. 'And ARCHIVE… and… and I don't want to be someone who Harry knows, someone he may have worked with.' She swallowed hard. 'I've lived here for *five weeks,* feeling so confused about who I am and where I belong, and… Amber's life just sounds more confusing than this one.' After a moment, she finally looked up expectantly at Luc's face.

His mouth fell open as it sunk in. *Five weeks? She's been wondering who she was all that time?* 'I—I'm so sorry,' he whispered.

Finally, Laura came to his rescue.

'You might find that a lot of things make sense when you come back here,' she suggested. 'I mean, we were able to explain how you lost your memory in the first place.'

'Harry doesn't work for ARCHIVE,' Shinichi added. 'He works against it.'

From the *o* that Amber's mouth made at hearing this, she hadn't had that piece of information given to her.

'ARCHIVE isn't reckless, either,' Luc said. 'It's about saving people. Just like you did for me today – saving people who may not even know they're in danger. I know you love that; you've told me yourself.' He pulled his ARCHIVE badge out of his pocket. It was a shield-shape of blue leather, with a bronze circle stitched onto it. Behind the circle was the word 'ARCHIVE', and cut out of the circle was the shape of a fox's head. Underneath, set into the leather, was a small bronze plaque with the words *Si Periculum* engraved into it. She took it wordlessly, staring at it and turning it over in her hands. 'ARCHIVE stands for Aid and Rescue Corp for Historical and International Victims and Emergencies,' he added. 'You were a psychologist. ARCHIVE picked you up when you'd only been working for three years.'

'How do you know that?'

'You told me,' Luc replied. 'We're partners – we do all our missions together. And Shinichi and… and Laura are helping us with this one.'

'And we need to get you back here,' Shinichi said.

Laura snorted. 'I think we should wait for Lucky to get back to at least 80% health before they Travel or we might have two amnesiacs on our hands.'

Amber nodded. 'I'll see if I can get Lucky to a doctor of some sort and see if we can help with his concussion,' she said. Her eyes widened as she realised what she'd said, and she looked at Luc.

See? he smiled. *Psychology degree.*

'No. No doctors,' Shinichi said firmly. 'ARCHIVE doesn't trust period doctors. You'll just have to monitor him, Amber, and if he takes a turn for the worse we'll risk a trip back.'

'But—'

'*No* doctors. He needs to keep all his blood.'

Amber sighed, but nodded. 'Okay.'

'Just keep us updated, okay?' Laura said. Quietly, she added to Shinichi, 'It's so weird hearing Amber call Lucky "Lucky", isn't it? I didn't realise how I'd gotten used to it.'

Amber looked at Luc quizzically. 'Am I not meant to call you Lucky either?' she asked.

Luc shook his head, resigned. He'd never liked anyone else calling him Luc, so he'd been looking forward to hearing it from her again. But when she'd forgotten about him, she'd forgotten about his nickname too. Oh well. It just wouldn't be the same if he told her about it, so he let it be. Hopefully she'd remember when they got back to ARCHIVE. 'No, Lucky's fine,' he replied quietly.

'Lucky,' Shinichi said quickly, the excitement of an idea coming through his voice, 'Lucky, when did you get your nickname?'

Luc looked away from Amber. His head hurt, his eyes hurt, his whole body hurt, and he didn't want to relive the story again. 'Amber made it up on our mission at London City Airport.'

'Yes, but where did it come from? It was a book, wasn't it?'

'Maybe? She didn't say; but she'd been reading a couple of books while waiting in the boarding rooms.' He frowned. 'Why?'

Luc couldn't see Shinichi's sly smile. 'It gave me an idea.'

The clicking of his keyboard came through the phone's speaker softly. 'I will have to go for a while,' he said. 'And possibly Laura too - we have something we need to investigate. Go find a place to rest. We won't be in contact for a few hours at least.'

'Wait, Shinichi—'

'This is very important,' Shinichi went on. 'Try not to get into any trouble. I might not be able to help you if you do.'

4:14PM 10 MARCH 2019, ARCHIVE

*The ARChronicles are available for all agents'
research on any topic to do with a mission.
Familiarise yourself with the resources available
in the ARChronicles: amongst other things, there
are newspapers, books, agent files, mission files
and obituaries.*

Laura followed Shinichi to the ARChronicles. If he had a plan, then she had no idea what it was. 'I'm still nervous about you being here,' she muttered.

It wasn't the first time she'd raised her concerns, and from the look on Shinichi's face, he wished she'd drop it. 'Laura,' he snapped as he walked confidently across the room. 'How long did it take you to notice I'd gone?'

'Gone permanently?' she said, feeling a bit guilty and hoping this made him think she'd thought he was sick. 'Well… maybe a few days before I wondered if something was up…'

'It's been a month now. Do you think anyone else has noticed I'm not supposed to be here?'

Laura hadn't known that Shinichi was so self-aware of his own invisibility. She felt lonely for him, wondering what it would be like to know that no one cared if you were there or not.

Not that he seemed very concerned about it.

According to Shinichi, all ARC-researchers had access to a large amount of the ARChronicles database on their own computers, but when he'd left ARCHIVE, they'd taken back his laptop. So, like every other field agent, they had to make the trip to the physical ARChronicles. Shinichi knew what he was looking for, and hadn't given her any instructions, so she followed him blindly around the computers to the rows and rows that made up the hardcopy sections of the ARChronicles.

'Is this going to take a long time?' she asked him.

'Yes. This may take all night and most of tomorrow morning,' he said easily.

Laura had, of course, heard the ARCHIVE adage that the ARC-researchers never sleep. She almost believed it; she'd seen Shinichi's average daily coffee intake, and couldn't believe he could sleep after that much caffeine. But she wasn't an ARC-researcher.

'Shinichi, I have to go home at five o'clock to take care of my family,' she said as he pulled out a yellowed agent's folder. 'Can't this wait until tomorrow?' He didn't look up from the folder. 'And why are you even looking through these files? Why not use the computers like a normal person?'

'The computers contain a record of everything you search,' Shinichi said quietly. He flicked a page. 'And I already know what I'm looking for, so this is much faster.'

The computers contain a record of everything you search, he'd said. *A record that Haste can access freely, to realise that we're onto him,* he hadn't said.

Laura sighed and glanced at the name on the file. 'That's the case file for Amber and Lucky's first case.'

Shinichi nodded.

'Is that linked to this somehow?' Laura prodded.

Shinichi nodded. 'I can't be sure, but I think so. Remember, Amber was at the airport, preparing to board the plane, when Agent Mendoza came and told her that he was her replacement. She'd never boarded the plane to New York, and the whole plane had gone down. He'd been sent to right things in her place. He left her at the airport and saved the plane with Lucky instead.'

Laura nodded. She was familiar with the case; she'd been told all about it when Carl had come for approval on his 1990s outfit.

'I was Amber's ARC-researcher on that mission,' Shinichi went on. 'And I remember talking her through her wait at the airport, telling her to stay and investigate anything that might help in the case. In the end, unknown to Mendoza, her findings were valuable to finding out more about what was going on behind the scenes.'

'So she was the one who found who damaged the plane?' Laura asked.

Shinichi closed the file and handed it to her. 'She found that two other ARCHIVE agents were in 1998 with her. Harry Goldwyn was one of them, and he had sabotaged the plane.'

Laura's eyes widened as she flicked through the agent report, finding the disciplinary section, which only confirmed what she'd just heard. 'However, Goldwyn disappeared from the airport before he could be located and arrested,' she read. 'So he's an ARCHIVE agent?' She looked up, but the space before her was empty. 'Um, Shinichi?'

'I'm over here!' he called from the alcove where the more sensitive files were kept. She closed the file and found him leaning over the bench at the files protected behind the desk. Laura followed his gaze, wondering if he was planning to jump over to get the file he wanted.

'It's not there,' he said, a small smile on his lips.

'What's not there?'

Shinichi pointed. 'There's no file for Harry Goldwyn.'

'So he's not an ARCHIVE agent?'

Shinichi rolled his eyes. 'Laura, you're acting like I would know that.'

'*You're* acting like you know that! Is he an ARCHIVE agent, or isn't he?'

Shinichi folded his arms. 'I assumed he was a future ARCHIVE agent because he was Travelling in time. He was certainly working on behalf of Haste in 1998. But now it seems like…' Shinichi trailed off, and Laura gave up asking for clarification as she saw the mental cogs wind up again behind his eyes.

'I never found out why Amber never got on the plane,' he said, lost in thought. 'I always assumed that it was because, in the loop of time, Mendoza stopped her before she could.' He shook his head, gritting his teeth in frustration as he went on. 'But this is unsatisfactory. If Mendoza hadn't gone, it could be assumed that Amber would get on the plane and successfully complete her mission. From Mendoza's point of view, something must have stopped her, then he had to go in her place.'

Laura nodded, though she only understood about sixty percent of it. Time travel was a reality at ARCHIVE, and with it came all the intricacies and paradoxes usually limited to novels.

'Did you ask Mendoza why she never got on the plane?' Laura asked.

'Yes, but he didn't know.' Shinichi shook his head resolutely. 'I refuse to believe that she was stopped from completing her mission due to the stupid reason that someone told her that she never completed it.'

Laura didn't agree. In any other profession, it would sound like psychological tell-yourself-you-can-do-it-and-you-can inspirational nonsense, but at ARCHIVE, if someone told you that you would fail, it was probably because they'd watched it happen. But that was an argument no one could win, so instead she decided to see where Shinichi would go with it. 'Look, that's great, but if Goldwyn's a future agent, why is he in 1868? I feel like we're concerned with different things here.'

Shinichi slowly reached out and took the file from Laura's hands. He flicked through it again silently. 'It's a smaller file than I remember writing,' he said softly.

Laura frowned. He was right. For such a complicated case, especially if it involved future agents as Shinichi was hypothesising, and paradoxical time loops, the file was quite small, about the same size as a file would be expected to be if it was an in-and-out case, straightforward and completed before lunch.

'What's missing?' she asked.

Shinichi shrugged. 'I can't remember the case well enough for details. It was an… eventful time for me. Most of it is sketchy. But it looks like someone has gone through this and pulled pages out.' He frowned. 'That's strange. The transcription is intact, but the profiles are not.'

'So whoever censored this wasn't very thorough.'

'Whoever did this? I think we can guess who did this,' Shinichi replied.

Laura frowned, lowering her voice. 'If you say Haste, you'd better have a good reason for it,' she warned.

He nodded. 'Amber was deliberately sent back in time, and we have good enough evidence to say that it was Haste's "experiment". I have a hunch that he did it because he was afraid that we knew something.'

Laura knew he'd hate her for it, but she asked anyway. 'Knew what?'

To her surprise, Shinichi smiled. 'I don't know. You're going to Travel back to 1998 so that we can find out.'

Laura raised her eyebrows. 'What? Two minutes ago you were all we-can't-use-computers-because-Haste-is-watching-us and now you want me to *Travel*? As though that won't raise eyebrows?'

'You're right. You'll need Haste's permission to Travel.' He looked at the paper he'd taken from the mission report and growled in frustration. 'Maybe if I can talk to Amber, I can get her to research it…' his eyes widened. 'Of course.'

'What?'

Slowly, Shinichi's mouth curved into a smile. 'It all makes sense.'

Laura blinked. 'What makes sense?'

'I didn't recognise Amber's voice just then,' Shinichi said to her, still smiling. 'Because on the mission, I didn't hear her voice.'

Laura hadn't been expecting him to say that. 'Then who did you hear?'

Shinichi started pacing up and down between the shelves. Ignoring her question, he started muttering to himself in Japanese. Laura shook her head and went back to the folder, reading through the commentary while she waited for him to finish.

'I think I've got a plan,' Shinichi said eventually.

'What is it?'

'We can't Travel without Haste's permission, can we?'

Haven't we established this already? 'No.'

'But we shouldn't need to.' Shinichi held up the paper he'd been holding, pointing to a small number in a box in the top-right corner. 'Because of this.'

Laura peered at the number. *1998-108654A.*

'That is the pin that ARC-researchers use. It is specific to one agent at one time in history.' Shinichi handed back the folder, a triumphant smile on his face. 'I can use that number to talk to Amber while she waits in the airport, and ask her to research what kept her from boarding the plane.'

'But if we do that, your past self won't be able to talk to Amber,' Laura protested.

Shinichi nodded. 'So I'll redirect my past self's call to some-one who's impersonating Amber, reading the transcript from the case.' He looked pointedly at Laura.

Laura blinked. 'Me?' She stepped back. 'I sound nothing like Amber!'

Shinichi smiled. 'That's okay. I have a voice-changing bowtie.'

This was getting stranger by the minute. Laura rubbed her temples, as though that would help her to keep up with him. 'You. Have. A. *What?*"

Shinichi shook his head. 'That was a good joke, and you didn't understand it.' He sighed. 'You know what? It doesn't matter if you don't sound like her. I didn't recognise Amber's voice when she spoke to me just then, because on that mission, I'd been talking to you!'

Laura kept rubbing her temples, thinking through the plan. 'So I'm talking to February-you, and you'll be talking to Feb-ruary-Amber?'

'Yes.'

'So February-you is talking to present-me, and Febru-ary-Amber thinks she's talking to February-you, but really she's talking to present-you?'

'Yes.'

It seemed like it would work… and they could do it under Haste's nose, without him finding out about it. All she'd have to do is put on an English accent like Amber's, and Shinichi probably wouldn't notice anything different, especially if he'd never heard her voice before. Considering that had been Amber's first mission, it was very likely that they'd never spoken beforehand.

She hugged the case file to her chest. If this worked, and they figured out what Haste was hiding, it would explain a lot, and would help them bring him to justice. She looked up at Shinichi, seeing her own determination mirrored in his eyes. 'Just one thing,' she said.

'Yes?'

'Can we do this tomorrow morning? I really need to go home at five.'

Shinichi nodded. 'We'll start at nine o'clock tomorrow morning.'

4:03PM 25 November 1868, Walhalla, Australia

Your ARC-researcher is always there to help you. Do you have a question? Do you need advice? Are you feeling discouraged? Never hesitate to talk to your ARC-researcher about anything. That is what they are there for.

Amber waited a moment after Shinichi and Laura hung up, trying to compose herself and give Lucky Holmes an opportunity to collect his thoughts.

Finally she stood and reached out to help him up too.

'Where are you staying?' she asked him. 'Do you have family here?'

'Amber, I'm—' he stopped with a sigh and shook his head. 'I don't have any family here. And I arrived this morning.'

'Where were you planning to stay?'

He smiled wryly. 'I wasn't.'

She thought for a moment. Johansson would not be impressed if she took him home; she was imposing enough on him as it was. The obvious option was the Walhalla Hotel, and she quickly resolved to take him there.

But when he tried to step forward, he stumbled onto a grave and she was forced to catch him clumsily.

'I don't think you'll make it to the hotel, let alone the hospital,' she said aloud. 'I don't think you'll make it anywhere.'

'I don't want to stay here,' he said dizzily, and she agreed. Spending the night in a cemetery was enough to make anyone uneasy.

But who else might take him? she wondered. There were plenty of caring people in Walhalla, but they all had families that they had to feed and take care of—

She smiled when she realised the answer. *I suppose* he *has no family,* she thought, *and he's self-employed, so he has no obligations. As a bonus, he lives the closest.*

'Mr—Lucky,' she said, still trying to keep him upright. 'I have a friend who lives about a hundred metres that way. Do you think you'll make it? He might be able to give you a bed for the night.'

Lucky grunted and mumbled something she didn't catch. Looping one of his arms over her shoulder, she led him out of the cemetery, past the church and right to the front door of Christopher Alpine.

Lucky was heavy, and they were both sweaty, which only made the waiting at Christopher's door more uncomfortable. She knocked a couple of times, wondering suddenly if he was home. *He may have gone out to find plants,* she thought, glancing worriedly at Lucky. He was still muttering, but she couldn't understand what he was saying. Something about water?

She knocked a third time, and finally Christopher opened the door. He seemed his usual self, unhurried but thoughtful, but now his shirt was untucked and his hair was slightly messy. He stepped back, blood draining from his face when he saw Lucky.

'He's been badly concussed,' Amber said urgently. 'Just in the cemetery.'

Christopher frowned at him. 'Isn't that—' he stopped himself. 'No, never mind. How does one get concussed in a cemetery? Did he run headfirst into a tombstone?'

'Harry attacked him. I saw it.'

Christopher flinched, and he looked again at Lucky. He inspected the wound on his forehead, then glanced into Lucky's eyes. Amber was surprised; she hadn't thought that anyone would know to check the pupils for concussion.

'He's concussed,' he said.

Amber forced herself not to snap at him. 'I don't think he'll make it to the hospital. Can he spend the night here?'

He looked at her for a long time, then his eyes flicked to Lucky's bloodied forehead. 'We could use the cart—'

Lucky toppled sideways, and Amber struggled to keep him from faceplanting into the ground. Christopher's eyes widened, his arms catching Lucky instinctively. 'I suppose he'd better stay here,' he said.

Amber thanked him and together they carried Lucky to a small bedroom. Christopher's house felt smaller on the inside, divided as it was into many small rooms, and it was cool and dark with the curtains drawn to keep out the heat. They settled Lucky on the bed, and Amber quickly checked his pulse.

'I just wanted somewhere to lay him down,' she said quietly as she watched him breathe. When she heard no reply, she turned around.

Christopher wasn't there.

***

Amber put the kettle on the stove to boil, wondering what boiled bandages would feel like. It was the best way to disinfect them, and it also gave her a moment to think while she waited.

Meeting Lucky had been even more of a puzzle than she'd anticipated.

He did *recognise me,* she thought, still wondering at that. *He was the first person to recognise me.*

But why did he have to be so sure that she was Amber Elkhoury?

There was a beep in the earpiece, and she jumped. *I didn't take it out?* she wondered. Getting Lucky to a bed had made her forget about it.

'Lucky? Are you there?' came Shinichi's voice suddenly through the earpiece.

'It's… it's me,' Amber replied quietly. She wasn't ready to try out her name, yet. She still wasn't sure that Lucky had got the right girl. No, that felt wrong. It wasn't that she wasn't sure he was right; it was more that she… hoped he wasn't.

She left the kitchen and waited just outside Lucky's doorway. She hadn't been able to find Christopher since he'd disappeared; she assumed he'd gone to get a doctor.

'Amber,' Shinichi said. He didn't sound surprised to hear her voice. She listened, but couldn't hear any sound from Lucky's phone. Apparently it had stopped working as a speaker when the phone had been turned off. 'Where's Lucky?' Shinichi asked.

Amber glanced into the room. 'He's sleeping,' she whispered, pivoting back around the doorway.

'Oh. Where?'

'A friend's house. It was closer than the hospital. Christopher's a botanist, so he knows a lot about herbal medicines and remedies.'

There was a clicking sound from the Shinichi's end of the connection.

'Is Laura there?' she asked.

'Laura's gone home. She'll be back tomorrow morning, but then we'll probably be busy for the rest of the day. It's just after five o'clock in the afternoon here.'

The statement surprised her. *Does that mean they're in a different time zone?* Amber knew it was about four o'clock; Lucky's phone had had the time on its screen. 'Where are you?' she ventured.

Shinichi chuckled. 'That's an interesting question to ask, Amber. We're in London.'

'Then how can you be an hour ahead of us?'

'It's four o'clock over there?'

'Yeah. If you were in London you'd be a long way behind Australia.'

Shinichi grunted his agreement. 'I'm not lying; I really am in London. I'm just not in 1868 London. I'm in 2019 London.'

Amber frowned. 'Oh.'

An odd sound came through the earpiece. It sounded like Shinichi was sipping a hot beverage, and didn't want to burn his lips. 'Just "oh"?'

'Well, I didn't expect you to be so far in the future, to be honest. I don't know why I thought you'd be from the future anyway.' Amber shook her head tiredly, leaning against the wall. 'Man, it's so frustrating.'

'Frustrating? What's frustrating?'

'What?' She hadn't realised she'd said it out loud, and as she realised it, a small uncomfortable feeling of dread settled in her stomach. She didn't want to tell this stranger – who for all she knew was an AI from the future – about her personal struggles from the past few weeks. She didn't know him – this mysterious friend of Lucky's.

But if I don't tell him, then who can I tell?

For the first time, people recognised her. Lucky had said that they worked together, that they were partners. And Harry had said the same thing to her before, too. Maybe Shinichi would be able to help her to make sense of everything.

She opened her mouth, but before anything could come out, an overwhelming wave of doubt washed over her, leaving her speechless. She closed her mouth again sadly. 'Don't worry, it doesn't matter.'

'There's no one else listening, if that's what you're worrying about,' Shinichi said. 'And I won't judge.' Again, there was the sound like he was sipping his drink.

'It's just… it sounds so weird.'

'Amber, you may not know this, but when people asked me what I did for a living, I said that I worked at a call centre, because it was too hard to explain that I worked for a time-travelling aid and rescue organisation that saves people who have already been saved, but I don't actually do any time-travelling or saving; I'm the little man in the earpiece.'

Amber hadn't known any of that. She couldn't help a small, amused smile forming on her lips.

'I know what it's like to say weird things,' Shinichi went on softly. 'And I know that some things are weird, but they're also true. So please don't lie to me because you think the truth will make an otherwise clean conversation a bit weird and awkward. I'm your ARC-researcher for this mission, and you know that you can tell me anything you want. It's what I'm here for.'

'Um, okay.' Amber glanced at Lucky once more. Yes, he was still curled up, fast asleep. 'The thing is… I know things that other people here don't know. Like I know what Blu-tack is, and somehow I thought Persia was called Iran. I mean, Harry knew those sorts of things too, so I assumed that we were from the same place. And I guess that made me… I mean…' Amber sighed. 'He kept saying I was Amber Elkhoury, but I didn't like him, so I didn't want to listen to him. In case that… made him… right.'

Shinichi didn't say anything. He sipped his beverage again.

'I was so determined to *not* be Amber Elkhoury.'

Amber didn't know what to say, so she kept quiet and hoped that Shinichi would reply.

'Well, whatever Harry, or Lucky, or any of us say, you can decide who you want to be,' Shinichi replied eventually. 'But we're all hoping that you decide to become Amber again.'

Amber nodded silently. *It's a decision I'm going to have to make eventually,* she thought. *To be or not to be.* 'What about you?' she asked quietly. 'What are you like?'

'Me?' For the first time since she'd talked to him, Shinichi sounded surprised. 'Why do you want to know about me?'

She shrugged. 'Well, at the moment, you're a voice in my ear. I'd like to know more about you.'

'Oh.' There was a small pause as Shinichi sipped his drink. 'Well, I… I'm from Tokyo.'

'I thought you were in London.'

Shinichi chuckled. 'I'm in London, but I'm from Tokyo.'

'Oh, so you're staying in London? When did you leave Tokyo?'

'When I started working for ARCHIVE twelve years ago. I was a detective there – in Tokyo – but I… I liked it better at ARCHIVE.'

Amber smiled. 'Do you have a family?'

'Um… no. I mean, my parents and sister are in Tokyo still, but I… I'm not married or anything.'

'Oh. What's your sister's name?'

'Misaki. She's twenty-two. She's in college, studying to become a pharmacist.'

Amber nodded. 'Sounds good.'

Shinichi sipped his drink again.

'Can I still talk to you tomorrow?' she asked.

'Maybe not tomorrow,' he replied. 'Laura and I are working on another case at the moment alongside this, and I don't want to talk about it over the earpieces. But if you need me, Lucky can send an alert to me through his phone.'

Amber nodded, rubbing her face tiredly as she headed back for the kitchen. 'Okay. I need to go now anyway.'

Shinichi took another sip. 'Look after Lucky.'

'I will.'

'And Amber?'

Amber bit her lip. *Amber. He really believes that I'm Amber.* 'Yes?' *Can I accept being Amber? If I do, will I suddenly remember everything?*

'You can trust Lucky,' Shinichi said. 'He wants you to.'

'Um… okay. I will. I'll be waiting for you to get back,' Amber said. She took a deep breath, then took the plunge. 'To take Lucky and me home again.'

There. I've made my decision.

I am Amber Elkhoury, an agent at the Aid and Rescue Corp for Historical and International Victims and Emergencies. I travel through time for a living, saving people who have already been saved.

'Good luck, Amber,' Shinichi said.

Amber smiled. 'Thanks. You too.'

*Travelling to the past can give you a new
perspective on the present. We often treat our
present as a special time in history, unique simply
because it is the 'present'. As you Travel, you
will realise that each and every infinitely small
moment in history is unique, and each one is a
'present', even if for you it seems like history.*

Amber quickly learned that Lucky was not one to call her when he wanted something.

She was still musing over her chat with Shinichi when he arrived in the kitchen doorway, leaning heavily against the wall and mumbling about being thirsty.

She sighed heavily, guiding him back to the bedroom. 'Just call me if you need something,' she said. 'The water's outside; there's no way you'll be able to get it on your own.'

His eyes half-closed, he nodded, so she sent him back to bed and went to get some water from the tank outside. It was warm from the sun, and she wished that she could chill it somehow. But there was nothing to be done; Lucky would just have to drink it as it was.

And he did. He downed the glass frighteningly quickly, and somehow managed to not choke on it.

'Thanks. Have you talked to Shinichi at all?' he asked when he was finished.

'Yes,' Amber replied. 'Briefly. He and Laura will be busy until the day after tomorrow, so you have until then to rest and get better.'

Lucky nodded again, then lay back on the pillows with a sigh, closing his eyes. The bed was small and low, void of blankets. Amber drew the heavier curtains over the window to darken the room.

'Are you hungry?' she asked Lucky. He shook his head.

The sound of the front door closing rang through the house, and soon Christopher was standing in the doorway of the room.

'Who's he?' Lucky murmured, opening his eyes again. 'A doctor? You know how ARCHIVE feels about period doctors, Amber.'

Amber glanced at Christopher's face. He was watching Lucky silently, his eyes full of unasked questions. 'Lucky, this is Christopher. He's not a doctor; he's a botanist.'

Lucky's eyes narrowed as he regarded the man. 'Oh, well that makes it okay for him to practice on me, then,' he said sarcastically.

Amber sighed impatiently. 'I haven't called a doctor, Lucky,' she said. 'Anyway, Christopher, this is Lucky, a… an old friend of mine, I suppose you could say.'

Christopher nodded to Lucky, whose eyes were still narrowed to suspicious slits. 'I know I am not trained,' he told Lucky, 'but at the moment it's either me or a four mile trek up a mountain for medical attention, whatever this ARCHIVE says about doctors.'

The kettle started to whistle from the kitchen, and Amber used the ringing to excuse herself from the awkward introductions. Christopher followed her to the kitchen.

'Miss Rachel,' he started, seeming unsure of himself. 'I… I know you're a private woman, but I have many questions.'

Amber nodded silently, using a cloth to take the kettle from the stove and pouring the water into a bowl. 'I know, Christopher. As do I.'

'Why do people keep calling you Amber?'

Amber put the kettle back on the stove with a sigh. *It's time to explain everything,* she decided. So she started from the night when she'd woken up with no memory of her identity, and filled him in on the events up until that day. She told him all she knew about ARCHIVE, Lucky, Shinichi and Laura, and tried to explain the earpiece and timebox. She matter-of-factly went through Harry's crimes, and finished with his disappearance into the future and her imminent journey back.

She used tongs to pull the bandages out of the kettle, spreading them over a cooling rack she'd found to help them to cool and dry slightly. When she'd finished, she looked up Christopher's face to see his reaction.

His eyes were wide, and his eyebrows were low. 'Miss Rachel, I must be frank. Either you're lying to me, or you're gullible enough to believe the lies that that… man has been feeding you.'

Amber tried to interrupt, but he held up his hand to silence her. 'No, Miss Rachel. I believe that you don't know who you are, as I can accept that a knock to the head can do that to a person, but no matter how desperate you are for answers, you can't believe that you're from the *future,* of all places, just because a stranger tells you so!' He was almost shouting at her, only keeping his voice down because Lucky was possibly asleep in another room. It was enough to make Amber's heart hammer, and she stepped back from him. 'But beside that, I don't believe a word of your story, and I would greatly appreciate you telling the truth, without your… embellishments.'

Amber shook her head. 'I swear, Christopher, I told you the complete truth.'

He folded his arms. 'If it's true, then I'll talk to this Shinichi, to confirm it.'

'Don't be like that, Christopher,' Amber pleaded. Everything had seemed to fit into place before – people had given her answers! But all too quickly, her certainty wavered, and the same old questions came back to her mind.

But I did *talk to Shinichi…. didn't I?*

'Shinichi told me that he and Laura were busy until the day after tomorrow. Then you can talk to them.' Amber lowered her eyes to the floor. 'Please believe me, Christopher,' she begged, her eyes filling with tears. '*I* believe Lucky! He's been the only one who's been able to give me answers that…' she stopped herself before she said *answers that make sense.* 'Anyway, if I can't believe Lucky, who can I believe?' Desperately, she raised her eyes to meet his. 'You don't understand what it's like! I didn't know who I was, but now I do!'

An idea came to her. 'Let me care for Lucky and make sure he's okay, and then I'll show you proof. Undeniable proof.'

Christopher's arms were still folded, like a physical wall he was building between them. He nodded. Amber sighed, wiped her eyes, then gathered up the bandages and hot water, carrying them to Lucky's room.

'Miss Rachel… Miss Amber…' Christopher said, stopping her in the doorway. 'I'll help him, as much as I can. Because he's a person, and it is my duty as a man to help those in need. But I will not tolerate lies in my house.'

Amber nodded. 'I'm not lying. I promise.' When he didn't respond, she shook her head, going to Lucky's room. He was still awake, and seemed stronger than before. Amber set the dish down beside his empty glass and sat on the bed next to him. 'Lucky, how do you feel? Any better?'

He nodded.

Taking one of the bandages, she started to wipe the blood off his face, starting with the blood furthest away from the cut, where it would sting less. Lucky closed his eyes again with a sigh. 'Are you coming back to 2019 with me?' he asked.

Amber had been wondering that herself. She'd built a life, albeit a temporary one, here in Australia, 1868. She shrugged. 'Is it really different from here?'

Lucky snorted. 'Yes.'

'Oh.' It was something she'd have to consider soon. *Tomorrow,* she decided tiredly, rubbing her own face. *Today has had enough questions.* She moved his head to the side, suddenly noticing something near his hairline. A small row of stitches, four in total. 'What's this?' she asked, tapping around it gently.

'Ow! That's an old battle wound; don't touch!'

'Looks fairly recent to me. Do you get knocked out often?'

Lucky sighed. 'Recently, yes. That's from our car accident.' *The accident that Harry mentioned. So it really happened?*

She dipped the bandage into the basin of water, washing the blood out. Watching the brown dissolve into the water, she considered swallowing her next question. Christopher was right, really. Lucky's story wasn't the most likely, and she didn't *really* have a reason to trust him. She took a deep breath, then made her decision. 'Lucky,' she said slowly. 'How old am I?'

He opened his eyes, watching her face as she worked. 'Twenty-five,' he replied promptly. 'Your birthday is on the fifth of October.' He frowned at her. 'Don't you remember how old you are?'

Amber shook her head, a small, rueful smile on her lips. 'No, I don't remember anything about myself, or you, or… anyone else. Weird, isn't it?'

He nodded, his blue eyes sad, but also compassionate. 'Any other burning questions?' he asked.

Amber touched the cloth to his head once more, this time directly on the large lump that had formed on the left corner of his forehead. 'Um… am I married?'

'Ow! No.'

She let out the breath. 'I was kind of worried I had a husband or something somewhere that I wouldn't recognise.'

Lucky smiled, quiet for a moment. 'You have parents in London, though, so you're not completely off the hook.'

She nodded slowly, tried to conjure a picture of parents. Strange to think they were two hundred in the future. 'Do you know how they are?'

Lucky shook his head. 'I don't even know how much ARCHIVE has told them.'

She nodded slowly. 'What did you tell your parents? Before you came here, I mean. Do they know you time travel?'

'Yeah, I told my mum,' he said. 'I know we're not meant to without cause, but… she's all I have now. That's my cause.' He saw her look, and seemed to remember that she didn't know him. 'My dad died four years ago. And I have a sister, in Dublin, but she has her own family now.'

Amber's hands paused. 'I'm sorry,' she said.

He shrugged. 'Mum lives with me. Legally, I'm her carer, but she's fairly independent about half the time. But I kept thinking, if something happened to me, she should know the truth.'

Amber wasn't sure what to say, but when she caught his eye, she offered a smile, and somehow, that seemed to suffice. She hoped her parents weren't worried. She hoped she'd get to see them soon. And she hoped that when she did, she'd recognise them.

'You'll see your parents again,' Lucky said. 'You and I know something they don't.'

Amber offered a weak joke. 'Time travel?'

He snorted. 'We know that you're okay. You're safe, and healed, and you're on your way home.'

There was a cough from the doorway. Amber turned with a start. Christopher was leaning on the doorframe with his arms crossed. 'She is going nowhere,' he said. 'Not with you.'

Amber glanced at Lucky's face. His eyes were flicking between Christopher and Amber, a small frown on his lips. 'Well, I haven't decided—' Amber started.

'No, Miss Rachel,' Christopher said, striding into the room. 'It doesn't matter if you've decided or not. I have. It would be different if he and his friends said that you were from a nearby town, but the *future*? No. Who knows where he'll take you? Or what he'll do to you?'

Amber opened her mouth to respond, but Lucky cut in first.

'Amber, what did you tell him?'

Turning back to him, Amber sputtered. 'I... I told him everything you told me.' Seeing his mouth fall open, she tried to justify herself. 'He's my friend, Lucky. He's been so kind to me, and people kept saying things he didn't understand...' she trailed off as Lucky pushed himself up on the bed to a sitting position.

'Amber, you...' He shook his head. 'You told him *everything?*'

'We can trust him!'

'Why wasn't I meant to know?' Christopher interrupted. 'You see, Miss Rachel? He's trying to steal you away secretly. His story is impossible, and yet you believe him.'

'Maybe I believe him *because* his story is impossible!' Amber snapped. 'If you were trying to kidnap a woman, would you tell her you were from the future?'

Christopher set his mouth into a stubborn line. 'Did you recognise him?'

Amber deflated a little at the question. She felt Lucky's eyes on her, and saw the curiosity turn to hurt in them. Miserably, she closed her mouth and shook her head. 'I don't recognise anyone, Christopher,' she replied.

'Stay here,' Christopher begged. 'I promise that I'll keep you safe.'

'Oh, so you're a police officer as well as a botanist and a doctor?' Lucky cried sarcastically. 'Do his talents ever cease?'

'Lucky!'

'At least I'm not a criminal.'

'Christopher!'

'Miss Rachel—'

'Just—' Amber stood up and stepped up to Christopher. 'Stop calling me that!' she yelled. 'My name is Amber Elkhoury!'

The room snapped into silence. The only sound was Amber's breaths, panting from her frustration. 'I know you don't understand, Christopher. Why should you?' she shook her head bitterly. 'Have you ever felt confused, like I have? Or lonely?'

Christopher held her gaze for a moment, his eyes hard and cold. *Challenge accepted.* She stared back at him, cocking her head as if asking the question again. Finally he looked away.

Turning, she asked, 'Have you?' Lucky was still sitting on the bed. He, at least, wasn't looking at her, but was staring into his lap.

Taking a deep breath, Amber continued at a quieter tone. 'Christopher, I know you're worried. I know you don't trust

Lucky.' She stepped forward and put her hand on his shoulder. 'And I know that you want me to stay.'

He nodded, still avoiding her gaze.

'And Lucky,' she went on, turning around. 'I *do* trust you. I know it's irrational, but I do.' She sighed. 'And I know that you want to take me home.' Slowly, Lucky's blue eyes rose to meet her gaze. He nodded, just once, and she risked a small smile back. 'Christopher, I offered you indisputable proof, and here it is.' She sat down again next to him on the bed, reaching toward his jacket pocket.

Quick as lightning, Lucky's hand closed on her wrist, and his shook his head. 'Amber, you can't do this.'

She frowned. 'No, Lucky. I need to.' Seeing the fear in his face, she pushed her hand harder. 'Lucky, if you want to take me back to the future, we need to convince him.'

After a moment, he nodded, and she pulled out his phone. Turning it on, she handed it to Christopher. 'This is technology from the future,' she said.

He took it curiously, a suspicious frown on his lips. He turned it over, touched the screen. 'You saw the timebox,' she went on. 'These are things that cannot be found here. They can only be from the future.' She watched his face cautiously. 'Do you believe him now?'

Christopher handed the phone back to Lucky, shaking his head uncertainly. Amber felt sorry for him. Time travelling? Future technology? That was earth-shattering news for him. Despite her indisputable proof, she saw the uncertainty deep in his eyes. 'Can I speak to you?' he asked suddenly. 'Alone?'

Amber nodded. 'Of course.' She followed him to the corridor outside.

'Miss Wint—Amber,' he shook his head emptily. 'Why… why are you doing this to me? You… you befriend me and now you're just… leaving me?'

Poor man. Christopher had been nothing but kind to her in the past few weeks, despite knowing nothing about her condition. Instead of replying, she pulled him into a tight hug. She wished she could say something comforting, but her throat felt full. 'I'm sorry,' she whispered. His arms tightened around her body, and she said it again. 'I'm so, so sorry, Christopher. If I knew…' she shook her head. 'I'm sorry.'

'You mean so much to me,' Christopher said, pulling away, his voice was thick. 'My father is arriving in Port Phillip Bay in two weeks. Will you stay, at least long enough to meet him?'

She nodded, brushing away a tear that fell from his eye. 'You're not making this easy,' she smiled.

'Good.' He bit his lip. 'I… Miss Rachel, I thought… maybe I meant something to you.'

'You do,' she said.

Christopher dropped his gaze again, then pulled her closer to him. With one hand on her waist and the other behind her neck, he leaned down and gently kissed her.

For a moment, Amber didn't know how to respond. She'd entertained a light crush on him, but hadn't thought he'd felt the same way. And now that the opportunity was in front of her, she realised, *I don't love him. Not like this.*

And yet, the kiss felt nice, for a moment, and she let herself relax. She couldn't have moved even if she'd tried to, so she decided to let him use the gesture to say his goodbye. Somehow the hidden message made it slightly sweeter.

Finally, he pulled away, with a soft sigh. 'Stay,' he whispered. 'For me.'

'I'm sorry, Christopher,' she whispered.

'I don't trust him.'

She stepped away from him with a small shake of her head. 'Let's get Lucky better first, anyway,' she said, her voice louder than before, as though it might erase the strange taste of the awkward kiss. 'I can't Travel without him. *If* I decide to go with him,' she added quickly. 'I'm going to bandage him up for now, then we won't talk anymore about this until tomorrow morning,' she promised. 'Please be nice to him.'

He scowled. 'I don't trust him,' he said again.

Amber sighed. 'Well, let's get to know him first.' She started back to his room, but Christopher caught her hand.

'Look, this sounds odd, I know,' he said. 'But no matter what he says, I'll remember you as Miss Winters. You mean a lot to me, Miss Winters.'

Amber wasn't sure exactly what he meant by that, but she decided to smile and take it as a compliment. 'And you to me, Doctor Alpine.'

8:58AM 11 MARCH 2019, LONDON

You cannot change history. History has a way of righting itself, and we are not powerful enough to change it, whatever we do.

D oubts had been filtering through Laura's mind all morning. *What am I doing? I've known Haste for so long, and he's never given me any reason to think he was hiding something. How did I get here anyway? This was supposed to be about Amber, not Haste!*

She tried to smother her doubts in indignation. *How dare the Commander try to cover up mistakes? I thought one of our "core values" was Integrity. He's betrayed us, the organisation, and everything we stand for by trying to deceive Lucky, Shinichi and I, and deliberately harming Amber.*

But, as she drove to work that morning, she didn't feel angry at her Commander, or indignant at his deceit.

She felt guilty. She felt like she was snooping around his past, like those annoying tabloid journalists looking for dirt on celebrities.

And she hoped that they were wrong.

As if to make her job harder for her, on the way into ARCHIVE, she met Haste in the elevator. He kept the door open for her so that she could duck in with him, steadying the coffee she'd bought on the way. *So my acting part begins now,* she thought, flashing a smile at her Commander.

'Ms Hamilton, how are you?' he asked.

Laura summoned the brightest smile she could. 'Fine, Commander. How are you?'

He nodded. 'I'm well. Looking forward to a busy day.'

You have no idea.

The elevator dinged and the doors opened to the offices of ARCHIVE. 'Commander,' Laura managed to choke as she stepped out. She wasn't sure how she was going to continue.

'Yes, Ms Hamilton?'

Laura bit her lip. *We know you lied to us and forced Amber into the past to cover up something,* she wanted to say. *Please just tell me this is all a big misunderstanding.*

But she couldn't say it. Not when she and Shinichi were so close. She couldn't let him down and make their job harder. Haste would certainly try to stop them if he knew what they were doing.

'Oh, just…' she forced another smile. 'I hope you get through everything you need to.'

'Thanks. You too,' Haste replied, as he left.

Laura was left by the elevator, coffee in hand, feeling like she'd dropped off a cliff. *How did I get here?* she wondered again, shaking her head.

She went to her workroom, half-handedly switching the sign on the door to 'Do Not Disturb on Penalty of Death' as she went past. The ARCHIVE sewing room was too small and too understaffed for everything it required of her. In one corner was a large desk where she set down her computer and coffee cup, then went to gather some supplies.

Gian had wanted embroidery on his 18th Century coat, and she could work on that at the same time as the mission.

She picked up the jacket, needle and a box of threads, then wound her way through the maze of racks, full of colourful clothes and bolts of wool, sitting at the desk in front of the computer. As if on cue, her phone pinged, and she set it next to her elbow, the text from Shinichi open.

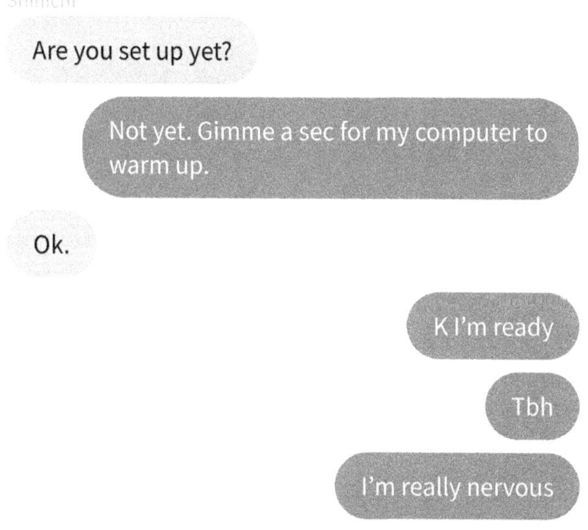

She stared at her typed response, hesitant to press *send*. She wondered how Shinichi felt – was he also nervous?

Did Shinichi have feelings?

She sent the message, waiting sheepishly for his response. *He's an ARC-researcher,* she told herself sharply. *He's used to agents telling him they're nervous.*

> It's a big mission. it's fine to be nervous.

> But I have a coffee so we're going to be fine
> ☒~(^w^)=b

Laura smiled, genuinely this time. *I'm so glad he's not really on a coffee detox,* she thought suddenly as she hearted the message.

A link popped up in a text from Shinichi, along with the message,

> Don't open that yet.

She sent a thumbs-up, and sat back in her chair, sipping the coffee to steady her nerves while she waited for Shinichi to get ready. *This will be fine,* she told herself.

She'd been practicing her Amber-accent all night, much to her husband's amusement. Shinichi hadn't known what Amber's voice had really sounded, but he would have become suspicious if she started speaking with an Australian accent, and he would recognise Laura's voice if she didn't disguise it. However, Shinichi's first time talking to Amber confirmed what she'd discovered during her rehearsals.

Her imitation of Amber sounded nothing like the real thing. She put the headset on, fitting it around her ears.

> Ready?

> Ready as I'll ever be I guess

> Good. Get your folder ready now so you
> don't have to turn pages. Be wary of other

> people talking to you in the office. Do you know how to turn off the headset?

> Um

> I don't know how to turn it on

> HAHA o_o

Two minutes later, after a lot of back and forth, Laura was set up, ready to go. Her leg bounced with jitters, and she silently practiced her Amber accent, cringing inwardly at how cheesy it sounded.

> I'm connecting you now. Good luck

> Hahaha yeh you too ⊠

There was a small beep. Laura's transcript was spread out over the desk so that she could read through it as quietly as possible. She focused on the first line, stabbing the needle into the fabric as she focused on taking deep breaths.

There was a beep that made her jump. She yelped as the needle went into her finger, her eyes widening. *That's an odd noise for an agent to make on landing,* she thought, wondering what Shinichi would say.

'Hi Amber, I'm Shinichi, your ARC-researcher for this mission. Were you hurt on landing?'

He sounded as calm as ever. Monotone, even. *Maybe he didn't hear,* she thought.

Laura swallowed and tried to reconnect to her year-8-drama-loving-self. 'Hi Shinichi,' she said. It almost sounded natural. *Oh heck, a longer sentence.* 'Yes, I've landed fine, just a bit queasy. Are we all ready to go?' *Man, I sounded like a Kiwi! English accent, girl. You're surrounded by the English! How hard can this be?*

There was a clicking as Shinichi typed. 'Yes, all good now. I thought I heard you yell when you landed.'

Laura licked her lips. 'Um… no…'

'It wasn't a local, was it? Were you seen landing?'

'No! It was…' *Oh wait, I don't have to make this up,* she realised, finding her place in the script. 'Me,' she read. 'It was me. I landed with a rock digging into my back.' She laughed an awkward laugh, then waited for Shinichi to stop thinking and get on with the next line.

Even the clicking had stopped. 'Fair enough,' he said finally. 'Where are you?'

You are Amber. Amber Elkhoury. Laura tossed her head theatrically, but it didn't help her confidence. 'Just outside the airport.' *Better.* 'I'll go in now.'

'Good. It's the 13th February, 1998, London City Airport. It's currently 26°C, with light drizzle later in the afternoon.' Laura stifled a laugh. He sounded like the pilot just after landing.

'Make your way to the boarding room and wait there,' Shinichi went on. 'You have no weapons for this mission, so boarding should be easy.'

'Where are you going?' Laura jumped as she realised what she'd done. *Stick to the script,* she thought furiously. *You can't afford to go off…* she glanced down and saw the next line on the transcript.

> AE: Where are you going?
>
> SG: I have to do something for the Commander. I'll be back in a couple of minutes.

In her panic, she'd missed hearing Shinichi's line. There was a short, awkward pause as she caught her breath and continued. Laura's heart was still pounding as she read out her next line. 'Okay. I'll let you know when I get to the boarding room.'

'Good.'

There was a beep as Shinichi disconnected the line. Laura sat, dazed, in her seat, already feeling tired. She risked a triumphant sip of coffee, then texted Shinichi.

> Everything seems to be going to plan. You don't suspect a thing.

She wondered how he was doing. Was he already connected? He had to copy the transcript for as long as possible to avoid raising Amber's suspicions.

Laura glanced through the coming pages of the transcript, her adrenaline starting to abate, leaving her tired, hungry and bored. She sipped the coffee. Suddenly there was a beep as Shinichi reconnected.

'I'm back. Any developments?'

Laura still had a mouthful of coffee that she was trying desperately not to choke on. She tried to swallow it as quietly as possible. 'I'm still in the entrance,' she said quietly. She felt very clever; apparently agents always spoke quietly when in crowded areas, if at all.

'Okay,' Shinichi said. 'I'll leave you be.'

Laura immediately saw a problem with their seemingly-ingenious plan. Silently, she glanced at her phone. No new messages.

She reread the next line on her transcript, dread filling her. As quietly as possible, she moved the microphone away from her mouth, then deepened her voice and put on a slightly posher accent.

'Can I see your boarding pass, ma'am?'

As quickly and quietly as she could, she moved the microphone back to her mouth. 'Ah, yes, here it is,' she said in her "Amber" voice.

Microphone away again. 'Excellent. Everything's in order. Please follow the arrows on the ground.'

Microphone went back to her mouth. 'Thank you very much,' she said. She heard typing through Shinichi's headset, and wondered what he was typing. *Maybe he's having a secret conversation with someone like he does with me.*

She had to repeat the roleplaying as Amber put her luggage on board and passed through security. Finally, she was in the boarding room, waiting for the announcement to board.

***

Shinichi checked his phone and noted the time.

No new messages from Laura, either.

About half an hour passed as Amber waited patiently for her plane to be called for boarding. She'd said she would read to pass the time. Shinichi hadn't been needed until Mendoza got there, anyway.

He got up to stretch his legs, wandering around his living room aimlessly. Laura texted to let him know all was well, and he quickly sent back a reminder to put her phone on silent.

His eyes widened. *No, no, no—!*

He stifled a chuckle. Her face when she thought he'd given up coffee… it almost made him miss working at ARCHIVE.

Almost.

He went to the bathroom while he had the chance, muting his microphone as he did so. Just as he got back to the couch, someone started to speak to Amber.

'Agent Elkhoury?' a man said, a thick Spanish accent colouring his speech. *Carl Mendoza,* Shinichi thought with a smile. Things were starting to get interesting.

'Just Amber is fine,' Amber said, her voice low. 'What's going on, Carl? What are you doing here?'

'I'm taking over this mission from you. According to ARCHIVE files, you never board the plane, and I take over this part of the mission.'

There was only stunned silence from Amber's end.

'Okay?' Carl prompted.

'Uhh…'

Shinichi took a deep breath. 'Just say okay, Amber. I'll explain soon.'

'But—'

'It's for the best,' he said gently. 'I promise.'

He heard Amber choke an 'Okay, Carl', and released the breath he'd been holding.

Carl didn't reply verbally, and from the sound of the ambience, Amber soon left the boarding room. 'Did I do something wrong?' she asked, the worry clear in her tone. 'What… what happened?'

Shinichi tried to calm himself. The thought of finding answers was exciting, but he needed to be patient or he'd make Amber more nervous than she already was. He shook his head, sipping a coffee. 'No, you didn't do anything wrong. In fact, I should congratulate you. Congratulations.'

'*Congratulations?* For what?' her voice was getting higher with panic.

'You have a paradox in your first mission.'

There was silence on the other end. Shinichi sensed that Amber wasn't feeling very excited about this achievement, even though most agents went their whole careers without ever encountering paradoxes. In a few years, it would make a great story to tell new agents. They'd be in awe of her immediately.

'What do I do?' she asked, bringing Shinichi back to the moment. 'Should I try to force my way onto the plane? Lucky's going to be so confused if I'm not—'

'Well, he told you that you never got on the plane, so what's the point of trying?' Perhaps he'd said that a bit too quickly, but Shinichi had lost his place in the script. He forced himself to calm down, find his place, and speak slowly. 'I would suggest that you stay here and find out what might be keeping you on the ground.'

He remembered saying those words last month. His heart beat a bit faster. *I'm going to leave the script soon.*

'You think there's something keeping me here?' she seemed surprised.

'Of course. Why not? Unless you think it's because you just decided to give up and go home.'

There was another short silence. A month ago, Shinichi had hoped that this was due to her contemplating what he'd said, and not because she was trying not to yell at him for his cheek. 'Okay,' she said finally. A boarding call for her plane sounded, echoing through the headset. He heard Amber take a deep breath. 'Let's see what's going on.'

Shinichi smiled. 'Good. Where would you like to start?'

He glanced at the next line on the transcript.

AE: It might be a threat here in the airport. I'll go talk to the security here.

'Well… I have no idea, to be honest,' Amber said in his ear.

That was the cue. Shinichi pushed aside his script and opened a notebook. He found a pen in a cup on the coffee table and clicked it open to start taking notes.

'I assume it would be something to do with whoever hijacked the plane in the first place,' he said slowly, wishing he could say everything he knew so far. 'At least we can start investigating that, and we'll see if you find something else.'

'Okay, that sounds good,' Amber replied, sounding a little bit calmer. 'So should I talk to security?'

That had been Laura's decoy, so Shinichi wasn't sure it would be helpful. He frowned, putting himself in the shoes of a person who had just successfully hijacked a plane.

'I'm about to miss the plane,' Amber said quietly. 'Are you sure this is okay?'

Shinichi smiled as an idea came to him. 'Go into the boarding room and wait there. But don't try to board the plane. Wait somewhere fairly hidden.'

He heard her footsteps on the linoleum, then a door opening. The ambience around her changed to the quiet of a boarding room where an announcement was being called over the speakers. 'Okay, I'm in,' she mumbled.

'Great. Now watch the doors everyone's going in to board the plane,' Shinichi went on.

There was silence and Shinichi hoped that she was following his instructions intently.

'A man just came in from there,' she mumbled excitedly. 'Is he our guy?'

Shinichi smiled. 'I can't say for sure, but all the same don't let him out of your sight. What's he wearing?'

'A grey suit and red tie. He looks about… thirty-ish?' She gave a small chuckle. 'I tell you what, he *looks* like he just did something sus.'

Shinichi sipped his coffee. 'They always do. It's impossible to completely hide it when you know you've just done something wrong. But he's not wearing a… uniform of some sort?'

'No, just a… just a suit. Like he's attending a conference of some sort.'

The swirling voices that were coming through her earpiece were fading now, and Shinichi could hear only a few excited far-away murmurs now. A final boarding call sounded over the loud-speaker, the amplified noise blurred and barely distinct through the earpiece.

'It's—Oh.'

Shinichi put his coffee down. 'What? What happened?'

There was a short pause, then she hissed, 'He's still here.'

The man in the grey suit. If it was anyone else, she wouldn't have been lowering her voice and keeping her answers to a minimum.

'Okay,' Shinichi tried to calm his voice, to sound as though he knew what he was doing. 'Do you have a… tiny camera?' Shinichi couldn't remember what they were called. Those tiny cameras were notoriously annoying and didn't work over a long range, and at some point Lucky had started calling them Pop-eyes, and the name had stuck, but he wasn't sure whether Lucky had coined the term by their first mission or after it.

'The ARCeye camera?'

Ah, that's the name. 'Yes, that one. Are you near a wall?'

'Yes.'

'Good. Stick it to the wall, somewhere where you can see a lot of the room, then find a hiding spot and wait.'

'But I can't see what it's transmitting,' Amber whispered.

Shinichi opened an app on his computer and entered the mission's code. 'Don't worry about that,' he replied quickly while the app loaded. 'Go and hide, quickly!'

'But my bag—'

'Leave it! Go!'

Amber was silent. Shinichi hoped that she'd found somewhere to hide. He didn't know who was coming through the door, but he didn't want to risk it. It was likely that that person was the one who was keeping Amber from boarding her plane.

The image loaded. The stupid Pop-eye transmitted a blurred, out of focus image through which he could see blobby chairs and vague whiteness that he assumed were walls. Shinichi had heard once that they had been tested transmitting only through space, and showed high-quality footage. It was only when transmitting through time that they became next to useless.

Nevertheless, Shinichi could see a tall man walk into the room. He didn't seem suspicious, judging by his appearance. He wore a grey suit and Shinichi thought he could see a red tie. The picture was too blurry to see his face.

He didn't walk around the room, but headed straight for Amber's bag.

Shinichi didn't want to ask Amber if she could tell who it was in case the man heard her reply. He would have to ask her later, after he left.

The man reached Amber's bag, but didn't touch it. Instead, he picked up a small red book, the book that Amber had been reading while waiting for her flight.

Shinichi started to write notes on his notebook, questions he needed to ask Amber.

His two questions were:

1) Who is he?

2) What were you reading?

The man flicked through the book. It looked like he was turning to the front page, reading the first chapter. Then, suddenly, he dropped it.

For a moment, Shinichi thought that he'd noticed Amber, but she hadn't made a sound, and instead of facing someone, the man had put the book on the chair and opened the bag. He rummaged through it, pulling out books, toiletries, clothes, and finally… something.

Stupid Popeye! Shinichi couldn't see what it was he was holding. It was small and blue. *A notebook?* Shinichi's heart seemed to stop. *A smartphone? What colour is Amber's phone case?*

Amber breathed in sharply. 'Should I confront him?' she whispered.

'No, stay where you are,' Shinichi replied, wishing he could see clearly what was going on.

3) What did he pull out of your bag???

'I thought so,' came the man's voice through the earpiece.

Shinichi racked his brain, trying to find out if the voice was familiar to him. The man sounded English, but aside from that, it was impossible to determine more.

Shinichi didn't know how old Goldwyn was, and had never heard him speak clearly. He'd heard a little bit when Lucky had been unconscious, but he hadn't paid much attention to it; he'd been thinking too much about his findings about Haste.

He knuckled his forehead, grunting in frustration. *I wish I'd known then that it would have become important,* he thought, frantically trying to remember. He took a deep breath. 'Do you… recogn—'

'Please not now,' Amber breathed, barely audibly.

Shinichi bit his tongue. His fingers tightened on his pen as he turned back to his notes.

Even if it *was* Harry Goldwyn, she wouldn't recognise him yet. After all, she'd first met him on her second mission. But… it would be too convenient for that man to be Goldwyn. Surely, too much of a coincidence.

The man flipped whatever it was closed and put it in his breast pocket, and Shinichi's heart seemed to stop. He felt the blood drain from his face as he realised what he'd taken from Amber's bag.

It's her ARCHIVE badge, he thought. *If my theory is correct, he would know what that is. That means he knows now that there's another ARCHIVE agent here.*

4) We need to confirm that he really is Goldwyn.

Though he didn't know whether he hoped it was or not.

'Shinichi,' Amber whispered frantically, and Shinichi's focus was pulled back to the screen. Goldwyn had left the bag on the seat and was now slowly strolling around the boarding room, opening side-rooms as though looking for something.

Shinichi's heart thudded in his chest. *Not something,* he thought. *Someone.*

Amber.

11:45PM 25 November 1868, Walhalla, Australia

The present will pull at you emotionally. This is not just a wish for modern convenience, but a deeper homesickness. It is normal for agents to feel this way while travelling in the past for long periods of time, and it is good to feel this way occasionally. Agents who do not feel homesick are often tempted to not come home.

Despite her bone-weariness, Amber couldn't sleep. She blamed the mattress – more of a pallet really, since Lucky had taken Christopher's only spare bed. Shinichi had told her to monitor him, and she wanted to make sure that if his condition did deteriorate, he would be whisked back to the future.

She hoped he wouldn't, not just because a concussion could easily and swiftly kill him.

But if she had to contact Shinichi to send him back, they'd expect her to go with him. And she still hadn't decided that was what she wanted to do.

Christopher would tell me that if I'm not convinced, I shouldn't risk it, she thought, turning over to look at Luc.

He was still asleep. He hadn't stirred since the early evening, but she could hear his breathing, so she was satisfied.

She'd promised to tell the Johanssons when she remembered something. But when she'd gone over to tell them where she was, she hadn't told them that this Mr Holmes knew her. It wasn't a lie; she hadn't remembered anything.

I'm from the future, she thought. It was so strange, but she believed it somehow. *How can I not? Lucky has so much technology; it makes sense. And Laura and Shinichi, too.*

And Harry.

So there are bad people in the future too, she thought. It hurt her that he got to go home while Lucky was now suffering and stuck in the past as he recovered.

And Christopher. What am I going to do about him?

She felt bad leaving him when he seemed to have fallen in love with her. She still couldn't get her mind around that – he'd always seemed to hold her at arm's length, even when he'd shown kindness to her.

Perhaps the urgency of her leaving had convinced him to take the chance.

Lucky had seemed horrified that she'd told him about ARCHIVE. She supposed that was probably a foolish thing to do. After all, who would invent time travel if people kept coming from the future? Everyone would just assume that someone else would do it, and that would create a paradox.

It's the middle of the night, Amber thought, closing her eyes against the darkness. *Too late to be thinking about paradoxes.*

There was something else bothering her about her day. It kept her awake, though she didn't know why.

Christopher's kiss.

It wasn't just that she'd never known about his feelings for her. it was more than that. She just couldn't put her finger on it.

Her eyes half-closed, she thought about their times together. When they'd first met, and he'd pulled her off the road so she wouldn't be run over by a horse. When he'd gone with her to Harry's house. When she'd given him the nectarines, and he'd given her a flower and said she was beautiful.

She sat up, suddenly realising what had been niggling her.

This is 1868.

And he kissed me.

Victorian men were very careful about maintaining their own and a woman's honour. Even before this, Christopher had let her into his house, alone with him. Johansson refused to be in a room with her without Mollie or Arthur present.

It was odd, but now that she'd identified what had been itching her, she didn't feel quite so bothered by it.

But that reminded her of something else she'd thought before: Christopher was quite middle-class, yet he introduced himself with his first name. He even allowed her to call him Christopher, not Mr Alpine, or Doctor Alpine.

And he hadn't seemed surprised when she'd told him about time travel, either. *'Miss Winters, I must be frank. Either you're lying to me, or you're gullible enough to believe the lies that that man has been feeding you.'*

He hadn't suggested that she was mad.

Amber shook her head, shocked at herself. *What am I thinking?* she asked herself. *Where am I going with this train of thought anyway? Christopher kissed me because he wanted to convince me to stay. It was his last-ditch effort. And he lets me call him Christopher because we're good friends. And he...* she stumbled with her last argument. He knew she couldn't remember her own identity; why hadn't it occurred to him that she could have started hearing voices along with it?

Because he's seen me and knows that I'm otherwise sane, she thought firmly. *There's nothing wrong with Christopher.*

She closed her eyes, hoping sleep would come.

And it did, restless as it was. She was still half-conscious when a creaking floorboard woke her completely. She rubbed her eyes and sat up.

Footsteps. Coming toward their room.

She frowned, glancing at Lucky. He hadn't moved. *It must be Christopher,* she thought.

And sure enough, the door opened with a light creak, and Christopher's shadowy head poked through. He glanced at Lucky, then at her, and he jumped.

'Miss Winters,' he whispered breathlessly. 'You look like a ghost sitting there in the shadows.'

'What are you doing?' she hissed.

He pulled his hand back from the door. 'I was just checking on Mr Holmes,' he whispered. 'You seemed so tired earlier, I didn't expect you would still be awake. And he could take a turn for the worse during the night.'

She didn't believe him, though she wasn't sure why. His words seemed a little too rushed, or too uncertain. 'He'll be fine by morning,' she whispered eventually. 'If he was going to die, he would have done so by now.'

Christopher didn't say anything for a moment. 'Well, that's good to know,' he replied, pulling his head back and closing the door. 'Good night, Miss Winters.'

'Goodnight, Mr Alpine.'

She felt rather than saw the look he gave her, felt it in the pause as he closed the door, and in his silence. The door clicked shut, and she released her breath.

Glancing at Lucky once more, she lay down.

Once more, Christopher had given her something to puzzle over until dawn.

11:19AM 11 March 2019, London

Integrity: All ARCHIVE agents must be above reproach, both in the present and in the past. ARCHIVE agents are of the highest calibre, and must always present this way.

'I have an idea,' Amber whispered.

'I—okay…' Shinichi had been about to lay down his own plan, but since she hadn't elaborated, he had to trust her. He leaned back into his small couch, annoyed as he had once always been at his own ineffectualness as an ARC-researcher with no visual information. Amber had gone full stealth, resulting in no sound going through his earpiece, and he couldn't see where she was from where the Popeye was. So he waited for the grand reveal of her plan.

Suddenly the sound of an automatic hand dryer buzzed through Amber's earpiece, loudly contrasting with the previous silence. A door opened loudly.

'What? Where is everyone?' Amber said loudly. Then, quieter, 'Oh no. Don't tell me…'

'Can I help you, miss?' said the man from the door. He sounded friendly enough, as though he hadn't just been through her bag.

'Did I miss my flight?' she asked quickly, her voice high with panic.

She walked forward a few steps until Shinichi could see her in the screen. The man hadn't left his position by the door.

'The boarding call was a few minutes ago,' he said. 'You've been in the bathrooms for a while,' he added pointedly.

Amber caught his tone and folded her arms. 'I couldn't help it! I had to clean up a bit after a…' she stopped suddenly. 'A minor crisis.'

Shinichi smiled. 'Nice one,' he said.

'Is that your bag?' the man asked casually.

Amber glanced at the bag in question, then nodded. 'Whose else could it be?' she asked. 'Anyway, what are you doing here? Did you miss the flight too?'

The man didn't miss a beat. 'I work here, at the airport. I'm meant to make sure no one's left behind, and I must apologise that there were no ladies here to check the female toilets. There's been issues with the loudspeakers in there, anyway. My sincerest apologies.'

'Ask his name,' Shinichi said quickly as the man rambled. *It can't be Goldwyn. That's too convenient.*

'Oh,' Amber said uncertainly. 'That's okay… uh… Mr…?'

The man stepped forward to Amber, holding out his hand. 'Alpine. Christopher Alpine.'

Shinichi rubbed his forehead tiredly, crossing out his first and fourth questions. *It's not Harry Goldwyn. Is that a good thing or a bad thing?*

But then, who's Christopher Alpine? The name sounded slightly familiar, but Shinichi couldn't think where it was from.

Curious, he sent a text to Laura to ask her to search his name in the ARChronicles while Amber told him a fake name.

Could it be Goldwyn giving a fake name? he wondered, switching off his phone. There was no way to know now.

Amber had picked up her books, stuffing them in the bag. She pretended to notice something, then searched through her bag and the surrounding seats.

'Lost something?' Alpine asked.

Amber grunted. 'Just a little badge thing,' she said. 'It looks a bit like a police badge. It's quite important to me, and I'd hate to lose it.'

She knelt and pushed a hand under the seat, feeling around the floor. Shinichi watched him carefully through the Popeye, waiting for him to reach into his pocket and hand it back to her. *If he's just a local, why would he keep the badge?* he wondered. It had no commercial value. Alpine watched Amber search for a moment, then stretched to check the row of seats directly behind it. 'What colour is it?' he asked.

Shinichi felt his dislike of the man grow with his every move. Amber straightened, watching him as he helped in her search, silently judging him. 'Royal blue,' she said stiffly.

'Hmm… well I can't see it here, but we can check lost property,' the man said.

It occurred to Shinichi suddenly that this Alpine must sincerely believe Amber's story that she had been in the bathroom the whole time, if he thought that he could steal the badge without her knowing.

Having realised this, however, Shinichi had no idea what to do with that information.

'Try confronting him directly,' he suggested.

Amber took his advice, planting her feet resolutely and folding her arms. 'What do you know about ARCHIVE?' she asked suddenly.

Shinichi's eyes widened. 'I didn't mean *that* directly.'

Alpine shook his head. 'ARCHIVE? What's that?' he asked.

Shinichi smiled, his eyes narrowing like an eagle that had found a cornered mouse. 'Go get him, Amber,' he said. 'People who know what ARCHIVE hear it correctly, and ask "What's ARCHIVE?". People who don't will assume they misheard, or you meant to use the plural: "archives". This man knows more than he's trying to let on.'

Amber shook her head, reaching forward as though to pull out the badge from his pocket directly, but Alpine was faster. His hand whipped up, caught her wrist and whirled it around until it was twisted around her back painfully. Amber grunted, and Shinichi could hear her breath straining as her ribcage was uncomfortably forced open by the manoeuvre.

'What do you know of ARCHIVE?' she asked again.

'I'll tell you what I know of ARCHIVE,' he whispered in her ear hoarsely. 'It's an organisation full of people who think they're going to save the world, saving it when it's already been saved and breaking it when it's already been broken.'

Shinichi's breath caught. *Breaking it…? What does* that *mean?*

Shinichi leaned forward. 'What on earth is he talking about?' he asked. His question was echoed by Amber.

The strange man laughed. 'ARCHIVE really is the perfect example of government bureaucracy. Let's bring together the best of the best of the world, and they'll be so busy orchestrating dead people's fate that they won't recognise coincidence. Those who pull the strings are often pulling more than we'd like, right?'

'Who?' Amber asked, but Shinichi already knew.

'Haste,' he murmured. He felt strangely numb. 'Amber, you need to find out everything he knows.'

'What are you—' she groaned in pain. 'Who are you talking about?'

'Fate and coincidence,' the man laughed. 'It always amuses me how much control he has. Like here, sending someone to bring a plane down, and someone else to keep it in the air.'

Shinichi couldn't imagine how confused Amber must have been feeling, hearing that. *This is why Haste sent her to 1868,* he realised suddenly. *We're close. He was so scared that she knew that he had to get rid of her.*

A small flame of fury started burning in Shinichi's stomach, close to a very fresh scar.

'But either way, it doesn't matter now,' Alpine went on. 'Unless you want to try going back thirty minutes to stop me bringing down that plane.'

'He hired you?' Amber grunted. Shinichi didn't know why everyone said she couldn't cope under pressure; she was doing wonderfully.

Unlike himself. He stood up and started pacing around his living room, his fingers fidgeting with his jumper and his legs refusing to be still. Laura still hadn't gotten back to him about who this man was, yet. Why did the name sound familiar?

'You are Fate,' Alpine said, and the sound hissed in Shinichi's ear. *His mouth must be very close to Amber's ear,* Shinichi thought, disgusted. 'Hired by Haste. And he hired me: Coincidence. Nothing wrong with that. Give the world fifteen hours,' there was a pause, and Shinichi imagined him checking his watch, 'and all will be righted.'

Shinichi glanced at the time his computer showed, the local time for Amber and Alpine in 1998, then quickly calculated fifteen hours ahead.

He frowned, shaking his head. It would be an hour and a half after the plane landed in New York. He checked his calculations again, but he was sure about it.

He picked up his pen and wrote the time and date down.

New York City, 1:00pm 14 February 1998.

8:45AM 26 November 1868, Walhalla, Australia

Try to be in contact with your ARC-researcher as much as possible. Remember that any ARCHIVE agent who is out of contact for four days will be presumed dead.

Just as Amber had predicted, Lucky looked much better when Amber woke up the next morning.

Medically, he looked better. His skin had some colour back in it, and he could stand on his own, even though he apparently hadn't eaten anything but an apple since he'd arrived. Everything else about him looked worse. He was dirty, he had grass and mud on his clothes and in his hair, and his jacket and pants were wrinkled and crumpled from sleeping in them. Amber almost asked Christopher to lend him some new clothes, but she knew what he would say.

Besides, something about last night gave her a feeling that Lucky be more comfortable somewhere else. And now that he could walk without support, she almost suggested he should get out of Christopher's way and stay at the hotel.

They'd have a spare room now that Harry's gone, whispered a voice in her mind, and that stopped her even while her mouth was open.

She hadn't wanted to stay after making sure Lucky was better. It was awkward being alone with Christopher now, after the evening before. He always looked at her expectantly, like he wanted her to say something important. Despite her tossing, she still hadn't made a decision. So as soon as Lucky went back to bed, she left the house and went home.

Johansson was unimpressed with her. She hadn't explained what had happened, and Johansson, holed up in his sewing room all day, hadn't heard the rumours of her visit to Christopher's house with an almost-delirious man she'd found in a cemetery. Nevertheless, he didn't scold her for her neglect of her duties. That was clearly Mollie's area of expertise, and he was content to leave it to her.

Arthur had politely thanked her for the peaches. Christopher had given her basket back to her after he'd taken the nectarines, and she'd given one to the child for his breakfast. But even the young boy knew that she'd done something wrong, and hadn't been *too* happy, in case that earned a black look from his father. He'd taken one from the basket and gone to enjoy it outside.

Mollie was the only one who dealt with her directly, spending the whole day ranting about trust and responsibility. Amber folded the clean clothes with her, nodding and shaking her head at appropriate intervals, trying to look like she really was listening and would repent of her faults soon.

It was enough to convince her that maybe life in the future would be better after all.

As Mollie talked, Amber considered her options. She could stay in 1868, in the middle of nowhere, with the flies and the dust and the lack of fresh water and where she didn't know herself, or she could move back to the future, where she wasn't sure she'd know how to live and where she wouldn't recognise people who knew her.

She sighed. The only thing that had been keeping her here was Christopher, really. Sure, she might miss Arthur, and some of the women in the town, and she was indebted to Johansson for his kindness, but her curiosity about the future was fast out-weighing her connections to the present.

And as for Johansson, she thought with a rueful smile, *I have the feeling that he would feel that I've repaid my debt to him just by disappearing.*

The only person keeping her in Walhalla was Christopher, and now even *that* relationship had gone sour. She liked him as a good friend, but now, he seemed to want her as his bride, which was… awkward. She would have thought he would have liked a nice, pious Christian girl instead of… well, instead of her.

She wondered how she would feel if Lucky left without her. If she would never see him again.

She didn't know him well enough to miss him. It would be like finding out that a person you'd walked past on the street had moved to the other side of the world. Interesting, but not earth-shattering.

Nevertheless, the thought of him leaving her behind left a small feeling of disappointment in her. She tried to investigate that feeling, see where it rooted from. Would she miss Lucky? She'd decided, no. Shinichi and Laura? She might feel sad that they were out of reach, but she'd get over it quickly. It wasn't a person she'd miss, she realised.

It was the opportunity. *This might be my only chance to see where I belong*, she thought. *And once Lucky leaves, if I don't go with him, I've missed the chance.*

And with that realisation came the decision to go with him.

After all, what have I got to lose? If I decide I don't like the future, I can always ask Lucky to take me back.

'Miss Rachel? Are you even listening to me?'

Amber's attention snapped back to what Mollie was saying. 'I'm sorry,' she sighed. 'My mind wandered. What were you saying?'

Mollie's eyes narrowed, and she glared at Amber suspiciously. 'What's been going on with you?' she snapped suddenly. 'You were out all yesterday, and you haven't told us where on earth you went. And – you may not know this – but this town's *teeming* with rumours about you and a suspicious man.' She folded her arms. 'In fact, your whole story's a bit suspicious, if you ask me.'

Amber held up her hands, palms forward, trying to pacify the maid. She looked up into Mollie's eyes, and her heart fell. In those eyes, she saw pain, betrayal, and anger. She hadn't realised that Mollie had cared enough about her to be hurt by her.

'I'm sorry,' she said quietly, though she needn't have bothered. Mollie went on over her.

'I sat by your *bedside*,' she went on. 'I nursed you back to health. I babysat you, teaching you how to do basic household chores. And this whole time I've felt there's something… something wrong with you.' Amber dropped her hands, turning back to pick up another item of clothing to fold it, trying to hide her own anger. *She's blaming me for things that I've been struggling with all this time. Of course there's something wrong with me! We've always known that!* 'It's not just that you inexplicably don't know who you are,' Mollie went on. 'It's that you say things and do things that are so strange! And now this? You won't tell us who he is or what you were doing with him!'

Hot anger flared up in Amber's chest but she didn't look up from the clothes pile. *I didn't explain,* she retorted silently, *because you won't stop to let me!*

She took a deep breath before she interrupted loudly. 'I don't know who he is for certain,' she said, harsher than she'd intended but milder than she felt. 'His name is… his name is Mr Holmes, and he was attacked, so I helped him.' She held her hands up in surrender. 'And I'm sorry that I'm so weird; honestly, I'm just as confused as you are. But don't worry, Mollie. After today, I'll be out of your hair and you'll never have to see me again.' Now she looked up, if only to make sure that her words had taken full effect.

Mollie looked stunned. She frowned, taking a small step back from Amber, confused. She opened her mouth to speak, but nothing seemed to come out.

Instead, a small voice behind them said, 'Are you leaving, Miss Rachel?'

Amber whirled around, finding Arthur standing in the doorway to the kitchen behind her. He too looked stricken. Tears formed in his large brown eyes, and his hands were clasped in front of his chest. His bottom lip quivered slightly as he raised his eyes up to meet hers. Her anger left her in a moment.

Putting down the apron she'd been folding, she went over to him and knelt to meet his level.

'Yes, Arthur,' she said gently. 'I'm leaving tomorrow morning, if all goes well.'

Arthur's face scrunched up into a frown. 'To go where?' he asked.

Tears came to Amber's own eyes, unbidden. She shook her head. *I can't tell you.* 'Back to England,' she said quietly, wishing her voice and resolve were as steady as they'd been a moment ago.

'Can I come too?'

She shook her head.

'Come now, Master Arthur,' came Mollie's stiff voice behind them. 'Stop that. Big boys don't cry.'

The effort the child made to stop his tears broke Amber's heart. She pulled him into a hug, rubbing his back as he sobbed into her shoulder, ignoring Mollie. 'But I don't want you to go,' he cried. 'I've already lost one mother. Do you have to go too?'

The meaning of Amber's assumed name fell around her shoulders like a heavy, wet towel. All those weeks ago, Arthur had been the one to choose it for her. *Rachel Winters. After his mother.*

Arthur had hoped that she would become his mother.

She wasn't sure if he'd expected her to replace her or to become her, but it didn't matter. Either way, it was a role she couldn't hope to fill.

'I'm sorry, Arthur,' she whispered. Maybe in the future, she could stop apologising for not being the person everyone wanted her to be. First Harry, wanting her to be his ticket home. Then Lucky, wanting her to be his long-lost friend. Christopher, wanting her to be his wife. Mollie, wanting her to be her assistant and confidante. And now Arthur, who wanted her to be his dead mother.

'Well, Miss Rachel,' said Mollie curtly. 'When were you planning to tell Mr Johansson about your departure?'

'Soon,' Amber said quietly, moving away from Arthur, who was attempting once more to dry his tears. 'I'll tell him when he comes in for lunch.'

★★★

Shinichi had been silent all day. *He did say that he and Laura would be busy until tomorrow.* Luc guessed that he would find out what they were busy with when he got back to 2019.

It better be important, he thought, annoyed.

He wasn't meant to have been in contact with Laura and Shinichi in the first place. But since worst had come to worst, he was hoping they'd be able to convince someone to bring them home, using the old ARCHIVE timeboxes. Surely Haste would allow it, if he promised to keep hunting down the timebox.

He sat on the front step of Christopher's tiny home, having nowhere else to go. He knew the family Amber was staying with, but couldn't see the point of imposing on them. *She'll be fine,* he told himself. Funnily enough, after all that had happened, he wasn't worried about her anymore, even though he had no guarantee of her safety. He'd spent weeks fearing she might be dead, then found her alive and healthy, even. Aside from some major brain damage. *Amnesia. I need to get her checked over by a proper doctor as soon as possible.*

It was frustrating. He had an urgent to-do list, and a lot to think about, but there was nothing he could do. With no timebox, and no official ARC-researcher, he was stranded.

The timebox.

As usual, the timebox was the start of Luc's list of problems, and only the start because it was what he supposed he, as an ARCHIVE agent, should be most concerned with. He wondered what Haste would say in light of these new developments.

Harry Goldwyn has taken the timebox back to 2019… at least, I think they're in 2019.

He supposed Haste would say he had failed his mission. Then he'd say something to do with *Si Periculum* and how he'd expected better.

Harry had the timebox. He'd started the hunt at the laboratory, tracked Amber back two centuries, and finally taken it home. To do what? Where would he go? Was that his plan, or was it a means to an end?

Luc shook his head tiredly. So many things to investigate, and he didn't even have a way home.

Three point plan.

Step one: Somehow get Amber back to the present and make sure she's okay.

Step two: Find out what Shinichi and Laura were working on and if it's important.

Step three: Hunt down Harry and get that silly timebox back to ARCHIVE.

11:45AM 11 March 2019, London

Not for the first time that mission, Shinichi wished that he had access to the ARChronicles. Google might have had the information he wanted, he supposed, but it was somehow too cluttered, and at the same time, not detailed enough.

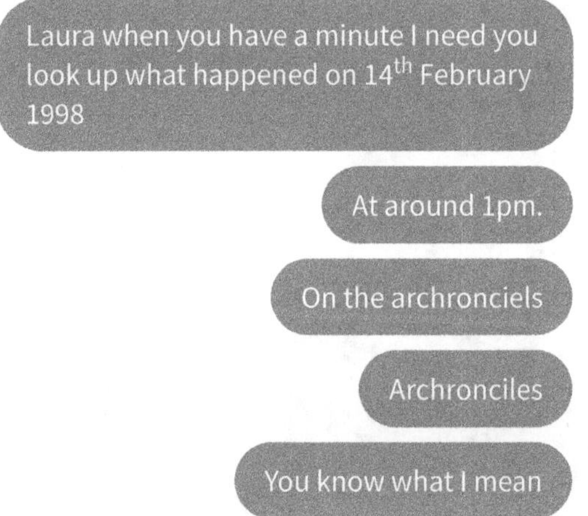

With a silent groan, he turned his attention back to Amber and Alpine. Alpine must know that Amber was in contact with ARCHIVE. He seemed to suspect he'd said too much, or that she didn't share his views on Fate and Coincidence.

'He's wasting your time,' Shinichi said quietly. 'You need to shake him off somehow and get back to ARCHIVE.'

He heard Amber sigh, and could almost hear the sarcastic question she didn't say: *Why didn't I think of that?*

There was a heavy *thwack,* and Alpine grunted. 'Trying to escape?' he asked.

'I have work to do,' Amber replied through gritted teeth. Another dull thump, and Alpine yelped. Shinichi hid a smile, wondering where she'd kicked.

'You little—' Alpine grunted, and Amber yelled in pain.

Her hair—? Shinichi wondered. He folded his arms, leaning back into his couch in frustration. ARC-researchers were so pathetically helpless in fights.

'Let go!' Amber screamed, and a loud thumping accompanied it as something brushed past the earpiece.

Yep, he's definitely got her by her hair, Shinichi decided, sipping his coffee. His experience as an ARC-researcher had come back to him like he'd never left, and he was surprised by how easily he remembered small details like how to tell what agents were doing based on how the sound of their movements was interacting with their earpieces. It wasn't a perfect system, but when there was a lot of fast-paced action, like when the agent was fighting, it was possible to at least have a guess at what was happening.

Shinichi's phone lit up, and he jumped, turning it on.

Laura

Sorry I was busy

His fingers tightened around the phone as she started typing again.

Can I get a coffee first? :/

No. this is more important

Brutal.

Come on, Laura, he thought. *Hurry up.*

Ok searching Christopher Alpine now

'Amber, I'm researching who this Alpine man is,' he said. 'Hold on.'

She grunted something intelligible, and he reflected briefly that perhaps his choice of words was unhelpful.

Anything yet???

Laura typed for a long time, during which Shinichi tried to calm himself. He picked up his pen and prepared himself to take notes of anything important.

This is going to be a long text, he thought, allowing his excitement to rise slightly.

A paragraph slid onto the screen, and Shinichi's eyes flicked through it.

Not really. There are a lot of Christopher Alpines in the world. Aaaand it doesn't look like any of them have done anything particularly interesting, especially around the 1990s-mark or earlier. But it also strikes me as a name someone would think up quickly?

I mean, it's probably not his real name; just one that he thought up on the spot.

He frowned, turning his phone off and putting it on the arm of his chair. The lack of information was discouraging, to say the least, but she did have a point about his name.

His phone vibrated again, and he glanced at the notification, then picked it up again.

Ooh

There's one Chris Alpine who's a bit sus

How?

Laura sent a few pictures of her computer screen, overlaid with the reflection of her holding her phone up to take the picture.

What do you think?

Shinichi wasn't entirely sure. He glanced at the blurry image of the boarding room on his computer screen, but the man – and Amber – were out of the frame. He had to compare the black-and-white CCTV frame Laura had sent him with his memory of the man.

He was fairly tall, with light hair and a sly physique.

The resemblance was unsettling.

He glanced at the timestamp from the ARChronicles and shivered despite himself.

4/03/2019, MOVARIAN LABORATORIES

The day of Amber and Lucky's mission, he thought. *He was there.*

And he had Amber's ARCHIVE badge.

'Amber,' he whispered. 'Amber, you need to get away from him.'

'I'm trying!' she screamed back, making him jump. Somehow in all his research he'd lost track of their fistfight.

But he didn't want to lose his train of thought. He'd felt like he was on the verge of a breakthrough.

Laura was typing; he hoped it was more on Alpine or her findings on Valentine's Day 1998, but from the sounds coming through Amber's earpiece, she'd finally been overpowered by Alpine, and was being pushed against a wall, hard. His teeth rattled with every thud, and as much as he told himself that he was close on Alpine, he couldn't quite pull his attention away.

'And before you get on your ARCHIVE moral high-horse,' Alpine said to her quietly. 'You ARCHIVE agents are just as much the puppets of fate as the rest of us.'

For a long time, there was only silence.

'Amber, is he gone?'

There was a small pause, then Amber replied, drowsily, 'Yeah, he's gone. Woohoo, I got away.'

He asked her some basic questions until he was satisfied that she wasn't concussed… *at least not as much as Lucky is,* he thought, rolling his eyes. Still, it provided him with a quick opportunity.

'Just wait there for a moment, okay? You can get up when you start feeling better.'

Amber groaned. 'Should I chase him?'

Shinichi shook his head. 'Just wait there. I'm finding a bit out about him.'

There was no reply from her end, but he imagined that she'd probably nodded. Okay. Back to Laura.

He opened his phone, quickly finding the message from Laura.

> Where are you looking at specifically on that date?

> New York, somewhere around the airport?

There was no response for a few minutes. Shinichi's fingers tapped his coffee cup nervously.

'Shinichi…'

He took a deep breath. Amber was sounding stronger, but he needed to stay calm so that she didn't pick up on his nervousness. 'Yes?'

'This is really random, but you're Japanese, right?'

Shinichi frowned. *Where did this come from?* 'Yes…?'

'Oh. That's what I thought. It's just… someone told me you weren't at the Christmas party last year. Because I'd thought everyone was there.'

He shook his head. 'I missed it. I was in the hospital. But I didn't mind missing it. I don't—'

Shinichi frowned, remembering that night. *The painkillers wearing off, leaving only agony. Too much pain to move. Too much pain to sleep. Unable to get the strength to call the nurse.*

That feeling, that he was on the edge of a breakthrough, returned, stronger this time. excitement rising in his chest, he reached into his breast pocket and pulled out a small notebook, flipping through the pages until he found the one he was looking for. Written on a blood-stained page, in his handwriting, were the words:

Christopher Alpine – 1868.

Nikola Lazarov, Italy 1900s

"Just saving lives"

NL: Haste's partner when he was a field agent. Died on mission in Castel Sain' Angelo Sul Nera, Italy, 27 July 1906.

-What does "four times" mean? ?

'I see,' he said quietly. 'That's how I know the name.'

He'd known this was connected since Lucky turned up at his door, asking for a favour. He'd known that coming back to ARCHIVE would only accelerate the inevitable. And he'd known, deep down, that no matter what he'd done instead, he would always find his way back here.

Cold dread settled over his heart, and suddenly, as though a switch had been turned off, his nervous jitters stopped.

I need to get Lucky back, he realised.

'Amber, when you're better, go and get a coffee,' he said.

'What?'

Shinichi sat forward in his seat, preparing to sever the connection. 'Something to wake you up. Give up on Alpine; he's gone. You need to take care of yourself.'

'But... you're acting like you're leaving.'

'I'll still be here, but I need to mute myself. I have a job to do.'

'What—?'

'I have to Transport someone back.'

7:42PM 26 NOVEMBER 1868, WALHALLA, AUSTRALIA

Until the release of the Timebox 3.0, only ARC-researchers had the authorisation to Transport agents. This meant that even an injured agent could be Transported back to safety if necessary, though this was not ideal. This is why it is important to stay in constant contact with your ARC-researcher.

The day had gone too slowly. It wasn't even nightfall yet, as the late spring had lengthened the days. The sun was almost at the horizon, despite the hour.

Luc had intended to explore, try to meet some people, and find out what Victorian Australia was like. He'd never been to Australia, but his sister had, and he had always intended to go. But after walking up the street and back, his head throbbing and spinning, he'd decided to take the afternoon off.

Christopher was reading through a book about plants, taking notes in a notebook as he flicked through the stiff pages. He didn't keep many live plants around; most were cuttings or fruits, hung up in his bedroom and dining room to dry them out and keep them preserved. Luc had looked around for a book to read, but the botanist only kept books on English plants, his own notebooks on the local flora, and a Bible.

Apparently early Australian settlers weren't big readers.

It was something of a relief when Luc heard Shinichi's voice in his ear. He jumped in his seat, earning a suspicious look from Christopher, then tried to walk calmly to his room so that he could reply.

'What, now?' he asked quietly. 'I thought we were leaving tomorrow.'

'Lucky, you have no idea what's been going on over here,' Shinichi said. He sounded tired, but there was a darker element to his voice. Almost… foreboding. 'This has become something bigger than we all thought it would be.'

'What are you talking about?'

'I need to get you back here so that I can explain.'

'Explain what?'

Shinichi huffed, frustrated. 'Are you and Amber ready to Transport?'

Luc sighed. Obviously pressing Shinichi wouldn't make him give up any more information. He grabbed his coat and left the room. 'I'll go get Amber.'

He decided he should go and say goodbye to Christopher. After all, the man had opened his home to him, given him food and first aid equipment, even though he clearly hadn't trusted him.

'Christopher,' he said at the doorway. The man looked up from his book. 'Christopher, I'm going home.'

He frowned. 'Now?'

'Yes. Something's come up, and Amber and I need to be back as soon as possible.'

Christopher closed the hymn-book with a small thud. 'Miss Winters hasn't agreed to go with you yet.'

Luc nodded. 'We'll see what she says. After all, I can't force her back.'

'No, you can't.' When Christopher said it, it sounded almost like a challenge.

Luc shook his head. He and Christopher had gotten off to a bad start together, and although Amber had tried to reconcile them, there was still no sign of friendship between them. Knowing he shouldn't be petty, Luc held out his hand. He owed it to Amber to at least try to be nice. 'Thank you,' he said as Christopher shook it reluctantly. 'For letting me stay here. And for your friendship to Amber.'

Christopher didn't say anything. As soon as Luc had finished, he went to the door and grabbed his coat.

'What are you doing?' Luc asked.

Christopher pulled his sleeve onto his arm. 'I'm coming with you. To make sure that "Amber" agrees to go before you force her to.'

'Does he think you're going to kidnap and murder her?' Shinichi asked in his ear.

'Apparently,' Luc muttered, leaving the house into the cool dusk air.

'Who is he?' Shinichi asked.

Luc dropped behind a few paces so that he could talk in private. The botanist continued on ahead, humming a song quietly. 'His name is Christopher Alpine. He's a botanist here in Walhalla. Amber befriended him while she was here, so I've been recovering at his house.'

Shinichi didn't reply. An uneasy feeling settled on Luc's stomach, as though it were seeping through the inter-time connection from Shinichi into Luc. 'Shi… Shinichi?'

'Christopher Alpine, did you say?'

'Yes…?'

Again, Shinichi seemed uneasily silent.

Abruptly, Luc realised where his feeling of dread was coming from. Shinichi wasn't completely silent; Luc could clearly hear his breathing. It was abnormally fast and ragged, as though he'd just run up a flight of stairs.

Except that Shinichi didn't run.

And Shinichi's never been afraid, Luc realised. His heart began to beat faster, and he couldn't stop the frown that worked its way onto his face.

'Um… Shinichi, what's wrong?' Luc asked.

'Lucky, you need to get Amber back here. Even if she refuses,' Shinichi said hoarsely. 'Her life is in danger if she stays with that man!'

'Who? Christopher?'

Christopher looked up at Luc as he heard his name mentioned. Luc glanced at him suspiciously. How did Shinichi know Christopher Alpine? And why was Amber in danger if she stayed with him? What was he, an assassin?

'Christopher Alpine!' Shinichi replied.

'What… how do you know him?'

'I don't know him,' Shinichi stammered. 'But I know the name.' He groaned. 'In all likelihood it is a different man with the same name, but I can't take this chance. Please, Lucky, for both your sakes, get Amber and get out as soon as you can!'

'Who is he?' Luc asked quietly, nervously. He turned his head, trying to keep the man in his sights as he rounded a corner. He seemed about as non-suspicious as men came, humming with surprising musicality and enjoying the brisk dusk air.

There was a short silence. Even Shinichi's breathing stopped. After a moment, Shinichi said, 'No, Lucky. If I tell you, it will go badly.'

'*What?*'

'Are you talking to me?' Christopher asked, turning.

'Not now, Alpine,' Luc snapped. 'What's been happening over there?' he asked Shinichi. Sweat dribbled down his forehead like cold blood.

Shinichi sighed hurriedly. 'Lucky, if he is who I think he is, he knows you're talking to me about him. And he knows who I am. He knows about ARCHIVE and everything.'

'Yeah, because Amber told him.'

'If I tell you more, he will know that his secret has been uncovered, and… and Haste will know… about me…'

'What are you talking about?'

'I told you that I will explain all when you get back. I want you to say this, like you're confused. Say, "Yes, he's a botanist. Amber has told me about him before. What about him?"'

Luc repeated the words, not needing to act confused. He knew what Shinichi was doing. Christopher could overhear Luc's side of the conversation, so he knew that he was the subject.

Why is he so important that we would be in danger if we knew who he was? Luc wondered.

'Now say, "No record? Why is that strange?"'

Again, he repeated it, looking up at Christopher, who was watching him suspiciously. As he said the words, he watched the man tense up, like a dog bristling its fur.

What a weird botanist.

'I wish I knew what was going on over there. How he's reacting.'

'Calm down, Christopher,' Luc said. 'You look tense. Did you know you have no historical record?'

The man blinked, but didn't relax at all. 'That's not unusual for someone of my position. I was Christened, but other than that, I'm just a scientist. I've written books, but I never expected them to last to your time. There's nothing exciting about my life.' He folded his arms. 'Is your friend at ARCHIVE researching me?'

Shinichi gasped. 'It *is* him.'

Luc didn't know what to say to Christopher. He shook his head and stepped forward, continuing the journey to Amber's house. Apparently that was the most important mission at the moment. Get Amber and get home.

They reached the tailor's shop, and Christopher motioned for Luc to knock on the door. He did so, and a willowy brunette opened the door, scowling until she saw Christopher. She blushed and motioned for them to come through. 'Doctor Alpine! Welcome – we're just in the kitchen. Please be quiet; Master Arthur's in bed already.'

Christopher nodded to her as they followed her through to the kitchen. It was dimly lit but large for a kitchen of the era, with a heavy wooden table in the middle and a wood oven set in the far wall. A man of about thirty years sat at the table. He had dark hair, a full beard and a sour attitude. Amber stood by the sink, her arms folded and her chin stuck out.

'Doctor Alpine's here, and he's brought a friend,' the woman said as they came through.

Amber looked up as they entered. She smiled at Luc, but pointedly ignored Christopher. 'Mollie, this is Lucky Holmes, the man I told you about.'

Luc inwardly groaned. *How much as she told* these *people?* he thought, nodding to Mollie and the man.

'How do you know Miss Winters?' the man asked him. His voice was deep and sombre.

'Who? Miss—'

'He means me,' Amber cut in, sounding exasperated.

Luc watched her face for a moment before he answered. She had smoothed her face to expressionlessness, but her eyes carried a look of pain. The man's question answered a few of Luc's own. Obviously, she'd told them that he'd recognised her, but not much more. He'd have to make up a story for them. 'Miss—Miss Winters and I work together.'

'As what?' the man's eyes narrowed.

Luc tried to come up with a reply that would make sense to a 19th-Century audience, with all their biases of gender roles, not to mention lack of time travel. 'Aid and rescue?' Shinichi suggested. That was the standard response, but it wouldn't work here. In colonial Victoria, there wouldn't be much in the way of organised search and rescue yet. 'Uh… we work in… in community services. You know, helping people after fires, supporting widows, that sort of thing.'

Johansson nodded once. 'And do you know how she came to be on our property, unconscious, bleeding and retarded?'

Retarded is a bit far, Luc thought. He struggled to come up with a response. 'I… no. My best guess is that she was visiting a local person in need of help and some… ruffians decided she might be easy money.'

'Miss Winters insists that a simple blow to the head cannot produce prolonged amnesia,' he said, still deadpan.

Amber snorted. 'So you *did* listen to me.'

The man ignored her. He watched Luc, waiting for his reply.

'Strange things happen in medicine all the time,' Shinichi said.

Luc shrugged. 'I am not a doctor,' he said. 'But I know that strange things happen in medicine all the time. Normally a blow to the head will not result in prolonged amnesia,' he looked at Amber. 'But in this case, it did.'

The man smiled a tiny smile, leaning back in his chair. 'You ducked that question well,' he said. 'You should go into politics.'

Funny, people are still making that joke in 2019. 'I—'

'One more, Mr Holmes,' the man said before he could continue. 'Miss Winters has been here for over a month. Where have you been?'

Luc took a deep breath. 'We were not aware—'

'We?'

'The…' Luc forgot what he'd said they worked as.

'Community services?' Shinichi said.

'The community services in the city were not aware that Miss Am… Winters was going to come here,' he said. 'So when she disappeared, we didn't know where on earth she could be. It took quite a lot of searching before I found her here.'

The man nodded, as though it made sense. Luc breathed a sigh of relief.

'I will take Amber back home now. We're going to take her back to England to recover with her family. We leave for the city immediately.'

'Not so fast,' Christopher said. 'That's not the story you told me.'

Luc's eyes widened. He shook his head quickly at Christopher, hoping he'd get the hint that what they'd told him was a secret that no one – including him – should know.

'That explanation makes much more sense compared to the one you told me,' the man went on, seeming amused at Luc's panic. 'It's much more believable than that she's from the future.'

Luc tried to watch Christopher, but his eyes were drawn to Amber as she laughed. 'Christopher, why would we tell you something like that? How could I be from the future? That's ridiculous.'

'Lucky, he's stalling for time,' Shinichi said. 'Trying to keep you there for as long as possible. You need to get Amber out of there.'

Right. Get Amber and get out.

Ignoring Christopher, Luc addressed the man. 'Sir, I need to take Miss Winters as soon as possible. Thank you for caring for her. Here is some money to repay your kindness.' He handed over his ARCHIVE allowance, a full £1 10s. *Hopefully the lack of inflation makes that seem like a lot.*

'What's the rush?' the brunette – Mollie – said. 'I thought you was leaving tomorrow.'

Amber watched Luc carefully. 'So did I.'

He nodded, aware of Christopher's suspicious eyes watching him. 'The plan was to leave tomorrow, but there is a ship departing tomorrow for England, and in order to get on it we need to be at the docks in time. Hence, we're leaving tonight.'

There was no way Amber could be satisfied with that answer; she knew where they were really going. So did Christopher. And he was seething.

Luc didn't care. He went to Amber and took one of her hands. He looked down into her brown eyes, hoping that she could read the urgency in his own. 'Amber, I need you to agree to come with me.'

Please. Please, Amber.

She held his gaze, for a moment, then her eyes flickered over his shoulder.

At Christopher.

Curses on that…

'Christopher, what are you—' she shrieked. Luc whirled around, catching Christopher's arm and deflecting the small pocket knife he'd aimed at his heart. He twisted his arm behind his back until he had to let go.

'Shinichi, what's with this guy?' he yelled, ignoring the others in the room.

'What's going on?' Shinichi asked urgently. 'Lucky, I can't tell you who he is here! But he's dangerous. I keep telling you, get out of there!'

Christopher threw his weight backwards into Luc, knocking him into a wall. His head started to spin, still tender from the blow yesterday, but he managed to dizzily kick the other man in the ribs, felling him. The man who'd been looking after Amber kicked the knife away so that it slid deep in under the table and went to help him. The woman screamed.

Though doubled over, Christopher still managed to throw a punch at Luc. Luc held up his arms. He knew that if the man got one blow to his head, he'd be out, and he suspected that Christopher knew it too.

Whoever he is, he's not just a botanist.

Luc stumbled away, around the chair the man had been sitting on, and Christopher followed him, his hands on the chair between them as though ready to throw it or use it in defence.

'I know you have a gun, agent,' he said slowly. 'Why don't you use it?'

Luc shook his head. 'The man's mad. Has he always been like this?'

Amber's eyes were wide as she shook her head, and even the other man looked stunned. Luc was only about a metre away from Amber now. If he jumped, he could grab her and run out…

Suddenly he remembered what Haste had said.

'Agent Holmes, make sure Amber is fit to Travel before you bring her back, okay?'

She looked fit to Travel. She looked in better condition than he did.

But in his time here, he'd learnt a new angle to the question. He had to make sure that Amber *wanted* to Travel. She'd created a new life here in 1868, with new friends and family that she would have to leave behind for the future. Luc couldn't force her into that decision; she'd have to make it herself.

Even if he couldn't explain to her that she could die if she stayed.

He watched the mad botanist closely, then, as suddenly as he could, he dived for Amber, grabbed her wrist and pulled her out of the kitchen.

Christopher chased them. That was good; it kept the inhabitants of the house safe for the moment. With Christopher behaving this unpredictably, Luc was glad that *he* was the one being chased, and not innocent locals.

He kept hold of Amber's wrist as they left the house and entered the cool night air. The main street was deserted; everyone was at home with their families, it seemed. That was also good.

Luc was faced with a dilemma, whatever Amber chose. He couldn't leave Christopher here; he seemed to have turned into a serial killer in an instant, and he couldn't leave the town of Walhalla with that. But on the other hand, he couldn't take him with him to 2019, where he'd be completely out of his depth. And he couldn't kill the man, either.

'Shinichi?' he gasped. 'Shinichi, what do I do with him?'

'Leave him,' Shinichi said immediately. 'Get away.'

'I can't. I can't leave him here,' Luc risked a glance over his shoulder. Christopher was close behind him. His face was in shadow of night, but it was easy to read the desperation in his posture, in the way he was running, in the slamming footfalls that echoed in double-time with the thumping quartz crushers. 'I don't know what he'll do to the people here.'

'He won't do anything,' Shinichi said, though he didn't seem sure.

'Shinichi,' Luc panted. He hadn't run in a while, and now it seemed like the worst mistake of his life. 'Is he from the future? I mean--'

There was a small pause. '2019? Yes, I think so.'

That settled it then. Amber pulled Luc onto a dirt track that veered off from the main road, only wide enough for two people to walk side-by-side. Luc didn't know where it went, but he trusted Amber. He glanced behind him once more. Christopher seemed just below them. If he reached out his hand, he could have touched Luc's back…

'Amber, do you want to go back with me?' Luc yelled suddenly.

'Yes! What did you think?' she yelled back. For a wonder, she seemed as puffed as he did, her shoulders heaving up and down as she struggled to breathe. Her level of fitness had always seemed unattainable to Luc. This was a girl who ran for *fun*.

'Good. Shinichi, whenever you're ready!'

Luc braced himself for the shock of Travelling. He hoped he'd survive; he still hadn't fully recovered from his beating the day before, and the steep running was leaving him dizzy. It occurred to him suddenly that Amber had no idea what to expect from this; she'd forgotten it all. They reached a white picket fence, and she went to jump it. Luc pulled her to the right, running alongside the fence instead. He stumbled as his feet got used to running along the hill instead of up it. Christopher ran into the fence, recovered himself, and continued the pursuit.

'Shinichi…?'

There was silence through the earpiece. Didn't they usually count down or something? 'Shinichi, you ready?'

'Well…'

Luc heaved air into his lungs, trying to keep up with Amber, the world spinning around him. He couldn't speak anymore. He'd just have to trust Shinichi.

They were reaching the corner of the yard. Whatever they did, they would have to jump the fence soon. Luc wasn't sure he would make it. His legs hurt, and his head felt dizzyingly light.

There was a beep in the earpiece. Luc's eyes widened. *What's that ARC-researcher doing?* 'Lucky, you ready?'

'Well, yeah, whenever you are!' *Take your time, no rush on my end,* he thought, rolling his eyes.

'Good. Anytime now,' Shinichi said.

Amber glanced back at him, pulling him forward. 'Jump soon!' she yelled. Luc nodded.

Amber jumped, pulling up her dress so that it didn't catch on the fence. Luc jumped too, though his jump wasn't nearly as graceful as hers. He stepped on the top of the fence, his foot wedging between the slats and pushing himself up higher into the air. He grabbed Amber's arm, pulling her up to him.

'Lucky, what—?'

He wrapped his arms around her body, trying to protect her from the brunt of Travel and tensed his body in anticipation. *Now, Shinichi.*

Everything disappeared.

PART TWO

Time

10:00PM 11 March 2019, Luc's Home

Time travel sickness (characterised by migraines, nausea and/or joint pain) may be experienced directly after Travelling. Generally, this goes away by the third or fourth trip. If symptoms persist, consult the ARCHIVE medical team.

It took a few minutes for Luc to remember who he was.

He opened his eyes. Wherever he was, it was dark. He seemed to be lying on… carpet. There was something heavy on his arm. It was large and warm, pressed against the side of his body. Something tickled his nose, and he moved his head away. He rubbed his nose with the back of his hand, then investigated the irritant. It was hair. Long, curly hair.

Not his hair.

'Shinichi?' he mumbled.

There was silence from the earpiece.

He tried to sit up, but as he did so he hit his head on something wooden. He dropped back down with a moan. 'Why is it always my head?'

Blearily he reached into his pocket with his free hand and pulled out his phone, turning the torch on. Bright, white light shone from it immediately.

He waved the torch around. He was in his living room. He'd hit his head on the coffee table, and the thing lying next to him was… Amber.

He closed his eyes for a moment, savouring the feeling of safety. Taking a deep breath, he sat up. The clock said that it was about 10pm. His mother would probably be asleep by now.

Amber had opened her eyes, but she seemed dazed and confused. Luc gently pulled his arm out from underneath her and put his phone on the coffee table.

'I feel sick,' Amber moaned.

Luc nodded. 'That's Travel sickness,' he said. 'It's always worse on the return trip, for some reason. How's your head?'

She frowned. 'It's fine. Just my stomach.'

Luc inhaled deeply, then looked down at her. The light was faint, but he could see her messy hair and pale face. He smiled. 'Remember anything yet?'

She caught his smile, but didn't return it. 'No,' she sighed. 'I know, I was hoping that going back would help too.' She looked around her. 'Where are we?'

'My house,' Luc replied, as he risked standing. 'Welcome to the living room.'

Amber sat up and looked around, seeming surprised. 'Why would we land here? Not at ARCHIVE?'

Luc swallowed. He hadn't explained yet that Shinichi technically wasn't meant to know about the mission, and it felt too late now. He didn't know how Shinichi had gotten them back, but he assumed he'd landed them here because he wasn't at ARCHIVE to welcome them back.

He didn't have the energy to explain. He just wanted to go to bed and explain in the morning. 'It's ten at night, Amber,' he said, as though they hadn't just travelled through time. 'ARCHIVE's closed now.'

Her flat glare showed she didn't buy it, but she didn't argue. 'So… how do I get to my… home?'

He sighed. He was in no state to drive, but he should call her a taxi or an Uber. But as he pulled out his phone, he hesitated. 'Do you know where you live?'

Amber shrugged, then looked away. 'I… I mean, two minutes ago—or two hundred years ago—my home was in Australia.'

Luc tucked his phone back into his pocket and touched her arm. 'I know you're trusting me completely blindly,' he said. 'And I appreciate it.'

She gave a weak laugh.

'And I know that at the moment, I'm the only familiar thing in this world. I'm sorry, for taking you away from everything you know.'

She nodded, rubbing her forehead and looking away. 'Thanks,' she said quietly.

'If you'd prefer not to go to an unfamiliar place, with an unfamiliar bed, you can… you can stay here for the night.' She didn't say anything, and he couldn't quite see her face in the dark. 'I'll get you a blanket, and a pillow. You can sleep on the couch. There's a cat somewhere; he'll probably join you. And in the morning, we'll talk to the ARCHIVE medics and get your head sorted out.'

She was silent for a moment. Then, she picked up her shoulders. 'There's a cat?'

Luc laughed. 'Yeah. His name's Pippin.' He offered her another smile, then tried to muster some fresh dregs of energy. 'I'll get your accommodation sorted, ma'am,' he joked. 'And the cat.'

When he came back, she was already asleep, curled up on the couch with her arms folded under her head as a pillow. He wondered if he should wake her up to get changed. Her dress was so tight and bulky and impractical, he was surprised she could have run in it, let alone fall asleep.

Oh, that's why she was as puffed as I was, he realised. *She was wearing a corset.*

Sheepishly, Luc unfolded the blankets and laid them over her, hoping she wouldn't wake up. He found the bag of clothes Laura had put aside for her, and set it next to the bed. Underneath, he saw her phone.

It had been in the car when they'd been driving back from the labs, and somehow it had survived the crash. He pulled it out and set it next to the bag of clothes. *I hope that helps,* he thought.

Next to the phone and book he placed a bottle of water and a muesli bar, in case she woke up hungry in the middle of the night. He munched on his own as he prepared the tiny bed-and-breakfast. While Amber seemed to have a stomach of iron, bad food always made him sick, and he'd long been advised not to eat historical food if he didn't want gastro.

He ate some cereal as well, finally curbing his hunger, and drank some water before showering. He could hardly hold his head up. He took an Aspirin, then fell into bed and slept.

8:12AM 11 March 2019, Luc's Home

*Usually, you will return to ARCHIVE
and immediately begin your mission
debrief. However, at the discretion of the
ARC-researcher, you may Travel instead to a
hospital or a discrete location.*

Amber opened her eyes blearily. She was lying on a couch in a normal-looking living room, covered in blankets with a small tan-coloured cat at her feet. She smiled. Normal-looking. It only looked normal because it had a television in one corner and a laminate bookshelf full of novels in another.

She was in 2019.

She spent a moment in contemplation, testing her memory, trying once more to picture her parents. Remember her address. Did she have any pets? What was her middle name? Where did she go to school?

Her mind was blank.

Oh well.

Light streamed into the room, outlining closed curtains. It was just light enough to make out details of the room, but everything was a shadowy grey.

Her gaze fell on the coffee table. It was within arm's reach of where she was lying, and on one corner sat a book, a phone, a water bottle and a muesli bar.

Opening the wrapper of the muesli bar, she munched on it and reached for the phone. It was strange; she recognised a television, but didn't know how to use a phone beyond what she'd seen Lucky do. Maybe when she saw a doctor, she would find out why.

She turned on the phone. The date and time appeared at the top. *8:15, 11/03/2019.* Underneath ran a long list of missed calls, unread messages, Instagram and Snapchat notifications, and even a few apps that were waiting for permission to update. *I guess people have been missing me,* she thought, slightly amused.

It was the same type of phone as Lucky's, so she figured it should work the same. She pressed the button at the bottom, and a number pad came up, asking for her passcode.

Uh… should I remember a passcode? she wondered.

Apparently not. The phone seemed to recognise her, and it opened automatically when she tried to press the button again. Shrugging, she started exploring the phone.

Photos, an app was labelled, and, her curiosity piqued, she tapped on it like she'd seen Lucky do. She spent a few minutes trawling through memes and pictures of books and clothes before she came to some with people in them. She clicked on the pictures and started to look through them one by one, stopping at the one with the most people in it.

It seemed to be a gathering of a large family. There were at least four generations in the pictures – from wrinkled, grey-haired elders to distracted babies. In the middle sat a man and a woman, both looking to be in their late-fifties to early-sixties. Though they were sitting in two different folding chairs, they were holding hands. The man was smiling uncomfortably at the camera, the woman was beaming. Standing around them were various adults, some with arms around each other, some with babies on hips, and there, on the right side of the picture, with her attention on a small child at her feet, was Amber herself.

She almost didn't recognise herself. That Amber – the one in the picture – seemed confident, relaxed, and happy. She checked the date of the photo, and her heart fell. It had been taken only two months ago.

The cat woke up and shook itself, meowing when it noticed that she was awake. Amber looked up from the picture, then reached out and tentatively scratched it gently under its chin. It started purring as it lay down again.

A gentle rumbling sound came from a different room. *That's a kettle,* she realised. Lucky must be awake.

Amber continued through the photos. There were a few of beautiful sunsets, and another of Lucky at a beach, with sunglasses on, reading a book on a towel in the sand. Amber checked the date on it, her unease changing. *Either he's telling the truth,* she thought, *or this lie has been very elaborately spun.*

But she knew he was telling the truth. He couldn't plant thoughts in her head; she'd been thinking all that time that she hadn't belonged in the 19th-century, and now she was in the 21st-century and everything felt more… familiar.

She didn't want to read the messages or phone people back. It looked like no one knew that she was in 2019, at least for now, and she was enjoying the peace and quiet. She knew that as soon as people knew, they would try to contact her, and a hurricane of confusing messages would ensue.

She looked through the other apps on her phone, eventually settling on the news app. Scrolling through the gossip and political headlines, she didn't hear the kettle as it turned off, or the footsteps clicking down the tiled hallway.

Or the door opening.

She *did* hear a woman's voice calling, 'Pippin! I have some—' before it cut off. 'I—oh.'

Amber jumped, looking around at a middle-aged woman, who was staring wide-eyed straight at her. She had short but well-styled dirty blonde hair that curled down around her well-lined face, wore tight jeans and a loose-fitting flannelette shirt, and carried a piece of what looked like bacon fat in her hand.

'Oh,' Amber said. 'Hello.'

The woman's mouth closed, and her face darkened. She straightened her back, narrowed her eyes, then turned around and stormed out of the room. Amber threw off the blankets, inadvertently throwing the cat into the air, and ran after the woman.

At least, she tried to. Her feet got caught in her skirts, and she twisted her ankle as she fell in a heap on the floor. 'Wait!' she called desperately, crawling to her feet. She threw the blankets back onto the couch and hobbled after the woman. 'Wait! I can explain!'

She found the woman in the kitchen's doorway with a sour look on her face. She looked her up and down, taking in her strange dress and messy hair. She raised an eyebrow and folded her arms. 'I'm assuming you're here because of Lucky,' she said. 'Do I want to hear this explanation?'

Amber swallowed and took a step back from the woman, trying to gather her thoughts. She was starting to panic as it dawned on her that she didn't have an explanation. She couldn't explain who she was, or what she was doing here. Lucky was right; she'd trusted him blindly. *Where is he?*

'My name is Rach—ah, not that one.' Her mind blanked. 'Amber! It's Amber.' Not a great start. 'And… Lucky said I could stay here for the night.'

'So he's back, is he?' the woman said.

'We got back last night,' she said. 'I… don't know where he is, though.'

The woman's eyes narrowed, and she turned and walked into the kitchen, muttering something Amber couldn't hear. She was left in the hallway, not sure of what to do.

But the phone is mine, isn't it? she thought, looking back in the direction of the living room. *It had a picture of me in it.*

She followed the woman into the kitchen. 'I'm sorry,' she said. 'I didn't mean to intrude, really.'

The woman was frying bacon and eggs. She flipped an egg. 'It's not you. You're most welcome, if you're Lucky's guest.'

Amber could feel the *but* hanging over her, and decided to save her response.

'But I wish he'd told me he was going to Travel,' the woman said. 'With his concussion, too!'

Ah. 'So you aren't mad at me?'

The woman shot her a dark look. 'No,' she said, but some-how, Amber didn't feel she'd answered the question.

There was a thump above them, then another, then a groan. 'Lucky's awake,' the woman said, turning back to the food. A shower hissed to life.

'What's your name?' Amber asked desperately.

'Loraine.'

'Nice… to meet you, Loraine.' She wanted to apologise again, but held her tongue.

'Breakfast?'

'Yes, thanks.'

Loraine set some food in front of Amber, then went back to the stove. 'Coffee?'

'No, thanks.'

She grunted, and they didn't speak after that.

A few minutes later, Lucky came downstairs in a shirt and slacks. 'Mum! Oh, you met Amber. Hi Amber.'

'You're back,' Loraine said, sitting down to eat her own food.

Lucky paused, his grin freezing. 'Yep. I… didn't want to wake you last night.'

Loraine glared at him. 'You didn't tell me you'd gone.'

Lucky released a sigh, then went to the kettle and poured himself a mug of hot water. 'It happened so fast,' he said, dropping a tea bag in. 'Haste gave me permission, and I thought if I didn't take the opportunity, he might rescind it.'

Loraine grunted, and Lucky seemed to take this as forgive-ness.

He launched into a detailed story of what had happened in 1868, with a lot of details Amber thought strange to include, but Loraine seemed to think important. 'The grocer had all kinds of fruit.' And, 'I was right, by the way, about the horse dung.' And, 'The best thing about Travelling is all the fun accents.'

Amber noticed that he left out Harry's attack, his stay at Christopher's and Christopher's last attack, though he still somehow managed to make a coherent story. His mother listened attentively, and when he had finished, she looked at Amber, and, for the first time, she didn't seem on her guard. 'Good,' she said, then turned back to her son. 'Now. What happened to your head?'

Lucky swallowed. 'Not… well, it… it's worse than it looks. But I may have been hit on the head by a man with a eucalyptus branch.'

Loraine rolled her eyes. 'Of course you did,' she muttered.

Amber set her cutlery down. 'Can I use your shower?' she asked.

Lucky nodded, retrieving the bag of clothes from the lounge-room and giving it to her in the hallway. 'You know how to use the shower, don't you?' he asked nervously.

Amber laughed. 'Yes, I do.'

★★★

While she was in the shower, Luc tried to explain Amber's story. He was realising just how little he understood of it, and how few questions he'd asked. Eventually, Loraine shook her head and told him to stop. 'She needs to meet her proper family,' she said. 'They can help her rest and recover in a calmer environment.'

Luc rolled his eyes. 'I know that, Mum. I just let her stay the night because we came in late.'

She sipped her coffee, avoiding his eyes. 'How long has she been your partner, anyway?' she asked casually.

Luc hesitated before answering. He knew where this was going. 'Since I started at ARCHIVE,' he said slowly.

Looking up, his mother leant her elbows on the tabletop. 'Then why didn't I get to hear about her?' she asked, shaking her head. 'I didn't even know you *had* a partner at ARCHIVE.'

Luc was surprised by how hurt she sounded. *Does she want to know who I'm working with? Working as a field agent at ARCHIVE is a dangerous job. Maybe she's worried about me?*

No, that couldn't be it. She'd sounded not like she wanted to make sure Amber was responsible, but like she…

Suddenly, he thought he understood. *Mum misses Francie. Since we moved to London, she hasn't had a daughter to… do whatever mums and daughters do together.*

Or maybe it's broader, he reflected. *Maybe she just misses female company in general.*

His mum hadn't gone out much since they'd moved. She'd always been introverted, preferring a night in with a movie, and being the first to leave large parties, so when they'd come to London, she hadn't joined any clubs or seemed to make many friends. With her chronic illness, she'd stayed inside most of the time, doing what she could around the house and talking to Luc when he was home.

'I'm sorry, Mum,' he said eventually. 'I didn't think of it.'

She nodded slowly, sadly, turning back to the bacon and eggs on the stove.

'Thanks for cooking breakfast,' he added.

'You slept in.'

He nodded, not sure what else to say. *How had I missed this?* he mused. *Of course she's lonely. She never goes out anymore.*

'You'll like Amber,' he said. 'She's really sweet.'

'Do you like her?' his mum asked.

'Yeah,' he said, adding a shrug. 'I do. She's a good partner.'

She didn't reply for a while. Upstairs, the water in the shower turned off. 'Did you get her a towel?'

Luc laughed. 'Yes, Mum. For goodness' sake, I'm not stupid.'

'You could have fooled me,' she said and, even though she didn't smile, he knew she was joking. She sat down in front of him, brushing his hair off his forehead to inspect his bruise. 'Get the doctor at ARCHIVE to look at that, okay?'

'I will.'

She nodded, satisfied, then smiled. 'I suppose that if you like her, then I will too.'

Luc returned the smile.

A few moments later, Amber came back downstairs. Her dark hair was still wet, but by brushing and towel-drying it the curls had flattened somewhat. She wore a bright red blouse and blue slacks. 'Lucky, thanks for getting these clothes,' she said uncertainly. 'But you forgot to put in a hairbrush, soap, make-up, and… shoes.'

'Laura packed it,' he said. He hadn't even thought to check if it needed anything more. 'Maybe she thought you'd use the stuff from 1868.'

'Did you find anything adequate?' Loraine butted in.

'Yeah. I hope that's okay,' Amber replied with a shrug. 'And I'm happy to wear my old shoes for a day at least. There's nothing wrong with them.' She shook her head. 'I'm not sure what to do about makeup, though.'

'Go commando?' Luc's mum suggested with a small smile.

'Ask Laura for some of hers?' Luc mumbled. Amber shrugged again.

'It'll be okay,' she said, sitting down next to him at the table. 'I appreciate the thought. And my phone.'

Luc smiled.

They ate breakfast, late as it was, and at the end of the meal Luc grabbed the plates and put them in the sink while Amber pulled out her phone to call her parents.

He glanced at the clock in front of the sink with a sigh. It was ten o'clock. *Oh well. I gave up on getting to work on time ages ago.*

I should probably text Laura or Shinichi though.

He went back to his room to change into something more suitable to work, inspecting his bruise as he did so. Frankly, he was impressed with himself; he hadn't had a bruise like that since he'd gone paintball-shooting as a teenager, and that bruise had been on his arm.

But this one hurt. Unlike a flesh bruise, this made his whole head throb if he moved too quickly, and though the painkillers had taken the edge off, his mind was still foggy. The swelling had gone down, but it had turned purple and ugly, with the half-healed cut from the crash running through it. He would have to get the stitches replaced again.

Sighing heavily at the thought, Luc grabbed his jacket and started back downstairs. It was now eleven thirty, and he needed to get Amber back to the doctor as soon as possible.

Saying goodbye to his mum, he quickly checked his phone to see if Laura had replied. She had.

:D :D :D :D :D :D :D :D :D :D :D :D

OOOOH I'M SO GLAD YOURE HOME ARE YOU COMING TO WORK TODAY

Quick as he could, he replied,

Yes. Leaving now.

ARCHIVE

It should not be taken for granted that being a field agent with ARCHIVE is a dangerous job. You will lose colleagues, friends, and partners as you Travel into the most perilous parts of history. "You don't appreciate your partner enough unless you've lost one," says Commander Haste. "So treat them well, never taking it for granted that you will both end each mission."

T he elevator doors opened, and Amber stepped out into a bustling office, full of people running around, talking through headsets and calling to each other over office dividers. Someone saw them as they came in, and soon people Amber didn't know were calling her name, telling her it was good to see her back. She forced a warm smile, nodding and grinning as she needed to. It seemed Lucky hadn't told them many details about the mission. She suspected their welcome would have been much different if they knew she couldn't remember who they were.

One woman seemed particularly excited. She'd been waiting at the door, and squealed audibly as they came in, sweeping her into a hug immediately. 'Hello, beautiful,' she said. 'Nice tan,' she whispered in her ear.

She was shorter than Amber, but thin and wiry, with dark skin and black hair that was swept up into a perfect messy bun on the top of her head. Her long green jacket looked cosy but formal, contrasting with her sneakers. 'And Lucky!' she beamed, letting go of Amber to pull him into a hug. 'Well done,' she said to him.

Finally, Amber recognised the voice. 'Oh, you must be Laura,' she said as the woman pulled away from Lucky.

Laura's smile faltered for a moment, but she recovered herself and nodded. 'Yep, the one and only.'

Amber looked around expectantly. 'So where's Shinichi?'

Lucky hushed her, and other agents gave her odd looks as they moved back to their desks.

'Shinichi?' Laura repeated, her face tense but her voice nonchalant. 'He doesn't work here anymore. Remember?'

Amber frowned, glancing at Lucky uncertainly. 'But—'

He shook his head. 'Not here,' he whispered. 'I'll explain... later.'

Maybe he actually was an AI from the future, Amber thought, confused. *No, Laura said he doesn't work here... so where does he work?*

'But... we can trust him right?'

Laura gave her an odd look. 'Goodness, trust Shinichi? Of course we can trust Shinichi, it's like trusting a block of ice not to tell your secrets to the dog. Even if he *did* talk to people voluntarily, he's more secretive than the bottom of the ocean.'

Amber's confusion only deepened. 'But he talked to me.'

'Laura's exaggerating,' Lucky replied, rolling his eyes at Laura. 'He talks to people. He just doesn't talk to her.'

Laura swiped at Lucky, and he ducked, laughing.

***

'It's so good to have her back safe and sound,' Laura said quietly, now that Amber couldn't hear her. Gian had pulled Amber into one of his heartfelt but barely audible conversations, and Amber was nodding along, smiling as though she knew what was going on.

Lucky nodded, but it seemed more of a dutiful nod, as though that were the right response, than agreement to the statement. He was watching Amber, a wistful kind of sadness in his eyes.

Laura studied him. 'You don't seem as excited as I thought you'd be,' she remarked.

He looked at her, as though he'd come out of a reverie, then shrugged his shoulders. 'Of course I'm happy to have Amber back, Laura. You know me too well to think otherwise.'

Laura's eyes narrowed suspiciously. She gave a low grunt.

Lucky stayed silent for a moment, and Laura let him watch Amber as she talked to the other agent. To look at him, you'd think he was watching a high-risk operation being carried out on his loved-one. His face was blank, but his eyes were watching with a detached kind of intentness. Focused, but not on what was in front of him.

'I suppose it's just not as exciting as I expected,' he said after a while.

Laura frowned. 'What do you mean?'

He shrugged again. 'I mean… I was looking forward to being back because coming back signifies the end of a mission. I thought that I would walk in here with a timebox in one hand and…'

Laura snickered. 'And Amber's in the other?' she teased. Lucky's cheeks turned a satisfying shade of pink.

'Well, I thought I would have the timebox and Amber, and I could start the next mission,' he said, seeming less embarrassed with the rewording.

She snorted, but after a black look from Lucky she calmed down and became serious again. 'You're halfway there. You have Amber.'

Lucky had been watching Amber again, but his gaze dropped to the floor in front of his shoes. Again, he nodded, as though it were the right response.

'She's more important than the timebox, Lucky,' she said gently.

'I suppose I thought it would be easy from here on,' he muttered.

Easy. Laura shook her head. Today would be many things, but it wouldn't be easy. If Shinichi went through with his plan, today would be one of the most challenging days of their careers.

She felt sorry for Lucky. He'd already been through so much heartache, and from what she'd gathered of his time in the 1860s, he desperately needed a few days off to rest. But from today on, it was only going to become more difficult, more hectic, more painful.

'Sorry, Lucky,' she said quietly. 'The easy part is over. I have a feeling it's just about to become more confusing.'

He rolled his eyes. 'Great,' he muttered. 'What *is* happening next?'

As if on cue, the elevator dinged, and the doors opened to reveal a middle-aged Asian man, tall and wiry, with a small goatee on his chin. He wore a familiar black suit and carried a slightly-worn computer satchel slung over one shoulder, and a 'Leon's' coffee cup in the other hand.

'Good, you're here,' he said when he saw Lucky.

'Shinichi,' Lucky gasped, then lowered his voice. 'You're not supposed to be here.'

'He's fine so long as he's quiet,' Laura replied, though the joke didn't make her laugh. Her stomach was feeling queasy with a nervousness she'd been feeling all night. 'Are you absolutely sure about this?' she asked Shinichi quietly.

The man shook his head, taking a sip of his coffee. 'Of course not. I understand Amber hasn't recovered her memories?'

Lucky shook his head sadly, and Shinichi sighed heavily. 'Well, at least she's still alive. Come on. We need to talk to Haste.'

11:29AM 11 MARCH 2019, ARCHIVE

For the eighth time, Luc checked his watch. He'd hoped to get Amber to the doctor as soon as they got here, but it was as though Laura and Shinichi had forgotten that she needed urgent medical attention.

'See?' Laura said, holding up her phone to Shinichi. 'It says I successfully booked my appointment with Haste for 11:00 this morning. He's legged it.'

Shinichi glanced at the screen, folding his arms. 'Maybe he did.'

Luc rolled his eyes. 'Are you still talking about the Commander? You threw me when you said he was late.'

Shinichi nodded. Unfolding his arms, he glanced around the office before opening the sliding glass door into Haste's office.

'Shinichi,' Laura whispered loudly.

'I'm just going to check his appointments,' Shinichi said.

'He's not coming, Shinichi,' Laura replied. 'And you shouldn't sneak into people's offices.'

'I snuck into ARCHIVE, didn't I?'

Laura threw her hands up in the air, but it seemed that she'd won. Shinichi closed the door and led them into a private meeting room.

They all chose a chair around the square table, Shinichi electing to stand behind one like a teacher preparing for a class. Setting his bag on the table, he unzipped a pocket and pulled out an unlabelled folder. Paper covered in small writing, newspaper clippings and torn-out notes half-slid out of the folder as he threw it onto the table.

Luc fidgeted on his chair. 'So this definitely can't wait until *after* we've done some medical check-ups on Amber?'

Shinichi nodded. 'She's survived this long, hasn't she? She can take a few more minutes.'

Luc shared a glance with Amber, who shifted on her seat. 'Sure, but if I ever knew who this Haste was, I don't remember him,' she said. 'I can't imagine I'll be that much help.'

Shinichi's lips curled slightly into a smile. 'Oh, you'll be more help than you might think,' he replied.

Laura rolled her eyes. 'Untheatrically, we need to bring you up to speed. A lot's been going on since you left.'

Luc narrowed his eyes but nodded. 'I got that impression when Shinichi left me stranded in the past for a day. What, was it your wedding day?'

'I would have told you if it was,' Shinichi said. 'This is much more important. I've been investigating the crash.'

Luc rubbed his face, vivid memories coming back to him even as Shinichi said the word. *The man at the laboratories. Wet, slippery streets. Amber's scream.*

He shook his head as though that could shake the images from his mind. 'The crash?' he managed to mumble.

'Amber was sent back in time with the timebox, and she lost her memories. I've been suspicious of this ever since you came to me, Lucky. How can someone Travel accidentally? Surely there would be safeguards in place. Beyond that, why did she lose her memories? But as I thought about it, I realised it was all a bit off from the start. The men ambushed the labs, didn't kill you or try to contain you there, but they chased you.'

'They wanted the timebox,' Luc said. This was the one part that *wasn't* confusing.

'Then they had an odd plan. I would have tried to kill you, then I would take it and Travel out of there.' The room chilled, but Shinichi didn't seem to notice. He opened the folder, pulling out two sheets. 'These lab records show that Movarian technicians left a Travelling Homing Device, or THD, on their last test trip. That THD was sent to make certain that the next time someone Travelled, they would find themselves in 1868, in Australia. It also shows that just before Amber Travelled, the timebox was remotely activated, at the request of Commander Haste.'

Luc's mouth went dry. 'What are you saying?'

Shinichi levelled a look at him.

'It was all deliberate?' Amber said in a small voice. 'What about the crash?'

Shinichi nodded. 'I'm speculating. My guess is that the pursuit was to supervise Amber's Travelling, and the crash was to cover it all up. Which leads me to ask, why? Why did Amber need to Travel?'

He pulled a third paper out of the folder, covered in highlighting. 'Would you like to read this?' he asked Laura.

'"Travel-Reliant Selective Memory Suppressant, or TRel-S MS."' Laura frowned as the title she'd just read sunk in.

'Selective Memory Suppressant?' Amber repeated in disbelief. 'Is that possible?'

Laura shook her head and continued reading. '"TRel-SMS is revolutionary new technology that allows for the suppression of certain memories in a specific individual, while leaving all other memories intact. A drug component must be ingested half an hour before the technological component is activated. By selecting certain parts of the brain, memories can be deactivated permanently."' She skipped down a few paragraphs to the next highlighted section. '"The drug component is reliant on the user Travelling past the date of the creation of the memories they are trying to forget. For example, to forget an event that occurred in January 2004, one must Travel back earlier than 2004. Similarly, the user must Travel back earlier than 2004 in order to forget a fact they learnt in January 2004. Tests are being undergone to determine the risks of using TRel-SMS without Travelling and the extent of memory suppression."' Laura's face went white. 'Did Haste use this on Amber?' she choked.

Shinichi ran a hand through his hair, causing a few strands to stick up. 'We assumed that Amber's loss of memory was due to her Travelling while concussed. However, Lucky has sustained multiple head injuries in the past few days, and the medic allowed him to Travel without concern. While this isn't definite proof, it's certainly suspicious. If he somehow managed to put the drug component in her food without her noticing…' he sighed, shaking his head. 'I have a statement that Haste sent *someone* back against his will, though no proof it was definitely Amber.'

Laura snorted. 'We'll have to keep an eye out for other people who were sent back in time suspiciously,' she replied.

Shinichi nodded.

Amber shook her head. 'I'm probably supposed to know this, but… why me?'

Shinichi grimaced, pulling a small notebook out of his breast pocket. He flipped it open to a particular page and stared at it for a moment. Luc craned his neck, wondering if he was about to be shown whatever was captivating Shinichi's attention.

But he wasn't. With a grim nod, Shinichi shut the book and placed it back in his pocket.

'Christopher Alpine,' he said quietly. 'A name that keeps coming up.'

'Who?' Laura asked.

'He was a friend of mine in 1868,' Amber said, and Luc squashed his annoyance at the way she said 'friend'.

One of Shinichi's eyebrows twitched, and he folded his arms across his chest. 'Your *friend*—'

'How could *I* know he'd—'

'—sabotaged a plane in 1998,' Shinichi finished, just as Amber said, '--try to kill us?'

There was an awkward silence.

'A great friend,' Laura remarked.

Luc felt slightly less jealous at that. 'He sabotaged a plane?' he asked, trying not to laugh.

Shinichi nodded, his face still as he opened his computer and selected a file. 'The plane that you had to save with Carl,' he went on. 'That's what he said to Amber:' he clicked on the computer, and a quiet buzz filled the air.

'What do you know of ARCHIVE?' came a voice on the recording.

Luc stopped breathing. *That's Amber,* he thought immediately. *But… a younger Amber.*

There was something different about her voice. It was the same accent and timbre as the voice of the woman beside him, and there was nothing different in her inflections or tone. But there was *something…* something that struck him as very different and made him incredibly sad.

And he couldn't quite put his finger on what it was.

'What do you know of ARCHIVE?' she demanded again.

Under the table, Laura put a hand quietly on his arm, and he let in a shaky breath. *Can she hear it too?* he wondered. *Can Amber?* He slid his hand up and gripped Laura's hand without looking at her. She squeezed his, and suddenly he remembered her words from earlier.

'Sorry, Lucky, the easy part is over. I have a feeling it's just about to become more confusing.'

'That's Christopher,' Amber murmured.

Luc forced his attention back to the recording. '…who think they're going to save the world, saving it when it's already been saved and breaking it when it's already been broken.'

Luc's eyes narrowed. It was definitely Alpine's voice. *Does he work for an organisation like ARCHIVE?* he thought. *That kills people who've already been killed?*

That sounds like something out of a sick sci-fi novel.

'What on earth is he talking about?' Recorded-Shinichi asked.

Alpine barked a laugh. 'ARCHIVE really is the perfect example of government bureaucracy. Let's bring together the best of the best of the world, and they'll be so busy orchestrating dead people's fate that they won't recognise coincidence. Those who pull the strings are often pulling more than we'd like, right?'

'Who?' that was Amber.

Concentrate, Luc.

Shinichi said something indistinguishable, then went on, 'Amber, you need to find out everything he knows.'

'What are you—' she sounded like she was in pain. 'Who are you talking about?'

'Fate and coincidence,' Alpine said. 'It always amuses me how much control he has. Like here, sending someone to bring a plane down, and someone else to keep it in the air.'

Luc hadn't realised he'd started shaking his head. 'What?' he whispered.

'He hired you?' That was Amber.

'You are Fate,' Alpine said. *What a jerk,* Luc thought. 'Hired by Haste. And he hired me as Coincidence. Nothing wrong with that. Give it fifteen hours, and the world will be righted.'

Shinichi stopped the recording, and for the first time Luc could take in a deep breath. Letting go of Laura's hand, he glanced at Amber uncertainly.

Her face was pale, and her eyes were wide. 'That was me,' she whispered.

A small ember of hope lit up inside Luc. 'Do you remember… it?' he asked.

Something in his face seemed to discourage her. She dropped her gaze to the table and shook her head. 'No, I… but… that was my voice. And Christopher's.'

Shinichi nodded. 'I hacked your earpiece yesterday.' Shutting the computer lid, he dropped his voice. 'I believe it was that discussion that scared Haste enough to try to eliminate you. I'm sorry, Amber.'

She shook her head, forcing a smile. 'Seems it did the trick,' she replied quietly.

Like a light going on, Luc knew what was different about her voice. *It's her confidence,* he realised. *In the recording she sounded… sure of herself.*

Somehow, the thought made him feel like a bully.

'What happened fifteen hours later?' Laura asked Shinichi.

Shinichi picked up his folder from the table and flicked through it. 'There was only one thing I could find that happened on February 14, 1998 at 6pm, and was connected to the plane.'

He pulled out a piece of paper and glanced over it, saying, 'Lucky, do you remember Stephanie Heile?'

Luc frowned. The name sounded familiar, and he had the feeling he'd been talking about that person recently. 'Stephanie Heile,' he mumbled, then remembered his dream. 'Wasn't she on the plane in 1998?'

Shinichi slid the file toward him like it was weighed down with bricks. 'Read this.'

He glanced down at the file, head swimming. It was a newspaper clipping, the small article in the corner of a page photocopied onto an A4 page.

Two Dead in Intersection Crash

Two people have died in a tragic crash on Valentines Day. A taxi was hit by a speeding sedan who failed to stop at the intersection of Liberty Avenue and Van Wyck Express Way, killing the driver and taxi passenger and injuring the taxi driver. Stephanie Heile (19) was seen getting into the taxi just at the airport before the taxi collided just ten minutes later.

Surely… couldn't it be a different Stephanie Heile? 'But… but she just got off the plane,' he mumbled. 'After that flight from LCA.'

Shinichi nodded. 'It was on the trip to her hotel that the crash occurred. Someone might say she was simply in the wrong place at the wrong time.'

Pieces clicked together for Luc, like a metal puzzle touched in *just* the right place. 'Christopher didn't kill her. He sabotaged the plane and let history run its course.'

Shinichi nodded heavily. 'And he used ARCHIVE to place her just where she needed to be.' He held up a hand, palm up. 'Fate—' his other hand raised, tipping the balances until they were equal. '—Coincidence.'

Luc shook his head, suddenly feeling an urge to throw up. *Stephanie—dead? But she'd just gone there on holiday…* 'But why her?' he asked hoarsely. 'She wasn't special… was she?'

Shinichi's fingers tapped the chair in front of him soundlessly. 'I don't know. I couldn't find anything particularly noteworthy about her, aside from her death. I'd hoped that Haste could explain. He was mentioned by Alpine as being important.'

Laura took a deep breath. 'So…'

'Where is he?' Shinichi nodded. 'Good question.' His body twitched, like someone had walked over his grave. 'Well, there are two options. Either he has, as Laura would say, legged it, or he's Travelled back in time. I asked Movarian Labs to text me if any of the timeboxes – including the 3.0 – was used today.'

Laura looked at Luc questioningly, and he returned the glance. 'And?' he said.

'They sent me their spreadsheet,' he replied, getting out his phone. He tapped it a few times, scrolled, then his eyebrows rose. 'Well, it's been updated.'

Luc's stomach turned. *Please, don't make me Travel again,* he whimpered silently. *Hasn't my head been through enough? And I need to get Amber to a medical officer soon…*

'*Someone's* Travelled,' Shinichi murmured. 'To—'

'Let me guess,' Amber said, standing. 'To 1868.'

C ommander Haste opened his eyes, only enough to let a sliver of sunlight through. His stomach did a flip as he sat up, and his head felt ready to burst. He wasn't as young as he once had been, and had never Travelled with this new timebox, either. The Travel sickness was worse than it had been for a while.

He waited for his head and stomach to remember which way around they were meant to be, then stood experimentally, looking around as he did so. The hot Australian sun reflected painfully off the tin roofs of the small townhouses, but he ignored the village down the road.

A cemetery. Alpine had said he lived next to the cemetery.

That's just like him, he thought.

He dusted off his pants and jacket, trying to look like he belonged in the past, and was definitely not trying desperately to walk in a straight line. Passers-by gave him an odd look, but he didn't notice as he squinted into the trees.

Where's that cemetery?

There. Halfway up the mountain, more a cluster of grave-stones than a cemetery, and just nearby was a small weatherboard house that branched off the cemetery's path. *That must be it,* Haste decided.

He knocked on the door and waited, already sweating in the heat. Heat in November. Even as a field agent, he'd never gotten used to the whiplash of time travel.

The door opened a crack, then wider, and Alpine's face came into view. 'Sir,' he said, holding the door open for Haste to enter. The inside of the house was dark and cool, but still hot enough that Haste itched to take off his jacket. He followed Alpine into a small, primitive kitchen.

'How's history?' he asked, glancing around the horrible kitchen.

'Dirty,' Alpine replied. 'Would you like a drink?'

Haste gave a tight smile. 'Thank you, but no. Do you have everything packed?'

'I didn't bring much to start with,' he said, folding his arms across his chest. 'Most of this I acquired when I got here. Including,' he gave Haste a pointed look, 'my partner. I thought he was going to be left behind.'

Haste nodded. 'Yes, Goldwyn's being here was an unfortunate accident, and I too wish he'd never picked up that timebox in the first place.'

Alpine turned and went into another room, leaving Haste awkwardly in the kitchen. 'Your ARCHIVE agents really are special,' he called from a corner of the house. 'It was right there next to them and somehow both of them forgot to pick it up.'

Haste frowned, going to the doorway. 'So they didn't go back with it?'

Alpine came out of a room, shaking his head, carrying a full sack. 'Harry went back with it.' He grinned, as if to say, *see? They're idiots.*

This piece of information put an uncomfortable weight on Haste's chest. *If Holmes didn't use that timebox to get back,* he thought slowly, *how on earth* did *he get back? I didn't give him an ARC-researcher.*

His eyes narrowed at the timebox on the table in front of him. He'd found it on his desk. *Holmes, what are you doing?*

'Is there any way for us to get fingerprint access?' Alpine was saying. 'I told Harry to steal Lucky Holmes' fingerprints, but of course, that only worked once. And… the agents have gone.' He ducked his head slightly, staring intently out the window behind Haste. 'I… may have botched the whole thing. I wasn't thinking ahead.'

Haste sighed, putting thoughts of Holmes aside for later. 'I've told you many times, agent, that you need to weigh your actions against their consequences. You managed to stay in character for weeks, it was only when Holmes came, wasn't it?'

Alpine hesitated a moment, then nodded. 'I needed to keep her here, and she wasn't listening—'

'Well discuss it later,' Haste said, holding up his hands to silence the man. 'For now, let's go back to 2019. I can't be found missing for too long, and we need to prepare to finish this mission.'

Alpine nodded, handing the timebox over to Haste. 'So you can't? Put my fingerprints into it?'

Haste shook his head, trying to put a regretful twist in his mouth. 'That job belongs to the labs, and it would look suspicious if I asked for a non-ARCHIVE agent to be added.'

Alpine shrugged, watching as Haste fiddled with the controls. *Besides,* he added silently, *I don't want to put this much power into your hands.* He spun the virtual year dial slowly, carefully… *2016, 2017, 201—*

'Nice timebox,' said a voice, distinctively accented, from the hallway. 'Reminds me of one I lost two hundred years from now.' Alpine spun, his arms ready to fight, while Haste turned more slowly. He recognised the voice immediately.

'Agent Holmes,' he said slowly, lowering the timebox. He considered turning to face him, but he wasn't sure if his face had gone white or if it was just his imagination. Potential excuses ran through his mind, anything that could make it all seem like a misunderstanding. *Did the Trel-SMS not work? Did Amber tell him everything?* 'There you are,' he said finally, forcing a smile and turning halfway. He could see Holmes in his peripheral, leaning casually in the back doorway, but something stopped him from turning further to look him full in the eye. 'I heard you'd been injured on the field, and since you didn't have an ARC-researcher, I wanted to make sure you got back safely. Couldn't you find Agent Elkhoury?'

Holmes folded his arms. 'Mm,' he said. 'You didn't give me an ARC-researcher. Which makes me wonder—'

Haste cringed, almost saying the words with him.

'—who told you I was injured?'

Haste thought quickly. 'You hadn't contacted ARCHIVE in a long time. The mission was so simple, and you'd already been injured in the crash—'

'Oh, stop it,' said another, female voice from behind Holmes. The agent moved aside, revealing his partner. Haste's body went cold. He could twist words with Holmes, but with Elkhoury… he was guilty as sin in her eyes.

The Trel-SMS didn't work, he concluded, turning slowly. The cold look in her eyes was worse than Holmes'.

Well, if I'm guilty as sin, I can't get any worse, he decided, grabbing Christopher's sleeve and pressing the timebox's transport button.

He saw Holmes step toward him, his arms outstretched and eyes wide, but 1868 disappeared.

Location Unkown

L uc opened his eyes, his head throbbing in a now-familiar
way.

Despite having just Travelled with a newly-opened wound,
he felt pretty good. Much better than Haste, who had his head
in a wastebasket.

Luc stood up, wavering slightly. Amber was only just opening her eyes, and Christopher was sitting up and looking
around. He saw Luc, and slowly reached for his belt.

Does he have a gun? Luc wondered. *Did he have a gun this
whole time, and yet didn't use it?*

Sure enough, Alpine pulled a gun out of his belt and aimed
it straight at Amber's head.

Luc's heart hammered, and he jumped toward the man, just
as Haste yelled, 'Don't!'

Everything froze, Alpine's finger squeezing the trigger
slightly, turning slowly toward Haste. Amber's eyes flew open,
and when she saw Christopher, she yelped and scuttled backward. Luc was frozen, as though the smallest move would be
trigger Christopher.

'Idiot. Don't you know where we are?' Haste asked, finally getting to his feet. 'We're at ARCHIVE. One gunshot and the best agents in the world will be arresting you.'

Luc looked around the small room. Yes, the skyline outside the floor-to-ceiling windows was familiar. Another wall held a flat-screen TV, and in the middle of the room was a large white table surrounded by comfortable swivel chairs. In one corner was a small table covered with a small tablecloth, with an urn and box of tea sitting on top.

It was an ARCHIVE meeting room, not unlike the one he and the others had just met in.

So… we're back in the present?

Haste straightened his jacket and tugged his cufflinks. 'Stay here and guard them, Alpine,' he said. 'I have a meeting to attend.'

Oh no you don't. 'If you leave, we'll call for help,' he threatened, pulling out his phone. Alpine swiped for it, but Luc was quicker, holding it just out of reach. 'And even if you take this, we can still yell. People will hear and come running.'

'They'll believe me before they believe you,' Haste said calmly, putting a hand on the doorknob.

'And when they look up who Christopher Alpine is?' Luc asked. 'And what he was doing in 1868, of all times?'

Alpine flinched, and Haste's hand dropped from the doorknob. 'Agent Holmes,' he said slowly. 'I would have thought that by now you would have realised that words are my weapon of choice. If it comes down to me providing a rational explanation, I will out-rationalise you, rest assured.'

Luc had no doubt the Commander would. He had a reputation behind him as Commander of ARCHIVE, whereas Luc and Amber hadn't successfully completed a mission yet. *But what should we do?* he thought. *Wouldn't it be best for him to go to his—*

Oh. The Commander's meeting was probably Laura's, which she'd booked for Shinichi. They were still waiting for him, somewhere upstairs.

No, wait. Haste hadn't turned up for his meeting with Laura; they'd had to hold it without him because he'd been ten minutes late.

Something must have held him up.

Luc's aching head cried out in resistance. *Can't "something" refer to… something else?*

Si Periculum, he answered, running toward Haste.

He grabbed Haste's collar and crashed into the door, feeling the breath going out of the man. As Haste struggled and fought, Luc pulled out his phone, finding Laura's name in his contacts. *Curses, why did the earpiece stop working?*

'Your call cannot be connected—' came the polite voice through the phone. Alpine's fist made contact with Luc's jaw, sending him into even more foggy confusion. *Not connected?*

He tried again, with the same result. *I'm sure I have data,* he thought, wrestling again with Haste. His fist was closed permanently around the suit collar, adrenaline lending him strength that would never let Haste leave. Haste punched him in the stomach, and though he was winded, Luc focused on his grip.

A shot ran out behind him, and with the sound, Luc remembered that he wasn't the only person in the room. Frantically he glanced around, seeing Alpine, smelling the burnt gunpowder, still half deafened from the noise but putting all his energy into making sure four people were still standing.

Haste started moving under his grip, arresting his reluctant attention once more. The Commander wriggled his arms out of the jacket sleeves even as Luc held onto it, and as soon as he was free, he reached for the door handle.

Before he could open it, the door flew open, hitting Haste in the nose and sending him backward into Alpine. Luc saw the distraction, and went to grab the pistol out of Alpine's hand.

But Alpine was faster. He whirled around, a shot fired, and Luc half expected pain to lace through every inch of him.

For a moment, he couldn't breathe, couldn't think. His whole body tensed, his head lowered, but no new flash of pain came. Only the old flashes of pain in his head.

'Idiot,' Haste wheezed from under him. 'Useless, *useless* idiot.' Suddenly his eyes widened. 'London City Airport, 13 February, 1998!' Haste yelled.

What?

Luc spun, trying to glimpse what he was looking at. Amber—*there you are*—had the timebox in her hand, and she pressed it onto Christopher's chest, then said firmly 'Transport!'

Christopher and Haste disappeared, and the timebox fell onto the table with a clatter. On its screen began a countdown.

'Cancel,' Luc panted, and the countdown blinked out.

The ensuing silence felt too loud. Luc took a deep breath, stepping back to lean against the wall, savouring the adrenaline. 'Where were you in all that?' he asked, harsher than he'd intended.

Amber slumped against the table, her head down and her hair covering her face. Blood dripped from her chin, and every breath she took made a wheezing sound in her throat. She put a hand over her face, and a strangled sob escaped.

Luc frowned. 'Um… Amber?'

The gunshot, he remembered suddenly, alarm shooting through his nerves. His eyes ran over her body, checking for bloodstains. But while there were spots, there was nothing big enough for a bullet-wound that he could see.

'Amber, are you hurt?' He stepped forward, awkwardly holding out a hand, but not courageous enough to put it on her shoulder. Her other hand went to her head. 'Shinichi,' she gasped, her fingers clutching her head.

'What?'

'Shinichi needs help.'

He shook his head. 'I don't—'

Taking a deep breath, Amber pulled her hand away. Her face was tight, and a final tear fell from her eye, but she didn't seem injured aside from her lip. 'Luc, it's *Shinichi,*' she insisted, pointing.

He turned to look where she'd pointed, but couldn't focus. *Did she just*—'What did you call me?'

'Luc!'

I wasn't hearing things, he thought, bewildered. 'Do you—'

He saw what she'd been pointing at. Dark blood spattered over the white door, smeared in a thick line leading down to a slumped shape.

Not just a shape, Luc realised, forcing himself to look closer. A man.

A man in a black suit.

Luc knelt in front of the man, checking his neck for a pulse. Of course it was there, fast and strong, it was pumping blood out through the man's fingers as he clutched his stomach.

He didn't want to. He wanted desperately to pull a mask or a hood over the man's face and never have to confront his identity. But he couldn't. He dragged his eyes up the blood-stained jacket, the wrinkled shirt, the tense neck and jaw until he beheld the man who was most definitely Shinichi.

He was muttering something Luc couldn't hear. Amber gently pulled off Shinichi's jacket as Luc leant in, trying to listen to what he was trying to say.

'*Anatewa… dare… nani…*'

Luc didn't speak much Japanese, and what he knew was from *My Hero Academia* and *Naruto*. But it didn't take a native to know that *nani* means 'what'.

And somewhere I learnt that dare *means 'who'.*

Luc glanced at Amber, and she looked back at him, but couldn't offer any answers. *Does…* Luc frowned. *Does he not know who I am?*

'Amber,' he muttered, his voice hoarse. He cleared his throat and tried again. 'Amber?'

Still, she didn't respond.

'Amber?'

'Yes?'

'We need to call an ambulance.'

She shook her head. 'There's no phone range here,' she said, turning on her phone and holding it up. 'See? No bars.'

Luc stared at the phone, then found his own and turned it on. Sure enough, no bars.

That can't be right… unless…

With a sinking feeling, he stood and picked up the timebox from the table. Dimly, he registered the words on it.

17th December 2018

***

ARCHIVE, 11 March 2019

Shinichi was, perhaps, too good at hacking earpieces. He put his earpiece in his ear, and soon he could hear a familiar voice, as clearly as if they were speaking into his own ear.

Is my voice really like that? he thought briefly. *I didn't realise my accent was so strong.*

It didn't matter. Soon enough he heard, 'Mission complete. Well done, Tamara.' He ended all his missions like that. Then came that painfully high, too-long, beep.

He had only a few seconds to interrupt before the connection would be lost. 'Shinichi,' he said clearly. 'Yes, it's you.

From the future. Listen carefully to me.' He tried to push down the uneasy feeling in his stomach, and ignore the itching scar on his stomach.

'Go downstairs. Meeting room number G3. I'd tell you there's no need to investigate, but…' he swallowed, then risked a half-chuckle. 'But I suppose that won't make a difference will it?'

His insides twisted uncomfortable, and his scar started to hurt, as though it knew what he was doing. 'And be careful. One of the men has a gun. You need to help the young man and woman.'

His younger self didn't say anything for a moment, but it was fine. Shinichi remembered being stunned, remembered the piecing together of the pieces. Finally, through the earpiece, he heard, 'I will record this ARC-researcher's code. Is there anything else I need to know?'

Don't make any plans for the next few weeks, Shinichi thought, but didn't say it. He couldn't imagine what he would do if he thought that he might not walk away from this ordeal. Besides, he didn't remember hearing it.

'Just one more thing.'

17 December 2018, Archive

Always check the date, time and location with a
local before you start your mission.

I n the words of another great time traveller, *this is heavy.*

Luc put as much strength as he dared into trying to staunch Shinichi's wound, using the man's jacket as a make-shift bandage. Amber was next; she seemed to be in shock, but was coping well enough to be useful.

Luc wondered if he should be third on the treatment list. He was having trouble concentrating, his mind ringing with the thought, *She called me Luc! Not Lucky… not "Mr Holmes"… Luc! Like she used to!*

He decided that he'd be fine.

Obviously, Shinichi would too. After all, this was 2018, and he was still alive in 2019. *You can't change history.*

Luc wasn't sure how far he was willing to test that 'fact'.

Shinichi was still mumbling in Japanese. He was only half-conscious, delirious from shock and blood-loss.

'What's he saying?' Amber asked.

Luc shook his head. 'I only know enough to know that he's saying 'who' and 'what'.'

Amber's mouth tightened into a tight line. 'So this is what he meant,' she murmured.

Luc couldn't hold it in any longer. 'Do you… remember…?'

She watched him for a moment, then her face broke into a grin. 'I remember,' she replied, nudging him. She shook her head. 'Haste saying that date just brought all these pictures into my head—including what I found out in 1998. And Shinichi saying that he'd missed our first Christmas party.'

Part of Luc wanted to ask why Shinichi had told her that on her mission, but he decided to ignore it. The rest of him was just a puddle of happiness. *She remembers,* he smiled.

'When I got back from the mission, I asked Haste about what Christopher had said.' Seeing Luc's confused face, she shook her head. 'It was before you got back; you were still sorting some things out. I asked him, and he told me he was saving lives. He said that you can't change history, and if you try to, you'll end up like Nikki.'

Luc frowned. 'Like who?'

She shrugged. 'I was going to ask more, but he got a phone call, so I left. I checked for a Nikki in the ARCHIVE agent lists, and the closest was a past agent – Nikola Lazarov – came up. She'd died on duty during a mission to the early 1900s.'

Luc's heart hammered. Unbidden, Stephanie's face came to his mind, and he pushed the thought away. 'You think she tried to change history and died because of it?'

Amber shrugged, putting a hand on Shinichi's arm. 'I wonder,' was all she said.

'You…' Shinichi gasped. 'You are from the future?' He tried to shift his weight with a groan.

Luc gave a small nod. 'How did you know to come here?'

A small smile formed on Shinichi's lips. 'I'm a genius,' was all he said. He reached up to his face, fumbling with his left ear. 'He said to give this to you.'

Luc frowned. 'Who?' He looked into the man's ear and saw a small earpiece, identical to the one he was wearing in his own ear, that had linked him to 2019 Shinichi. Curious, he pulled out his earpiece and gently pried the small speaker from Shinichi's ear. His fingers were slippery with Shinichi's blood, and he swallowed, throwing a nervous glance at Amber, before transferring the earpiece into his ear.

'He—Hello?' he stammered.

'Lucky,' came a familiar voice. 'So it's over.'

Relief flooded through Luc. It was Shinichi. 'Are you the Shinichi from 2019?' he clarified, despite his confidence that he knew the answer.

'Yes, yes, I'm from 2019,' Shinichi said. 'Where's Amber?'

'She's here. We were going to call an ambulance—'

'Don't worry about that now,' Shinichi snapped. Luc blinked. *Don't worry about an ambulance? Does this man have a death wish on his younger self?* 'Where's Haste?'

Well, I know that one. 'LCA, 1998,' he replied. Shinichi could guess the specifics.

'Okay,' Shinichi said. 'That's your next destination. Use the timebox to go there.'

'Are you sure he'll be okay?' Amber asked as Luc stood up.

'Yes, someone will find me eventually,' Shinichi replied, and Luc relayed the message. '*You* need to find Haste. He's becoming more and more reckless. More dangerous.'

'What about our earpieces?' Luc asked. 'It doesn't work now we're not in 1868.'

'Give this one back to me, there's more I need to do. I'll reconnect, but it might take a moment when you get there. I'll connect Laura to Amber's earpiece too.' The clicking of a keyboard came through the earpiece, then there was a pause. 'Oh, Lucky, what's your address?'

Luc frowned. 'What do you—'

'I'll explain later. What is it?'

He slowly answered, then, at Shinichi's direction, pulled out the earpiece and gently stuck it back in the injured man's ear, silently apologising as he did so.

'What now?' Amber asked, and Luc held in a smile.

She sounds like her old self again, he thought, and didn't feel so bad this time. 'Now, we need to follow Haste,' he replied.

A mber opened her eyes, feeling numb and foggy. Sounds were muted, and the world spun in front of her. *Stupid Travel sickness.* As she woke slowly, the numbness was taken over by the blinding headache that had accompanied her memories. It had eased slightly, but as she sat up, it throbbed a steady rhythm in her temples.

She was in a large industrial cleaning room, and just a few metres away, Luc was still out cold.

'Shinichi?' she asked tentatively. They'd stocked up on earpieces just before going to 1868 to pick up Haste. *What a strange trip that turned out to be,* she mused. 'Laura?'

No reply. The earpieces must not have connected yet.

She closed her eyes, leaning her head against a cupboard until her head cleared somewhat. When she opened her eyes again, everything was less misty.

'Luc,' she called softly, but he didn't respond.

I wonder if his head hurts more after Travelling, she thought. In the midst of everything, they still hadn't made it to the doctor.

He must have had that bruise even before Harry attacked him, she remembered, frowning slightly. His chest rose and fell slowly; he could almost have been asleep if he wasn't on the cold linoleum floor of a cupboard. 'Didn't you stop and wait to recover from the car crash before you came to get me?' she said aloud.

'That's what I said!' came a voice in her ear.

Amber winced, the pain lancing from one temple to the other. 'Ah, Laura, you're back,' she said.

'Yep. You on the move yet?'

'Not yet. Lucky hasn't woken up. He needs to see a doctor.'

'You both do,' Laura said. 'You don't have any memories later than 1868.'

Amber smiled, going through moments in her mind that had previously been shut off. Birthdays with her parents, her first day at ARCHIVE, and the first time she'd met Luc. 'It was an eventful time in 2018,' she replied.

'*2018?* How did you end up there?'

She shrugged. 'I told you; it was eventful.'

More moments flashed in her mind, ones that she wished she didn't have to remember. She held up her hand, blood drying and congealing on her fingers. She swallowed. 'Shinichi's still there, right?'

'Yeah, he keeps texting me asking for coffee. It's quite alarm-ing.'

'Sounds like him,' Luc said, sitting up and rubbing his fore-head. Dried blood came off, but it was hard to tell what was his and what was Shinichi's. 'He knew what he was doing.' Suddenly, he grinned. 'Oh, oh! Laura! Guess what else happened in 2018!'

'Did you *finally* ask Amber out?' she asked.

He rolled his eyes, and Amber laughed. 'No,' he snapped. 'But she remembers everything now!'

Laura squealed, sending a jolt through Amber's head. Luc winced too, pulling out his earpiece. Amber wished she'd thought of it too. 'Oh, that's such a relief,' she said, her pitch so high it would be inaudible to anyone over seventy. 'I think I'm going to cry.'

'Laura,' Shinichi said, and she stopped, though her happy vibes continued to radiate through the earpiece.

Amber's heart gave a thud. 'Shinichi,' she said. 'You're okay.'

'I'm more than okay, I'm brilliant,' he replied. 'Now. Where are you?'

Despite herself, tears welled up in Amber's eyes. 'I know you're okay,' she said quietly. 'But still… we practically left you for dead—'

'I'm fine,' he said bluntly. 'I had other things to do.'

Luc raised his eyebrows. *What things?* Amber wondered, frowning.

'Where are you?' Shinichi asked again.

Amber scrambled to her feet. 'We're in a cleaning cupboard somewhere,' she said, moving for the door.

'Not too fast,' Luc complained, leaning back against a wall, an arm on a mop bucket. 'Some of us are concussed, you know.'

'So you admit it now?' Amber joked.

She wasn't sure if she had offended Luc. He looked at her with a strange, wistful look in his eyes, a small smile twitching his lips, then quickly looked away. 'Okay, I think I'm ready to go now.' He pulled his feet in under him and, leaning on the bucket, attempted to stand. Amber watched him carefully. She took a step forward, in case he toppled into the brooms, but he didn't even waver.

'Well done,' she said.

Luc nodded, tugging on his cuff-links with great bravado and assuming the air of a sheriff from a Western. 'Well, miss, when you've done that as much as I have, you don't really think about it so much as an accomplishment,' he said, and she had to laugh.

He grinned. 'Now, I've been thinking…'

'Wow, he *was* concussed,' Laura snickered.

Amber hid her smile and forced herself to focus on what he was saying. Luc seemed to ignore her. '…to find Haste, we need to know what his objective is. Now, Alpine already hijacked the plane, right?'

'Right,' Shinichi said. 'He'd just come back from that when Amber confronted him, and he didn't seem to recognise her.'

Luc nodded, his shoulders squaring. 'So they're here for another reason.' He looked at Amber, his eyes dark. 'Considering what Haste said in 2018, we can guess who he's after.'

Amber felt a rising coldness in her chest, and she gave a small nod. 'You think he wants to kill me?' she said slowly.

Luc nodded. He opened his mouth, as though trying to say something he wished wasn't true.

'I can bring her back,' Shinichi offered.

'No!' Amber said, perhaps too quickly. 'Well… can't we use this to our advantage? If he wants *me,* you'll need to know where I am… right?'

'You can direct us safely from 2019,' Luc said.

Good point. 'But… but what if something happens to you?' she asked desperately. 'Isn't that why we're sent in partners? In case something happens to one of us?'

Come on, Luc, she willed silently. *I've never finished a whole mission with you, and I really want to.*

But Luc just shook his head, seeming more certain now. 'Amber, you of all people should know by now that arguing about my safety isn't going to convince me.'

'Well maybe that's exactly *why* I should stay!' she pressed, stepping forward. 'Because *you* have so little concern for your own safety!'

Luc fell silent, but his jaw clenched and he looked away. *Stupid, stubborn…*

'You nearly *died* in 1868,' she went on. 'I took you to Alpine's house, and I watched you and made sure you didn't get worse. In fact, during the night, Christopher was going to try to kill you, I know he was, but he didn't, because I was there, and he realised he wouldn't be able to convince me it was your concussion. If I stay, we might survive. But if I'm not here, Haste will kill you and then come back for me.'

'If you hadn't taken me to Christopher's house, he wouldn't have tried to kill me.'

Amber opened her mouth to let him have it, but after a second of indignant spluttering, a cool Shinichi came to her rescue.

'I don't know how much of 1868 you remember, *Mr Holmes*,' he said with a chuckle. 'But I was trying to get something intelligent out of you and failed.'

Laura laughed. 'I've been trying to do that since I met him.'

Luc's eyes narrowed.

'Lucky, she has a point. But Amber, don't forget who brought you here,' she added gently. 'Lucky didn't go to 1868 with a bung head because he couldn't feel pain; it was because he was worried about you.' Amber tried very hard not to look at Luc's face, curious as she was. She stared at the bottom of the wall, and guessed that he was probably looking the other way too.

She tried to think of something to say, either to Laura or to Luc, but everything her mind thought up she rejected immediately. *Thank you, Luc,* seemed cheesy; *I know* seemed curt; a plain and simple *sorry* seemed best. But before she could say anything, Luc stepped forward and wrapped her in a hug.

He hugged her tightly, protectively, making it almost hard to breathe. But his body was warm and sad, like a doona on a cold morning, and for a moment she just closed her eyes and allowed time to stop.

I thought I wouldn't be able to do this, he seemed to be saying. *And I'll hug you a bit longer to make up for that.*

She gave him a squeeze. *Thanks.*

After a moment, he pulled back slightly, lightly touched her chin and smiled. 'All in a day's work.'

She knew she was smiling back, and wished she could say something witty, as though this was no big deal, and she was glad to be back. But her mind was frozen, her skin still tingling even as he moved away.

'Speaking of,' he said, as though nothing had happened. 'We need to find Haste in this airport, somehow.'

Amber tried desperately to come back to the moment. 'Haste knows I was at the boarding room after everyone got on the plane; so I think he'll be planning around that. I think we should wait there.'

There was a silence from everyone for a moment. *What happened? Did I speak too fast? Am I being weird?* she thought, glancing at Luc. He was beaming.

'Good thinking,' Shinichi said, and she could hear his wry smile through his tone. 'Lucky, you heard her. Boarding room.'

'Boarding room,' he repeated, finally moving to follow her. 'But if Haste gets too close for comfort—'

'We'll get backup,' Amber finished with a sigh.

'Good. Where is the boarding room?'

She made sure the hallway was clear before she stepped out, Luc just behind her. 'I remember,' she said, with a flush of excitement at being able to say the words. 'Follow me.'

Shinichi was typing something. 'And may the luck of the seven coffees I've had today be with us all.'

L uc followed Amber through the wide, echoing floor-space, finding it somewhat hard to concentrate on the mission. *She remembers,* he thought, feeling his face break into a grin.

Travellers and would-be tourists swirled around them looking up at signs and down at tickets, forgetting luggage and small children as they tried to find where to board. The people passed with alarmed looks, as though they knew at a glance that Lucky and Amber didn't belong in that time.

We kind of stand out without our luggage, Luc thought, but he realised that they weren't the only ones without bags. He looked at his hands, and realised what the problem was.

'Amber,' he said, and she turned around. 'I was thinking we should wash our hands.'

Amber looked down, her eyes widening. 'Your head was bleeding a lot,' she said loudly, which didn't quite help the stares.

Shinichi directed them to a nearby pair of bathrooms.

Luc watched the pink water wash down the sink, still mulling over what had happened in 2018. *Why would Shinichi send his past self to help us, knowing it would end in failure?* he thought. *At least tell him to get more backup.*

'Lucky,' came Laura's voice. 'You alone?'

Luc glanced around the bathrooms and confirmed it. 'But the others—'

'I had Shinichi put us on a different line for a moment. You said you wanted to talk to me about something.'

He turned off the tap, trying to think back through the eventful past few hours. 'What were we talking about?'

Laura hummed. 'About getting back to 2019 with Amber? You'd just come in to work.'

Luc nodded as he remembered. 'Oh, yes. About my mum.'

'Your mum?'

'Yeah. I'm worried she's a bit lonely since we moved here. I mean, she hasn't *told* me she's lonely, but she doesn't talk to anyone but me.'

Laura snickered; he knew what she was thinking and pointedly chose to ignore the insult.

But all she said was, 'There are worse people to be stuck with. But why do you want to talk about it now?'

Luc shrugged, pulling out some paper towel from the dispenser and wiping his hands. There was still some black under his fingernails, but not enough to concern any security officers. 'Well, Amber was at my house this morning, and… I think mum just liked having a woman to talk to. It made me think, maybe she misses having my sister around to… I don't know, do woman-y stuff with.'

Laura snorted. 'Maybe this is the world's way of telling you to get a girlfriend.'

Luc rolled his eyes as she laughed at him. But once he'd gotten over the initial dismissal of her suggestion, he realised that it actually held some merit. It would probably help to bring a new person into the house who could befriend his mum, give her someone to talk to, all under the guise of her being his girlfriend. It was a subtle enough ploy that she might not realise what he was trying to do.

The only problem was, he didn't know anyone he'd want to date.

That's not true. He forced the thought out of his mind.

Nevertheless, Laura's had been a good suggestion, and he was glad he'd asked her for help. 'You know, that might work,' he muttered.

Silence echoed through the connection, which meant he wasn't sure what expression she wore, or what she was thinking. Pride? Excitement?

'What, you'll actually do it?' she asked. 'I don't believe it.'

Luc shook his head. 'I didn't say that. I said that it *might work.*'

'Great,' Laura said. 'No time like the present. Go and ask her out.'

Luc sighed. 'Laura, have you ever considered that you might be hindering your cause by trying so hard?'

'You came to me for advice.'

Fair point. Luc stared at his stitches in the mirror, brushing some cold water over them to try to dull the pain. 'What are your thoughts on… asking someone twice? If they've already said no.'

There was silence as Laura tried to sort through his implications. After a moment, she seemed to give up and answer the question. 'It depends on when you asked her.'

He wasn't willing to give more information than he already had. He kept his mouth shut.

'I think twice is the limit,' she said. Because that backed up her advice.

Great, Luc thought numbly.

'Give it some time between asking, and it shows that you're still interested. If she changes her mind later, she'll know to come to you.'

Luc ran his fingers through his hair, trying to pull it down over the bruise.

'You've been through a lot together recently,' Laura said. 'And you have a dangerous job. There's no guarantee you'll live through the mission. Surely it's better to ask respectfully, than let the opportunity pass? The worst she can do is say no.'

There *were* worse things she could do. She could ask for a new partner. She could drop all contact with him. She could say yes, date for a while, then break up with him.

But Laura was right – they weren't guaranteed a trip home. Of all the ARCHIVE agents, Luc knew that best. After all, he'd lost his partner on a mission that consisted of a drive down the road to pick up a timebox.

But all the same… He shook his head. 'I don't know, Laura.'

'Lucky,' she said quietly. 'How will you know until you've asked her?'

I have asked her. He opened his mouth to say it, but he wasn't sure he trusted Laura with this information. He didn't want to embarrass Amber, and if Laura knew, she'd definitely bring it up with her. Probably in a confrontational way, like a mobster confronting a mole in an alley.

'I'll give you twenty-four hours to ask her out,' she said, before he'd formulated a plan. 'That's twenty-four hours according to your timeline.'

He sighed. 'And I have to ask her out before that time is up?'

'Yep.'

Luc raised an eyebrow. 'Or what?'

'Or I'll tell your mum about this conversation.'

Hmm. That's an effective threat. 'I'm telling you, Laura, she won't date me—'

'Luc?' Amber called, poking her head in the door. 'Are you talking about girls with Laura again?'

Laura laughed. 'Amber, this is the men's,' he called out. 'And what do you mean *again?*'

'You're a high fall risk,' she said. 'I had to make sure you were still conscious.' She flashed him a smile, and he felt everything he'd lost when she'd said no. 'Come on. Let's go get Haste.'

He threw his damp paper in the bin and sheepishly followed her. 'Right. Haste.'

Haste checked his watch, trying to do so without looking impatient. Of course, he was in 1998, and his watch was wrong.

'Where is he…?'

Finally, a staff-only door opened and Alpine came out, looking both ways as he stepped into the hallway. He held the door open, and behind him came Goldwyn. Both had changed into mock black security uniforms, with a cap hiding Alpine's blonde hair.

Goldwyn planted himself in front of Haste. 'Chris said you could explain,' he said bluntly.

Haste nodded. 'We've been found out.'

The man shifted his jaw, looking away. 'Who knows?'

Haste shrugged his shoulders, forcing his eyebrows to not frown. 'Just a few ARCHIVE agents. Nothing to worry *too* much about.'

Alpine grunted. 'No, it's not like ARCHIVE agents are any good, are they?' he said sarcastically.

Haste's eyes flicked over to watch him until he shifted his feet. 'Sorry sir,' Alpine said finally.

'Yes, ARCHIVE agents are good, but these particular ones are still green,' Haste said. 'You two don't realise that Holmes and Elkhoury haven't finished a mission yet. You two have completed more than fifty between you. Together you're worth at least ten ARCHIVE agents. This shouldn't be hard.'

Alpine nodded, to Haste's disappointment. He'd hoped the man would pick up on the disappointment in their worth being in their combination. He wasn't impressed with Alpine on his own.

It's going to be hard explaining Samejima's death when we get back, he thought, running a hand through his hair. *Why was the man at ARCHIVE anyway? He resigned about a month ago.*

He closed his eyes for a moment, taking a deep breath. At least now he didn't have to worry about the ex-detective. Perhaps he should be grateful.

Haste glanced at the assassin and all gratefulness left. 'The woman is the biggest liability,' he said. 'She's a witness.' *Because of you, Alpine,* he wanted to say, but he held his tongue. 'We're going to have to keep them quiet permanently. Obviously, this is a last resort. But a necessary one if we don't want our good fight to be stopped.'

Alpine frowned. 'The whole reason we went through the wiping of her memories and trying to keep her in 1868 was because you didn't want her to die.'

'Things have changed,' Haste snapped. 'You need to adapt, follow my orders. Yes, that's what I said last time, but *last time* everything was still confidential. Now, we can take more risks, be more open. Holmes is already injured. We'll deal with

Elkhoury here, and use his injuries against him in 2019. No one would be surprised if he, say, passed out while driving. Had a horrible accident. What a loss.'

'But sir,' Goldwyn said slowly, his eyes looking anywhere but him. 'I… don't see why we have to kill them. We're saving people's lives, aren't we? Keeping them from trying to change the course of history and making it worse. That's what you always told us. So if we're doing the right thing, why should we try to cover it up?'

Haste sighed deeply. 'Because others don't see it that way,' he replied. 'These agents are naïve and short-sighted. Like someone going into debt for a loved one, . And there's no way to convince them otherwise. They'll lock us up, and then no one will know the truth.' He shook his head. 'It's not ideal, but if it's what it's come to, it's the way it has to be. This way, we can go on keeping things as they should be, and no one has to know. They didn't have ARC-researchers; it will all be fine.'

Alpine didn't look at Haste, but he nodded once, and he decided he'd have to take that as good enough.

At least, I didn't assign them ARC-researchers, Haste thought, a small seed of doubt growing in the back of his mind. *Yet somehow they Travelled from 1868 to 2019.*

Somehow, he repeated, gritting his teeth. *I know how. I'd bet my life it was that Samejima's doing.*

Procrastination.

Being able to do something, having the means, motive and opportunity to do something, and yet, for no rational reason, not doing it.

It was a new experience for Shinichi.

Usually, he didn't see the point of it. He knew what needed to be done, whether it be housework or investigative tasks, and when he needed to, he found it easier to do it than worry about the task.

But as he lay in the meeting room, blood pumping rhythmically through his fingers into the ever-growing pool in his lap, his foggy mind contemplated how strange it was to procrastinate for the first time. He couldn't say why he wasn't getting up.

Why didn't I tell myself to get a bulletproof vest? he thought, annoyed. *Probably because there wasn't enough time between the end of the mission and the start of this.*

Well, I could just make a note to tell myself to get one when it's my turn to give the orders, he thought dizzily. *That'll test if I can change history or not.*

An interesting experiment.

He shook his head. Enough.

But he couldn't help lying there a moment longer. Lying in pain, almost hoping that the door would open and someone with heavy-duty painkillers would come and take him to a hospital.

He sighed. *I don't know if I can do this.* 'It doesn't matter,' he said to the empty room. 'I already have.'

He nodded to himself. *On three.*

One, two, three.

He rolled onto his side, using his elbow to prop himself up. *One, two, three.* Pushing all his strength into one arm, he snapped his arm straight until he was wobbling on his hand instead of his elbow. He swallowed, panting in pain and exertion. A bead of sweat dripped from his chin onto his shirt. He rolled onto his hands and knees and, painful step by painful step, crawled along the floor until he reached Haste's jacket.

I don't know the agents' names, and I don't think they're even agents yet, he thought. But technically he didn't have to. There had been something important dripping from the man's face.

He picked up the jacket, inspecting it carefully. Yes, there it is. Inside one pocket, and on the shoulder.

Blood stains.

Gripping the jacket in one hand, Shinichi leant on a chair and, before he could count in his head, pulled himself into a standing position. He stood for a moment, gasping in pain and wondering if he was about to black out and end up on the floor all over again.

His head cleared somewhat, and he took a step toward the door.

He glanced around the room with a numb sense of pity. There was a trail of red drips along the floor, decorated occasionally with smudges and handprints that made him feel sick. He buttoned his jacket in an effort to hide the damage, then went to the door.

Walking was somehow easier than standing still, so he used his momentum to carry him all the way to the elevator without stopping to talk or comment on the dripping trail behind him, even as he felt the eyes of everyone in the corridor watching him.

You're invisible, he told himself. *They won't notice.*

He pressed the elevator button with his one clean finger and wobbled as he waited. Finally the elevator dinged and the door opened. He stepped inside, sliding to the floor just before the doors started to shut.

It was a good thing that no one at ARCHIVE noticed him. He'd been working for ARCHIVE for eleven years now, and had helped agents with countless cases, but afterwards, they always went back to their cliques and left him be. It was quite lonely normally, but now it worked in his advantage.

Wouldn't you like someone to ask why you're pale? asked an annoying voice in his head. *They could complete your mission instead of you, and you could get to the hospital.*

Yes, he answered the voice, striding between the ARC-researchers' desks as quickly and casually as he could. *Yes, I would love for that to happen. But it won't. And it doesn't matter, because I can do it myself.*

The tricky part would be in the Travelling floor. There were always other ARC-researchers waiting, and they were bound to notice if he was acting strangely.

Maybe they can help.

One of the timeboxes was out of order, as it always had been. The other two, predictably, were in use. Nothing ever changed in the Travelling floor.

Taking a deep breath, Shinichi leaned tiredly against the wall of the room, Haste's jacket in one hand and notebook in the other. Thankfully no one was waiting in front of him; as soon as one of the ARC-researchers was done, it would be his turn.

While he waited, he opened his notebook, flipping through the pages to find one that was empty. He pulled a biro from the same pocket and, his hand trembling, wrote down everything he remembered.

Christopher Alpine – 1868

Nikola Lazarov, Italy 1990s

"Just saving lives"

One of the ARC-researchers – as he walked past, Shinichi realised it was Neil – finished his work and left the Travelling room, giving Shinichi a quizzical look as he passed. 'You alright, mate?' he asked.

As he spoke, the other ARC-researcher, Annastasia, looked up from her work and noticed him too. 'Goodness, you're very pale,' she said.

Shinichi wanted to shrug and say that he was fine, but it was all he could do to remain standing. He thought he muttered something in reply, but he couldn't have repeated it.

'He must be sick or—' Annastasia must have noticed the blood over his shirt. 'Oh, Samejima,' she said slowly, quietly. 'What on earth happened to you?'

'Just…' Shinichi tried to emphasise his words. 'Just let me… use the timebox…'

Wordlessly, the two agents moved aside and let him through.

Okay. Jacket. Notepad.

Shinichi signed in and selected Manual Travel on the time-box's tiny screen, then selecting Travel - Return. A few options came up.

Agent's ID | Agent's DNA | Select agent manually

His finger trembling, Shinichi chose Agent's DNA. A small red fingerprint was left on the screen, but he didn't have a clean piece of cloth to wipe it away.

He pulled up the jacket, stuffing the blood-stained fabric into the slot and not quite believing it would be enough. A few excruciating, exhausting moments went by before the machine finally beeped and told him that it accepted the sample.

The timebox clarified the agents, and he selected the two he'd seen before. Lu—lucky? And Amber? He shook his head. Westerners have such strange names. *Now. I want them to return, apparently.*

He glanced at the notebook. They were returning from 1868. He didn't know why he was doing this – was his future self so busy that he couldn't finish his own mission?

But there was one thing his future self had said had been taken care of.

Coordinates.

'Just get them to return,' he'd said. *'I'll do the destination part myself.'*

Is that why he needed the man's address? Shinichi wondered dizzily, pressing the button to confirm everything. He checked the time curiously. 'I'm ready,' he slurred.

'What happened?' Annastasia asked quietly.

Tiredly, Shinichi shook his head. 'I can't begin to explain,' was all he said.

He pulled the jacket out and stumbled backward, his eyelids and limbs heavy. *How much blood…* he thought dizzily.

Niel was saying something to him that he couldn't make out. A black haze closed in at the edge of his vision, and as Niel and Anna leaned over him, he realised he was back on the ground.

'Just—just wait a moment' came a voice in his ear. His voice, he realised. Not his voice, his future…

He gave up, and closed his eyes. Finally, the sounds around him faded into a comforting silence.

★★★

'Shinichi?' Lucky said, annoyed.

'Just—just wait a moment,' he replied, quickly muting the earpiece so that he could focus on his other ear.

Neil was still talking, and Shinichi ignored him. He couldn't even understand the man's New Zealand accent even when he was trying to, so it was easy to block out. He typed Activate into the code in his computer. Next to his desk was his notepad, with Luc's address scrawled across a random page.

He smiled, remembering posting the parcel to Luc's home as soon as the man had turned up at his house asking for him to be his ARC-researcher. It was a bit embarrassing that it had taken Shinichi so long to piece everything together.

A green light came on somewhere in the depths of the complicated program. *There,* he thought. *The THD in Lucky's home is activated.*

In his dizzy haze, he'd forgotten most of what had happened that day. He'd woken up in hospital, a note written shakily in his own handwriting and a painful wound in his stomach. No one had been able to explain much to him.

But he'd remembered the call from his future self. He'd had nightmares, hearing his own voice repeating the order to go to that room and beware the man with the gun.

I can't do it, he'd decided one morning, having woken up sweating and panting from one such dream. *I can't put anyone through that, not even myself.*

But he knew he'd have to one day.

So, in a last-ditch effort to change the unchangeable past, he'd resigned from ARCHIVE and left all the earpieces behind. *If I can't call the past,* he'd reasoned, *I can't call my past self.*

Shinichi felt sick, and foolish. He'd travelled across the world for this job; learnt a language for it; and now he was giving it up, telling himself he could change the course of history because to him, it was still his future.

As though he were any different to everyone else in history.

He shook his head as he left the Travelling room, his head down to avoid being seen by the ARC-researchers crossing the hallway ahead of him.

He himself had wondered how Lucky and Amber had gotten home. Now he knew.

He sat down at an empty desk like it was his own, and opened his laptop. He'd already done most of the hard work hacking his own earpiece from that mission; now he had to complete the final step and he'd be in.

After a moment, he could hear Lucky's heavy breathing. 'Lucky, you ready?' he asked.

Despite his panting, the agent still managed an exasperated sigh. 'Well, yeah, whenever you are!'

'Good. Anytime now,' Shinichi said. *Neil, when you're ready,* he said through to 2018.

It took a minute before finally the earpiece beeped and there was silence. Shinichi sighed in relief, closing his laptop.

They're safely on their way home now.

Luc shook himself, trying to force his concentration on the mission as he followed Amber and Shinichi's instructions through the labyrinth of an airport.

Haste sent Amber back to 1868, he told himself, though he still couldn't quite believe it. *He forced her to forget who she was.* It still felt like a dream, or the plot of a book.

The more he thought about it, the crazier it seemed. He was second-guessing all of Haste's actions and decisions now, and he didn't know which were rational and which were paranoid. *He sent us to Movarian Labs without ARC-researchers,* Luc remembered. That was pretty sinister. *Then he sent me to 1868 without an ARC-researcher too.* Definitely sinister.

Then he forgot about Laura's meeting.

He shook his head. That was Haste being sinister elsewhere and forgetting to be normal.

And now I have to ask Amber out before Laura tells my mum I'm matchmaking her friends.

He grimaced, rubbing his eyes tiredly, avoiding the bruise on his face that, despite everything, throbbed like an old annoying neighbour.

Really, Laura? he wanted to yell. *It's a bit off-topic at the moment.*

He risked a glance at Amber, striding confidently beside him. Her jaw was set stubbornly, and her eyes were directly forward, her stride fast enough that he had to speed-walk to keep up. Despite everything, he felt proud of her.

'Something on my face?' she asked.

He looked away, trying not to smile. 'Nothing,' he replied.

Laura snickered in his ear. *Would she really tell Mum though?* he wondered, then had to shake himself again. *Stop getting distract—*

What he saw immediately brought his mind back to the mission. They'd come to the line for passport checks; Amber had made to push through the crowds, ARCHIVE badge in hand, but Luc grabbed her wrist and pulled her to a halt.

'What—'

He shook his head, his eyes wide as he discreetly pointed ahead. Amber followed his gaze and her eyebrows rose.

Halfway down the line for the tickets stood Amber. Though she was a few months younger, Luc was surprised that she looked exactly the same now as she did there. Sure, on closer inspection, her skin might have gotten a little bit darker, maybe she'd lost a tiny bit of weight in 1868, and if he'd taken a ruler to her hair, it would be slightly longer now, but somehow he'd expected her to be... more different.

'So that's what I look like in third person,' Amber said quietly. Luc had to laugh.

But if Amber's here… his gaze travelled up the line slowly, person by person, until he found her.

A painful lump caught in his throat at the sight of the young woman, with her short red hair and glint of wanderlust.

Stephanie Heile.

He didn't realise he was moving until Amber caught his wrist. 'Where are you going?' she hissed, and he opened his mouth to give an answer before realising he didn't have one.

'I need to warn her,' he muttered, feeling dazed. 'I need to stop her from getting on the plane.'

'It's Stephanie, isn't it?' Shinichi asked.

Amber sighed. 'For your benefit, Shinichi, Luc just nodded.'

'Ah. Lucky, listen to me. You can't change what happened to Heile—'

'I could steal her passport,' Luc said slowly. 'Then she won't get through security.' It wasn't as though he had quick fingers; he'd probably get arrested if he tried. But wouldn't it be worth saving the poor girl's life? Even if she never knew what he'd done, it would be worth it.

I wonder what the punishment is for stealing someone's passport, Luc thought.

'Luc, no,' Amber said. 'To get to her you'll have to go past me. I'll recognise you immediately!'

'Then *you* go.'

Amber shook her head. 'No, Luc, that's not the point.'

'Then what *is* the point?' Luc snapped, pulling his wrist from her grasp. 'We're going to "finish our mission" and leave her to *die?* What's the point of finishing the mission then? Amber—'

he swallowed the lump in his throat, glancing at the oblivious woman again. 'I talked to her, just before she left for the hotel. She wanted to buy lunch for me and Carl, to say thank you for helping the plane's passengers. And we refused.' He stepped back from her, and tears started to fall from his eyes. He let them fall; he didn't care that he was scaring Amber or making a fool of himself, all his guilt and shock finally forming itself into words. 'No one else on the plane thanked us,' he said quietly. 'And no one else died.'

He turned back to Amber, grim determination settling in his eyes. 'I have another chance to stop this, and save her life. I can do it. Just give me two minutes. Haste won't go anywhere, I'll… I'll just talk to her or *something* and then we can keep—'

'Lucky,' Shinichi said quietly, but Luc gritted his teeth. He knew what the man was going to say, and didn't want to hear it. 'Lucky, you can talk to her.'

Luc blinked, frowning slightly. *Surely I misheard—*

'You can talk to her, but it won't change anything,' Shinichi went on. Luc rolled his eyes. *Nope, I heard correctly.* 'We know from history that she will get on the plane, the plane will be delayed, and when she gets to New York she'll be killed in a crash, and—'

You can't change history, Luc thought as the man finished his sentence.

'You need to get Haste,' he continued. 'Leave her to her fate; it's what's best. Even if you think that you've changed history, it will just right itself.'

Amber was watching him carefully. Tentatively, she put a hand on his arm, but he shook her off.

The guilt and sadness in the pit of his stomach had turned to a cold anger. *I don't want to work for an organisation that gives up as soon as something's written down,* he thought, his eyes narrowing. *I want to work for somewhere that fights for people's lives, even when it seems hopeless.*

As he put that nameless feeling into words, he realised something else.

'You're the same as Haste,' he said quietly. A million things ran through his head; explanations and evidences and defences, but he left it at that. It was a challenge, left open for whoever was brave enough to take him on.

Nobody said anything for a long time.

Finally, Shinichi sighed. 'Almost,' he said quietly. 'Almost, but not quite.'

Luc's anger slowly died as he contemplated Shinichi's response. Somehow, it helped to know that he wasn't the only one who hated himself. Not just himself, but his job, his boss, his mission.

And his decisions.

'Shinichi,' he said, wiping his eyes with the back of his hand. 'If I'd agreed to have lunch with her…' he took a deep breath. 'Would it have changed anything?'

Shinichi swallowed. 'I don't know.'

Luc nodded. 'So isn't it worth a try? In case it *would* have changed something?'

Shinichi didn't say anything, though Luc could hear him rubbing his face.

Beside him, Amber nodded. 'I'll go,' she said quietly.

Luc blinked. 'What—what do you mean?'

'I'll go talk to her,' she said, stepping back with an unsteady smile. 'She doesn't know who I am, so it shouldn't be a problem later on, whereas she'd recognise Luc.'

'I—I don't know what to say.' He hadn't expected to actually convince anyone that he was right. It felt like a very new experience.

'Don't say anything,' she smiled. 'Leave the talking to me.' Her forehead creased slightly and she bit her lip. 'Though I don't entirely know how this is going to work either. Which one is she?'

Luc glanced back at the queue, quickly finding her again. She'd moved up a few steps, and was studying her passport as she waited. 'She's the red-head in the grey cardigan,' he replied, trying not to lose sight of her.

Amber nodded, giving him a last squeeze on the arm before setting off for Stephanie. She threaded through the queue, between families and suitcases, apologising as she went and occasionally flashing the ARCHIVE badge at indignant travellers.

Finally she made it to Stephanie's side. 'Is this her?' she breathed, her voice coming clearly through Luc's earpiece.

'Yeah, that's her,' Luc replied, wishing he *could* breathe.

'I feel like I'm asking her out for you,' Amber muttered, then reached forward to tap her on the shoulder. 'Hey—'

Stephanie turned, and Amber took a small step back. 'Oh, I'm so sorry. I thought you were someone else. My mistake.'

Stephanie gave a smile, shaking her head at Amber's apology. 'Don't worry, I do that too,' she said. 'Is this your first time going to New York?'

Amber's smile wavered slightly. 'Visiting a friend there,' she said after a beat. 'Hey, do you…' she trailed off, shrugging one shoulder uncertainly. 'Do you ever get nervous flying?'

Stephanie shook her head. 'Not really, though to be honest, this is my first time flying without my parents. I'm more nervous of customs than anything, though. It's such a pain.'

Amber nodded politely, and Luc gritted his teeth. *What could we say that would make her give up?* he thought. 'Wasn't there a major flying disaster recently?' he asked desperately.

'I'll check,' Shinichi replied. Luc could hear the keys clicking on his keyboard as he did a search. 'Just ten days ago a plane crashed in Mindanao,' he said. 'One hundred and four people died in it.' A moment later, he added, 'That's the best I can find here.'

Luc watched Amber give a small shrug. 'Yeah, I suppose it's just me. It's only, since that plane crashed in… um…'

'The Philippines,' Shinichi said.

'…in the Philippines about a week ago, I just can't help but think that… maybe the next plane I get on might not land safely.' Amber swallowed and continued slowly. 'Sometimes things happen that we can't expect, and then, even though the consequences are painful, it's not our fault. Still, it takes a lot of courage to follow through with it, knowing the danger.'

Stephanie didn't say anything. She looked at Amber suspiciously, even after Amber finished talking and all that was left was an awkward silence that hung in the air.

'Are you trying to tell me not to go?' she asked eventually, sounding vaguely hurt.

Amber's head swivelled as she looked back at Luc. She turned back to Stephanie and licked her lips. 'Would you listen to me if I said yes?'

Stephanie's mouth smiled even as her eyebrows frowned, and she gave a shake of the head. 'Nope,' she replied confidently. 'Enjoy your stay in New York.'

Amber nodded as Stephanie moved up the queue, leaving her behind. 'You too, Stephanie,' she said quietly. Her head came up and she stepped back up to the other woman. 'Hey, just…'

Stephanie turned around, but even from the distance, Luc could tell she was just being polite.

'Just don't take public transport for granted while you're there,' Amber said, forcing a smile. 'The Tube is cheaper than taxis.'

The Subway in New York, Luc thought, though he wasn't sure why she'd brought it up.

But Stephanie was nodding. 'Thanks. I'll keep it in mind.'

Luc hadn't spoken a word to Amber since she'd come back from talking to Stephanie. She wasn't sure if it was because he was still angry, or disappointed, or just didn't know what to say.

'You're the same as Haste,' he'd said. The words were on repeat in her mind, like she was a punching bag and he kept pummelling into her. Those words, and another phrase she remembered being attributed to a few men. *All that's needed for evil to succeed is for good men to do nothing.*

She wasn't sure she'd ever know whether walking past Stephanie would make them as evil as Haste's orchestrating her death. But she'd attempted to silence the debate by agreeing to talk to Stephanie.

They were close to the boarding room now. Luc followed her through the halls to the room she remembered, crowded with its sliding doors and dated décor.

'Luc,' she said, just before they went in. 'Are you still mad at me? Because we're about to meet Haste, and I don't want to do that if we're not on the same page.'

He shook his head. 'Why would I be mad?'

'You're very quiet.' She looked away. 'I'm worried about you. You're not usually this…' she tried to think of the right word. Depressed? Quiet? '…pessimistic?' she finished, though it didn't feel quite right.

He inhaled deeply, rubbing a hand over his face. 'It's been a long day,' he said finally, and she nodded sympathetically. 'But I'm not mad at you,' he said quietly. 'I'm really proud of you. And glad that you're my partner.'

Amber glanced at him, a reply ready, but forgot her words as soon as she looked at him. He was smiling at her, a warm, proud smile, but behind his eyes, he was still hurt. *No, not hurt,* she realised. *Conflicted.* But even that didn't seem like quite the right word.

Too late, she realised she was staring. 'I—' she cleared her throat and tried again. 'Thanks and… um…' She forced a confident smile. 'Same, Luc.' She glanced away, but not quick enough to see how his eyes changed.

He's really expressive, she thought to herself, risking another glance his way. The resignation had gone from his eyes, and his smile was genuine now.

She cleared her throat again, hoping it would somehow clear her brain too. 'Well, let's get this over with,' she said briskly. 'I met Alpine in the boarding room, when he came back from the plane. I doubt they'll wait *in* there, in case they meet a younger Alpine, or myself. If they *are* looking for me, I suspect they'll wait until everyone else boards the plane.'

'It makes sense,' Laura confirmed. 'They know you're going to stay behind. It seems like the perfect opportunity.'

Amber nodded. 'So all we have to do is search around the boarding room, and if we don't find them, we'll just wait a bit longer and search again.'

Luc nodded slowly, standing straighter as they clarified the task. 'We'll search together,' he added.

'Of course.'

Too nervous to go into the boarding room where her younger self was waiting, they started in the hallways surrounding the boarding room. It didn't take long to find the pair – plus a less-dishevelled Harry – having a meeting just around the corner to the boarding room.

'We've found them,' Amber breathed.

'They seem to be having a meeting,' Luc added.

'Can you hear what they're saying?' Shinichi asked.

'No, they're speaking too quietly.' Amber clenched her jaw in determination. 'Alright. I have a plan. Luc, you have the timebox ready to go home. You need to run up to him quickly and Travel back to 2019 with him, before he has a chance to run.'

Luc raised an eyebrow. 'And you'll take on Harry and Christopher on your own? Seems fair.'

If she was honest, Amber hadn't thought her plan through that far. 'That's a good point.'

'Haste has nowhere to run,' Shinichi said, sipping yet another coffee. Amber tried her best not to judge him and be thankful for all the luck he was bringing them. *We're going to need it.* 'Just corner them and they'll either fight or surrender.'

'It's the fighting I'm afraid of,' Laura argued.

Luc glanced at Amber uncertainly, and she shrugged. 'It's our only option,' she said after a moment. 'If we wait much longer, they'll be gone.'

Luc nodded, and quietly counted to three. On three, they stepped out from the corner, Luc yelling, 'Surrender and put your hands in the air!'

Harry jumped, whirling, and Alpine reached for his pistol. Haste just turned silently, cocking his head when he saw them. 'Or… what?' he asked.

Luc glanced at Amber, nudging her behind him, then held up the timebox in front of his chest. 'Okay, we don't have a weapon, but we have a shield.'

'That won't stop a bullet,' Haste argued, and Luc's eyes hardened.

'I'm counting on it,' he said quietly.

No, Luc, Amber wanted to say, but his face was so serious, his eyes were so determined, and his stance was a challenge directed at Haste. *Go ahead,* he seemed to be saying. *Tell Alpine to shoot me and he'll destroy the timebox.*

And you too, Amber wanted to add, tears coming to her eyes. 'Luc—' she hissed.

'You might be able to get around killing Stephanie Heile by calling it "fate",' he said, ignoring her. 'But if you shoot us, it's downright murder. And—' he turned his head, showing Haste his earpiece. 'You can't hide it from ARCHIVE anymore.'

Haste's eyes flashed. 'Who is it?' he demanded.

'Like we'd tell you.'

Haste grabbed Alpine's pistol, shot it into the ceiling, making both Luc and Amber jump. He levelled his arm to Luc's head, plaster dust flittering around them and mingling with the smoke from the pistol. Luc watched the barrel of the pistol warily, keeping the timebox level with his chest. 'Tell me who you're in contact with!' Haste demanded.

'Sir—' Christopher said.

'Shut up. Holmes?'

Shinichi and Laura said nothing, but Amber could hear their uneven breathing through the earpieces. 'No!' she spat back. 'Why would we? You'll just kill them, or take away their memories, or—'

Haste stepped forward, moving the gun to her. 'You. I should have made Goldwyn kill you in that car crash. It would have saved me that much stress *and* it would have definitely worked.'

'Woah, that's a confession and a half,' Laura said. 'Shinichi, can we record this? I just want to watch him worm his way out of it in court.'

'I'm recording it,' Shinichi replied.

Don't get too smug yet, Amber wanted to scream. *He's holding a gun to our heads.*

She wanted to see the court case too. Or at least live long enough to miss it.

'So tell me who you're in contact with,' Haste said smoothly. 'Or I'll find out later one way or another. Everything you say will be on record.'

Amber stepped behind Luc. 'Distract him,' she whispered to him, hiding her mouth with his shoulder. He glanced at her, his eyes wide, then his eyes flickered back to Haste. 'I'm counting on that too.' he said firmly. 'It's over.'

'Hey, ARC-researcher,' Amber whispered under her breath.

'Uh… yes?'

'Can you have the timebox ready just in case? We can't get ours ready without Haste catching on. Just be ready to pull us back to 2019 if we say so.'

'Okay,' Shinichi said, and she heard chair wheels rolling on the floor. 'And Haste too?' he asked.

Amber glanced at the man. More than anything, she wanted to leave him here, or, better yet… 'Can you prep him to be sent to the Antarctic in 400BC?'

Shinichi chuckled. 'Of course, but no. Justice is here.'

Amber sighed. She'd known that would be the answer, knew it was the *right* answer, but it still felt too much like poetic justice to put it out of her mind completely. 'Yes, sure. Um, yeah, if you can, prep him, Harry and Christopher too.'

'What are you stalling for?' Haste asked suddenly, pulling Amber's attention back to their conversation. 'Is back-up coming?'

Amber took a deep breath, wishing her hands would stop shaking and stepping out from behind Luc. 'We're ARCHIVE agents,' she said. 'We don't need backup.'

Haste's mouth curved in hatred, and his hand shook. 'Like I said,' he said quietly. 'I should have killed you when I had the chance.' He swivelled the gun to Amber, and, as though in slow motion, she watched his finger tighten on the trigger. Her breath quickened involuntarily, and she wanted to run, but for some reason she couldn't move.

'Now!' Luc yelled.

Everything continued like the world had slowed down for commentary. Amber watched Haste flinch, watched his hand convulse, pulling the trigger, and, most horrifyingly of all, watched as his body, and hand, jerked around to Luc's head.

The sound of the gun was deafening, yet somehow also muted. The bullet swam through the air toward them, slower than Amber had expected yet still impossibly fast.

'No—'

The last thing she saw was Luc's body jerking back in the air before 1998 disappeared.

11 March 2019, Archive

Amber opened her eyes. The room around her was fuzzy, as though she was looking through a dirty camera lens. She blinked and sat up, and the blurriness slowly disappeared.

'Don't move,' said a voice. She looked up. There was a pistol levelled at her head, close enough that she could feel the heat still radiating from the barrel. At the other end was a man, turned away from her to watch something to his right.

Haste.

Amber blinked again and her vision cleared. *Tears?* she realised.

Why am I crying?

Horrified, she looked down at her clothes, held up her fingers. The wetness on her face wasn't just tears.

It was mixed with red too.

And her clothes were spattered with millions of drops of blood.

A lump caught in her throat, choking her. She wiped her face, making her hands red and slippery. As hard as she tried, she couldn't get rid of the stuff; every move she made seemed to make it worse.

'Don't move!' Haste ordered, moving the gun closer. She jerked her head away from the heat angrily.

'Where is he?' she choked, trying to crawl around him. *Maybe he Travelled just before he was shot,* she thought. *Maybe he's still—*

Haste grabbed her arm and wrestled until she was still. 'Alpine!'

From behind him, a groggy Christopher came forward and knelt next to her. 'You did something to her,' he muttered, then pushed her shoulders back against the wall.

'Where is he?' she shouted. She couldn't breathe. Her chest was too tight; her throat felt like someone had shoved rocks down it and she couldn't stop shaking. *Why is the world so fuzzy?* she wondered. *I can't see!*

She blinked, and the fuzziness left once more. 'Where is—'

'He's there,' Alpine said, pointing toward the floor-to-ceiling windows. She followed the direction, but could only see chair and table legs. On the carpet was a dark stain, a trail leading away from it and under the table.

There was a beep in her ear, then a familiar voice. 'Amber?'

Shinichi, she thought. Her chest tightened, and this time the tears didn't hang around long enough to blur her vision.

'Where are you?' she whispered, her mouth away from Alpine's line of sight. 'He—he killed Luc. He—'

'Amber, pull yourself together and listen to me,' Shinichi said. 'Back-up is on the way. Haste wants to kill you, but he doesn't know who your ARC-researcher is. So don't tell him that, and he can't kill you. Understand?'

Somehow, his logic penetrated, and she whispered, 'I understand.' Swallowing painfully, she focused on breathing deep, even breaths.

Slowly, her mind cleared. *Don't tell him who my ARC-researcher is and we have the upper-hand,* she told herself.

Okay. I can do this.

Haste tossed the gun to her, telling Alpine to leave it. 'Don't even think about it,' he warned Amber. 'I've taken all the bullets from it, and if you try to use it as a weapon, it's three against one. But if you cooperate, no one else will get hurt.'

Amber looked at the gun, her mind whirling. *Deep breaths. Don't say anything.*

Haste dropped the gun under a chair and went to the door. Glancing around the room, he nodded once, then opened the door and yelled, 'Call an ambulance!'

Amber's head came up. *An ambulance? So… Luc's still alive?*

She looked around, straining against Christopher's hands. His face looked so horribly hard now, she could remember thinking he looked kind and welcoming, but now the scene he'd just witnessed in 1998 was searing itself into his features. It wasn't an improvement, but, she supposed, it was more truthful than the kind twinkle in his eyes.

Is that…? Her throat tightened again, and she jerked forward against him. There, beyond the table, guarded by Harry, she could see Luc's shoes, his legs, the colour of his shirt…

Her heart stopped.

A dark red puddle was soaking into the carpet around Harry's feet. He stepped to the left, and she could see Luc's head.

No.

She slumped back against the wall, the now-familiar tightness forming in her chest. *His hair's supposed to be blonde,* she wanted to scream, but the words locked up her throat.

Haste was talking, she realised, in that calm, patient tone that Luc had once described as patronising. Like he was talking to teenagers about the importance of doing their homework, he'd said.

She'd found it funny at the time.

'It's because she was trying to change history,' he was saying, shaking his head. 'I've always said that we can't change history. Always.'

Someone was at the door, and they said something; it was too quiet for her to hear.

'Exactly,' he replied. 'The past doesn't change, but the people from the present do. And it's always for the worst. Like here, she tried to save a young woman, and ended up killing her partner.' He shook his head. 'But please, find security and call an ambulance. She needs to go to a hospital; and if she tries to escape, I don't want her to hurt herself.'

Amber's eyes narrowed. Something Haste had just said stuck in her mind, like the lump in her throat that stopped her from speaking. *The past doesn't change, but the people from the present do. And it's always for the worst.'*

She remembered thinking once that Haste pretended to be eloquent, but really he only said the same things over and over again.

Like now.

The past doesn't change, he'd told her once. *And,* she remembered, *he mentioned Nikki.*

Nikola Lazarov.

'She'd died on duty during a mission to the early 1900s.'

'You think she tried to change history and died because of it?'

Pieces started clicking together in Amber's mind.

'Nikola Lazarov,' she said.

The door closed, and Haste turned to Amber, watching her with an eyebrow raised. 'So you did listen to me,' he said.

Goldwyn's head came up. 'Who's Nikola Lazarov?' he asked. Alpine rolled his eyes.

Her head had felt like it was spinning, like she couldn't keep up, but with that name, everything seemed to grind to a halt. Haste stopped moving, he just watched her.

'Nikki is the proof that you can't change history,' Haste said quietly. 'And believe me, we tried.'

Amber didn't trust herself, so she closed her mouth.

'There was a little girl, about seven years old, caught in a house in the landslide,' Haste said. 'Every time I tried to save her, I was too late. I Travelled back four times to save her, and in the last time, Nikki decided to try it together.'

He sighed heavily. 'She made it inside, which was more than I could have done. And the house collapsed and killed them both.'

His eyes flashed. 'Elkhoury, you can't change the past. Only the present. That's what I learnt then, and that's what you've learnt now. That girl needed to die. If she didn't, someone from the present would have died with her.' He swung his arm like an auctioneer with a piece of art, his gesture taking in Luc's motionless body. 'As he did.'

Amber knew there was some ARCHIVE adage that Haste's logic always made sense, even if it was wrong. Her mind raced through possibilities, rebuttals, exceptions but it was all too sound. *You can't change history. You can only change the present. But…*

The sound of chair wheels rolling backwards distracted her. She turned her head toward it, but of course, the chairs in this room had steel legs, not wheels. Besides, it was too quiet and distant.

Shinichi, she realised, hope forming in her chest. *Is he coming?*

Just a few more minutes, Shinichi had said. *Surely that was a few minutes ago now.*

She looked over at Luc's body. It was true; he *had* died for Stephanie. And they hadn't saved her, either. She had still died in that horrible crash. So—

'Then what is *the point?'* Luc had asked. It felt like so long ago, but the words were still ringing in her ears painfully. *'We're going to "finish our mission" and leave her to die? What's the point of finishing the mission then?'*

Amber swallowed. 'I'd rather die trying to save Stephanie than live knowing I caused her death,' she said quietly.

Haste shook his head. 'Wonderful sentiment,' he replied, deadpan. 'But it only works when it's *your* life in the balance. I'm the one who has to explain to agents' families what happened.'

Amber looked up, the cold anger returning and squeezing her chest. 'So you're going to tell Luc's family what happened to him?'

She forced herself not to glance at the door. *Shinichi's coming,* she told herself, forcing deep breaths. She wasn't sure how long she could keep herself together.

Haste glanced at her, then nodded. 'I'll tell them about your efforts to change history,' he replied. 'And that they got him killed.'

Shinichi, where are *you?*

'*My* efforts got him killed?' she yelled. She tried to stand, but Christopher pulled her down roughly, forcing her still. Well, he could immobilise her, but he couldn't silence her. 'Who held the gun, Haste?' she screamed. 'Who pulled the trigger? You blame *his* death on *me*, and Nikola's death on "history". When will it become *your* fault?'

'I do what must be done,' Haste replied, with that infuriating calmness of his. 'I save lives. If you hadn't stepped in, only Stephanie would have died!'

Shinichi! Where are you? she wanted to scream. *I can't do this any longer!*

'If you hadn't gone back all those times—' something stopped her, something that left her cold, though she couldn't say why. 'Wait, how *did* you go back four times on that mission? I didn't think ARC-researchers could do that.'

Haste shook his head. 'They can't. And when I talked to mine afterwards, he knew nothing. He insisted that he lost connection with us and only reconnected just before the accident.'

An idea came to her, but she pushed it away. *No, Shinichi wouldn't do that,* she thought. *He wouldn't meddle in something from so long ago…*

But he'd meddled in his own past life. Sent himself into a room when he *knew* he'd end up injured.

She couldn't wait any longer. Her head was pounding, and she wanted to cry, scream, and sleep. She was *so* tired. Where was Shinichi? What was taking him so long?

She couldn't help but wonder if he was next to a Timebox, listening to Haste's conversation with Nikola Lazarov, and facilitating their Travelling from so far into the future.

You're as bad as Haste…

She shook her head, trying to stop it from spinning. 'Where—' No. She couldn't let Haste know that she was still in contact with her ARC-researcher.

'I'll just be a few minutes more,' Shinichi replied. 'Hold on there, Amber, you're doing well.'

She could hear the tension in his voice. The distractedness. The guilt.

'Don't you dare,' she whispered. 'Don't even think about it.'

A beep came through, a distant one, and she heard his breathing pattern become more ragged, uneven.

'I have to,' he replied hoarsely. 'If I don't, then none of this will happen. Nikola will still be alive, and Haste probably won't even become Commander.'

You're as bad as Haste, Luc had said. At the time, she'd thought he was being dramatic.

But now she understood.

'She's still in contact with her ARC-researcher,' Haste said, his eyes widening.

Christopher shoved her against the wall. He locked one arm across her chest and pressed it back, then with his other hand he pulled out her earpiece and put it in his own ear.

Amber struggled, but with each movement he just pressed harder, and she was pushed painfully back into the hard plaster. She tried to snatch it back, but her arms were pinned, and she could only reach feebly with her hands. 'No! No, Shinichi you—'

'Ah, it's Agent Samejima, back from the dead,' Haste said, a smile twisting his lips. 'I should have known.'

Christopher nodded. 'I think that's who she said they were talking to in 1868, too. This is definitely Sammy-whatsit,' he said, pulling out the earpiece and crushing it.

Haste nodded to Goldwyn. 'You know what to do?' he asked, not turning to see the man's nod. Harry left his post by Luc's body, winking at Amber as he opened the door and left.

Amber was struggling to keep up. Her head was spinning, throbbing. *I…* the truth came crashing down on her. *I've just killed Shinichi. He's going to die, and it's all my fault.*

But maybe Harry will kill him before he gets a chance to help Haste, she thought.

She felt horrible for it, but it gave her a little hope.

Shinichi was killing Nikola. He was setting up Haste to kill Stephanie, send her to 1868, and kill Luc.

And, to make it worse, he *knew* that what he was doing was wrong.

You're as bad as Haste, Luc had said.

No, Amber thought, clenching her fists. *You're worse.*

But… the door closed with a slam. *But what about me? My carelessness just sentenced him to death.*

It felt like walking past Stephanie all over again.

'Maybe I should just kill you too,' Haste said quietly, shaking his head. 'See what you've done, Elkhoury? The whole point of sending you to Australia was that no one had to die.'

'Why don't you just send her back?' Christopher suggested with a shrug. 'She's already made friends there.'

The only friend I had there was you, Amber thought, throwing him a sullen glance. *Though it'd be better than what I deserve.*

Haste was nodding. 'Agent Holmes had the timebox,' he said, stepping around the table. 'He landed right—'

His pause made Amber look up. There was Shinichi's old bloodstain; there was Luc's new one.

Her eyes widened. *Maybe…* she thought, her chest finally loosening. *Maybe this isn't the end after all.*

Luc's body was gone.

H aste straightened, glancing around the room with small, tentative steps. Amber watched his eyes slide around the room, momentarily investigating every potential hiding place, as though the room was haunted.

Amber could see under the table and out the other side; and he wasn't there. The rest of the floor was clear, except for one place a grown man could possibly hide.

Under the small table with the urn.

It was covered with a long black tablecloth that probably hid boxes of teabags and sugar sachets, but if he'd packed them up the right way there might have been just enough space for him to hunch in under the table and wait for an opening.

Maybe even develop a plan.

Haste stared at the small table, reaching the same conclusion. Amber watched him, her heartbeat loud in her ears.

He stepped forward, bending over to pick something up from the floor.

The timebox.

Luc? Amber rolled her eyes. How did he forget about it *again?*

'I'll set it to leave in a minute,' Haste muttered, fiddling with the buttons. 'Done.' He came over to her, leisurely setting the timebox as he came. 'Do you want to know where you're going, or should I keep it a surprise?'

She wanted to know, but to say so seemed to be resigning herself to her fate. 1868? Or maybe earlier? He wasn't trying to remove her memory this time, so there was no guarantee she'd land near civilisation, or even on land. She started struggling, wrestling her arms from Alpine's grip, pushing her elbows in the hope that she'd somehow inflict enough pain that he'd let go.

Haste came closer, pressing a button with a special, final force. 'Transport,' he said as he pressed it. 'Good bye, Elkhoury. And this time, you won't have Christopher Alpine to protect you.'

Alpine laughed, and for a moment his face looked like Christopher again. Kind, open, friendly. 'We had some good times,' he said. 'I might come and visit you someti—ow!'

Amber's shoulder found a rib, and *that* shut him up. He thumped her back against the wall, snarling again. Somehow, Amber preferred that to his kind face. 'But not until I've had my turn killing your partner,' he growled. 'Maybe I'll be the successful one out of the three of us.'

'Ten seconds,' Haste said, dropping the timebox into her lap. 'Nine. Eight.'

Amber kicked at him, but he was standing too far away. 'Seven.' The timebox fell from her lap, but Alpine picked it up and leaned it against her stomach like she was a primary teacher displaying a picture book to her students.

'Six.'

'No!' Amber screamed.

'Five. Apologies for the early end to your career. Four.'

Amber raised her elbow a bit higher, pushed a bit harder, angled a bit sharper, and her elbow found Alpine's nose. Blood gushed everywhere, and he swore at her.

'Three.'

Her right hand now free, she threw the timebox away and under the table from her. Haste made a lunge for it, but she caught his leg and he crashed down onto the table, hitting his head and falling motionless.

'Two,' she said.

Alpine, holding his nose, gave up on Amber. He crawled forward and under the table. There was a loud smash, and he fell too, his hand on the timebox and his head surrounded by shards of glass, wooden shrapnel and tea bags.

'One,' Luc said.

Leaning on the table, he stood, holding the remains of the tea box in his right hand. Alpine disappeared, leaving a small spattering of blood to match Shinichi's and Luc's. 'Cancel,' Amber said, and the timebox switched off.

Leaning heavily on the table, Luc stood, swaying slightly. The right side of his face was covered in blood; it dripped from his hair and chin onto his shirt and every so often he blinked it out of his eyes.

Amber stared at him for a moment. She'd suspected it – hoped it – since she'd first seen the empty puddle, but even so, she couldn't quite believe that it was really Lucky Holmes standing in front of her. 'You—wait…'

He smiled at her, but his smile was vague and distracted. She stood, her own head spinning a bit. She wished she could be ecstatic, dance around and hug him; after all, just before she'd thought he was dead! But her eyes filled with tears, and as she stepped forward, all she could think was, *Poor man.*

'My… my head hurts,' he said, and collapsed.

orking the timebox would have been much easier if Shinichi's hands stopped shaking. The ARC-researcher before him – she must have come after he'd left, because he didn't recognise her – waved as she closed the door. He caught it, but didn't respond.

The case file was open on top of the timebox, the papers inside flicked haphazardly until he'd found the page he'd wanted.

It was the last case file under Haste's name.

'Craig,' Haste said in his left earpiece. He'd assumed that it was his ARC-researcher who was letting them go back, and Shinichi hadn't spoken up to correct him. 'Can we do it once more? And if it doesn't work, we'll give up. I promise.'

He sounded so different to the man speaking in his right ear. Younger, less used to authority. Less mature.

Amber knows, he thought. Somehow, that was worse than Goldwyn knowing. The thought of Goldwyn hunting him only made him work faster; the thought of meeting Amber after this made him cringe.

She's young, he told himself as he reset the coordinates for the fourth and, according to his note, last time. *Everything's so black and white to her. I need to do this.*

But a small voice that sounded something like Amber's whispered, *do you?*

He pulled out the earpiece from his left ear. He didn't want to hear what happened next; reading it in the file was terrible enough. He pulled it out and set it on top of the stack of papers; then put his hands on the timebox and leant against it.

He was so tired. But this tiredness felt deeper than a caffeine crash, or a symptom of his terrible sleep the night before. That kind of tiredness was easily remedied.

This tiredness seemed to go deeper. His *soul* was tired. Tired of him.

What I wouldn't give to be someone else right now, he thought. *I wish…* he shook his head, picking up and straightening the files. *I don't want to finish that sentence.*

But his mind did it for him.

I wish I saw things like Amber did.

The door burst open, and the ARC-researcher on the other timebox yelled. Shinichi closed his eyes. 'Ah, Goldwyn I presume?' No ARC-researcher would open the door so dramatically. 'Perfect timing. Let's take this elsewhere.'

'Agent S… Sema…'

'Samejima. Say it after me: *Sa-meh-ji—*'

'Shut up. Show me the recording.'

Shinichi raised an eyebrow. He was already sick of himself; he might as well help everyone else feel the same way. 'Recording? The one of—'

'The more you say, the more people will get hurt,' Goldwyn growled, nodding at the other ARC-researcher. Shinichi frowned. He hadn't resigned himself to damage-control *quite* yet. *Though I should find out where that back-up is soon,* he thought.

He picked up the folder, earpiece and empty coffee cup and led Goldwyn to the room he'd been using as a temporary office. The table here was even messier than the timebox had been. His computer sat open, waiting patiently, and next to it was his notebook, open to the all-important blood-stained page; a pen; the 1998 case file; the newspaper report of Stephanie's death; and a few other miscellaneous pages he'd pulled out and scattered around in the likely event that he'd need to stall Haste or his men while deleting something.

'Find that file,' Goldwyn said. 'And show me what it's called.'

Shinichi sat down at the computer and opened his files. *I wonder if Amber's still alive,* he thought as he found his recordings. 'This is it,' he said, and Goldwyn took the computer to delete the file.

'Any backups?'

Yes, I've made five. One on my phone, one on my USB, one on the cloud, one I emailed to the head of police (who's on his way), and the one I emailed to Laura. Oh, and all conversations through earpieces are recorded automatically and stored in the ARCHIVE database, and I don't have access to it to be able to delete it.

Wordlessly, he pulled out his phone and showed the file. Goldwyn deleted that too.

'Come on, don't think I'm stupid. Where else?'

Shinichi sighed. 'I didn't have enough time to upload it anywhere, so it's just on my hard-drives.'

Goldwyn watched him for a long time. 'You must have at least started an upload. Show me.'

He opened the cloud and, sure enough, there was the same file, though he'd named it differently. Goldwyn pointed to the .mp3. 'Is that it too?'

For a moment, Shinichi contemplated lying, but rejected the idea. If he said no, Goldwyn would just listen to it, and then he'd be much more careful. So he nodded, and the file was duly deleted.

'Where else?'

This could take a while, Shinichi thought, already bored. *Where is that detective inspector? He said he'd come right away.*

He shook his head. 'That's it.' *I wonder if he's getting coffees. Maybe he'd get me one too.*

He looked down at his hands, his fingertips *tik tik ticking* on the keys as they shook uncontrollably, and wondered if he should really be blaming fear.

Goldwyn watched him for a moment. 'Sir, I've gotten Sammy-jimmy here to delete all his files. Should I destroy his computer and phone too?'

Sammy-jimmy? Shinichi folded his arms. *That's worse than my pronunciation of his name. I guess I won't try so hard to get it right.*

'Sir?'

Hm, Haste wasn't replying. That was interesting. Had he Travelled somewhere? Or was he dead? Shinichi chuckled to himself. *Or maybe he just doesn't want to talk to Goldwyn. I understand the sentiment.*

'Sir? Can you hear me?'

Maybe it's broken. Police sirens crescendoed in the distance, and Shinichi perked up. The small room had no windows, frustratingly, so he had to listen and hope they wouldn't go past. The sirens stopped, and a car door slammed. His hopes rose.

'Sir?'

'Dead battery?' he asked with a smile.

Goldwyn glared at him. 'I was told to kill you,' he said. 'If you keep this up, I'll do it slowly.'

Shinichi's smile widened. 'Please, take all the time you need.'

They must be in the elevator by now, he thought. *Or would they take the stairs?*

Goldwyn was watching him, his eyes wide. His last comment must have unsettled him. That was strangely satisfying.

'Sir?' Goldwyn said again.

Where are they?

'Excuse me,' Shinichi said, pushing back his chair and standing.

Goldwyn grabbed his arm roughly and shoved him back in his seat. 'Hey, no, where are you going?'

'To get another coffee. Don't worry, I'll come straight back.'

'Another coffee? Seriously? You need *another* one?'

Shinichi froze. Slowly, his eyebrows lowered as he took in what the man had said. *Did he just…* 'What on earth do you mean?'

Goldwyn tossed his head. 'Not now. Sir? Are you there?'

Shinichi rolled his eyes. *If you're that worried about him, go and see what's wrong.* He stood again, pushing his shoulder into Goldwyn's chest and storming out of the small room before the man could react. He *would* get another coffee, whether he "needed" one or not.

The room outside was the usual calm but busy environment, with ARC-researchers getting on with their research. *If only they knew what their Commander had done,* Shinichi mused. But the elevator doors opened, and out strode a tall man in a smart suit. His hair was blonde despite the lines on his face, and he was surrounded by five officers in uniform. Laura hung back, her usually laughing mouth in a stiff line and her eyes hard.

I'm sorry, Laura, he thought, his stomach twisting.

'Mr Samejima?' the man in the suit said.

The door crashed open, startling everyone in the room. Laura was staring over Shinichi's shoulder at who he knew had just entered. He ignored him.

'Ah, Detective Inspector Scortch, follow me.' ARC-researchers on either side looked from Goldwyn to him, their eyes widening and mouths opening as they saw him leading the group of officers. More policemen and women came from the emergency stairwell, until he stood surrounded by a group of about twenty.

Images flashed in his mind, memories of police inspectors and officers, forensic scientists, suspects, evidence…

And the body.

He shivered, turning with a grimace to the open door behind him. Goldwyn stood in the doorway, his face dark and his eyes narrowed, calculating. They flicked through the faces of officers, then finally landed on his face.

Goldwyn snarled.

'Yes, Mr Goldwyn?' Shinichi said.

The man took in the police officers surrounding him. A few were moving toward him, one young man pulled out handcuffs. Goldwyn backed away.

He gestured to DI Scortch. 'Whatever you have to say to me, you can say to both of us.'

A few ARC-researchers laughed, and Shinichi risked a smile. Goldwyn's eyes flicked between his face and DI Scortch's, his face turning red.

But he could leave Goldwyn to the police officers. Amber needed him.

Amber. The thought of facing her tied his stomach in knots. He led the squad downstairs and showed them the room, considering leaving and disappearing without another trace. Both Laura and the chief of police had copies of Haste's incriminating evidence; what more did he need to do?

You need to face Amber, he thought, straightening his jacket. *Come on, Shinichi Sammy-jimmy. Be a man.*

'Police, open the door!' Scortch yelled. The officers stood in a fan around the door, guns at the ready, legs slightly apart and eyes staring straight down the barrels.

For a moment, nothing happened, and a terrible picture crossed Shinichi's mind, a picture where they opened the door to a room full of corpses and blood—

The door opened. 'Please don't shoot,' Amber said quietly as she stepped aside.

Shinichi stared, his mouth falling open. He'd seen horrible corpses and distressed people countless times before, but somehow when it was someone he knew, all the techniques he'd taught himself to keep himself distanced from it just didn't work.

Her face was covered in blood, dirt and tear tracks, and her already-red shirt was spattered with darker stains. She held the door for them, but Shinichi couldn't go in.

There was something about her that was… *wrong.*

What was it?

Laura gave a sob and ran toward Amber, wrapping her in a hug despite all the dirt and blood. Slowly, Amber put her arms around Laura, hugging her as she cried.

And Shinichi knew what was wrong.

Her eyes were dry.

He smiled. 'How is he?' he asked.

Her eyes flicked his way, and he immediately regretted his question. Stiffening, she replied, 'He's alive, and that's enough of a miracle for today. Did you call an ambulance?'

'He's alive?' Laura gasped, pulling away. 'But… but how?'

Amber shook her head. 'I'm not sure. Shinichi?'

He took a deep breath. 'Well, I'd have to think—'

'Did you call an ambulance?'

His heart stopped. Staring into those hard, dark eyes, he wished he'd been a coward and left without saying good bye. *You idiot,* he told himself. 'I… no. I'll do it now.'

He stepped to one side and pulled out his phone, closing his eyes. He went through the motions, told them the information they needed, but he could just hear Laura say, 'Don't be too hard on him. He's been busy with his own life-threatening circumstances.'

Amber mumbled an acknowledgement and went into the small room.

DI Scortch came out leading a small parade. Behind him was Haste, his hands handcuffed behind his back and his forehead bleeding. Shinichi noted the bruise, and the irony, but somehow, couldn't get any satisfaction from it. Behind him was an officer, pushing him forward, and a few other policemen tailed behind.

Hmm. No Alpine.

He watched them go into the elevator, watched the doors close, lost in thought.

'Excuse me, sir? Sir?'

Oh, right. He put the phone back to his ear. 'Yes, sorry, I'm here.'

He went into the small room and found Lucky on the ground.

'He's in the recovery position,' he reported. 'Apparently he's been unconscious for—' he threw a questioning glance at Amber – 'about four minutes.'

He knelt in front of him, peering at him from different angles with a frown. He couldn't see under the blood coating his face to see if there were any bumps or new cuts on his head.

'Shinichi, he's not dead,' Laura said. 'You're allowed to touch him.'

Oh right. This isn't a murder investigation, he realised. *Old habits.*

He flicked the man's fringe out of the way, the dried blood crunching a bit under his fingers as the hair moved. *Hmm, curious.* A round scar sat just above his right eyebrow, the skin raised slightly with jagged edges and rough burned tissue around its edges.

But it looked like it dated from when he was a child. The skin wasn't broken; just scarred and bumpy. *Didn't he get shot just an hour or so ago?*

Shinichi's eyes widened. *No… he was shot* twenty years *ago.*

'Sir? Can you see any bumps or bruises? Anything at all?'

Shinichi stared at the scar, swallowing. 'Well…' His gaze moved a few centimetres across the agent's temple, to the ugly bruise Goldwyn had given him in 1868. 'Yes, I found one.'

He answered a few more questions, nodded and 'yes'ed a few more, then finally hung up. 'He said six minutes,' he replied, turning to Amber and Laura.

Amber nodded. 'Did you see it?'

He swallowed. 'Yes. It… answers a few questions.'

Laura's eyes widened. 'What? What is it? Can I be a detective?'

He stepped aside, allowing her to examine the scar for herself. Standing, he put his hands in his pockets and tried not to fidget or look at Amber. He could see out of the corner of his eye that she was staring at Luc, her face emotionless.

'Shinichi,' she said quietly, after a moment.

He closed his eyes, focusing on taking deep breaths. *I deserve whatever she gives me,* he told himself.

'I'm really, really sorry,' she said.

His mind blanked, and he opened his eyes curiously. 'S—sorry? For… what?'

She lowered her eyes. 'I told Haste your name. I… I think he already suspected, but—it was careless of me. I'm sorry and… and I'm glad you're not dead. I was really scared you were.'

He watched her for a moment, wishing he knew what to say. 'It's okay,' was all he could think of. 'And…'

And what? 'I'm sorry' didn't cut it for him. His actions had effectively caused Nikola Lazarov's death, Stephanie Heile's, Lucky Holmes', even her own exile to 1868. Haste had been the one to carry them out, but Shinichi had driven him to it.

And she knew.

'I'm sorry' wasn't enough.

But what was the alternative? Saying nothing at all?

Wasn't that somehow worse?

'Shinichi, please,' she choked, her eyes brimming with tears. 'Tell me you didn't do what I thought you did. *Please.'*

His heart pounded, his chest tightening as he watched her. 'What… what do you think I did?'

She glanced at Laura, then whispered, 'Someone sent Haste back in time to let him try to change history on that mission with Nikola Lazarov. And you left, and I heard you—you weren't doing that, were you?'

Despite himself, his eyes filled with tears, and he turned away. He took a deep breath, blinked them back, and clenched his fists.

Be a man. The words echoed in his head, berating him.

'No,' he whispered. 'Of course not.'

She watched him for a moment, and he forced himself to hold her gaze. *She studied psychology, you idiot!* he yelled at himself. *She'll see through you!*

Part of him hoped she would.

But finally she smiled, tears dripping onto her cheeks as she gasped, 'I knew it! I knew you wouldn't!' Stepping forward, she clasped him in a hug and sobbed into his shoulder. 'I was so scared. But I knew—'

He closed his eyes, wishing he could curl up into a ball and shrink into nothing. *I should never have come back to ARCHIVE,* he thought. *I knew this would happen as soon as Lucky came to my door, but I came back.*

Idiot. Stupid, stupid idiot.

The last nurse had been around only ten minutes before-hand, but a vague boredom was settling into Luc.

He didn't have the energy to set up the television, or to focus for any length of time, so he settled down and dozed for a while.

For an hour, his sleep was light, and without dreams. But then, as the late afternoon sun darkened, his sleep went deeper and vivid memories filled his mind. Racing through the streets at night. Amber's face as she smiled at him in 1868. The blurred image of Harry, bringing a branch down on his head. Christopher Alpine, chasing them through the grass. Shinichi, pushing a paper toward him with the words *Stephanie Heile* written on it.

And Haste. Telling him to find the timebox. Leaving Shinichi crumpled and bloodied to kill another agent twenty years before.

Holding a gun level to his head.

Somehow, in his feverish dreams, Luc had an epiphany without realising it. Si Periculum *is fine,* he thought, *but Haste and I want different things 'at whatever risk'.*

Haste fired the gun. Luc's eyes flew open, glancing wildly around the room as he tried to remember where he was.

'Oops, sorry,' came a voice from the doorway.

Surely that's not…

But who else had her olive skin, her black curls and kind, adventurous eyes? He'd know her anywhere.

But the crash, she should be in a hospital too…

'Laura,' he croaked, then cleared his throat and glanced at the chair next to the bed.

Laura wasn't there.

Slowly, memory by memory, his mind caught up to the present. The hospital had muddled his mind, sent him back to the morning after the crash, when he'd woken up and found out that Amber had been lost.

'How are you feeling?' Amber asked, pulling up a chair next to him.

'Fine,' he said, pushing himself up on the pillows. The fabric was so stiff; did they wash the pillow-cases in hand-sanitiser between patients? He swallowed, his throat dry. 'A bit… confused.'

She smiled. 'About how you survived?'

Luc's mind was foggy, but he knew enough to know that he wasn't confused about that. *Well, now I am,* he thought. He shook his head quickly, but it just made it hurt more. *Argh, now I'm confused about what I'm confused about.*

'I thought we'd just Travelled before the bullet hit,' he said slowly, looking back up at her face.

Her raised eyebrows were confirmation enough that it hadn't been that simple, but she gave a smile and nodded. A part of him was grateful that she didn't launch into an explanation there and then.

'Whatever happened…' he squeezed his eyes shut, shaking his head again. 'They made my head hurt *more*, then gave me something that's made it hurt *less* but also made me slightly giddy in the meantime, so please don't hold me to everything I say.'

Amber laughed. 'I don't usually listen to you anyway,' she teased.

'It's probably a good thing.'

She nodded, then glanced down at the floor, catching her breath. She bit her lip, and after a moment, wiped at her eyes impatiently.

Is… is she crying? he wondered, slightly terrified. *Did I say something wrong?* 'What—what's wrong?'

'Nothing,' she said quickly, but couldn't hide a sob. She stood, leaned over the bed and hugged him awkwardly, her arms around his neck and her cheek pressed up against his. 'I thought you were dead,' she whispered.

'You don't have to be so heartbroken that I'm not,' he replied, slightly irritated. Still, the hug was nice, he supposed.

She laughed. 'Yeah, try harder next time.' She pulled away, wiping the tears from her cheeks.

'It's okay,' he said automatically, wishing his mind would wake up and say something cleverer, something the love interest of a rom-com would say when the heroine was crying.

According to Laura, they always knew what to say in every circumstance.

He started, his eyes widening as he remembered. *Laura's challenge! How long have I been asleep for? What if I missed the 24-hour time frame and she's going to tell my mum—*

He took a deep breath. *Calm down, Luc,* he told himself. *It's unlikely that Laura would go to talk to Mum considering everything that's happened. Unless you've been in a coma for a few weeks – in which case it would be unfair to consider the challenge closed – she hasn't had a chance to see Mum. So if you ask Amber out now, it should be fine, right?*

Right. Except that just meant that he had to ask Amber out *now.*

He turned his head to look at her. She was checking something on her phone; and she quickly wiped her eyes before putting her phone back into her handbag and looking back up at him.

'What?' she asked.

He shouldn't have, but he said the first thing that came to his head. 'You look nice.'

He was probably imagining it, but he thought he saw her blush. Her mouth twisted in a funny way, like she was trying not to laugh. 'Are you feeling okay? Should I leave you to rest?'

'No!' He blinked, lowering his hand. 'No, I… it's nice to have someone to talk to. Sorry. I…'

She shook her head, not even holding in her laughter now, which made Luc smile. He didn't know why she acted like she shouldn't laugh at him; it was fun and strangely satisfying to be the one she was laughing at.

It'll be a nice memory for after she disowns you for asking her out again, an unhelpful part of his brain said.

He sighed. This wasn't hard. He'd ask, she'd say no again, he'd go to Laura and say he'd tried, he really had.

'Where are the others?' he asked instead. Procrastinating.

'They're back at ARCHIVE taking care of stuff,' Amber replied. 'Laura asked me to tell her when you woke up, but,' she leaned forward, 'between you and me, I decided to keep you to myself for a little bit.'

Luc wondered if she could see the heat that was rising in his cheeks. *She wants to spend time with me alone,* he realised. *Isn't that as good as saying she'd agree to a da—*

'I wanted to ask you something,' Amber finished, and Luc's newfound hope went crashing to the ground like a dog trying to fly.

She didn't want to spend time with me. She just wanted to ask me something.

He licked his lips. *Well, let's get this over with.* 'That's a coincidence; I wanted to ask you something too.'

She smiled wryly. 'Do you want to go first?'

He closed his eyes. 'I really don't. Go on.'

'Okay.' She shifted slightly on her seat. 'In the bathrooms in 1998…'

Oh no. No, no, anything but that.

'You said *"she wouldn't date me".* Do you remember?'

Say no. 'Yes.' It came out more of a whimper, but she clearly understood.

'Who were you talking about?'

For a long time, Luc lay on the bed, feeling immersed in a puddle of a feeling he could only describe as:

(o′·□·)□ *why*

Finally he let out the breath and tiredly rubbed his eyes. 'I really thought you'd have guessed,' he said. 'I changed my mind,' he said louder. 'I want to go first.'

'You can't back out now! I already asked the question – you have to answer it!'

Luc held up his hand. 'I will. But… by asking my question, you'll answer yours. No. I'll answer yours by asking my—'

'What's your question, Luc?'

Luc opened his mouth, then hesitated. A horrible realisation came over him that he hadn't prepared how he would say it. He'd thought about it, wondered how he would approach the question, but he'd always assumed that he would know when the moment arose.

The moment had arisen, and he still had no idea.

Great. Good one, Luc.

'Well…' He decided to go for the simple approach. *Will you go out with me?* It would be better for her to refuse him if he said that, than if he started by telling her how he felt. *Okay. I can do this. Will you go…*

The words died as he looked up at her face. She was watching him expectantly, impatiently. But, he realised, this was too important to pretend he didn't care. When she rejected him, she needed to know that he was serious. This wasn't just to get out of Laura's blackmail. He really cared about her, and he wanted to be with her. Even if she didn't feel the same way, he needed to tell her.

And then he would blame Laura.

He pushed himself up on the pillows till he was sitting up, and looked her straight in the eyes.

'After the car crash, I was out until about ten o'clock the next morning,' he said. Somehow, now that he'd started, it was easier than he'd thought it would be. 'Laura was there when I woke up, and she looked like she'd been crying. I asked her what had happened and she explained everything, including that you had disappeared.

'I was so shocked, and… and confused; I couldn't say any-thing. All I could think was… where is she? What if she's not safe? What if she's dead?'

Luc shook his head, staring down at his hands. 'Laura will testify to this: I was a zombie for days. She told me to go home, but even then, I read the whole timebox manual, and as soon as I found out you had gone back to 1868 I…' he swallowed. 'I wasn't very well, but…' Reluctantly, he looked up at her face. She seemed confused, but she was listening attentively, despite her tiredness. 'All I could think was that if you were dead – and there was such a huge possibility that you were – but if you were, I would… I'd never get over it.' He looked away, suddenly feeling a bit embarrassed. 'And then, when I found you and you were alive, I was so excited to take you home and make sure you were safe again, but you didn't recognise me, and as I realised that you weren't pretending… it felt like… like a whole section of my life had gone missing and… and I'd never get it back.'

He bit his lip. 'Now, you've got your memories back, of course, but I spent days coming to terms with you not remembering everything, and I just couldn't accept it.' He hadn't wanted to tell her how that had felt, but now he couldn't stop himself. 'Amber, the thing is, I can't imagine life without you. I don't *want* to imagine life without you. I know you're out of my league, but would you…' He paused to gather his thoughts.

Amber laughed. The sound was so confusing to his ears; for some reason he hadn't expected it. 'Luc, you're funny,' she said, giggling.

Here it is, he thought, bracing himself. *Well, Laura, I tried.*

'Sorry, finish your sentence,' she said. 'Is that the question you were going to ask me?'

Luc nodded, feeling miserable. 'Yes, that was the question,' he sighed. Now that he'd said so much more than he'd intended, he wanted to go home, crawl into bed and sleep for a week. He'd never come back to ARCHIVE – well, he'd have to for work, but he would put it off as long as he could. But Amber would be at ARCHIVE, and he wasn't sure he could handle the torture of seeing her every day, knowing that… he'd one day have to say goodbye to her.

'Luc? Are you going to finish your question?' she asked.

He shook his head, rousing himself from his thoughts. 'It doesn't matter,' he said, wishing he could feel as indifferent as he was acting.

She almost seemed disappointed, but he decided it must have been her new cruel streak, disappointed that she couldn't laugh at him more. 'Were you going to ask me out?' she asked after a moment.

Wishing he could be anywhere else than where he was, Luc sighed, nodding reluctantly. 'But—'

'Why did you stop?'

He stared at her, confused. 'Because… you laughed at me…?'

She laughed again. 'I'm sorry,' she said. 'I'll tell you why I laughed a bit later. Please, continue.'

Luc didn't say anything. He hated himself for getting into this situation. *I knew she'd reject me, but I didn't think she'd be this cruel,* he thought suddenly. *It's not like her.*

His first thought was wondering if she'd been switched with a double, a spy who was impersonating her. He shook off the idea as soon as it came to him. *I've been reading too many spy books,* he thought.

His second thought was to do as she said and see where she would go with it. At least that approach would get the pain over quickly and then he could go back to sleep.

At least I covered my hide earlier by saying that I was effectively high on painkillers, he thought, and that brought some comfort.

'Don't laugh at me,' he said eventually. 'This isn't easy for me to do.'

'I'm sorry,' she said. 'I won't laugh.'

He watched her suspiciously for a moment, then shrugged. 'Would you ever consider going out with me?'

'Sure.'

He looked up abruptly, stunned. 'What?'

'I said sure,' she repeated, laughing again. Honestly, this woman.

'Then… then why did you laugh?'

'I'm sorry,' she said. 'Were you talking about me? In the airport bathrooms?'

'Well… yeah…?'

'I asked you that because I was wondering who you were interested in,' she explained. 'And who you thought would reject you, too.'

'You didn't think it was… you?'

Amber shook her head. 'Of course, not,' she said, reaching out for his hand. 'You doofus. It never occurred to me that you thought I wouldn't date you.'

He took a deep breath, rubbing his eyes with his free hand. 'Amber, I asked you out *ages* ago, and you said no. How was I meant to know you'd changed your mind?'

'What? When?'

'When—At the Christmas party.' He dropped his hand. 'Did you forget?'

Her eyes unfocused as she tried to remember. 'Oh, I remember. To be honest, I wasn't sure if you were asking me on a date, or to an afterparty. But I was tired that day, and I didn't know you, so I said no.' She smiled at him. 'If you weren't going to ask me again, I probably would have asked *you* eventually.'

He stared at her, his mind blanking. He tried to picture Amber asking him out, but his drugged mind was struggling to keep up with both imagination and reality. And her hand was so soft, and it was in his, and it fit really well, and it occurred to him that now he could ask to hold it whenever he liked, and it wouldn't be that weird.

This was great. *Good job, Laura.*

'See, I told you you would answer my question… no, I would…'

She shook her head, standing and sitting next to him on the bed. The mattress dipped slightly uncomfortably under her weight, but Luc didn't care. 'You need to sleep,' she said firmly. She leaned down, incredibly close to his face. His head started spinning. He felt like a ship sinking into icy water.

He leaned forward slightly and kissed her. Gently, a small bob on the surface of the sea before it all pulled him under. He wanted to kiss her more. He wanted to rewrite time for her. He wanted to gift her prehistory, to stop the spinning of the world until they were ready for it to begin again.

She pulled away with a smile. 'I won't tell Laura you're awake,' she whispered.

Luc nodded vaguely, trying to catch up with where he was and what had just happened. It felt so good to be able to talk to her again, let alone…

Wow, he thought, with a small smile. *Let alone kiss her.*

'Sleep well,' she said, letting go of his hand and picking up her handbag. 'I'll come back tomorrow.'

He nodded, still a bit dizzy and disoriented. *Stupid painkillers,* he thought with a small smile.

He closed his eyes. *I can't believe she said yes,* he thought. *I can't believe it.*

★★★

Laura couldn't stop grinning to herself. *I did this,* she smiled.

She hugged Shinichi, not caring that he didn't hug her back. Pushing her away, he picked up his phone and texted her, adding to the silent conversation they'd been having for the past ten minutes.

Laura also picked up her phone as his text slid silently onto the screen. They were sitting in a meeting room that was fairly isolated. There had been absolutely no noise in the room since they'd entered, and that was the way they'd wanted – no, needed – it.

Laura scrolled down the conversation from where she'd been checking the first text Shinichi had sent.

Shinichi

> Okay. I've hacked Amber's earpiece so we can hear what they're saying. They'll be able to hear anything we say so we need to communicate this way. Your phone's on silent, isn't it?

> Yeah.

> Good. No noise, okay?

Ok

Ooh yay Lucky's awake <3 <3

Wow but he's so out of it HAHAHAHA

Aww he just said she looks nice

It's a good start

(◖◗ω◖◗) <3

I can't remember if I told you what I told lucky to do XD

What?

I told him to ask Amber ou

t

he wasn't going to do it anyway?

Idk I don't understand that man

ugh this is the most painful love confession I've ever heard

I can't imagine you'd have a lot of experience in this area

':0

DID YOU JUST ROAST ME

HOW DARE YOU ROAST ME

There was an opportunity

o(⌗⌗⌗)o

AWWWWWW

Man lucky is so darn CUTE when he's sincere

This is still painful

It's CUTE

What are you talking about

SHUT UP YOU MAN WITH NO SOUL

YOU KNOW NOTHING OF LOVE

-_-

Fair enough

He just sounds… drunk?

I wonder what that hospital put in him XD

Wait why is she laughing

NO AMBER DON'T DO THIS

Stop texting me

I'm trying to listen

Sorry

Tbh tho I've actually never heard lucky be so sincere in my life

Im so made at amber for ruining the moment and lucky's life

*mad not made

Stop texting me

Hehehe

"doofus"

What does it mean

I've never heard that word before

It means like an idiot

But affectionately

HE'S ALREADY ASKED HER OUT??

HE DIDN'T TELL ME

This surprises you?

I BLACKMAILED HIM INTO ASKING HER OUT

What??

KISSKISSKISSKISSKISS

You blackmailed lucky??

WHYWONTHEKISSHER

How many people have you blackmailed in your matchmaking?

It's important for me to know this, Laura.

are you afraid that you're next? :P

Hey if you sigh too many times he might hear you

…fair point.

Finally, she reached the end of the text thread and found his new message.

There. She kissed him. Are you happy?

Her eyes widened. What? When did she…?

What??????

I MISSED IT

ARE YOU SERIOUS

Щ(ºﾛº)Щ

NO NO NO I MISSED IT

Shinichi rubbed his face, visibly trying not to sigh.

(* —n—)

Now stop texting me or you'll miss it again

I WONT I WONT I PROMISE ☒x☒

Through Amber's earpiece, Laura heard her voice, in a slightly breathless whisper, saying, 'I won't tell Laura you're awake.'

She bit her lip hard to keep from laughing, or squealing, or bursting into song. How long had she known? How long had she planned this? And now it was finally happening. It was a bit unromantic, sure, but it got the job done.

> If you squeal, I will forcibly remove your earpiece.

> Nah you wont

> Amber will hear

> -_- you're insufferable when you're right

> You too <3

> WAIT SHE'S LEAVING SHE'S ON HER WAY BACK

Laura looked at Shinichi expectantly, waiting for his eyes to widen, for him to get up and start frantically packing up equipment. He caught her eye, his face hardening.

> We cannot let them know what we know

Laura nodded solemnly.

> I will guard this secret with my life.

Very carefully, Shinichi shut his computer.

It took all of Laura's willpower to not grin as Amber knocked on the door of the meeting room. She welcomed her in, putting her phone down with what she hoped was a natural-looking, welcoming smile.

Amber's eyebrows rose. 'What are you so excited about?' she asked uncertainly.

I guess it wasn't that *natural,* Laura thought. She tried to think quickly. 'You're not crying; Lucky must be okay.'

Amber let out a breath, and inwardly, Laura smirked. *You can try to hide from me,* she thought. *But I know everything.*

'The hospital says he'll be fine,' she replied, sitting down. She glanced at Shinichi. 'Is he okay?'

Laura nodded. 'Don't worry. He's just tired.'

Exhausted seemed to be the better word for him. His arms were on the table, and his head rested in his arms, and although his eyes were closed, Laura wasn't sure if he was actually asleep or just resting. He'd managed to disconnect the earpieces silently before Amber left, and had closed his computer and pushed it to the side.

'I wonder how he can sleep with all that caffeine in his system,' Amber said. 'Eight coffees, did he say?'

Laura shrugged. 'I lost count a long time ago. I'm sure it's not healthy.'

An awkward lull descended on the room as Laura watched Shinichi's breathing deepen.

Amber shifted on her seat. 'Where's Haste?' she asked finally.

'He's been arrested, charged with kidnapping, attempted murder, murder... I can't remember them all.' Laura waved her hands around. 'Anyway, agents have retrieved Alpine from Walhalla, 1868, and now all three are due in court in a couple of months.'

Amber nodded slowly, but she was frowning.

Laura fiddled with her lanyard, feeling a bit sick. 'Apparently, a few years ago Haste proposed to the governing committee that ARCHIVE should not only be saving people who have been recorded as saved, but organising the flow of history more broadly.' She hunched over on herself. 'They rejected the idea, or rather, did nothing about it, it seems. So he must have found Alpine and Goldwyn to... do the dirty deeds.'

Amber nodded. 'Shinichi and I came close to finding all that out in my mission to 1998,' she said quietly. 'Shinichi was injured at the time, and Haste sent me to 1868... he silenced us.'

Laura didn't know what to say. She felt like she was going to throw up just thinking about what was going on in ARCHIVE... the Aid and Rescue Corp that had been turned into an organisation for compassionless killing. *Haste knew that what he was doing was wrong,* she realised. *Otherwise he wouldn't have gone so far to keep it secret.*

But, she realised at the same time, *what's wrong with helping fate kill someone it's already singled out to kill? Isn't it the same as saving people, just… not?*

She glanced at Amber, troubled by the question. Was it *really* Haste who had killed Stephanie… and not just Stephanie, but all the other people whose deaths he'd also orchestrated… or did he just happen to fit all the pieces together, and someone else killed them?

Laura shook her head tiredly. Technically that was for the jury to decide.

Still, the question was unsettling.

★★★

The question still troubling her throughout the months through which the trial took place. It didn't matter how many times she told herself that they were doing the right thing, or that it wasn't her decision; the doubt was always in her mind as to whether Haste was getting what he deserved.

He hijacked a plane, she told herself angrily. *Just to make sure one girl died.*

Throughout the months of alternating in-person and online hearings, Laura would have thought that going through it with Lucky, Shinichi and Amber would have made it easier, but somehow that just made it worse. She found herself wanting to avoid them outside of real life, and couldn't even bring herself to ask how their first date went.

It occurred to her more than once that she could leave ARCHIVE. It was said to be easy for ex-ARCHIVE agents to find work, and she could probably have easily set up a costume-making business online.

Luc could see that the trial was affecting her friend, but felt powerless to help. And it wasn't just Laura who was hurting from it – it seemed that everyone was carrying around an extra emotional weight. He felt humiliated – not just from when they announced him as a witness:

'Mr… um… Luckworth? Holmes?'

Luc sighed.

He still cringed whenever he remembered the surprise on Laura's face when he stood up, heard Amber badly hide a snicker, then force her face into something innocent and supportive. So, his secret was out.

His dates with Amber hadn't seemed to go too well, either. She hadn't complained, but they'd both been too tired to do anything special, so they invariably ended up getting takeaway and crashing at home. Sometimes he'd try to plan a nice dinner out or at least a movie somewhere, but when it came down to booking it, he'd always put down the phone at the last second.

His mum told him not to worry too much, but he felt like he was letting Amber down in a way.

For her part, Amber didn't mind Luc's low-stress dates; it felt nice to not have to dress up and pretend to be a cute couple, when they were in the middle of a harrowing court case. Though she might have preferred a large dinner with her extended family, or even just going to a crowded night-market, it seemed that Luc was exhausted just at the thought of it, and she didn't mind spending time with him.

Besides, finishing the day with light-hearted banter with him almost removed the trauma of going through the events of the mission again and again.

As for Shinichi, he bore the events of the trial with the same attitude he bore most things… a cup of coffee and a stoic expression that betrayed nothing.

The only time he gave anything away was when the jury asked Amber why Mr Luckworth Holmes, allegedly murdered, hadn't actually died in 1998.

'I've… talked to various ARCHIVE medics and time travel researchers on this issue,' Amber answered. 'And from what I gather, while we can't be sure, our best guess is that, well, essentially Luc was Travelling while the bullet was entering his head.'

A thoughtful silence descended on the courtroom. 'But you said that there was blood,' one of the jury said.

Amber nodded. 'There was. I…' she glanced at Shinichi, as though she hoped he would explain. But he looked as baffled as the rest of them. As many theories as he had, none of them fit for that exact reason. He too was curious as to what the experts had come up with.

Amber took a deep breath and held up her hands as though showing specific points in history. 'Maybe it hasn't been explained yet,' she said. 'Travelling is an ARCHIVE term for time travel, not travelling through space, so much.'

The jury nodded, slightly impatiently.

'Well, Luc started Travelling just as he was shot. That's why there was so much blood,' she went on. 'So he was Travelling… departing, I suppose you could say, just as he was shot. But because the timebox had already picked him up, it was somewhat tricked into healing it because of the Dorrivan Effect.'

This time no one nodded. The jury stared at her, completely confused. *You're going to have to explain that one, Amber,* Shinichi thought with a small chuckle.

'The… Dorrivan Effect is a theory created by a… uh… Dr Dorrivan, I think… who realised that agents who had never been vaccinated or contracted certain illnesses still had the antibodies for those illnesses. Similarly, sometimes they would land and have old scars that weren't there before. He hypothesised that by Travelling through certain times and places, they contracted illnesses while Travelling. However, their bodies also healed themselves at an increased rate while Travelling.

'So Haste shot Luc, and while the bullet was entering Luc's head, Shinichi turned on the timebox to bring him home. Luc's body thought that the bullet was sustained from Travelling, and healed itself while he was still in the flow of time. At least, that's our best guess.' Her eyes fell. 'It's so sad to think that it took all that planning, a plane hijacking, three ARCHIVE agents and two cars to kill Stephanie Heile, yet it was only a split millisecond that saved our Lucky Holmes.'

'Rather convenient, isn't it?' the judge asked, raising an eyebrow.

Amber shrugged, glancing at Luc. 'Or just lucky.'

9:00AM 13 November 2020, ARCHIVE

'Shinichi's not here yet?' Laura asked as she came up to Lucky and Amber. They waited outside the ARCHIVE elevator, regrouping before they went inside to work.

Amber shook her head. 'He's probably still getting coffee,'

Laura frowned. 'Shinichi plans his life around coffee. He knows to check when the cafe is busy and allow extra time.'

'But he wouldn't give up on it just because it would make him late,' Amber pointed out.

Together, they entered the elevator. It was a curious day today. Rumours had been flying around the office about Shinichi's reappearance, Haste's conviction, and what would be happening moving forward. Specifically, who would be crowned the next ARCHIVE Commander.

'Who do you think it will be?' Laura asked.

She hadn't given any context to her thoughts, but everyone knew what she was talking about. Lucky shook his head. 'I've heard they're getting someone new in,' he said. 'Someone we don't know.'

Laura snorted. 'Well, I've heard it's going to be me, so I'm not willing to believe any rumours.'

Amber laughed. 'I can't imagine you as Commander, sorry, Laura.'

'I never wanted to be Commander.' She thought about it, then shrugged. 'I wouldn't mind being second-in-command, but not Commander.'

They reached the floor of desks of ARC-researchers, and Laura's phone vibrated in her pocket. She pulled it out and checked the message. It quickly turned into messages.

Shinichi

> Laura I really need a coffee

> I'm going to die from lack of caffeine

> Please

She sighed and replied.

> Where are you???

> We thought you were getting coffees

> I can't. I'm busy.

> Please get me one. Even instant is fine

She couldn't believe it. Shinichi couldn't be *that*—

> No. I'm not that desperate. Just one from the coffee machine is fine.

> Bring it soon.

Laura frowned. 'I… have to grab Shinichi a coffee,' she said. 'I'll be right back.'

Amber and Lucky looked as confused as she felt. 'Isn't he getting his own?' Amber asked.

'He said he's busy.' She turned to go to the kitchenette that had the espresso maker.

'We'll wait for you outside Haste's—well, outside his old office,' Lucky called after her.

Hurriedly, she prepared his coffee, surprised that no one was using it despite it being so early in the morning. *Everyone probably bought theirs on the way here,* she thought, rolling her eyes as she added milk.

> I can't remember. Do you have sugar?

> Not with me, no.

> Is that normal for westerners to carry sugar with them? I get that question a lot.

> No I mean in your coffee.

> Do you like sugar in your coffee?

> Oh

> No I don't.

She picked up her handbag and the mug of coffee and went over to his desk—

But it wasn't his desk anymore. *Where am I meant to meet him?* she wondered suddenly.

She pulled out her phone and called his number, counting the rings.

It went through to voicemail.

She gritted her teeth, her fingers tightening around the handle of the mug. *That man—*

Laura went back to Haste's old office, steam coming out of her ears. The four of them had been called in to meet the new Commander before anyone else did, though if they didn't like them, Laura wasn't sure what they could do.

She'd give Shinichi a piece of her mind when he deigned to join them.

Lucky and Amber were waiting for her, as promised. They all paused, gathering their wits, then went into the room together.

Lucky frowned. Amber smiled, as though she thought it was a joke.

Laura laughed. 'I brought your coffee, *Commander,*' she said, handing Shinichi his coffee.

'Oh, thank you Laura,' Shinichi replied, taking the mug and sipping the coffee lovingly. 'Oh, I should give you a salary rise,' he murmured.

Laura thought he was joking, but just in case he wasn't, she said, 'I'll take a pay rise.'

'I was talking to the coffee,' he shot back.

Amber shook her head. 'Wait. Wait. *What?* Shinichi, *you're* the new commander?'

He shrugged. 'Temporarily. But I moved all my things in here because I expect it will be a long "temporary" position.' He held up his hands. 'But why do you all look so surprised? Don't you think I'd make a good Commander?'

Amber shrugged. 'No, it's not that—'

Laura interrupted her. 'You'd be terrible. It's a good thing it's only temporary.'

But Lucky looked like he was thinking it through. 'Did Haste suggest you?' he asked.

Shinichi shook his head. 'Haste didn't want me at all, apparently. But they were looking at a few people, but I had worked here the longest out of the candidates, so I suppose I was chosen. I can't help but wonder if Haste's word had worked in my favour, though.'

'Maybe he was right,' Laura said. She hadn't been joking when she'd said that he wouldn't make a good Commander. His leadership skills would be spread too thin; instead of leading an agent step-by-step through a mission, he'd struggle with the more distant and general leadership that being Commander would require. *But then again,* she thought, *maybe he'll surprise me.*

'Yes. They're looking to employing someone who's new to ARCHIVE to take over permanently,' Shinichi explained. 'And then I will go back to being an ARC-researcher.'

They all looked at each other, then burst out laughing. Even Shinichi was laughing at the ridiculousness of the situation.

'I did *not* expect this,' Amber laughed after a moment. Lucky shook his head, and Shinichi shrugged.

'Neither did I. But I couldn't say no.' He shook his head, pulling out a piece of paper. 'It's my punishment, in a way. Now, I know you all have questions about how your missions will run from here, considering the… legacy Haste left.'

Laura knew that the board had been in deep discussions about how to answer the questions raised by Haste's actions. The court had required they write up a detailed response to Haste's actions, and it had ended up being a good-sized book. Laura hadn't read it all; she was only about a third of the way through, and it was dense.

But one thing they'd mentioned was whether ARCHIVE should work harder in attempting to save individuals who had *not* been recorded as saved. Whether the adage *you can't change history* was true, or just ARCHIVE theory.

'Laura—oh, do I have to call you Agent… uh…'

'Please don't.'

Shinichi shook his head, raising his eyebrows. 'I can barely remember all the names as it is, and I haven't even started on last names. Except yours,' he said, turning to Lucky. 'I remember Holmes. It's like Sherlock Holmes.'

'Lucky's fine,' he said quickly. 'Did you call us here just to show off your new position?'

'No,' Shinichi replied, then pointed to his collar. 'But look, I got a new badge too.'

Laura laughed. 'Did you have *anything* to say to us?'

Shinichi looked at her. 'Of course I do. A few things. Firstly, before I forget, the court has ordered compensation for each of you, if you fill out certain forms that I'll give to you later.

It will be a painful process going through the paperwork, but it's ARCHIVE's apology for the emotional, and physical, stress we've been put through on these missions.' He glanced at Laura. 'I don't know if you qualify, to be honest, but if you want to apply…'

Laura shrugged. 'I don't deserve it anywhere near as much as you three do,' she answered gently. Though it had been hard losing Amber, and watching her Commander betray them, Laura couldn't imagine the pain the other three had gone through on these missions. They deserved her share of the compensation, and then some.

'I don't have the paperwork with me yet,' he said, glancing around his new desk. 'It's been quite a morning.'

'That's fine,' Lucky replied. 'We can do it later.'

Laura glanced at him, a twinge of sympathy twisting her heart. His face was completely neutral, and his voice sounded numb, like he'd just stopped caring.

Somehow, it made her feel worse.

Shinichi nodded. 'Well… I'd also like to give you both something more… personal. From me.' He took a deep breath, staring at the desk in front of him. 'Amber, I… I remember you saying once that you hoped that one day we'd be able to have desks for field agents.'

Amber frowned, but nodded.

'We've decided to hire out a floor in a nearby apartment building. It's less than ideal, but the plan is to move the ARChronicles' physical copies over to that building and use that floor as desk space for field agents who aren't yet on mission. I hope to have that done by the end of the year.'

Laura glanced over at Amber's face. 'You… you did that for me?' she asked, her mouth open.

Shinichi shrugged. 'Technically I did it for all the field agents, but it was your idea.'

Lucky grinned at her, and she beamed back. 'I can't wait! That's amazing, Shinichi!'

Shinichi smiled, and Laura felt herself relaxing. She hadn't seen him smile like that in years.

'Lucky,' he said, pulling out a sheet of paper. 'This took quite some organising, but I think it's all good to go now.'

Lucky took the paper, an eyebrow raised. 'Does this mean… I can become an ARC-researcher?' he murmured. Laura's eyebrows rose.

Shinichi nodded. 'You're booked for a trial. Then the agents you worked with will give feedback and, based on that feedback, we'll decide—' he coughed—'that you're fine to be one.'

Lucky stared at the paper in his hand, his mouth smiling but his eyes puzzled. 'Thank you,' he said. 'But… I don't know that I can.' He lowered the paper and looked around. 'I mean, I was warned against Travelling too often after this—' he pointed at his forehead, where his scar was mostly hidden by his fringe—'and I suppose this solves that, but…' he shrugged. 'I'd love to trial it, I suppose.'

Shinichi put his hands on the desk and leant on it. 'Is there a mission in particular you'd like to be involved in?' he asked.

Lucky smiled sheepishly. 'There's a few, sir. Amber and I heard about the so-called Heile Missions.'

Laura's eyebrows rose. 'They're the missions where you try to—'

'To do the impossible and change history, yes,' Shinichi replied, rubbing his face tiredly. 'The board has decided to put forward a few people who will be dedicated to these missions, at least at the start. In fact, they have suggested you two specifically.'

Laura's heart dropped, and she slowly shook her head. But Shinichi wasn't looking at her.

Slowly, she followed his gaze to Lucky and Amber's faces, almost dreading what she was going to see. Lucky had wanted to forget the whole thing; he wouldn't want more of the same missions… and it would continually break Amber's heart to have to fight, tooth and nail, against the course of history.

But she was smiling. Amber glanced at Lucky, her smile breaking into a grin. 'We were just talking about this the other night,' she said.

Laura rolled her eyes. The two had never finished a mission successfully before, and at this rate they never would. The Heile Missions were more likely to prove that nothing could be done, and back up ARCHIVE's old excuse – you can't change history, therefore, you shouldn't bother trying.

'Because I looked up Stephanie Heile's death,' Luc said, a twinkle in his eye. 'In the ARChronicles.'

Laura's eyes widened. 'No way,' she said, before she could stop herself.

Lucky caught her words and nodded excitedly. 'Yes way. Amber did the trick.'

'She survived? But—'

Lucky's mouth turned into a self-satisfied smile. 'We found her return ticket. And many more records after that.'

Laura's mind churned, working through possible explanations. But her passport… that had to be her, or they wouldn't let her through. And a return ticket? That would be after the accident. 'How?' was all she could say. Even Shinichi's eyes were wide as he waited for Lucky's answer.

'As far as I can tell, without having access to CCTV to confirm this, it seems that she took the taxi to… somewhere… then got off and the taxi continued on before it crashed. She was seen getting into the car, but we think she took the Subway the rest of the way home.'

Amber gave an apologetic shrug. 'It's not much, and it's still tragic that someone else died, but I guess… it just gave us hope.'

'You can't change history,' Lucky said with a chuckle. 'But you can use the loopholes.'

Laura finally managed to close her mouth, but her head felt like someone had filled it with helium. *So this isn't so daft after all,* she thought numbly. Loopholes. She rolled her eyes.

'Take a break, first,' Shinichi said. 'Spend your compensatory money. Then, when we all come back for good, you two will have first pick of the Heile Missions. For now, Laura and I have work to do.'

They shook hands, then Lucky and Amber left, chatting excitedly. Laura reached for the door, but Shinichi called her back.

'Laura.' He put his hands on the desk. 'We can't pretend that you weren't caught up in this too. Is there anything ARCHIVE can do to try to make it up to you?'

Laura watched him for a moment. It wasn't like she'd gone through anything like Lucky and Amber had. She didn't deserve ARCHIVE's compensation like that.

But she also saw something deeper in Shinichi's eyes. This was his personal apology, not ARCHIVE's.

She shook her head. 'You don't owe me anything,' she said, waving her hands.

'I'm serious, Laura.'

She looked away, licking her lips in thought. 'The truth is…' glancing behind her, she stepped forward, fidgeting despite herself. 'I don't want to stay at ARCHIVE forever,' she said quietly. Shinichi's eyes narrowed slightly in confusion, and she retraced her steps. 'I mean, I love it here, and I don't want to work anywhere else, but…' she sighed. 'But I have a family, Shinichi. And… I…'

He nodded slowly. 'I understand.'

She wasn't sure that he did, but at least it meant she didn't have to explain any further. 'I haven't told anyone about this,' she went on quietly. 'But I've been thinking of asking for a… an assistant. That I could train up to—eventually—take my place.'

'How long?'

She shrugged. 'A year? Maybe eighteen months?'

He leaned back from the desk with a baffled sigh. 'Honestly I…' he shook his head. 'I wasn't expecting that.'

'I know,' she replied softly.

He stared at the desk for a moment, lost in thought. Laura waited patiently, licking her lips and feeling somewhat guilty. But it wasn't something new for her. She wanted to grow and focus on her family; shouldn't she have the right to do so?

Finally, Shinichi shook himself and gave a firm nod, as though in answer to her unasked question. 'No, this will be good. Do you have anyone in mind?'

She hid her smile with a hand to her chin, as though she were thinking. 'Well, there is someone…' *please don't catch onto me,* she thought, watching his face carefully.

'Hmm? What's their name?'

He doesn't suspect a thing, she thought, grinning inwardly. 'Her name's Koo Yu-na, and she's an old friend of mine. We studied together in university. She's even brighter than me—'

Shinichi nodded, writing the name down in his little notebook. 'Hmm, good.'

She rolled her eyes. 'Anyway, last I heard from her she was studying ancient fabrics in a Chinese university.'

He noted that too. 'Her name's Korean.'

She nodded. 'But she's been all over the world. Not many have her breadth of knowledge in historical costume-making.' *Plus, she's thirty years old, single, smart as a whip, and would be a perfect match for you.* 'So what do you think?'

'I think you've been thinking about this for a long time,' he said, still looking at the name in his notebook. Laura nodded, suppressing her grin. *Ages,* she thought. 'Which gives me confidence that she'll be good for the job,' he went on. 'I'll see if I can get in contact with her. Do you think she'll be happy to come here and work for ARCHIVE?'

Laura nodded. 'I think she'll love it here. We used to dream about going back in time and seeing ancient clothes and how they were made. She'll jump at this.'

He closed his notebook. *Checkmate, Shinichi.*

3:22PM 21 FEBRUARY 1998, NEW YORK CITY

S tephanie stepped out of the taxi and stared up at the airport, her heart beating loudly. What had that woman said, just a week ago?

'I just can't help but think that… maybe the next plane I get on might not land safely.'

Stephanie stared up at the glass doors and swallowed.

'Sometimes things happen that we can't expect, and then, even though the consequences are painful, it's not our fault.'

She shook herself and took her bags. *It was just one plane,* she told herself firmly. *It won't happen on the way back.*

It had been an exhausting week; her first week away from her parents, in a different country, and she was looking forward to seeing them again. There was a lot to catch up on.

She went up to the glass doors and, just as she was about to push it open, stopped.

Surely… surely not.

She peered through the tinted glass door, wishing the sun wasn't at her back so that she could see outside her own outline, see inside the airport lobby, between the passengers passing in front, to see… where did he go?

What was his name? It was a strange one.

She turned over name after name, rejecting each one as she thought of it. *It's on the tip of my tongue…*

Throwing up her hands, she rolled her eyes. It was gone.

She gripped her suitcase handle and opened the door, her smile ready for him even if his name wasn't. *He probably doesn't remember my name either,* she thought as she glanced around.

Yes, it is *him!* She started toward him, but at the same time he moved away, behind a pillar, talking to someone. His face broke out into a grin, but her smile faded. He wasn't looking at her.

He didn't recognise me, she thought, her spirits falling.

She turned back to the queues for ticket checks, dragging her suitcase behind her and feeling a little bit less lonely. No one else was nervous flying, but in the airport, she and he both knew what could go wrong.

She looked after him with a last smile, and this time he saw it, smiled back, and gave a wave. She couldn't stop herself from beaming back, waving enthusiastically, and the man laughed.

What is *his name?* she wondered. *This is going to drive me nuts the whole trip home.*

She stepped toward him, half-wondering if she could get through an entire conversation with him without having to say his name. *I'm sure I've done it before with others,* she thought with a smile.

A family with their luggage moved in front of her, and she side-stepped to avoid them. The mother apologised, picked up her child and hurried to follow her husband, spluttering apologies while watching frantically after her other child. Stephanie smiled, but when she looked up, the man was gone.

No, not again.

She ran toward the pillar, not caring who else got in her way or who she ran into. *He was right there!*

But when she got there, as she'd already known, he'd gone.

A small bubble of annoyance rose in her stomach. Why hadn't he stayed around to say hello? Didn't he want to talk to her? Or was he just waving to be polite?

She shook her head, walking back to the counters with a heavy sigh. *I wonder if I'll ever meet him again,* she thought, then shrugged, a small smile breaking onto her face. *Maybe if I'm lucky.*

Random things I Googled while Researching This (With Little to No Context)

- When were hand dryers invented? (In the 1960s, so I *could* include them in the airport bathrooms.)

- I'm proud to say that I remembered I was alive in 2018 BEFORE I Googled if flat screen TVs had been invented by then

- "Kookaburra" etymology (the word became popular in the 1920s, which led me to…)

- What were kookaburras called before they were called kookaburras? ("Laughing jackasses" or "Laughing kingfishers".)

- What is a suit bag called? (Believe it or not, it is indeed called a suit bag, or a garment bag.)

- I also took multiple trips to Walhalla, because it's a

lovely place and there's really no better way to get a feel for the town. <3

Bloopers:

Find the Mistakes in These Dates

Walhalla, 11:65pm 25 November

12:15pm 7th November 1969, Walhalla, Australia

[I think my finger missed the 8?]

There was a black stamp over the front that read, *Agent resigned,* and the date *19/02/2020* was scrawled on the line beneath it.

[Honestly I wouldn't put it past Shinichi to resign in the future, effective in the past.]

She turned on the phone. The date and time appeared at the top. *8:15, 11/08/2019.*

[This one's subtle, but the month on Amber's phone didn't match the month in the heading of the chapter (March). It did match the Walhalla month, so maybe I just got them mixed up.]

General Typos:

She folded his arms

Amber tried her best not to judge him and be thankful that technically for all the luck he was bringing them.

"'Climbed' seems wrong. 'Clumb'?"
—Me, editing

"If she wanted to live a quiet life in rural Australia, in a goldfish town that promised all the wealth she'd ever wanted, she could."
(Autocorrected from goldrush)

Throughout the months of alternatingly in-person and on-line hearings

Plus, she's thirty years old, single, smart as a whipe, and would be a perfect match for you.

Acknowledgements

My only apprehension in writing this is that I started *AEITAM* about six years ago, and so many people have had input since then that there's no way I could remember you all. I'm sorry if I forget to acknowledge you. Please write me an angry email.

I'm first going to thank Jesus, the ultimate ARCHIVE agent, stepping into history to save all those recorded as saved. You gave me this dream, and the story to tell, and then provided everything I needed to accomplish it. This is a big privilege. Thank you.

I have to thank my family, despite (for?) their continued disinterest in my career. Dad, you first brought me to Walhalla, and now I share your love for the beautiful town and its cemetery. Mum, your thoughtful questioning of my career choices keeps me accountable and confident that I'm thinking everything through. I'm incredibly grateful to have you both as parents. I love you, which I don't say often because I'm afraid you'll think someone's dying. But I do. Love you, that is.

Thank you Jenny Ann, the first reader of this book, and the only one whose opinion I really care about. I'm sorry for making you pay $15 in postage when you literally live with me. My bad.

Thank you to Beks, Kirsten, Bethany, Uzzielle and Jenny Ann (again!), the enigmatically named Uncle Tony Band. I dare say we have the most fun of any writer support group anywhere. Thanks to Uncle Tony himself too, I guess. (Sorry about the helicopter.)

Thank you to the Young Writers' Workshop for introducing me to the concept of editing (yeah, thanks a lot.) and writers' support. There are many writers I met there who need to be mentioned: Bojidar, Elsa, Nicole H, Cara, Evangelyn, Ben, Kimmi, Karissa, Jem, Jasmine, Nicole (NJ), Lulu and so. Many. More. Emma Rose and Meghan get special mentions as my AEITAM Undercover Street Team. 8)

Thank you to Lauren D Fulter, AEITAM's "book aunt", and Brianna Campbell. You inspired me and convinced me I could do this, and in a lot of ways, that's why we're here. Thank you to Meghan Dzurichko, the amazing artist who did ALL my character art. Your surprise nearly made me cry on the train. And thank you Katarina, for the FANTASTIC cover!

Thank you Marina, who stayed in Walhalla with me, as well as Megan, Rose, and Ruby, for your excitement over the book's release.

Thank you to all the people who supported me on Kickstarter. Through the chaos, you believed in me enough to support me with your money, and I'm so grateful. Thank you to Beks (again!), whose first online purchase was my book, and one of the first supporters. To Andrea (THE first supporter!), Bojidar, Rebecca Taba, Evangelyn, Jenny Ann, Gavin and the Williamson family, B Rose, Cat Corben, Stephanie Richey, Rory McGraw, Stephanie Raines, and Callum (sorry I didn't realise it was you!). Also, HAPPY BIRTHDAY to Jessica Wakefield! I hope you had a fun day and enjoy your present.

You guys are the best. You have done nothing less than delivered my dream into my hands, and I'm so grateful for you taking a risk with this book.

Finally, thank *you,* for reading not only the book, but also these acknowledgements. I hope you had a good time. You're the best.

About the Author

Photo by Ruth Baaco

Debbie Coll is a Christian writer, composer and songwriter from Melbourne, Australia. She's claiming that *AEITAM* is her debut despite having already written one season of *Ballads of Beyond* (a fictional podcast about banshee-banishing bards) and having composed the songs for *The Piper's Mountain* (a musical about the Pied Piper of Hamelin that was performed in 2022). She's also been writing books since she was eleven and is now twenty-four (still writing about spies), so while this isn't her first book, or her first release, it is her first *book release.*

She's never won an award for her work, but she *did* win a pair of socks in a Disney trivia competition in New Zealand, which she's very proud of, and she can count all the way up to twelve, which she's less proud of.

Debbie works as an instrumental teacher, and is studying to be an Allied Health Assistant in her spare time. When she's not writing, teaching or studying, she likes watching sit-coms, and op-shopping, which means thrifting, but is more fun to say.

For more of Debbie's work:

Ballads of Beyond (podcast): https://balladsofbeyond.podbean.com/

The Campfire (email list): https://deft-builder-384.kit.com/afbb810687

Instagram: @the.book.balladier

Find all of these and more on her website, debbiecoll.com.

P sst—if you want to hear a song Debbie wrote especially for *An Experiment in Time and Memory*, check out her song, *Everywhere for You.*